SOME FAR ELUSIVE DAWN

Also by Emma Drummond:

SCARLET SHADOWS

THE BURNING LAND

THE RICE DRAGON

BEYOND ALL FRONTIERS

FORGET THE GLORY

THE BRIDGE OF A HUNDRED DRAGONS

A CAPTIVE FREEDOM

SOME FAR ELUSIVE DAWN

Emma Drummond

LONDON
VICTOR GOLLANCZ LTD
1988

First published in Great Britain 1988
by Victor Gollancz Ltd,
14 Henrietta Street, London WC2E 8QJ

Copyright © 1988 by E. D. Partnership

British Library Cataloguing in Publication Data
Drummond, Emma
    Some far elusive dawn.
    I. Title
    823'.914[F]   PR6054.R785

ISBN 0-575-04241-9

Photoset in Great Britain by
Rowland Phototypesetting Ltd, Bury St Edmunds, Suffolk
Printed in Great Britain by St Edmundsbury Press Ltd,
Bury St Edmunds, Suffolk

Chapter 1

"A shell-shocked army captain! Oh, Austin, how could you?"

Casting his complaining wife a look of intense irritation as he mopped his brow with a silk handkerchief, Austin Beresford then accepted the delicate porcelain cup and saucer from his white-coated Chinese houseboy dispensing tea on the verandah.

"I will allow that I extended the invitation at very short notice, Margery, but I heard you this morning bewailing the fact that your numbers were uneven." He sipped his tea gratefully before adding, "I have solved your social dilemma very neatly, at the eleventh hour."

"You have done nothing of the sort," came the incensed retort from a woman ruled by excessive maternal responsibility. "Half a dozen of Lydia's friends will be here within the hour. How can you contemplate exposing them, to say nothing of your own daughter, to such a person?"

Austin grunted. "If Lydia's friends can survive some of Alexander's they will hardly be damaged by an hour or two in company with Sir Hartle Weyford's godson, my dear. Young Linwood has come to Singapore to take up a post in the Civil Service."

"The Civil Service? He is no longer in the Army?"

"After a year in hospital to put him back on his feet, he was given a medical discharge."

Margery Beresford let out a strangled cry. "The Army refused to keep him! Oh, Austin, how could you?"

"Will you please stop saying *Oh, Austin, how could you?* and accept the fact that I have?" snapped her irate husband. "You have never before baulked at welcoming new arrivals. Indeed, you are the acknowledged leader in taking unattached young men under your wing. This poor fellow knows no one in Singapore save the Weyfords, and must be finding it difficult to adjust to his new life. Sir Hartle assured me the boy plays a decent game of tennis—he was champion of his public school—and is a good all-round sportsman." Biting into a biscuit, he waved the remainder in the air. "I have invited him for four-thirty, and that is the end of the matter."

A visible shudder ran through his wife's ample frame. "It is *not* the end of the matter. Who knows what he might do when he has a racquet in his hand?"

"Oh, *really*, Margery!"

Alex had been lounging on a cushioned settee beside his sister Lydia,

5

lethargic and bored until the exchange between his parents had aroused his curiosity. He had returned to the large white stone house on the outskirts of the mercantile centre only thirty minutes before his father, after a long day at his office in the usual temperature of around ninety degrees. No man was in the right frame of mind for feminine argument until he had downed several cups of tea, cooled off under the shower for ten minutes, donned fresh clothes and embarked on a sundowner. He sympathised with his father, whose arm must certainly have been twisted by Sir Hartle over the disputed invitation. The shell-shocked godson would doubtless also have gained his Civil Service post through more arm-twisting by an old warhorse well known for getting what he wanted from those unwilling to offend him. By the same means, Linwood would be systematically thrust into every club, and every social group with influence, until he was accepted by all those who could make or break a young colonial's career. The Beresford family had plainly been chosen to perform the task of introducing this misfit to the younger element of the European community, by including him in their sedate tennis party. Alex felt resentful, even as he reasoned that the affair might be lifted from the dreary routine of giggles, gossip and good behaviour, for once.

"The fellow is probably quite harmless, Mother," he murmured. "Billy Frampton's cousin suffered from shell shock. He was awfully messy when eating or drinking, and apparently laughed for hours on end. Apart from that, he was no trouble at all."

His father rounded on him. "Your attempts to be amusing often border on the grotesque. Martin Linwood is perfectly sound. His experiences have made him a trifle withdrawn and shy in company, that's all. Sir Hartle wishes the boy to meet the right kind of young people with whom he can mix socially."

"I could cancel, I suppose," put in Margery thoughtfully. "It's not as if it were a dinner party, or a ball."

"Mummy, you *can't*," cried Lydia, sitting forward in swift protest. "I'd have to explain, and what would I say? Besides, we're all longing to see the engagement ring Jack Northolt brought over from England. Melody says it has been in his family for *centuries*."

Waiting to see how his mother would proceed, Alex groaned inwardly. With all the girls eulogising over a diamond ring, and Jack Northolt standing around looking fatuous, even the presence of a shell-shocked public school champion might not save the afternoon.

"I really don't know what to do," declared the ruffled hostess. "I had everything beautifully planned and now . . . ! I suppose the girls could play first while the boys have tea. Then Lydia could bring her friends

6

indoors leaving Alexander to ensure that the . . . the *visitor* plays a set. No one could then accuse me of failing in my social duty toward new arrivals," she finished, casting a dark glance at her husband.

"The boys'll eat all the tea," protested Lydia immediately. "You know what appetites they have."

"We'll have a better game without the girls," countered Alex. "They're so damned slow."

"Language, Alexander," admonished his mother absently.

"Mummy, please let's do what we always do. It'll look so . . . so *odd*," concluded Lydia, with strange signs of embarrassment.

Austin signalled the houseboy to refill his cup then, stirring the tea with unnecessary vigour, said, "Sir Hartle confided to me a little of young Linwood's background, of course. The boy inherited a sizeable sum from his father's estate last year. Frere Linwood was a brilliant politician with a fine career ahead of him, but ignored medical warnings not to overburden a weakened constitution. The loss of his beautiful Italian wife in a hunting accident six years ago had left him ill-equipped to bear the news of his younger son's death in action at Ypres, in addition to the seriousness of Martin's mental condition at that time." He dabbed at his moustache with his napkin whilst submitting his wife to deliberate scrutiny. "A tragic story, is it not, my dear? With his entire family taken from him, the Weyfords had no option but to draw young Linwood into their midst and do their bounden duty as his godparents. Incidentally, Sir Hartle is the sole trustee of Frere Linwood's estate until Martin is considered fit enough to manage his own wealth."

Until that moment, Alex had found the situation diverting. When he saw the expression on his mother's face change from one of vexation to that of glowing gratified speculation, the familiar flame began to burn within him. Straightening from his lounging position against the bright cushions, he waited tensely for what he knew would come next. He was not mistaken.

"Austin, you have just provided me with the explanation for the sudden arrival of Lady Weyford's niece on an extended visit," said Margery triumphantly. "If the Linwood boy is no worse than withdrawn and shy, then naturally the Weyfords would be anxious to . . . but why would they then wish to thrust him into a social circle where unmarried girls abound, and where he is likely to . . . ?" Lost in her butterfly reasoning, she continued almost to herself. "A wealthy bachelor unable to manage his affairs . . . an uncle who is the sole trustee . . . yes, an extremely attractive prospect for the sharp-tongued little Fay Christie! So what reason could Lady Weyford have for launching the boy before her niece's future is secure?"

"You'll find the answer to that when Linwood starts laughing and can't stop," said Alex tautly.

Lydia swung round to face him, her colour considerably heightened. "That's a beastly thing to say! In any case, I don't expect he'll come this afternoon. Invitations from perfect strangers are not normally sent at such short notice. He's likely to be already engaged."

Alex put his cup on the low table beside the settee with a bang. "He'll come, all right! If Sir Hartle can force Father to invite him here, he can certainly force his half-witted godson to toe the line."

"That's quite enough, Alexander," cried his father, throwing down his crumpled napkin and dismissing the houseboy with a nod. "Your opinion on this matter is superfluous, especially as you must be well aware that I was obliged to yield to pressure from Sir Hartle after asking him to perform a service for me on your behalf."

Into the sudden silence, Margery said, "Time is flying, Lydia. I think you should slip into your tennis frock, dear, while I just check that Ling has cut the cucumber thin enough for the sandwiches."

They rose to make an exit which was a study in feigned nonchalance. Alex reached forward to take a cigarette from the sandalwood box, his gaze resolutely fixed on a *chichak* on the wall just above it. He knew what was in store for him, and betrayed his anger by the force with which he struck the match on the side of the box encased in cloisonné enamel. Lighting his cigarette, he took a deep draw on it before his father opened battle in his usual fashion.

"It pains me that your mother and sister plainly knew to what I referred, and felt obliged to invent a pressing need to leave us."

"They could hardly escape knowing," Alex pointed out. "There's not a thing happens on this damned island which escapes the sharp eyes and tongues of the residents. I daresay every time I change my underwear, the fact is relayed from Raffles to the new causeway. When that is completed, the news will be over the Straits a hellish sight quicker, too."

"Resorting to vulgarity does not add to your credit, you young fool," his father snapped, mopping his brow again. "People are prepared to make allowance for high spirits; recklessness can sometimes be regarded as a praiseworthy trait. Your conduct yesterday was a total disgrace, however. Not only could you have broken your own neck, you endangered the lives of others present, to say nothing of risking the loss of an expensive horse."

"Credit me with some sense," Alex responded tight-lipped. "I never accept wagers unless I'm certain of my success. I agree that the jumps were dangerously high, but Romus is an exceptionally good jumper and

I'm an exceptionally good horseman. The risks to us both were negligible. As for the men who erected the fences for me, they couldn't have been safer from the positions in which they watched me clear all three in triumph. I can't be held responsible for the one fool who almost rushed into my path in his excitement before I'd calmed Romus."

"You can and you were," his father insisted forcefully. "Raymond Conninghame read me the rule book, where it clearly states that members are forbidden to issue or accept challenges to participate in feats designed to bring the good name of the club into disrepute, that monetary wagers apart from those on the official tote are banned, as being against the true sporting nature of the club. Lastly, no member is permitted to direct club employees to set up jumps, mark a course, or in any way use the track without the full knowledge and consent of at least three members of the committee." Sitting back in his chair, Austin glowered from beneath his thick brows. "You broke all those rules. I credit you with enough wisdom, however, to admit your guilt without further argument."

"Yes, I'm guilty of breaking their damned rules," Alex cried, "but no lives were at risk. I suppose Old Conninghame failed to admit that it was a first-rate piece of horsemanship which set up a record for the club."

"*A first-rate display of tomfoolery which set up a record for contempt for the club and all it stands for*, was how Lord Conninghame expressed it."

"He means to disallow it?" demanded Alex incredulously.

"You acted without his permission."

"If I had asked, he would have refused it."

"*Quite!*" Allowing the emphatic comment time to explain itself to his son, Austin then continued. "If you did it to make a point, I'm damned if anyone saw it. If it was to demonstrate your riding skill, you failed lamentably."

Alex was almost lost for words. "I don't believe . . . my God, I cleared three jumps which ten men wagered I would not."

"*You failed lamentably*," his father repeated with cold anger. "No responsible rider would act in such reprehensible manner, especially on the premises of a club which counts amongst its members some of the most renowned horsemen in the East. What was the reason for what you did? Tell me, if you can."

Alex rose restlessly and went to lean against the stone pillar of the verandah, smoking his cigarette and staring out over the tropical garden. Austin Beresford was universally known as a very prosaic man. He would never understand what had driven his son to commit what he saw as an act of dangerous folly. Alex sometimes found it difficult to

9

believe his father had ever been young, for it seemed he had acted with meticulous correctness from the cradle, if he was to be believed. Easing the damp shirt from his body now perspiring from the heat of the tea he had enjoyed, Alex sighed. How could he explain why he had deliberately ignored the rules in order to pit his youth, his strength, and his skill against almost impossible odds? It had been not only the challenge of those three highly testing fences, but the knowledge that the decision had been his own so that he had been master of his own life for the space of five brief but supreme minutes. He could still feel the sun, hear the utter stillness as he had sat astride Romus facing those fences, gauging the distance between each and the exact moment to gather the horse for the effort required to clear them. The turf had stretched out ahead of him with the shimmer of rising heat above the surface of the track, making it difficult to estimate the height and depth of each jump. His friends had been watching, yet he had been aware of nothing during those elating moments but the feeling of freedom. His father asked why he had done it. He had done it because it had been there to do, and no one could deny him the opportunity. If he had been making a point, it was to protest against his lack of such freedom.

The scene he had just witnessed between his parents perfectly reflected a way of life against which he rebelled with increasing inner ferocity. His mother's over-protective attitude toward the young had led her to see a shell-shocked soldier as a threat to vulnerable virgins. Yet mention of the possible violator having inherited a fortune had immediately transformed him into a sad victim being exploited by godparents bent on marrying him to their mercenary niece. Complete reversal of opinion within minutes!

His father's attitude was little better in pretending that he was sincerely trying to help a socially undesirable youngster to establish himself in the colony, when he was really buying forgiveness from the Turf Club for his son's behaviour—behaviour he was at a total loss to understand. What right had his father to make such a deal? What right had he to promise his son's participation in a game or two of tennis with some poor bastard who had lost half his wits, in return for Sir Hartle's arm-twisting at the Turf Club? They made their damn silly conventional rules, then covered up for each other when they were broken. Alex would far rather they blackballed him from the club.

"Have you any intention of answering my question?" asked his father sharply.

Alex shook his head. "You wouldn't understand my explanation if I offered one."

Red in the face, Austin stood up. "I can perhaps forgive foolishness, but not deliberate insolence. Doesn't it ever occur to you to apologise for the pain your exploits cause me?"

The cigarette butt cut a glowing arc in the air as Alex tossed it into the dense green foliage below, then turned to lean back against the stone balustrade.

"I apologise for the fact that you have been forced to invite to this house Sir Hartle's undesirable protégé, but not for what happened at the Turf Club. I didn't ask you to get me off the hook, sir, nor do I care that you have. Membership of that damned club is not the epitome of greatness."

"I know that, you self-centred puppy! It was not to get you 'off the hook' that I made the bargain with Sir Hartle. I did it for the sake of your mother and sister. It's a great pity you don't think a little more of them when you're tempted to indulge in immature antics which cause tongues to wag."

"Do they ever think of me when they indulge in their antics?" he retaliated. "I'm obliged to bring my friends to partner Lydia's simpering set for tennis parties, afternoon teas, and watered-down cocktails. I have the devil's own job to persuade them to suffer giggles and juvenile conversation time and time again. If that's not enough, I'm expected to flatter and dance attendance on all Mother's committee and charity ladies. They utter nauseating platitudes on how handsome I have grown, or how much I resemble my dear mama. The wonder is that I have somehow contained the urge to tell them I'm really a foundling, or your bastard by a music-hall dancer—*anything* that will put an end to their cooing." Running a hand through his hair in exasperated fashion, he demanded, "Is that what you want your son to be, a pet dog who performs parlour tricks?"

His father appeared slightly abashed at being faced with the other side of the coin. "No . . . no, of course not, Alexander. I am well aware that demands on you are sometimes rather irksome. All men suffer in that manner, and learn to make the best of it when it cannot be avoided." Sighing heavily, he continued in a tone Alex knew all too well. "Your mother has never wholly recovered from the loss of Charles so soon after Eleanor's tragic death, and has become a trifle over-possessive with you and your sister. I own it may be undesirable, although perfectly understandable, but simply ask that you bring her no further unhappiness through your wildness."

Alex hit back with long-standing bitterness. "That's always the unanswerable argument, isn't it? The blow to the heart. Charles and Eleanor were victims of an epidemic. I was in no way responsible for their deaths, so why am I expected to surrender my soul by way of atonement?"

There was a long silence before his father said stiffly, "You have every advantage under the sun. A long, successful career lies ahead of you, culminating in succeeding me as head of the company. Many a man must envy you. When you meet Martin Linwood, thank providence that you are not now like he is, shattered in mind and spirit. Sir Hartle was very decent and promised to soothe ruffled feathers, so I'd be obliged if you'd join me in doing something for his godson. An invitation or two from your friends would suffice to show that you are making the effort." He began turning away. "Cut along and get into your flannels. Guests will be arriving shortly, and your mother will expect you to be there to greet them."

Alex glared at his father's retreating back, fighting the familiar sensation of impotency. Confrontations between them always followed the same pattern: references to the family's double bereavement in 1912, his obligations to his mother and sister, to his father, to the company, even to society. That was unfailingly followed by the reminder of his enviable secure future, with the glittering prize of control of a shipping line when he reached the age of silver hair and thrombosis. This afternoon, it was harder than usual to quench the fire of rebellion. He stood for some time punching the balustrade with a gentle but agitated fist until he realised, with a sense of shock, that tears were threatening. Ashamed and furious, he headed through the house and ran up the stairs to his room before he made a complete fool of himself.

His boy, Fong, was in the airy adjacent dressing room laying out tennis clothes. He greeted Alex with a broad smile. "You late, Young Master. Tennee guests come soon."

"Too bloody soon," grunted Alex as he tugged off his Cricket Club tie and began unbuttoning his limp shirt. "Pour me a drink, like a good lad, and be sure to put in plenty of ice," he directed over his shoulder as he padded across the wood-block floor to the shower cubicle.

"Velly early for G and T," Fong pointed out in scolding tones. He had looked after Alex since he had matured beyond the capabilities of a female amah, and felt entitled to admonish his charge when he thought it necessary.

"I need it," Alex yelled above the thunder of tepid water on stone floor as he pumped the handle vigorously. "I'll probably need several," he added savagely as he offered his body to the deluge, closing his eyes against the sheet of wetness sliding relentlessly over his face. For once, he did not sing during his shower. Instead, he soaped his body generously, working it up to a lather that made his skin as smooth and slippery as an Ancient Greek wrestler before a contest. For a brief moment, he found satisfaction in feeling the strength of his torso and limbs beneath his soapy hands. Then his anger returned to still his movements as he thought of the row with his father. What did Austin Beresford require of a son, for God's sake? Did he feel no pride in a young man with a good virile physique? Did he have no appreciation of skill and daring, or a personality which craved the opportunity to express its individuality? Did his father truly want no more than a shadow of himself, a puppet without a single thought or desire of his own? Did he want an unctuous sycophant who would marry to produce yet another, who would continue to run the *Berondel Line* with extreme caution, no imagination, and certainly no emotion for years to come?

As Alex watched the suds sliding from his lower body, he wondered that Austin Beresford had ever begotten four children. Copulation was not an act he could easily associate with the frigid man he knew. On the only two instances that the subject had been mentioned between them, his father had simply read him a lecture on the penalties a man could incur for abusing his own body, especially in the East and, another time, had stressed the responsibility Alex held for protecting Lydia from licentious conversation or behaviour at all times. The latter he most certainly did. At eighteen, his sister was far too pretty and much too innocent, thanks to their mother's protection. Although they wrangled now and then, he was fond of her to the extent of being more than ready to take on any man who overstepped the line with her. His friends knew this and respected it, although their tastes in women were more erotic than cloistered virgins.

If his father considered "abuse of his own body" an occasional hour spent with a willing and reliable Chinese girl, then Alex was guilty of it. Being young and eager in a climate that heightened passions, made relationships with European girls difficult unless a man could find an outlet for his repressed emotion elsewhere. Alex did not have a regular mistress, as had most of his friends, and there was no girl in the colonial set who had captured more than his passing fancy. His sights were set on more athletic pastimes, and the masculine pursuits of rowing, steeplechasing, cricket and high-diving provided him with partial fulfilment. In control of a horse, wielding a bat, or high on the diving board, he was free for a brief, stimulating period.

The slatted doors swung open as Fong arrived with his gin and tonic. He held it clear of the running water. "You hully! Car come aleady. Plenty young missy downstair for tennee."

"Oh, lord," sighed Alex, taking the glass and downing half its contents, before turning off the shower and draping a towel one-handed over his shoulders to soak up water running from his thick curly hair. As he walked naked across his dressing room, leaving a wet trail on the floor, Fong fussed alongside him to fasten another towel around his waist.

"Too muchee fliend put money on Young Master horse," the Chinese told him in worried tones. "You sure you win?"

"Of course I'll win," Alex told him, taking another gulp from the glass. "I shall be riding the best horse in Singapore. I told you that at the start."

"You tell me many thing, but some thing lie," Fong replied accusingly.

"Rot! I never lie to you. Your friends'll make their fortune on me, then cut you dead next time you meet because they'll be wealthy enough to impress their ancestors." Alex held out the empty glass. "Fill it up, there's a good chap."

Fong shook his head. "No more. You no hit tennee ball."

"I've no wish to hit the damned tennee ball," he claimed with a sigh. "I'd rather skip the party and go for a swim."

"Missy Lylia no likee you go for swim," Fong told him, taking a pair of cotton undershorts and some cream flannels from the rail and holding them ready. "Mem no likee you go for swim. Old Master no likee you go . . ."

"Don't go on and on," Alex interrupted testily. "Even you are aware of the situation in this family. No one ever considers whether or not *I* no likee. They run my life, Fong, and the minute I break out they close ranks around me and tell me I'm selfish. Is it too much to expect to have what *I* want, once in a while?"

The round face of the boy grew distressed. "You wanchee more G and T, I get. You no hit tennee ball, but I get."

"Well, it's a step in the right direction." A rueful smile touched Alex's mouth as he drew on the undershorts, then the flannels which he secured at the waist with one of his club ties. Fong was a good friend who had covered for him on many occasions, despite his real fear of incurring Austin's wrath and being dismissed. The Chinese had also nursed Alex through youthful illnesses, and the epidemic which had killed his older brother and sister. He still suffered from bouts of tropical fever which, once in the system, recurred every few years with hardly any warning. The worst of the attacks had deprived Alex of his one opportunity to prove himself and, five years after the event, he still felt that ache of frustration.

Lost in thought he slipped his arms into a cream silk shirt, buttoned

14

it, then fastened a club cravat at the neck before taking up his silver-backed hairbrushes. When war had begun in 1914, he had been eighteen and fired with patriotism. Some of the younger colonials had immediately booked passage for England to volunteer, and Alex had declared his intention of joining them. Family opposition had been total and crushing, however. Every form of emotional blackmail had been used against him until he had been silenced. The ship had sailed without him, and he had never recovered from that inner anguish of watching the great white vessel pulling away from the island to the strains of "Auld Lang Syne" as the fragile streamers linking ship to shore broke, one by one. He had cried that night as only an adult man can cry, and had believed tears could never be forced from him again. Yet they had run helplessly down his cheeks a year later, when Indian troops in Singapore had mutinied and run amok through the city. The Singapore Volunteers, of which Alex had become a member, had been involved in the fighting, during which civilian residents had been transferred to ships in the harbour until the mutineers had been subdued. Throughout the brief affair Alex had been delirious with fever, and only heard of it when calm had already been restored. His friends had come to his bedside with tales of bravado and excitement, the insensitivity of their youth preventing them from seeing that their every word turned the knife in a wound he had hidden so well. It had seemed the cruellest stroke of fate that he had been denied even a glimpse of a small battle.

Fong's reflection appeared beside Alex's in the mirror. He ceased the vigorous brushing that never entirely tamed his unruly hair, then took the drink from his boy with an abstracted nod of thanks. From the verandah below came the sound of female laughter and assured masculine voices. With the glass in his hand Alex, moved across to the slatted doors folded back to allow access to his own verandah. Late afternoon in this steamy exotic island always filled him with inexplicable restlessness. The going down of the sun and the onset of night were separated by so short a time, and day never died more gloriously than it did in the tropics. The drink forgotten, Alex gazed out over the expanse of lawn to where flame-of-the-forest trees rioted scarlet before a row of fan palms which marked the boundary of the garden. The sky was already faintly tinted with gold as the sun lowered, and the great curving fronds of the palms made an impressive dark-green pattern against the gilded light filtering through the fingers of leaves. Within two hours the sky would have become a shimmering golden-rose, and the fan palms would then form a black silhouette of breathtaking beauty. Soon afterward, the gold would deepen to a blood-red glow lasting no more

15

than fifteen minutes. At seven o'clock, the glory would be gone; the graceful shape of the palms lost in the blackness of a noisy oppressive night.

All at once, the surge of life within him became a physical pain. There would be three more hours of daylight, then sudden inevitable darkness. Three hours during which he would do no more than play tennis, drink tea, exchange social inconsequentialities. Another day was ending, and he must stand impotently aside to watch it go. Time was passing, taunting him with glimpses of the unattainable. Those three short hours were life; the sudden darkness death. Desperation clawed at his throat. If only his family had been in England in 1914. If only his mother had not lost two of her children and consequently clung obsessively to the remaining pair. If only his father were a shopkeeper instead head of the *Berondel Line*.

With a savage movement he reached out to close the shuttered doors against the haunting, taunting scene outside. Ten thousand twilights would mark off his life until he reached his father's age, then ten thousand more, while he played tennis, drank tea and waited to become head of a shipping line he did not want. Only when he took up a brace of tennis racquets ready to go downstairs did he acknowledge the true reason for the ache of rebellion within him that afternoon. Within minutes he would come face to face with Martin Linwood, a man who had done all those things Alex would have given his soul to have experienced.

By five-fifteen it looked as if the star attraction was not intending to put in an appearance. Two sets of mixed doubles had been played in half-hearted manner, and the youngsters were drinking iced barley water as they grouped around garden tables, or draped themselves over cane chairs at the side of the court. The usual bright conversation and mild flirtation were missing, and the guests seemed disinclined to go on court again. Alex's mood darkened further. The party was falling flat because Sir Hartle Weyford's godson had declined their invitation. Martin Linwood had been the cause of friction between Alex's parents, and had indirectly sparked off a hefty lecture on the subject of reckless riding. How dare he fling their magnanimity back in their faces? The fellow would find himself totally ostracised if he failed to observe the rules of common courtesy, however determinedly Sir Hartle thrust him into Singapore society. Did Linwood imagine he was superior to mere colonials because he had fought in the war? Maybe he regarded himself a hero, and the withdrawn manner he adopted was merely to draw greater fuss and attention from those around him.

Giles Fancot offered Alex a cigarette. He took it moodily, leaning sideways while his friend lit it for him.

"You seem off-colour today," Giles observed. "Is it a sense of anti-climax after that superb jump yesterday, or have you had a wigging from the pater?"

Alex cast him a sour look. "You know I abominate mixed tennis. The girls are so damned slow, and make such a bally fuss if the ball thumps them. They don't even have the generosity to go in and leave us to get in one decent set of men's doubles before it grows too dark to play," he grumbled, glancing across to where the row of fan palms had become silhouetted against the golden-rose of early evening. Night was creeping inexorably nearer to end another in a succession of identical days.

"My people are none too pleased about yesterday," Giles confessed. "Old Conninghame made it sound as though entire fortunes were changing hands while you diced with death on the race track. They believed him, and read the Riot Act to me. They even told me to give back to Lionel the bally money I won." Shifting his position against the low wall surrounding the court, he grunted morosely. "What the older generation can't see is that reneging on a wager is a worse confounded sin than egging you on to perform a superb feat of horsemanship. It'll be a long time before I forget the thrill of watching you clear those jumps."

"Artificial intoxication," ruled Alex, his gaze still on the fan palms.

Giles goggled at him. "By God, you *are* off-colour today!"

What little conversation there had been at the two circular tables bearing the jugs covered with bead-edged doilies, seemed to have petered out into lethargic silence. The guests looked bored. Lydia suddenly detached herself from her friends to approach Alex, and he was perturbed to discover that she looked near to tears.

"Alex, I feel terrible."

"Go indoors and lie down," he advised briefly. "Mother will explain to the girls and give them tea."

His sister's large blue eyes gazed at him disparagingly. "I meant that I feel terrible about Mr Linwood."

"Why? What reason have you for feeling terrible?"

Giles pushed himself away from the wall and wandered off, hands in pockets, to where his and Alex's other friends were swinging racquets idly as they drank from glasses filled from the jug Alex always persuaded Ling to secretly "ginger up" with a dash of gin.

"Whatever must he think of us?" demanded Lydia.

"Who, Giles?"

"No, *Mr Linwood*. It isn't the thing to issue an invitation only an hour or two before a party. With close friends it's not so bad, but we are

17

strangers to him. It must have been obvious to him that we only did it because we had been asked to by Sir Hartle.''

''Then he'll think badly of Sir Hartle, not you,'' Alex pointed out roughly. ''Forget it, Lydia.''

''I can't. Mummy has been saying the most frightful things to the girls, warning them that his behaviour will be very odd.''

''Luckily, they've been spared it.''

''You boys have been as bad. I thought Ferdy Hancock was perfectly beastly to tell that story about someone's brother who now thinks he is Lord Kitchener. It's so very sad,'' she declared, dashing a hand across her eyes. ''Well, I admire Mr Linwood for showing us all he doesn't need our charitable invitations. If I am ever introduced to him, I'll die of embarrassment.''

''You idiot. He's a mental case.''

''He's a war casualty,'' she contradicted heatedly. ''We should all be especially understanding. Millie's sister was a nurse in France, and she said that . . .''

''Lydia, you're surely not getting one of your silly fancies for this man, are you?'' demanded Alex, weary of the subject of their absent guest.

The giveaway flush stole into her cheeks even as she denied it. Alex grew angry. His sister was ridiculously romantic, like most of her set. The unusual circumstances surrounding Martin Linwood had plainly conjured up an image of an enigmatic young man with a tragic past, haunted by the ghosts of war and contemptuous of those who tried to patronise him. Her current literary heroes were Darcy and Rochester —cold, arrogant blighters, in his opinion—and she had only recently recovered from a phase of melodramatic mourning for a Singapore banker, who had shot himself when his wife ran off with a Eurasian gem merchant. Yes, Lydia was ripe for a new hero.

''Don't clad him in armour and put him on a white charger, old thing,'' he advised with brotherly kindness, putting a hand on her shoulder. ''He's no more heroic than anyone who volunteered just for the fun of it.''

''He is,'' she insisted breathlessly. ''Sir Hartle told Daddy he won the MC at Arras.''

Letting his hand slide from her shoulder again, Alex straightened up. ''Every officer won an MC somewhere. It was an inducement from the Government to get them back from leave to the trenches.'' Tossing his cigarette stub away he went on firmly, ''I suggest we forget all about him and get this party going again. They're all sitting around like wet towels. That's all the thanks we get for trying to oblige Sir Hartle Bally

18

Weyford." He lunged forward determinedly, crying, "Come on, every-one. Who's for three-a-side? Two chaps and one girl."

The vigour in his voice raised a response in their guests, and conflict ensued as the males saw an opportunity to get a decent game without being accused of ignoring the girls, and the females cried that it was pointless as all the boys poached their shots. The argument was settled when a girl called Cecily, always eager to be outnumbered two to one by the opposite sex, volunteered for the first game.

"So do I," cooed another of Lydia's friends with more imagination than the rest.

"Right-o," said Alex with growing enthusiasm, pointing to four of his own friends who had partaken of the gin and barley water very liberally. "You chaps must have a handicap in fairness to the girls, since we've been accused of poaching all their shots. You must play left-handed, with a blindfold over one eye."

To a chorus of baritone groans, the delighted girls clustered around the four victims to loosen the cravats from around their throats and start tying the striped blindfolds across their right eyes. The afternoon came alive with giggles and protests, as the sexual overtones of what they were doing began to affect them all. Iced drinks and boredom were forgotten. Alex urged them on to greater excitement with the promise of a special prize for the winning trio. Gradually, however, the girlish shrieks began to die; the happy chatter petered out. One by one, all glances were drawn to the far end of the court, where a pergola provided a blossom-covered entrance from a small gate on the west side of the garden mostly used by the servants.

Alex was one of the last to become aware of the figure in immaculate flannels and the pale blazer of a top public school. The sudden silence and complete immobility of those who had been so animated, halted the new arrival several feet from the end of the pergola. He stood, very plainly ill at ease, the subject of universal fascinated scrutiny. The moment dragged on and on, no one appearing able to break it, until Lydia began walking around the tennis court toward him. The petrified scene continued until she reached the man and held out her hand.

"Mr Linwood, how nice of you to accept our invitation," she said in clear tones which reached the silent majority. "I'm Lydia Beresford."

If he replied it was too low to be overheard. His gaze seemed to be locked to her face as he advanced beside her toward the others. Alex stared at them, resentment growing to uncontainable proportions. Having ruined their party by his non-appearance, he had turned up in the most damnably casual way through the servants' gate just as they were about to enjoy themselves. Martin Linwood would pay for his contemptuous attitude!

Lydia led her hero toward Alex, completely absorbed in him. Why, he could not understand. Tall, with a frame that needed more weight than he presently carried, the man was hardly impressive. His thin face was paler than that of the average new arrival from England—deathly white, in fact—and suggested an age ten years more than his supposed twenty-four. Dark hair swept across his brow, heavy and straight, and he appeared oblivious to anything save Lydia's softly-glowing upturned face as they halted a few feet away.

"This is my brother Alex," she told him in tones that sounded almost maternal.

Dark unfathomable eyes swivelled to stare at Alex as if in shock. Neither man spoke as they stood regarding each other, and it was only Lydia's next words which broke the curious hiatus.

"I'll introduce you to our friends when we have tea in a moment."

Her ridiculous solicitude goaded Alex into action. "Tea and introductions can wait. We were just about to go on court, Linwood. As you missed the first two sets, you can go into this one."

Looking desperate the newcomer stammered, "No, I . . . I can't break up a set which is already arranged."

"Rot!" cried Alex with gusto. "Giles will gladly drop out, won't you, old chap?" he demanded, touching his friend's foot meaningly with his own. "It's not every day we have a public school champion gracing our court, and we're eager to see you in action."

Through a jaw grown almost rigid, Martin Linwood managed to say, "You mustn't expect . . . I mean . . . well, it's a long time since I . . ."

"No false modesty, old chap," chaffed Giles, rising to the rare occasion. "Get out there and show us all how it should be done."

"Come on, Linwood," urged Ferdy Hancock, enjoying himself hugely. "I'm to be your partner. Can't tell you how good it feels to know the set is ours before playing a shot." Slinging an arm around his victim's shoulder, he continued confidentially, "Let me know what you want me to do. Don't want to cramp your style, old sport."

In visible confusion Martin Linwood was surrounded, and hustled on to the court clutching a well-worn racquet so tightly his knuckles looked white.

"Don't, oh don't," whispered a voice beside Alex. "Please stop them. It's *cruel*."

He glanced down to see Lydia in such distress there were tears on her long blonde eyelashes. It put the finishing touch to his vow to show

Martin Linwood that he could expect no special treatment from him, or from his friends.

"Don't be so damned melodramatic, Lydia. He wants to be treated like any normal chap, doesn't he? That's what we're doing." So saying, he followed the group on to the court, where the new arrival had grown further confused by the presence of five other players, two of them girls. "Sorry, Linwood," he called cheerily. "I forgot to mention that it's a three-a-side game. The chaps have to play with the left hand."

"That won't worry a public school champion, will it, old sport?" declared Ferdy Hancock.

The dark shocked eyes stared at Ferdy, and the hesitant voice said, "I'm naturally left-handed. I suppose I should use the other . . . the right . . . shouldn't I?"

"That's right, old bean," chirped Ferdy.

"You also have to wear a blindfold," squeaked Cecily, over-excited by the bizarre situation. "Let me do it for you."

Her hands went to the knotted cravat at her partner's throat, soon pulling it free to tie across his right eye. Instead, she gave an audible gasp and gazed in fascinated horror at an elongated puckered scar, which had been hidden by the scarf. In total silence, everyone on court regarded the scar with varying reactions, until a loud clatter broke the stillness. Everyone then stared at the racquet at Martin Linwood's feet.

"I . . . clumsy of me," the owner muttered, and bent to pick it up with hands that shook.

As he straightened up, his gaze met Alex's and held it. As Alex gazed back into the intense depths of eyes grown wary, he experienced something he had never known before. Martin Linwood was telling him that he now understood what was happening and, in telling him, somehow reversed their roles. The vindictive jest had to be carried through to its unknown end, but Alex knew he was now as much a victim of it as the man confronting him. Lydia had been right. It was cruel.

The set went ahead because no one knew how to avoid it, but it turned into a feat of endurance for those taking part as they grimly battled through six games. There was not a single laugh or clap from the players or spectators, each of whom longed for it to end yet could do nothing to shorten the agony. Alex watched silently, conscious of Lydia beside him, as Martin Linwood's face slowly changed from white to greenish grey and his movements grew more and more erratic. He appeared to have no control over the racquet at all. The other three men playing with the wrong hand were not much better, but their movements were at least coordinated and deliberate, unlike the helpless

21

floundering of the man who seemed to keep going only by a super-human effort of will. The ordeal magnified until they finished the set, then shook hands with solemn relief prior to walking off court.

Lydia went forward before Alex could move, and smiled at the man who looked in imminent danger of collapsing. It was a very strained smile, however.

"Now that silly nonsense is over, come and have some barley water. Then I'll introduce you to Mummy and Daddy." Tucking her arm into his, she walked him over to the table and filled a glass from the jug she was unaware contained a large measure of gin. "Your name is Martin, isn't it? May I call you that?"

The young man gazed speechlessly at her as he clutched his racquet under his armpit and the glass in his hand. The rest of the players began donning blazers or cardigans ready to go indoors for tea, quietened by something they did not begin to understand. Only Lydia managed to cope with the situation as she held a one-sided conversation with the man she had decided to befriend. Then, as Martin Linwood took a gulp of the drink she had given him, the tennis racquet shifted beneath his arm. In trying to stop it from falling, he lost his grip on the glass instead. It shattered on the flagstones at Lydia's feet, and he stared down at it in visible misery, as did everyone else.

With her colour heightened, Lydia said clearly, "Don't worry about that, Martin. Ling will clear it away. Come in and meet my parents before we have tea."

Alex knew he would not easily forget that afternoon. As he watched his sister lead a stumbling, shattered man up the broad flight of stone steps toward the house, his own sense of humiliation was complete. His silent friends picked up their racquets and towels, then headed for the verandah where tea was set. Alex remained by the tennis courts, the significance of the coming night affecting him even more strongly than usual, as the sky behind the fan palms turned from golden-rose to blood-red.

Chapter 2

Martin reached the crumbling stone bungalow not a moment too soon. Thankful that the man with whom he shared the accommodation appeared to be out, he waved aside the houseboy's offer of service, and went straight to the bathroom. A bout of violent sickness was followed by the usual twitching, and he forced himself to go through the routine of breathing exercises and mental recitations they had taught him at the hospital. Stripping off his tennis clothes with unsteady hands, he filled the triangular stone bath with tepid water, then sat in it to swamp himself with continuous deluges from the giant ladle.

When he felt calmer, he fastened a towel around his waist and went through to the bedroom to throw open the shutters to the darkness filled with the shrill chorus of cicadas. For some time he stood gripping the sill, then he turned into the room to confront the bottle of brandy on the dark, ancient chest of drawers which had been used by many a colonial servant before him. That bottle was a symbol of his recovery. All the time it remained full . . .

Putting back his head and closing his eyes to temptation, he acknowledged that this was the worst attack he had had since leaving the hospital. The loss of his brother at Ypres, and the shell explosion that had turned eight months of his own life into a comparative blank, had left him unable to accept the early death of his father. Only just back on his feet and learning to cope with the horror of war once more, it had seemed to him that the unbearable rhythm of grief and pain was starting all over again. He had run amok in battle, and his superiors had returned him to hospital with other men shattered by their experiences. A year later, he had been discharged from the Army. The military doctors had told him that total recovery was in his own hands now and, in a suit bought for him by Sir Hartle, he had walked through the hospital entrance into peacetime England, terrified by his sense of isolation.

The distant past had been a golden era in a great rambling mansion, with a vivacious black-haired mother, a clever, laughing father proud of his two sons, and a young brother who had shared all Martin valued. They were all dead. The recent past had been indescribable hell made bearable only by the close companionship of those who had shared it. They were all dead. That emergence from hospital beside his godfather had taken place three months ago, and the sense of isolation was still as terrifying. A visit to his old home had proved so upsetting they had not even stayed overnight, as planned. A conference with the family solicitor had revealed to Martin the clause in Frere Linwood's will, which stipulated that the estate should be administered by the trustee until such time as medical advisers gave assurances of the heir's fitness to handle his own wealth. Those assurances were not yet forthcoming.

Like a leaf in the wind, Martin had found himself installed in a sombre apartment presided over by a woman who never entered the room without something heavy to use as a weapon, while Sir Hartle had used his influence to obtain a colonial post for his frail protégé, and booked passages for Singapore on the first available sailing. The voyage had been quite pleasant in that it had allowed Martin the opportunity to relax for hours, just watching the movement of the sea. The occasional albatross which had followed the ship for a while had given him great pleasure, seeing in the huge white birds other creatures in isolation who sought communion with those who had no understanding of their need. He understood, however, and found comfort in their presence above him.

During those days at sea, Sir Hartle had set about preparing his godson for a new life in Singapore, urging him to cultivate determination and strength of mind. The older man had seen action in South Africa at the turn of the century, and appeared ignorant of the way warfare had changed since then. To him, shell shock was merely a medical term for lack of stamina. He did not go so far as to suggest that the sufferers were actually *afraid* to fight; he regarded them more as involuntary cowards, who basically needed only to pull themselves together. Airing this opinion frequently, he had lectured Martin on the wisdom of his advice.

"No use hiding yourself away, boy," he would always conclude. "We have all been through it, you know. At the Modder River I saw great brutes of men cry like babies over what they had seen and done. Felt it myself, I must confess. Every military man has moments when he feels he can't go on, but it's simply a case of pulling oneself together. The war is over, Martin. You must forget it and put that period behind you. Reticence is no answer, I assure you. You must mix with others; take your rightful place in society. Your father had begun a brilliant career serving his country at the seat of Parliament. We all expect great things from his son, so square up those shoulders and remember who you are."

Martin had listened to the lectures in silence. If he could have "pulled himself together" he would have done so long ago. As it was, he often seemed to be standing outside his own body watching helplessly as it fumbled and groped in humiliating fashion. The assured Sir Hartle would never understand that sensation, which was why he had immediately arranged quarters for Martin in a bungalow shared by an administrative colleague with a large circle of rowdy friends who used the place like a second home. Such an atmosphere was supposed to help Martin tread the road to recovery.

This first week at the bungalow had been a terrible strain. Damien Lang used the communal dining and sitting rooms with inconsiderate frequency for entertaining his friends. Martin had been invited to join them, but he was not yet ready for crowds, party clamour, freely-flowing alcohol, and loud gramophone music which muddled a man's thoughts on sultry evenings. He had made a fool of himself once by falling over a low stool he had not noticed, and had kept to his own rooms during the other revels held by his fun-loving colleague.

Today's invitation had thrown him into something of a panic when Sir Hartle had told him about it. Resistance had risen like a solid wall, but his godfather had insisted that he must attend the tennis party because the Beresfords were people of quiet influence who could help him socially. Despite that, Martin had had no intention of going there, until a sense of guilt had overtaken him. Sir Hartle had been very good to him. With the bungalow to himself that afternoon, his confidence had risen to persuade him that little could go wrong on such an occasion. A tennis party took place in the open, where there would be few obstacles to trap him. The atmosphere would be casual, and any social clamour would be muted by the surrounding afternoon. Tennis was his game and, although he had not played since his second spell in hospital, he would surely not have lost his skill. The Beresford house was within walking distance, and he was too new to the colony to take a rickshaw even that short distance. Setting out tardily, he had felt an assurance he had not experienced for many months. Passing a gate in the wall, he had heard voices and laughter just the other side of it. Certain that he would find the court there, he had entered through the gate and walked beneath a long curving pergola.

At that point in his thoughts, the dread nausea began to return. He opened his eyes quickly, and the first thing he saw was the bottle of brandy. It had been on the chest of drawers for a week. As a symbol of recovery it was pathetic; as a promise of oblivion it beckoned irresistibly. Untucking the mosquito net from around his bed, Martin settled on it beneath the slowly rotating fan and downed several stiff tots. Then he abandoned the glass to drink straight from the bottle as he relived the last few hours.

He had entered the Beresford grounds, plagued by no more than slight nervousness when finding himself confronting a dozen or so surprised youngsters who had plainly not expected him to appear from

25

that direction. Whilst he had been regretting his error of protocol, a girl had come from their midst . . . a girl with large violet eyes, long pale hair caught back with a blue ribbon, and a mouth slightly parted as she had approached him. Something quite shattering had happened at the sight of her. Overwhelming sexual desire had raced through him, bringing the inevitable appalling result. Knocked totally off-balance and unable to think straight, he had then been faced by the girl's brother, whose undisguised belligerence left Martin in no doubt that his condition was apparent, to him and to everyone present. Retribution had come swiftly. He had been surrounded by people mouthing things at him, and the old terrors had returned. He remembered little of what had followed, save that something he had once done extremely well had then turned into a stumbling, fumbling marathon watched by the girl and her sadistic brother.

Tipping the bottle again, Martin's dulled senses tried to come to terms with the implications of what had happened. Since he had emerged from his limbo of shock a year ago and found himself in a ward with fellow-sufferers, he had been immune to sexual response. Where some patients made violent and uninhibited overtures to every nurse in sight, Martin had been completely unmoved by the female form. His doctor had produced erotic pictures, passages of obscene prose, and even bawdy trench jokes, all of which had failed to arouse any interest in him. Passion was apparently a thing of the past, where he was concerned. The medical staff had assured him that it was unlikely to be permanent, but he had been unprepared for it to return so immediately and violently after twelve long months. He could still picture Lydia Beresford's stunning invitation to ravishment as she had approached through that pergola. He could also still see the expression she had worn as he had blundered down the front steps of her home after a wildly garbled exchange with her parents, during which, to their obvious relief, he had refused tea. Recovery? It was out of the question. He would be a stuttering, twitching misfit for the rest of his life.

Wah woke Martin at dawn, setting on the bedside table a tray bearing a glass of milky liquid, which he assured his master was good for sore heads. Martin raised his from the pillow and found it was more than sore. He groaned. What a state to be in on the first day of his new job. Through eyes narrowed by the piercing stabs of pain behind them, he watched the little Chinese go through to fill the bath then return to take from the wardrobe with a creaking door, cotton undershorts and vest, a white shirt, sober tie, and a starched white suit on a hanger. Socks and a handkerchief were set with precise movements on a chair, beneath which highly-polished brown shoes were placed side by side. The tasks completed, Wah turned toward the bed with a wide smile.

"Blekfast leddy soon. Floot, baconegg, toast and larlalade. Allite?"

Martin shook his head, then wished he had not. "Just coffee, Wah."

The man's smile broadened as he pointed to the glass beside the bed. "This one good. You eat blekfast allite."

The miracle was achieved. By the time Martin had submerged himself in tepid water for five minutes, brushed his teeth vigorously, dressed and combed his damped hair into place, he felt like a new man. Early morning in Singapore was strangely pleasant to him. The *kebuns* were watering gardens and hosing down verandahs, so the air was filled with the smells normally encountered in European hothouses—warm earth, damp giant foliage, and the overpowering scent of exotic blooms. The trees were filled with chattering cockatoos, whose raucous screeches mingled with the lovely liquid melodies produced by the orioles. Small monkeys chased through the branches, filled with the exuberance of a new day. In clearings reached by the sun, and on exposed stone walls, lizards lay soaking up the warmth necessary to make them active, and the cicadas reduced their endless chorus to half volume.

Martin walked through the central sitting room to a dining room furnished with dark solid furniture polished to a rich sheen. Breakfast was set on the verandah, as usual, where lush vegetation shielded it from the sun and where Martin had eaten it alone after his colleague had departed for the office during the past week. Damien Lang was already seated at the table, and appeared irritated at having his attention drawn from the scene outside.

"Good morning," greeted Martin, sitting in the other chair and shaking out the starched napkin.

"Forgot you were getting down to some honest toil today," grunted the other man. "I must warn you I'm very anti-social on rising. Can't abide chit-chat at the breakfast table."

Urged to express lack of surprise, since the man indulged in an excess of it most evenings, Martin confined himself to saying, "That suits me, Lang."

They ate chilled papaya, bacon, eggs and tomatoes, toast and marmalade without exchanging a word, either with each other or with Wah, who served them with dedicated efficiency. Martin found it an ideal arrangement. He did not care for the sardonic Lang, or the set he brought to the bungalow. If it were not for the fact that he found rapport with no one these days, Martin might have thought Sir Hartle guilty of great misjudgement in his choice of accommodation.

The contemplative breakfast period allowed Martin time to think of

27

the day ahead. He had been taken to the old administrative building several days ago, to be introduced and shown over the department in which he would work. With Sir Hartle beside him, Martin had found his future colleagues pleasant enough, but he had detected a subdued resentment of someone they would regard as a usurper. He had no illusions about the change in their attitude he might find today. The one cheering prospect was that his office would be shared by a middle-aged medical adviser, who was more often than not at the nearby hospital, he had been told. Dr McGregor had been absent last week, so Martin fervently hoped he would see little of a man reputed to have become eccentric after a lifetime spent in the East. Maybe the head of his department, Sir Frederick Wildernesse, had unwittingly put the two lunatics on his staff together, thought Martin wryly.

Exactly at seven-thirty, Wah positioned himself by the open front entrance ready to assist his two masters into their jackets, hand them their topees, then signal the waiting rickshaw-men to approach the foot of the steps. It was while Martin was in his room collecting his notecase and small change, that his neighbour appeared from his own quarters on the other side of the bungalow. In his hand was Martin's blazer.

"Must have been quite a party you attended last night," he drawled. "You left half your clothes behind."

"How did you get that?" asked Martin, humiliation washing over him anew at the evidence of further idiocy yesterday.

"The Beresfords' boy brought it round. Thought it was mine. I forgot about it until now." A knowing smile crossed Lang's face. "There's also a billet-doux. Engaged some virgin's fancy, did you? Have a care, Lothario. Fathers come down hard on upstarts who think that having an influential godfather will guarantee them *everything*." Dropping the blazer on the floor, he murmured, "Adieu, until this evening," and walked out to descend the steps to the waiting rickshaw.

Picking up the pale-coloured coat, Martin plucked an envelope from the breast pocket before hurrying out to occupy the second rickshaw. It would not help to be late on his first day. The runner in loose cotton clothes set off down the crescent-shaped drive on bare feet, swinging into the road where an entire procession of white-suited Europeans in topees was heading toward the commercial centre in rickshaws, horse-drawn carriages or motor-cars, all of which had to thread their way between the trams. Ignoring those around him Martin slit open the envelope, half afraid to read the contents. The thick decisive hand-writing conveyed a message he had little expected to receive:

I shall be going to the Swimming Club on Sunday morning, as usual.

If you'd care to be introduced as a new member, be at the *Berondel* wharf between eight and eight-fifteen.

Alex Beresford

Into his mind came a vision of a man around his own age, sturdily built and good-looking, with brown curly hair, assessing green eyes, and an expression of hostility as he had set out to punish an unwanted guest for having carnal thoughts about his sister. Who could have forced him to pen such an invitation? Not the upright, respectable parents who had been unable to disguise their aversion during the introduction and short garbled conversation. Not the lovely sister, whose honour Beresford had leapt to defend. Not Sir Hartle; there had been no time for that. If young Beresford had made the gesture without duress, what was behind it? Further public humiliation? A verbal warning to stay away from Lydia Beresford? Not whilst recommending him for membership of a club, surely. The puzzle occupied Martin all the way to the two-storeyed building set amid immaculate lawns, frangipani trees and beds containing hibiscus and poinsettias.

The first occupation of the administrators was apparently to drink tea by the open windows, while their individual messengers watered the plants on the sills. As Martin walked through the stone corridor to his small office, he saw the identical scene through every open door he passed. No one looked his way, so he made no attempt to bid a good morning to any of his new colleagues. It seemed that, like Damien Lang, they were anti-social in the morning. A board bearing his name had been nailed on to his door, which stood ajar as if awaiting his arrival. Inside, order was strictly observed. The new desk stood squarely central, suggesting that those who had placed it there had measured the distance from each of the four walls. The blotter was placed equidistant from the ends of the dark wooden surface; the ink pots containing black for normal messages, red for urgent ones or for stressing important passages, and green for those concerning ethnic matters, were lined up regimentally at the top of the blotter. A wooden tray marked IN lay on the right corner. Another marked OUT lay on the left. A selection of pens with shiny nibs rested in the felt-lined rack. A swivel chair with cane seat and back rest faced the kneehole in the desk at a correct ninety degrees.

With a faint sense of amusement Martin stepped inside, likening the scene to the first day back at school after the holidays. It had seemed like sacrilege then to mar the blotting paper with a smudge, or make an inkstain on the desk. He felt the same way now. The prospect need not have worried him. An hour after the young Malay allocated as his own messenger had brought his tea and watered his plants, Martin was still sitting at the tidy desk with nothing to do. He had looked in all the drawers and found them empty save for a dead *chichak*, and a faded map of the island. The messenger sat on a stool outside the door, enjoying the idle quality of his morning as he watched his colleagues passing back and forth on frequent errands. For the seventh time, Martin wondered whether to take action or sit it out all day. He had expected a slightly cool reception, but not ostracism.

Another half an hour passed, and his patience ran out. The situation was ludicrous. Better to face them and have it out than to allow them to think him gormless. The Head of Department's assistant was an urbane youngster with straw-coloured hair and a moustache of the same shade. He regarded Martin from behind a desk piled high with papers shifting in the breeze from an overheard fan.

"Someone should have explained that one makes an appointment first, Linwood," he said smoothly, in reply to Martin's demand. "Sir Frederick's schedule is extremely heavy, you know. One can't expect to walk in at any old time and request a hearing." Consulting a large diary, he looked up with a frown. "I could just *squeeze* you in at twelve-thirty next Friday."

With one of the flash explosions of anger common to men in his condition, Martin said, "*Go to hell, Grayston!*"

The man coloured, but held on to his control very well as he offered, with a touch of frost in his voice, "If the matter is that urgent, I could pass a message to Sir Frederick."

Knowing that his hands were starting to shake, Martin thrust them into his pockets while he took a deep breath. "I'm sorry, but I'm inclined to get very angry over other people's stupidity . . . and it's the height of it to give me a brand new office and a decent salary, then ignore me. Contrary to the opinion you plainly all have, I am not a millstone Sir Hartle has tied around your necks. I may be new to Singapore and its problems, but I'm well able to take responsibility. I commanded an entire company for two years at Arras and the Somme, so I imagine I could cope with the routine business of this department, shouldn't you?" Growing calmer, he added, "I'd be obliged if you'd pass that message to Sir Frederick when the opportunity presents itself. Now, if you'll excuse me, I must get back to my office where mid-morning tea is doubtless about to be dispensed. I'd hate to miss it."

A cup of tea was certainly awaiting Martin, and so was a man in his early forties, with thick tawny eyebrows, shrewd eyes and a craggy pleasant face deeply browned by the sun. He wore a crumpled linen suit and exuded the odours of sweat and antiseptic.

"Hallo," he greeted from the adjoining chamber. "Could you be the M. W. T. Linwood announced on that door?"

"Yes," replied Martin defensively.

"I'm McGregor, George Arthur Henry Herbert. So I beat you by one initial, young Linwood. Finding it hot, are you?"

He nodded. "In more ways than one."

"Take your tea. It makes a man sweat, but it does him more good than alcohol. Imbibe, do you?"

"At times."

"Which times?"

"When I decide that I will."

Dr McGregor rose smiling, and walked into Martin's area of the dual office, teacup in his hand. "Give us time. We grow on new arrivals, after a while."

Martin relaxed his rigid shoulders and took up the cup and saucer from his desk, rubbing the spot where it had stood and saying, "Can't have this perfection marred. I've been admiring it since seven-thirty."

The thick eyebrows rose. "Nothing to do? You can help me, unless you like idling."

"I'd be glad to help, believe me. Trouble is, I know nothing of medical matters."

"I know a little, but not nearly as much as I'd like. Medicine is changing all the time, but I'm in a backwater here. However . . . er . . . what do M. W. and T. indicate, by the way?"

"Martin William Trevor."

"Which do you prefer?"

"The first."

He nodded. "So do I. However, Martin, I am no longer in general practice, and the work I do here is well fitted for a layman like you to join in."

As Martin drank his tea speculatively, the other man began to chuckle. "I can see the romantic thoughts passing through your mind: struck off for operating whilst drunk and killing a patient; broke the rules and married a woman of the country, which would put me beyond the pale. No, my dear fellow, nothing like that. I have a grave disability. I throw fits and foam at the mouth without warning. Can't possibly run a practice any longer. Very unromantic. Disappointed?"

Martin shook his head, but the confidence he longed to express remained unspoken as he quietly finished his tea, enjoying the gentle ruffling of his hair caused by the circling fan above.

"What exactly do you do for the department?" he asked.

"My official title is General Dogsbody," McGregor responded with a grin. "I've had fifteen years' experience in the East, ten of them at mission stations in some fairly inaccessible places, the rest in hospitals specialising in tropical medicine. Three years ago, symptoms I had been

31

trying to ignore magnified into a serious attack which forced me to face facts. I was fortunate enough to have intelligent friends, who knew my experience and knowledge of this part of the world were invaluable. With poverty, overcrowding and squalor comes disease. The native people die, of course, but not at the appalling rate at which the Europeans succumb. I have to keep a tight check on medical conditions in the native quarters in order to prevent possible epidemics." He slapped at a mosquito on his neck, muttered a curse on all its relations, then went on. "We have a team of doctors, and a beautiful modern clinic, but I'm known and tolerated by the local people, so I'm accorded the doubtful honour of doing the field work." He gave a short laugh. "I had a minor attack down at a sampan colony once. They saw me in paroxysm, foaming at the mouth, and became convinced that I was some kind of high priest going into a trance. Fascinating how they can do it at will, you know. I'll take you to witness the phenomenon one day, if you're interested in that kind of thing."

Martin could hold back no longer. "I don't actually foam at the mouth, but the effects of shell shock still reduce me to a state of acute nervousness, at times."

George McGregor perched on the edge of the desk and looked up at him frankly. "Well, lad, it took you a while to open up. Didn't the doctors tell you that the best way to cope with it is to admit it openly and often?"

Martin stared. "You knew about it?"

"Every European in Singapore knows, I should imagine. That kind of news is fallen upon by social vultures."

Everything suddenly made sickening sense. A private word from Sir Hartle in influential ears had resulted in the facts of his own condition being relayed throughout the colony. His new colleagues imagined him to be witless; Damien Lang had treated him as if a child in telling him to be quiet during breakfast and not to show interest in the colonial girls. It was then he realised that the Beresfords must have known before he arrived at their house yesterday. Small wonder everyone had stared at him, and Alex Beresford had played such a pitiless game with him. The lovely Lydia had also known, and had merely been treating him as one would an idiot for whom one felt compassion.

"Oh, God!" he exclaimed in despair. "They all expect a dolt, and I've given them every justification for that belief. Some chance I have of being accepted out here."

The other man wagged his head, smiling. "Much depends on whom you really wish to accept you. The sticklers for protocol probably never will; as men who have lived here all their lives the mercantile class will resent your intrusion into their enclosed paradise. Some of your administrative colleagues will probably snarl "nepotism" as they turn their backs. The ignorant will claim you are halfway to bedlam, as I am believed to be."

"So, if you're General Dogsbody, I shall be Major Misfit."

"Only to a section of this community, Martin. There's more to life out here than the Cricket Club, afternoon tea at Raffles, and exchanges of smouldering glances during the monsoon season. The mixture of cultures and religions is fascinating, the flora and fauna are some of the most varied in the world, and it is possible to find on this small island a study of human nature which is at once amusing, dismaying and perplexing. If all the world's a stage, this corner of it produces more than its quota of dramas and comedies." He rose to grip Martin's arm. "My advice, for what it's worth, is to forget your own weakness and look for that in the people around you. I guarantee you'll not find Singapore dull or disappointing."

By the end of the week Martin was finding more than enough to occupy his working hours. Tom Grayston had responded to his outburst quickly, although within two days it had dawned on Martin that he was being given all the unpopular outside work. He spent very little time in the immaculate office where it was cool and pleasant, for he was no sooner back in it than he was obliged to set out again in one of the rickshaws always waiting in the shade of the trees near the main entrance. The men who pulled them set off with an air of assurance when he stated his destination, and he had no choice but to put his trust in their ability to take him to the right place. To someone who had been in the colony only two weeks, the long hours out in the heat of the day were a severe trial. He returned to his bungalow exhausted, but he slept without the usual nightmares as a result.

George McGregor was also frequently absent during the day, so meetings between them were rare. Their initial conversation stayed in Martin's mind, however, and it was partially responsible for his decision to accept the invitation for Sunday morning. Alex Beresford was all Martin had once been. Vital, confident, possessor of a family, a home based on wealth, and a future bright with promise. If the young shipping heir had a weakness, Martin would like to know what it could be for he appeared to have everything a man could want. Something had prompted the enigmatic invitation on the heels of public disparagement. By accepting it, Martin might solve the mystery. He might also correct the impression he had made at the disastrous tennis party, for Lydia Beresford would not be present at the all-male Swimming Club to inhibit him in any way.

33

They greeted each other warily on the jetty where *Berondel* ships tied up, and Martin was further mystified by the unsmiling man who led the way down the steps to where a company launch bobbed on a lively sea. The blaze of hostility had gone from Alex Beresford's eyes, but it had been replaced by an evasiveness that disguised what he might be thinking. The boatman put to sea, and Martin settled on one of the slatted seats, reflecting that his host would surely normally join a party of his friends for such an outing. Where were they today? The launch should be filled with a laughing crowd anticipating the pleasures of swimming, not two silent men unsure of why they were there together.

Even so, Martin derived pleasure from the progress through water turned opalescent green by the sun from a cloudless sky. They chugged past the steep dark sides of merchant ships flying the *Berondel* flag, rocking wildly each time they crossed the wake of other boats. The Javanese at the helm was expert at dodging the nautical jam ranging from ponderous ocean-going junks with brown sails, and eyes painted on their prows to enable the vessels to see possible hazards ahead, right through to the hooded sampans housing entire families, tongkangs impossibly laden, and a myriad narrow craft carrying rotting vegetables, piled fish caught too long ago, coal in broken baskets—anything which would bring in a meagre sum to sustain life. He was quite relaxed as he sat back against the side of the launch, one arm along the rail. It was beautifully peaceful. Water slapped rhythmically against the hull, a light breeze lifted his hair from his damp brow, and the sun burnt into his face and hands already assuming a toffee-coloured shade from his hours spent in the open that week. A sigh of contentment broke from him, and he decided that it was time he found out a little about his companion.

"I think I should have joined the Navy in 1914," he began. "This seems vastly more interesting and comfortable than soldiering."

"I don't suppose it's much better under fire," Alex replied, then resumed his silence once more.

Martin tried again. "I suppose you sail with your own ships of the line, whenever possible."

"No, not if I can avoid it. Noisy cumbersome vessels. There's no romance attached to freighters."

"I doubt your captains would agree with that."

Alex gazed at the several company vessels alongside the main jetty, where winches squeaked as large laden nets were swung up and over into the holds. The godowns beyond were a scene of activity, the sound of altercation floating seaward from them as native porters argued over their loads.

34

"The captains? Plying the same coastal waters year in, year out, they know every sandbank and hazard, every channel, every tidal flow and wind pattern. Those ships are so solid and dependable they can ride out monsoons like rubber ducks in a bath. The only risk they have to concern themselves with is whether or not the cargo will be waiting at their ports of call when they arrive."

Sensing that he had somehow touched a nerve, Martin asked casually, "Not a dedicated shipping man?"

Slowly, Alex turned back to face him. There was a great deal of expression in his green eyes now. "My great-grandfather started the *Berondel Line* with two other men—Onslow and Delman—hence the amalgamation of the three names. It was a line of sailing ships then, of course, great square-riggers armed with cannon to fend off Chinese and Javanese pirates who used to plunder these waters. Their cargoes were mostly rubber, pepper, tin and spices, although some captains risked carrying opium to run the gauntlet of the authorities.

"Old Beresford's son—my grandfather—fell out with his partners and created a false scare on the market in order to buy them out cheaply. When society realised what he had done, his business integrity was damned and other merchants refused to deal with him at a time when competition was intense. Having acquired the company, he found himself without the funds to run it. That was when he was driven to bring in revenue by other methods. Piracy, to be accurate. He fitted out two fast clippers with cannon and false flags, then began the lucrative sideline of robbing his competitors, details of whose cargoes and sailing times he well knew."

He paused to offer Martin a cigarette and light them both. Then he continued the story. "Grandfather made a vast fortune before his luck ran out. Naval gunboats finally caught up with his pirate clippers. The true owner of the brigantines was then identified. There was the most fearful scandal, and Grandfather shot himself, leaving his family to carry on as best they could." He looked away again as if unwilling to let Martin read his feelings. "My father has dedicated his life to bringing respectability to our name and the line again. *Berondel* is now the epitome of solid and sound trading." There was a pause before he murmured, "Grandfather must be turning in his grave."

"No romance in the business any longer?" suggested Martin, with interest in this insight into the other's character.

"Cargo vessels don't dance over the water. They can't lie on their sides in a great racing turn; they don't have wills of their own. There's no sense of conflict, no challenge, no *risk*. Where's the satisfaction in knowing exactly what you'll be doing in ten or even twenty years' time?"

35

To Martin, who had lived for too long in the knowledge that each day might be his last, the prospect seemed highly attractive. With a frown, he asked, "What kind of challenge are you seeking?"

The other man faced him, and a return of the evasive look told Martin the confidential mood had vanished. Had he probed too far?

"We'll be there in a minute or two. You'll find the members are quite a decent crowd, because they're mainly young. There are some elderly sticklers at other clubs who cut up rough over the slightest thing, and spoil a chap's enjoyment."

"Sticklers like my godfather?" Martin asked deliberately.

Alex Beresford flushed a little. "Well . . . yes, as a matter of fact."

"I suspected that he might be a little out of touch with youth. He was a close friend of my father at school, and they soldiered together in South Africa, but Sir Hartle came East when I was still at prep school so we've seen very little of each other in the interim years. He has a strong sense of duty and of honour, and has been exceedingly kind to me since my father died. However, his knowledge of progress is scant, which suggests to me that the world has passed him by out here."

"It has passed us all by. Isn't that what you're really saying, Linwood?" the other man demanded aggressively.

Martin looked him directly in the eye, sensing that he had again touched a nerve. "I haven't been here long enough to make a judgement like that, Beresford, but I'll take your word for it."

The launch approached the steps leading up the sea wall to the grounds of the club, and they climbed up to join a large number of men sitting around in groups with towels draped across their shoulders to avoid burning in the direct sun. Alex Beresford appeared highly popular with most of them, and Martin was left to absorb the scene as his host's attention was taken by those who had arrived earlier. The large two-storeyed clubhouse faced the sea, where swimmers were either enjoying the lazy pleasure of floating on their backs or were out on the diving platform for more energetic exercise. On the terrace, most of the tables were occupied by those who had taken a dip and were now embarking on breakfast. With vague mental visions of trenches, machine-guns and diving aircraft superimposing themselves on these images, Martin was inclined to believe that the world *had* passed this entire colony by.

The morning proved very enjoyable. Relaxed and feeling confident, Martin alternately swam and lazed the hours away in undemanding company. It was undemanding because he was a silent observer for most of the time, which suited him very well. Although no one made it obvious that he was regarded as in any way different from most men, there was a certain amount of reticence on the part of other members who nevertheless accepted that Sir Hartle Weyford's godson must be allowed to join the club, especially when introduced by one of their own number. For some time, Martin watched the young shipper executing daring dives from the highest board on the raft which heaved on the swell, and recognised an athlete of no small ability.

From the conversation of those around him, Martin learned that young Beresford was a skilled, fearless horseman who was the star of his polo team. He was also the finest fast bowler at the Cricket Club, besides being an accomplished sprinter and tennis player. If the adjectives *impetuous*, *rash* and *daring* were often used, they were all part of the general recognition of sporting skill, culminating in speculation on the forthcoming Gentleman's Stakes, a race in which all aspiring jockeys competed each year. Alex Beresford was rated second only to a captain of artillery named Reardon. With the honour of his regiment riding with him, this military firebrand was believed to have the edge on the young shipper, who nevertheless confidently expected to be presented with the cup. The subject of the discussion returned from the diving platform to emerge, dripping, in time to augment his claim with cheery bravado. A lively argument ensued until the boastful jockey realised that noon was not far off.

Turning to Martin, he said, "We'd better towel down, I'm afraid. The time seems to pass twice as quickly on Sunday mornings."

They went to the changing cubicles, and emerged almost simultaneously, neatly dressed and with their hair slicked down. As they strolled away from the clubhouse, Alex said casually, "My sister said she would join us for curry tiffin at the Seaview."

Martin's heart raced. It was the last thing he had expected. His confidence evaporated swiftly as he thought of the impression he must have given her at their last meeting. He dared not face her again, in case the same frightful thing happened.

"Sorry, I can't . . . I mean, I didn't expect," he began in the dreaded stammer. "Another engagement, you see."

"Oh. Well . : . fair enough," his host conceded, almost in relief.

Martin expressed his thanks clumsily when they parted. On the journey back to the harbour he told himself the peacefulness of the morning had been an illusion. All the same, he had several clues to ponder on for the remainder of the day. Alex Beresford excelled in the most active and dangerous sports, yet they apparently did not provide the challenge he was seeking. Despite having everything a young man could ask for, the young shipping heir had his eyes on horizons beyond this colony. Why did he not pursue them? If the traits of his rip-roaring pirate grandfather were also in him, he could easily end up destroying himself, too.

Chapter 3

Sunday supper was the one meal of the week which Margery Beresford preferred to keep as a purely family occasion. It was not a time when English residents tended to entertain, in any case, but Alex nevertheless regarded the obligation to be present as one of the invisible apron strings his mother had tied to her two surviving children. That particular evening seemed more irksome than usual. His father was preoccupied during the meal, still smarting from the outcome of his obligatory invitation to Martin Linwood, no doubt. Lydia was sulking because Alex had not delivered the man on a plate to her for tiffin. His suspicion that she had embarked on a fresh melodramatic infatuation seemed dismally justified by her behaviour.

He was already regretting the impulse that had led to that morning's meeting with the person who seemed to be in all their thoughts. It had been designed to salve his own conscience over the tennis party, but had only resulted in pricking it further. Doubting that Linwood would turn up, Alex had then been treated to a glimpse of a vastly different man from the stumbling fool on the court. Knowing that he had been mainly responsible for that pathetic display made Alex recognise the courage it must have taken for the other man to face his tormentor again so soon. Only mention of Lydia had brought a return of the nervous stuttering, and Alex did not blame him for wishing to avoid a confrontation with a girl who had witnessed his humiliation.

Whilst the committee members of the Swimming Club had been obliged to admit Sir Hartle's godson, they had heard what everyone in Singapore had heard—stories backed by the accounts of those who had been present at the Beresford tennis party. They were all doubtless as baffled as Alex was now. Although Linwood had appeared relaxed and normal, he had given no extravagant displays of swimming like those in which many of the younger members revelled. There had been evidence that he was a strong swimmer with considerable stamina, but he had contented himself with no more than a little enjoyable exercise. Out of the water he had participated in the conversation of those around him only when drawn into it. His comments had been intelligent and concise before lapsing into silence again. Yet, even when sitting quietly, Alex had been aware of the man's presence amid his noisy friends.

Halfway through curry tiffin eaten in company with his sulky sister, Alex had realised that Martin Linwood was a quiet man because his voice had already been heard by the world. He had been to the very brink of existence, and returned shattered but enlightened. What must he have thought of Alex's bravado words in the launch, when he had referred with contempt to the *Berondel* captains and suggested that they faced no risks or challenge? His own days were spent no more dangerously than dictating letters, checking figures, buying cargoes and searching for more profitable routes. How immature he must have sounded, how arrogant. The strange lapse which had prompted him to confide the history of his trading family meant that he had not freed himself, after all, of the man who had a disconcerting knack of reversing roles.

"Alexander, you're not listening to a word we are saying tonight."

He looked up to find his mother's eyes filled with affectionate admonition, and Lydia's filled with lingering reproof. Really, females were the bane of a man's existence, he thought moodily.

"Sorry. I have something on my mind. Business," he added hastily, before his father could unite with them in condemnation.

"No business on Sunday evening, dear," his mother ruled firmly. "It is my favourite period of the week, you know that. We are so rarely *en famille* these days."

"That's the way Alex likes it, Mummy," put in Lydia. "He much prefers the company of wild cronies like Ferdy Hancock."

Alex scowled at her. "Ferdy isn't wild. He happens to have more life in him than your insipid crowd, that's all."

"I'll never forgive him for what he did at the tennis party . . . and you were egging him on."

"I wish to hear no more about the tennis party. I believe I made that plain immediately after the event," said Margery through a prim mouth.

"Hear, hear," put in Austin heartily. "That affair is best forgotten. Shall we adjourn to the verandah for coffee? A breeze is springing up, and I must say I enjoy Sunday evening quietness with the stars over my head and the tropic moon over my shoulder."

The poetic outburst caused Alex to raise his eyebrows at Lydia as they left the dining table to walk out on to the broad verandah, where a boy was lighting ornamental lanterns. His sister, still unforgiving, gazed back at him mutinously. With a sigh he walked to the balustrade, where the blinds had been raised at sunset to allow the passage for an evening breeze. As he gazed toward the fan palms, the usual ache in his breast intensified at the sight of the frieze of curving fronds now silvered by a brilliant moon. What he would give to be in the midst of a desert, like T E Lawrence, one man in a huge ocean of silvery sand overhung by that moon? What if he were at the controls of a Sopwith Camel, flying through a silent silver-blue night, with that great moon staring him in the eye? Imagine standing on the deck of a long graceful clipper which flew over foaming florescent sea, setting a triumphant course by that moon and riding as high as any free spirit. Next minute, a new image superimposed itself on the others. He saw the white face and dark secret eyes of Martin Linwood, who was standing in a trench with a host of dark, silent men. What had it been like to stare out across a no-man's-land made as bright as day by the sudden emergence of the moon through clouds, and see the silhouettes of an advancing enemy horde for a few brief moments before darkness descended again? What were a soldier's thoughts and feelings before battle? Was there a sense of fear or of curious elation? What supreme quality allowed him to face it again and again until his mind could take no more? Martin Linwood had the answers to all those questions, yet Alex knew he could never bring himself to ask them.

"Alexander, your coffee is growing cold. Come along!"

Responding to his mother's command made the ache within him barely containable, and he sat heavily in the chair beside her to stir his coffee with unnecessary vigour.

"I have decided to refurbish that large airy room on the west side of the house, Austin," his mother said then. "A new counterpane will have to be bought, for the present one is quite unsuitable. I have spoken to Ah Toy on the subject. She will be responsible for that room, in addition to Lydia's, and I feel it is most important to make her *au fait* with the arrangements right from the beginning. The furniture is a little too heavy for a young lady's use, so I shall have it exchanged with the suite presently in the third guest room. A selection of pretty cushions, new silk shades, and several cream and blue rugs should create the effect I am after. It will look delightfully welcoming for Dorothea, don't you agree, Alexander?"

Alex came from his thoughts to ask, "Agree about what, Mother?"

"The arrangements for Dorothea."

He shrugged, saying irritably, "I'm no authority on such things. Lydia's the one to speak to about what girls like and don't like. In my opinion, this one should be exceedingly grateful that you've even agreed to put her up for an indefinite period. It's not as if she's really related to us."

"Of course she is, dear. Not a blood relative, perhaps, but she must surely be some kind of cousin to you."

She will be if you have your way, he thought gloomily. Any excuse to gather another child under your maternal wing! Dorothea du Lessier was the daughter of Margery's brother's wife's sister, and only his mother could make a close relationship out of *that*. It had taken no more than one rare letter from her brother to persuade Margery to agree to play hostess to this girl who, according to Uncle George, needed to get right away to a different environment after a difficult period following a bereavement. Alex dreaded the advent of another female in the household, especially one requiring sympathy and understanding, and could foresee the indefinite period of the visit extending into permanence.

"Lydia has already written addressing her as Cousin Dorothea, so I think that is the best way to continue," his mother ruled. "I am expecting you to do your utmost to help her feel at home here, Alexander. I know her father only died six months ago, but I daresay it will do her good to go to an occasional party with one or two of your more responsible friends."

"Oh, really," he protested hotly. "Can't a man have a life of his own? First the Linwood fellow, now this girl we don't know who needs to recover from something about which we are unclear. Why do we have to entertain all the waifs and strays in Singapore?"

Lydia turned on him, cheeks pink. "Martin Linwood is not a waif or a stray. How beastly of you to suggest that he is."

"There is no justification for jumping down your mother's throat, Alexander," put in Austin, signalling for his cup to be refilled by the houseboy standing in the shadows several yards away. "Miss du Lessier is to be our guest for at least six months, and there is certainly no suggestion of being charitable to an unfortunate creature, as you suggest. The young woman has very adequate private means." Fixing Alex with a stern look, he added, "Your behaviour comes unpleasantly close to boorishness, on occasion, young man."

"But, sir, it really is the limit when I am asked . . ."

"You are asked to do very little," came the snapped response. "Life is not the long selfish round of pleasure you appear to expect. We all have social obligations. Some of them may be tedious and not entirely to our liking, but unless you wish to follow in the footsteps of your reprehensible grandfather you will fulfil them to the best of your ability. Is that clear?"

Alex let silence be his answer. He could not bring himself to agree in meek filial fashion, especially with Lydia smiling smugly over the reprimand. He sat burning with resentment. Damn Martin Linwood, and damn Dorothea du Lessier. The only hope was to introduce the pair as two fish out of water who might find mutual comfort in each other. It seemed a promising solution until he realised that, instead of sloughing off the cousin who was not a cousin, the Beresford family would probably end up also entertaining Martin Linwood indefinitely.

The conversation centred on Dorothea for some while, then Lydia mentioned that her friend Grace Reynolds had added the girl's name to the guest list for her birthday ball next month. Alex was then reminded of something he had been told at the Seaview earlier that day, and made a bid to change the subject.

"I met Ricky Reynolds today, Father, and he mentioned something I thought worth investigating. His firm handles the *Rochford-Kendal* account, and it seems their finances are rocky, in the extreme. Since *Bergua* went down in the South China Sea last year, their fortunes have been going steadily downhill. They lost several rich contracts, besides the ship which had only been in service three months. Ricky says they have debts of some hundred thousand, and will have to sell off a few of their assets in order to stay solvent." He half turned in his chair as he warmed to his theme. "They have a group of godowns on the South Jetty which would be jolly useful for us. They also have a prime contract they now cannot fulfil with an exporter in Manila, which would be just the thing to augment our cargoes there. If we put in a bid now, before the whole thing is made public, we could gain two valuable boosts to our Indies trade. I thought one of us should approach old man Kendal as soon as possible."

Austin looked thunderstruck. "Do you mean to tell me young Reynolds discussed the confidential details of one of his firm's clients' accounts *in the bar of the Seaview Hotel?*"

On the immediate defensive, Alex said, "No . . . I mean, of course he didn't speak about it *publicly*. It was a private word in my ear, that's all. He knows we are anxious to increase our contacts in Manila, and that we are also on the look-out for extra warehousing. It was a friendly tip. I thought it very decent of him."

"Oh, you did, did you? Then I must inform you that, on no account, will I have any part in underhandedness. The fellow has no sense of loyalty to his client whatever, and neither one of us will approach Tom Kendal like a vampire out to suck his blood."

"Kendal has to sell if he wants to remain in competition," Alex cried heatedly. "Once he puts assets like that on the open market, we won't stand a chance. The big names like Jardines will step in, and we'll be left sniffing around like dogs who have seen a bone and been denied a lick."

"Your phraseology smacks of the gutter, young man, and so does your sense of integrity. I will have nothing to do with business practices that are questionable or clandestine. *Berondel* will stand or fall by that principle. I have spent my entire business life wiping the stain of such things from our name, and *nothing* will induce me to sink to sharp dealing."

Alex was furious. "It has nothing to do with sharp dealing! Any shrewd businessman takes advantage of early information. Stock Exchange tips, or the advice of a sound friend who is in the know. We need those godowns; we need that contract in Manila. Really, sir, you're so terrified of being tarred with grandfather's brush, you let chance after chance go by. *Berondel* will stand or fall by your attitude, you say. Then it will *fall*, believe me, and who is going to respect your rigid principles when the company crashes due to overwhelming competition? Business involves taking risks, and I am prepared to take a few."

"I am not," snapped Austin coldly. "While I am the major shareholder in *Berondel*, that is the way I mean to continue. Let me remind you that I have no intention of retiring until I am absolutely satisfied that you will be a worthy successor to all I have devoted my life to build."

Alex rose swiftly and went to lean against the balustrade, gazing at the moon as the storm which had been gathering all day within him reached its zenith. Next minute, he swung round to face his father.

"You might have no successor. Every idea or suggestion of mine which doesn't fit in with your inflexible policy is tossed aside, or condemned as sharp dealing. You give me no leeway whatever. You credit me with no instinct or individuality in a profession that is a legacy of birth, not my free choice. Mother and Lydia are as bad. They expect me to trot around their friends like a trained poodle. There is never any question of asking what *I* want to do, of any of you doing something to oblige *me*." Breathing hard, he held back no longer from the resentment he had never before expressed. "The one thing I desperately wanted, the one chance I would have sold my soul for, was denied me by your combined efforts. You, Father, told me I owed loyalty to the company you had sacrificed your own youth and hopes to rebuild. You, Mother, called me heartless to even think of causing you further grief after the tragic loss of Charles and Eleanor. You said it was utterly selfish and cruel of me to want to go to war; you charged me with loving you so little I could offer myself to be killed without any thought for those I would leave behind to mourn for the rest of their days. Lydia made herself ill with melodramatic anxiety, and you held me to emotional ransom because of it."

His voice grew husky with his anger as he continued. "I cancelled my passage to England, but none of you ever knew what it cost me to do it. I stayed here, as you all wished, but I have regretted the decision every day since then. Yes, I might very well have been killed . . . but I should at least have *lived* before I died."

The outburst silenced his family. Their mute outrage emphasised the chorus of cicadas and bullfrogs, and even highlighted the soft pattering of moths' wings as they fluttered around the lanterns. Austin stared at him with colour heightened, his lips clamped together. Margery sat with her head bowed, as if he had rained blows upon it. Lydia gazed at him with misty condemning eyes as he realised, with incredulity, that they were all waiting for him to apologise for exposing their selfishness. He could take no more.

"I wish to God Charles had survived," he cried. "He would be heir to *Berondel*, and I'd be free. I'd rather be a rascal, like Grandfather, than a bonded slave to a company with no pulsebeat."

A moment longer he looked at them, then he turned away to take the steps into the garden in one leap as he went in search of the moon. He hardly noticed the emptiness of the streets as he drove his new car at top speed alongside a muddy river. The moon hung, huge and inviting, at the end of it, and he fixed his gaze on the great silver disc instead of on the surface ahead. Total impotence filled him. That same moon looked down on a world where men were achieving, creating, finding fulfilment. He thought of Lawrence of Arabia, one Englishman leading a foreign nation to its destiny. He thought of those pioneers of the air who had shown that the aeroplane was the machine of the future. He thought of explorers who trod where no white man had previously been, and mountaineers who defied the elements and the law of gravity to reach the glittering white pinnacles. He thought of Martin Linwood, and the MC he had won at Arras. Yet Alex Beresford, bounden by an obligation to his father, chained by the ghosts of a dead brother and sister, had done nothing save dance to the tunes his family played. What more did they want of him? Would they never be satisfied and release him?

He drove on, lost in the rising volcano of rebellion and longing. Suddenly, the moon tipped sideways and he was thrown over the steering wheel as the car hit the railing beside the river, tried to climb vertically, then thumped back on to the road with its engine racing noisily. For the first few seconds he was too dazed to think straight. Then he became aware that the floor was tilting at an angle, and the dark gleam of water was racing past the bonnet.

Slowly, warily, he switched off the engine and opened the door. The front nearside wheel was in space above the river, and water was dripping from the radiator which had been pierced by the bumper.

44

Locking the door, he gave the vehicle a malevolent glare before slouching off with his hands deep in his pockets. Even the damned car was against him!

Time passed unrecorded, until he came from his preoccupation and grew aware of sounds and activity in the near distance. He glanced around swiftly. The street he was in was little more than a lane, dark, narrow and full of pungent smells. He did not know his exact location, but almost certainly it was in the Chinese quarter—an area Europeans avoided at night, knowing they were unwelcome. No other person walked in the dimness of that thoroughfare, and it soon became obvious why.

At the end of the lane he could see leaping scarlet lights, flashes of vivid gold decoration, and undulating waves of green, blue and yellow. Up there, the sinister silence in the surrounding hovels had been banished by deafening cracks, resounding crashes of cymbals, the high-pitched nasal voices of Chinese singers, and the cries of a crowd carried on a tide of hypnotic excitement into near frenzy.

Alex's heart lurched; his bruised spirit responded to the call of that excitement. Eagerly, his eyes straining to take in the widening vista, he went forward like the moths which had been drawn to the irresistible light of lanterns on his own verandah. The voice of caution was silenced by him before it had a chance to speak. Here were the pulsing rhythms of his longings, here was the bright dazzle of the moon, here was the full expression of his yearning, his cry of frustration: a living kaleidoscope showing him the way in his darkness.

On reaching the top of the lane, Alex was swallowed by the night crowd with eyes only for the spectacle of celebration. Vivid paper lanterns swung in undulating patterns, like small blood-red satellite moons in the velvet darkness. They mingled with banks of golden flame-tipped candles atop poles adorned with rippling gold-embroidered silken banners. The leaders of the procession were spreading out as the street widened and, over the heads of others, Alex could see the approach of the cause of greatest excitement. Caught up in a desperate need to be part of it all, he pushed his way through to the front just as the ceremonial dragon drew level. Its head was enormous and painted with vivid slashes of colour to emphasise great rolling green eyes, thick black brows, red-lined flaring nostrils, a hinged mouth which clicked open and shut to reveal fangs jutting from a cavernous scarlet throat. Emerald-green hair flopped madly around scaly horns as the head was jerked and swung in triumphant semi-menacing manner. The body stretched back along the street for as far as Alex could see. Yards of shimmering blue, green and yellow patterned silk in garish design undulated and wriggled through the gap in the teeming lines of spectators, to the accompaniment of deafening red-tasselled cymbals, the wailing falsetto of handmaidens, and stuttering fire-crackers to ward off evil spirits.

The head of the dragon passed Alex, tossing its mane arrogantly. Then the body started to slither past in a dazzle of colour, as those around him jostled and shifted mesmerically. With an acute pang, he knew the creature would pass him by; would vanish into the night with all its colour, noise and challenge, leaving him once more alone in the darkness. The tail of the dragon was approaching when some curious impetus sent him lunging forward to scramble beneath the silk-covered bamboo rib-cage, which he immediately gripped with both hands. He was swept inexorably onward, the alien smothering darkness illuminated only at ground level.

The creature governed him completely from then on, as he found himself in a mystic world of black-shod feet treading fast and sure throughout the winding ceremonial journey. It was dim and tremendously hot under the dragon, yet the smell of bamboo and ancient fusty cloth which mingled with that of his own sweat became heady, as he surrendered to the demands of the symbolic pagan beast. Tramp, tramp, tramp went his feet, and his heartbeat soon pounded in a matching rhythm. His ears rang with the crashes of cymbals held by those running alongside the dragon, and he began to pant from heat and exertion. Sweat ran into his eyes so that the regiment of feet ahead blurred into ten times the number. His senses began to swim, but he was a prisoner of the creature now. On and on it progressed, until sound and sight mingled into a sensation of being in that world beyond the world which he so longed to reach. The night was no more than a sway of brilliant colours before his aching eyes, his head thudded with the pain of effort, his heart hammered agonisingly in his breast to drive out the old familiar ache.

Next minute, he was gazing straight at the moon he had set out to find. It hung right before his eyes, huge and yellow, tantalisingly near. Yet, as he reached out for it, it occurred to him that his moon had been silver, not amber. He tried desperately to focus clearly, but the yellow light was swinging up and down in a confusing series of movements. The pounding in his head slowly lessened, and he then realised that the night had become very quiet. Fighting down a feeling of nausea, he passed a hand over his brow. It came away wet. His clothes were sticking to him in an uncomfortable manner, and craving for a drink grew stronger and stronger. The bright yellow light was now right in his face. From behind it came voices, angry voices speaking a Chinese dialect he did not know. Then he realised the legion of feet had vanished; the smell of the silken dragon was no longer in his nostrils. In confusion, he tried to make sense of the situation.

Gazing around him, he saw that the crowds had dispersed. Lanterns and banners lay on the ground; the cymbals and sopranos were silent. The fearsome beast, which had rioted for an hour in triumph, was now no more than a beheaded heap of curved bamboo and coloured cloth in a dingy backstreet. Surrounding him was a group of hostile Chinese, glaring in the light from a single yellow lantern. The men began to advance on him, shaking their fists in protest against his unforgivable intrusion in their ritual. Scrambling to his feet, his bemused brain tried to think of the right words to explain why he had done it. His halting basic Cantonese was insufficient for the task: it did not appease them in the least. The unpardonable had been committed and no amount of apology would compensate. The intruder must be driven away, as all devils had been driven away that night. One man picked up a stone and threw it at Alex. Another did the same, causing him to turn and run from a veritable hail of missiles which began to rain down on him.

The area he was in was a tortured maze of alleyways, as dark as Hades and as hot. It was impossible to select a route because his enemies were hot on his heels with howls of abuse, giving him time to do no more than run as fast as possible wherever an opening yawned in the darkness. It was like a living nightmare, and he was beginning to feel almost ill with effort when dark figures emerged from the night ahead, blocking his escape. He slowed to a halt, knowing he was trapped. Incredibly, those pursuing him slowed to a halt, also, then drifted away into the night as if they had never been there. With cohesive thought returning in a flash, Alex realised that the four men ahead of him were infinitely more dangerous than the stone-throwing dragon-men. These four were some of the night inhabitants of the Chinese quarter, who lived by crime. A man could vanish from the face of the earth, leaving no trace, after falling into the hands of such people. They were organised, vicious, and conducted a reign of terror.

In real fear, Alex began running back the way he had come when pursued by the dragon-men. The street was silent and totally deserted. It was as if the people of the East had turned their backs in fatalistic acceptance of his plight. He raced blindly through dark swathes which cut through the darker night, scattering scavenging dogs and a multitude of rats, squelching and slipping through garbage which had been left unswept for days. Light, running footfalls kept pace with him until he finally rounded a corner and glimpsed the lights of a main thorough-

47

fare at the far end of an unlit alleyway. Desperate, he sprinted for that illuminated street, knowing his only hope lay in the brightness his attackers shunned.

Two yards along the narrow way, they brought him down with a blow behind his ear which almost knocked him senseless. Somehow he found the strength to scramble to his feet as they lunged forward, and turn on them with flying fists and feet. His superior strength and build told for a few seconds, but the odds were against him. He was pinned against the wall by two of the men, then a third drew out a blade which flashed in the light from the moon visible over the rooftops. Alex was mesmerised by that blade while the fourth man expertly rifled his pockets and person. That done, his assailant moved slowly forward with the knife at the ready. Before that bright blade could slit Alex's throat, however, the alleyway was suddenly flooded with light. Startled, they all turned to see the headlights of a car, which was making a turn in the main street. Blinded by the beams, it was a moment or two before Alex could make sense of the situation. When he did, he realised that he was standing alone against a light-washed wall. The four had vanished into the regions of their kingdom.

Several outlines of running men appeared at the top of the narrow lane, illuminated by the headlights of the car. An English voice called out, "I say, are you all right?" and Alex knew the danger was over. They took him home in their car, bombarding him with questions on what had happened. He said nothing, and hardly heard their words. Possessing him completely was the memory of that moment when the knife had been poised over his throat; that vital second between life and death.

Martin paid off the rickshaw-boy, and stood for some moments looking at the drive leading to the main entrance of the Beresford home. He could hardly believe that fate had sent him back to the one place he had never wished to enter again, and he prayed that no one would be at home so that he could leave immediately. The houseboy who answered his knock assured the visitor that the young master of the house was there, and ushered Martin into a large room on the south side of the house to wait for him. The faint smell of cigar smoke suggested that it was used by male members of the family as a study, or for business meetings. He breathed a sigh of relief. It was unlikely that he would encounter Lydia Beresford here. He glanced appreciatively at the furniture gleaming richly in the cool dimness created by trees almost touching the verandah beyond. That enclosing vegetation gave a welcome suggestion of privacy, and he told himself it should be possible to deal with the problem quickly and leave by this side exit without encountering any more of the Beresford family.

Martin had put up strong resistance to this errand, but Tom Grayston had stated firmly that Sir Frederick's wishes must be obeyed, apart from the fact that no one else was free to do the job and Martin's friendship with young Beresford made him the ideal person to clear up the mystery. One visit to the Swimming Club with the shipping heir hardly constituted friendship, in Martin's view, and the humiliation suffered on his previous visit to this house still rankled enough to induce the dreaded nervousness during those few minutes he waited. Swallowing hard, he ran his fingers around the inside of his collar to ease it from the clamminess of his skin. They stilled for a moment on the ridged scar at the base of his throat. He remembered the taste of choking blood as he had lain beside the barbed wire waiting for nightfall, when stretcher-bearers would come for him and the other wounded. It had seemed like a lifetime of waiting.

"Hallo."

Martin spun round, jumping nervously, having been so lost in that other time he had not heard anyone enter. "Er . . . hallo. I . . . look, I'm sorry to disturb you at home, but I tried your office and was told you had not been in all day."

"No. I felt a bit off-colour."

As the other man came further into the room, Martin looked at him for signs of cuts or bruising. Apart from shadows beneath his eyes and definite coolness in his voice, Alex Beresford looked fine. What was clear, however, was that he did not welcome this visit so soon after yesterday morning's gesture in introducing him to the Swimming Club. Hands deep in the pockets of casual slacks, he halted a few feet from Martin, regarding him warily.

"Well, what can I do for you?"

"You can answer a few questions, if you don't mind," Martin said, beginning to resent an attitude which suggested that the other man suspected him of becoming a social nuisance. "I feel certain a mistake has been made somewhere along the line, however."

The wariness increased. "This all sounds highly mysterious."

"I'm here to ask you to clear up the mystery, Beresford. We received a memo from the military garrison this afternoon. It stated that the three officers who witnessed the attack on Alexander Beresford are *en route* to Hong Kong, but will provide written statements before they sail tomorrow morning. It posed something of a problem to my people, because no report of an attack had been made. I've been sent along to straighten out the misconception."

49

Rolling his eyes heavenward, Alex sighed heavily, saying, "Trust the bloody Army to report everything . . . in triplicate, no doubt."

"There really was an attack on you?"

"No, of course not."

"So the three officers have mistaken you for someone else?"

"No-o. Look here, whom do you represent, Linwood?" he demanded aggressively. "Have you some kind of official status, or have you come here as a damned administrative spy?"

Martin began to suspect the truth. It was possible the young shipper was in some kind of scrape which would blow over if ignored .Three signed statements and an official investigation could enlarge the affair out of all proportion in a colony where gossip and scandal thrived. The supposition aroused an element of sympathy in Martin, who had experienced the same kind of thing at public schools and in the Army. He was always on the side of victims of pompous sticklers for rules, whatever the circumstances. Because of that, he said, "I am supposed to be here in official capacity, but I can always go back and tell them you were out when I called, if it will help you to sort out your thoughts on the matter."

Alex took a long time to weigh up the significance of that, then he indicated a chair, saying wearily, "Now we have established that I'm not here, take off your jacket and sit down. It's too hot to stand around formally." He flopped into the corner of a sofa, adding, "Would you like a drink?"

"Not at this hour of the day." After a moment's hesitation, Martin slipped off his jacket and sat facing his reluctant host.

"How about some tea, then?"

He remembered the last tea he had declined to drink in this house. "No, thanks."

Alex gazed back broodingly from his slumped position. "They'll only tell you to come back. Your kind of people never give up."

"They do when they receive a satisfactory answer." Pausing significantly, Martin went on, "It doesn't necessarily have to be the right one."

The other's green eyes narrowed; his brow furrowed. "You'd lie?"

"Not exactly. I'd simply wobble the truth a little." Confronting him frankly, he added, "I'd need a good reason for doing so, mind you."

There was a short brittle silence before Alex said, "I don't understand. Why would you, of all people, do such a thing?"

Anger raced through Martin, driving him to his feet again to say explosively, "Because I'm a normal bloody human being who has covered up for those in trouble before. I haven't spent *all* my life in a mental hospital, you know."

Such attacks always took him by surprise, and started the distressing bouts of shaking symptomatic of shell shock. He was shaking now as Alex got slowly to his feet, looking set and strained. For several moments they confronted each other silently, and Martin tried to control his spasms, in vain.

"That blast was long overdue. You should have made it at the tennis party. I deserved it even more then, didn't I?"

All Martin wanted was to get out of that house. Reaching for his jacket, he managed to say, "I'll tell them I was unable to track you down today. Perhaps you'd send an account of what happened to my bungalow later on, so that I can work out something I think will satisfy them enough to end the matter."

Alex blocked his way as he made to leave, and confessed hesitantly, "If an inquiry into this is made, the parents will become impossibly Victorian at a time when I am already wearing a hair-shirt. I did something on impulse, that's all. No harm was done, but my family would be scandalised. Thanks to the arrival of those military chaps, serious trouble was averted, but I *was* robbed. It's impossible to get the stuff back—it'll be on a junk or sampan by now—so there's little point in making an official *brouhaha* which will ruffle administrative feathers. If you can do anything, Linwood, I'd be extremely grateful."

With his gaze on his means of escape, Martin murmured, "Give me a day or two. I'm sure I'll manage something. Goodbye, then."

There was no escape for him, after all. The door opened to admit Lydia Beresford, whose delighted gaze flew straight to Martin and rendered him motionless. In a dress of lemon-coloured silk with rows of covered buttons on the shoulders, she looked stunningly lovely; a vivid, vital creature lighting the dim, musty room with her presence. The pale hair was arranged in two shining coils at her neck, giving her a suggestion of Quaker purity. Her sun-gilded cheeks had an evening blush on them, explained by the ingenuous betrayal of her feelings in eyes brimming with excitement of an unmistakable kind.

"Hallo, Martin," she greeted breathlessly. "Ling told me you were in here with Alex."

"I was just leaving," he said, excited yet appalled to experience the same sexual reaction he had known on first meeting her. It was imperative to get away.

She had other plans, however. "You can't leave yet. I've told Ling to serve tea for us on the verandah. You wouldn't have tiffin at the Seaview with us yesterday, so we have no intention of letting you slip away now, have we, Alex? Come on.''

Linking her arm through Martin's she took him out across a hall to an elegant dining room, where doors were thrown open on to an airy spacious breakfast verandah. Chairs with bright cushions were arranged in groups around cane tables on the polished wood floor, and large stone jars containing climbing plants ranged along the open ends of the verandah. The front wall, where steps led down into the garden, had half-lowered blinds to deflect the glare of the afternoon sun. A slowly-rotating fan stirred Martin's hair pleasantly as he was led to a table containing a tray of tea. Beside the table was a three-tier stand bearing plates of sandwiches and a plain cake. It looked normal enough, but Martin was still anxious to leave before disaster struck in one form or another.

"I'm certain your parents would prefer to have tea without the bother of an uninvited guest," he said, resisting Lydia's attempts to make him sit at the table.

"Mummy and Daddy are out," she replied with a smile. "We can be as informal as we wish." Taking the jacket from his hand as he made to put it on, she literally pushed Martin into one of the chairs. "Alex is in shirtsleeves, silly. Do relax and stay cool."

Stay cool? If she only knew how his temperature had risen at the sight of her, or how his heart still raced at her nearness. He felt almost sick with the strength of his desire to reach out and touch her, feel the smoothness of her bare skin, subdue her body beneath his own.

"I daresay you find the heat something of a torment," remarked Alex. "Most new arrivals suffer."

Martin fastened his gaze on the good-looking face in the hope of curbing his lusty thoughts. "We lived in the open a lot in France. A man grows used to being in the sun. Of course, we had the rain, too. That was a worse torment, because the welter of mud made it impossible to move around for months at a time. We could never decide whether or not we wanted the rain to stop. When it did, it usually meant another offensive."

Realising that he had unthinkingly spoken of something best forgotten, he stopped abruptly. Alex was looking back at him with an indecipherable intensity, yet did not encourage him to continue. A cup and saucer were pushed across the table to him, and he glanced up to see Lydia regarding him with misty longing.

"Poor Martin. You mustn't think about things like that any more."

"Wait until the monsoons start," put in Alex briskly. "You'll see rain

52

then. Roads are flooded, mould grows on everything, the cockroaches appear in droves, and no one goes out except on business."

Lydia sighed. "Life becomes awfully boring."

"That's the period when strong men have been known to put a pistol to their temples," continued Alex, biting into a sandwich ferociously. "Failing that, they run off with another man's wife . . . or even go out of their minds."

"*Alex!*" cried Lydia, flushing painfully.

The interchange between brother and sister had given Martin time to relax, and he took up his tea with hands that were perfectly steady, saying, "It sounds anything but boring, with all that going on."

From that point on the conversation was undemanding. The Beresfords did most of the talking, and Martin could not help reflecting on how insular they were in outlook and opinions. Singapore might have been the whole world from the way they spoke of it. Alex revealed a cynical sense of humour, and appeared to have few illusions about his fellow men. He was extremely subdued in comparison with the other times on which they had met, and Martin wondered about the attack which had been made on him. What was the truth behind the affair the young shipper wanted played down?

Lydia's approach to life appeared naïve to the point of fantasy, but her simplistic world sounded immensely attractive to a man who had seen and experienced the extremes of horror. He longed to share her Arcady with her, longed to surrender to the ideal of good and evil being so far apart they could never meet and intertwine. Throughout that teatime he was acutely conscious of the girl in the chair facing him. She sat gracefully against the bright cushion, her soft arms brown against the yellow silk sleeves, and her skirt pulled down modestly over the flesh-coloured stockings. Her innocence was devastatingly belied by the glowing message in her eyes each time they looked into his, and he bathed in an enchantment as sensual as the notes of a distant golden oriole, wanting the afternoon to last forever.

Darkness came with its usual suddenness, but they chatted on as the houseboy lit lanterns all around them, oblivious of all but the pleasure of discovering each other. Only when they heard the sound of a car approaching up the driveway, did Lydia then rise quickly, as if in guilt.

"Heavens, that must be Mummy and Daddy," she said in a faint alarm. "Hasn't time flown?"

Martin was on his feet immediately, reaching for his jacket as he recalled his dreadful jabbering departure from the older Beresfords a week earlier.

"I'm not really dressed . . . I mean, I came from the office. Didn't mean to stay," he stammered, furious with himself for doing so.

Lydia stood next to him in the seductive low light from the lanterns, and the fragrance of her nearness made him even more nervous.

"Don't worry," she soothed. "We'll go out through the garden. Alex will keep them occupied."

"Oh, no," corrected her brother swiftly. "I have no wish to meet the parents until dinner. I'm off."

So saying, he jumped the steps and ran off round the outside of the house, waving to Martin as he went. Lydia seemed upset by his behaviour, but headed down the steps into the garden inviting Martin to accompany her to the side gate.

That walk with her brought a return of overwhelming desire. She strolled so close beside him that the sweet perfume of her beckoned irresistibly, and the demure sexuality of her body increased the drive in him he had thought never to experience again. The frangipani trees beside the pergola were dusk-heavy with fragrance as they formed a bridal archway of white blossoms over their heads. Whilst struggling to answer her comments made in tones of husky awareness, Martin found his mind reeling with thoughts of all he longed to do.

She stopped speaking abruptly when his hand brushed against hers. Opening his palm he cupped it around her curled fingers, sliding his thumb with caressing slowness over her skin until the clasp was complete. Although Lydia had tensed beside him, she made no attempt to free herself from the tingling contact as they neared the gate by which he had entered for the tennis party. They instinctively slowed, then turned to face each other in that beguiling, hushed moment between the passing of day and the onset of night. Desire became a physical pain as Martin sought and captured her other hand, drawing her closer so that her face was faintly lit by the street lamps on the other side of the wall.

"I'm so glad you came today," she whispered.

"So am I. So am I."

The breath of her sigh fanned his cheek. "You are going to be one of our friends, aren't you? A *special* friend, Martin."

Restraint was no longer possible. Pulling her against him he kissed her with all the fervour a passionless year had built within him. His trembling hands buried themselves in her soft pale hair, and the sensation of the silky strands against his skin drove his need beyond containment. The yielding roundness of her body responded to his searching hands. His mouth opened and bruised hers in the desperation to release something which had been locked away deep inside him by

54

psychological shock. Total release was so near, it demanded the only possible action.

In the act of lowering her to the ground, the sound of voices calling loudly and repeatedly shocked him back to this senses. She had heard her name, and began to struggle free of him. His hold on her slackened instinctively, giving her the chance to back away. She was panting and clutching her skirt convulsively as she moved unsteadily backward, her lips still parted and her hair tumbling around her face. By the faint light from outside, he saw her eyes, huge and dark with shock.

He took a stumbling step towards her. "*Oh, God!* Lydia . . . I . . . ."

She ran from him beneath the frangipani blooms, until he could no longer see the pale yellow of her dress in the surrounding darkness. He remained by the gate, his cheeks wet with tears for what he had done, knowing her father would come for him at any moment. He remained there alone, however, prey to his thoughts. It began to rain, suddenly and torrentially, falling in huge fat drops that smacked on to the leaves around him like the sound of bullets. The earth was too dry to absorb it, and there was soon a stream running through that pergola, sending liquid mud over his shoes as he stared at the lights on the distant verandah. Thunder began to rumble in the distance, and Martin stood motionless in the downpour as memories swamped him. His hair stuck to his head, sending runnels of water down his cheeks and neck; his clothes were saturated and clung to his shivering body. As the rain thundered down on him, and the branches of the surrounding trees waved madly in the wind, he was back in a French wood waiting to attack the moment the artillery bombardment ceased.

He could hear someone playing the piano, and the voices of all those safely back at headquarters. He longed to be one of them. He was sick of killing—always killing. His friends were dead. So was his dearly-loved brother. Soon, there would be no one left on earth alive. The mud was sucking him down, and he was wet to the skin yet again. He did not know where his tin-hat had gone, and felt very vulnerable without it. He would have to take one from the first casualty when they began to advance. Crouching there in the darkness waiting for the end of the thundering sound of guns, he knew it would take every ounce of resolution to rise up and lead strange young boys, who had come up the line as reinforcements after his company had been wiped out the week before. Something told him his own time was up now; some extra sense told him he would walk out of this wood and die. He had thought a lot about dying lately. Since his brother had been blown up and scattered over a field, death had not seemed so terrible. If Giles could meet it, so could he. Yet, now he knew it was waiting for him a short distance away, he wanted to live—wanted it so desperately he found himself crying for all the chances lost.

The gunfire ceased, and the signal came. For one brief moment he felt impelled to turn and run back to those lights and the comforting sound of that piano. Yet he went because the others expected him to lead the way. They were so young and frightened, looking to him to give them confidence. Because of them he went, but every step he took was a step toward annihilation; a walk toward the end of everything. His breathing grew laboured, as if life was already being drawn out of him. Then, through the dim shapes of the surrounding trees, it came with a roar and a blinding flash. Crying out, he threw up his arms to cover his unprotected head.

When the rain stopped, he was still crouching in that position. It was then he realised that he was still alive, and in a garden. The Beresford house was now ablaze with lights, and someone was playing a piano in an upstairs room. He hardly registered the details of the walk to his bungalow but, once there, he dropped on to the bed feeling utterly drained. He slept and awoke to find Wah had left him a supper tray. Immense hunger overtook him, so that he devoured everything with no thought other than quelling it. It was much later before he faced up to what had happened in the grounds of the Beresford house, and he realised that there had been something other than shock in Lydia's eyes as she had backed away from him. Elation, wild excitement, the birth of uncontrollable passion? Whichever it had been, instinct told him he had awoken something potentially dangerous—dangerous to them both. The only way to avoid it was to stay away from that family, although how he could on such a small island seemed an insuperable problem.

Chapter 4

The run of ill-luck continued to dog Alex during the next few weeks. Those who had backed him to win the Gentleman's Stakes all lost their money when he fell at the first fence. His friends were shaken, and Fong wore an expression of reproach for a week or more, his loss of face with those he had encouraged to back his master being in no way lessened by a doctor's pronouncement that the jockey was suffering from delayed concussion following his car accident. Only Alex knew how he had received the blow to the back of his head, and had no intention of revealing the truth. During the several days he was confined to his bed with giddiness and loss of coherent thought, his mother fussed over him incessantly. His plight did nothing to mollify Austin, however. The cost of repairing the car had halved Alex's allowance that month, and inspired another lecture on behaviour which undid all the work toward making the Beresford name respectable again. It was as well the whole truth of that evening did not come out.

As soon as he was back on his feet, Alex invited Martin for a sundowner at the Tanglin Club while they discussed his official report on the affair. Luckily, his concussion perfectly explained the military officers' statements that "Mr Beresford seemed stunned and bewildered during the journey to his home". The version Martin promised he would submit was that Alex had been concussed by the crash, and had wandered in a state of semi-consciousness deep into the Chinese quarter, where he had been robbed of his watch, wallet and cuff links. The story sounded so feasible, Alex felt no obligation to mention the dragon and the anger his interference in the ritual had aroused. That escape into bravado seemed tawdry by the light of day. He could never explain, particularly to Martin Linwood, the yearning induced by that full moon, or describe the pulsing throbbing excitement that pagan creature had created in him at a moment when the future had seemed so colourless.

Martin was as good as his word, and the matter was closed. Yet Alex found the young civil servant withdrawn, almost curt, at that meeting and at all others during those next few weeks. In view of the hour or so the fellow had spent with himself and Lydia, chatting and drinking tea in the friendliest fashion, Alex found the man's coolness inexplicable. However, he had problems of his own, and put the change of attitude down to the mental condition which produced extremes of behaviour he had already witnessed. He thought it most probably also accounted for the absurd means Martin used to avoid the Beresford family at the racetrack, at cricket matches, and at hotels favoured by Europeans. With a curious sense of disappointment, Alex left the man to his devious behaviour and tried to concentrate on work.

Even in that direction he was dogged by bad fortune. The ailing *Rochford-Kendal Line* suffered another blow when old Tom Kendal went up-country, and there died from snakebite on a remote plantation. The godowns Alex had wanted were offered for sale and bought within minutes by a Chinese merchant with interests throughout South-East Asia. The contracts in Manila were taken up by an agent on behalf of an anonymous client, so *Berondel* missed the best opportunity to expand that it had had in years. Alex was furious, and made no secret of the fact to his father. Since the end of the war, the great trading houses and shipping lines of the East had seized every opportunity for renewed business, and were still seizing them. Normality was returning and, if Britain was now bankrupt, and full of broken, dazed young men unable to take up life where it had ended in 1914, her outposts were on the brink of a boom.

The major change to motorised traffic meant a great demand for rubber for tyres, and the khaki years had given birth to extravagance in the fashion world. Women wanted silk as never before, the luxury fabric being used as the basis for clothes in extremes of colour, style and ornamentation. The commencement of the Twenties had fostered a rebellion against convention, moral standards, and anything that repressed individuality. Yet, in the first half of 1920, the social innovations begun at home had hardly touched the residents of the Empire's trading outposts. They were too busy expanding their markets and making their fortunes. All save the *Berondel Line*.

Caution was the byword of Austin Beresford's nature. Alex knew why, but knowing did nothing to curb his impatience. In the privacy of their respective offices, and at home, father and son argued bitterly over company policy. In the boardroom, Alex struggled to control his tongue in the presence of the other directors, an innate sense of filial loyalty keeping him silent when he longed to raise his voice, thump the table, or in any way shock them into awareness of the word "progress". However, as the members of the board were also elderly, cautious, satisfied men, a fiery outburst from Alex in a room in a building which had not changed since the days of Great-Grandfather Beresford would have been considered bad form. They would have shaken their grizzled heads, tut-tutted and told each other that young Beresford had a lot to learn about the conduct of business, if not about good manners.

Alex could not forgive the loss of the godowns and the Manila contract, which they could have secured with an early approach to their impoverished rivals. To ease his anger and renewed frustration, he indulged in further daring but pointless escapades with those of his friends who found him excellent company when in such a mood. His reckless behaviour set tongues wagging, the more elderly or prim residents wondering once more whether the bad blood of the piratical Justin had reappeared in his grandson. Many predicted that Alexander was going downhill fast, and it would be amazing if the colony was not shaken by another scandal in the family before he was much older. The rift between father and son created by Alex's passionate accusations on the evening of the Chinese dragon, widened further. Alex was deeply depressed, less by the fact that his father could not forgive what he had said, but because he could in no way understand that it had been true.

At the office, Alex did all he could to avoid his father. At home, he could not, and the atmosphere was made worse by the two females in the family. Lydia had not been herself since the bad fall she had apparently had in the garden after letting Martin out through the side gate. Their parents had created a great fuss over her wandering in the grounds after dark, and Lydia must have felt that a greater fuss would have been made had they known why she had been there, because she did not mention the young civil servant's visit. Alex remained silent on the subject for reasons of his own, but he wondered if his sister could also be suffering from concussion after the incident which had caused her mouth to swell and bruises to develop on her upper arms. He did once ask her if she had hit her head in the fall, but her reply had been that she wished everyone would leave her alone. In his more thoughtful moments, his sister's preoccupation puzzled Alex, however. He had never seen her moon around the house in listless fashion, as she now did. Instead of surrounding herself with groups of giggling girls, she was either reading a Bronte novel, or wandering alone in the garden gazing at the frangipani trees as if she had never seen them before. He did not know what to make of it, and missed the easy companionship they had once had.

Plaguing him further was his mother's non-stop chatter on the subject of Dorothea du Lessier. As the date of her arrival drew near, the excitement over the prospect of having another young person under her roof grew to the point where she spoke of little else. The room had been prepared in four different ways before she could feel satisfied with it, and everyone had been informed that future invitations should include Miss du Lessier as one of the Beresford family. The cousin who was not a cousin was already practically a sister, thought Alex gloomily. A girl

59

straight from England, who was being sent to them to recover from the death of her father, sounded a dismal prospect. She was certain to complain about the heat, the smells, the insects. She would imagine snakes in her bedroom at night, and swear there were Chinese climbing up the verandah to peer in at her when she was asleep. She would be pale and lethargic, and all the young men in the colony would pursue her because she was new to the scene.

He had encountered a number of girls out from England for a visit. Lady Weyford's niece, Fay Christie, was a good example, although he suspected that that girl was not as demure as she pretended to be. Dorothea du Lessier was sure to be worse than any of them, he told himself heavily. He would be expected to dance attendance on her, introduce her to suitable young men or partner her himself to sedate affairs. He would also be told to keep his rowdier friends away from her. Might as well put him in a strait-jacket for six months!

It was in a mood of deep resignation that he prepared to accompany his family to the docks on the morning of the girl's arrival. It was not a successful start. His mother had ordered a new dress and hat for the occasion, and was well pleased with it until five minutes before setting off. Then she concluded that her dressmaker had failed to ease the fastening at the neck, as she had directed. Flustered and irritated, she vowed that the dress would choke her before she was halfway to the docks.

"Go upstairs and put on a different dress, my dear," advised Austin soothingly.

"What, meet my niece in last year's dress?" she challenged, pinker in the face than ever.

"I hardly think Miss du Lessier will be able to tell that it is last year's dress," came the mild response which annoyed her further.

"*I* would know, Austin . . . and so would any of our friends we might encounter at the docks."

"Ah, I see. It is not Miss du Lessier you mean to impress with your elegance, but our friends."

It was a typical example of male perception, which females would call tactlessness. Still dressed in the unsatisfactory frock of green Shantung silk, with rose-trimmed matching hat, his mother sat in the car maintaining an injured silence as the syce drove away from the house. Alex turned to catch Lydia's eye, but she was gazing from her window at the passing scenery. In cream muslin banded with blue satin, and a demure straw boater, his sister appeared wan and abstracted, when she should be full of excitement at the advent of another girl to live with them, he thought. Glancing back at his father, Alex wondered why he

60

was so chirpy this morning. In his immaculate tropical suit, with gold tiepin and cuff links, and the silver-topped ebony walking cane, Austin Beresford was the epitome of quiet wealth and respectability. His clipped moustache looked very brown. Alex had often suspected that it was dyed, and thought it a silly vanity in a man whose hair was thinning and liberally sprinkled with grey.

For the first time, he wondered what the du Lessier girl would make of them all. Rather a daunting prospect to be so far from home amidst a group of strangers, when trying to recover from a bereavement, he supposed. Still, as she had practically invited herself, she only had herself to blame if she hated them all and felt homesick. It was excessively hot that morning. He ran a finger around the inside of his collar, reflecting that he would probably choke before his mother did. Why they had all been obliged to dress up in this fashion he could not understand. As the girl would be living with them for several months, she would see them in all states. It seemed pointless to meet her as formally clad as they would be for the Governor's garden party. His depression deepened. There was no more than an obscure link between them, so why all this fuss just to impress her? His suit was uncomfortable, his collar too stiffly starched, and his topee was making his hair damp already. It was only his mother who saw the slightest relationship with the du Lessier creature. Why could she not have gone to the docks on her own?

By the time the syce drove through to the jetty, he had worked up a strong sense of martyrdom. Margery had not recovered from her pique, and alighted from the car with no more than aloof acknowledgement of her husband's assistance. Lydia had to be reminded of the fact that they had arrived, before she showed languid interest in leaving her seat. On the jetty, there was a period of dress straightening by the ladies, and adjustment of topees by Alex and his father. Then they moved toward the gangway leading from the boat deck of the liner, which had crossed the world from west to east, and from north to south.

On the jetty a regimental band was playing rousing melodies, and there was an air of festivity in the waving flags, handkerchiefs and hats as passengers and those arriving to welcome them caught sight of each other. The atmosphere tightened Alex's throat with sudden unexpected intensity. He recalled the occasion when he had stood in a waving, cheering crowd whilst a great white ship had slowly pulled away to the strains of military music, and his aching heart had yearned to be on it with those returning to fight for their homeland. Climbing the gangway with his family, he remained lost in that other occasion, the echo of that ache in his heart settling on him.

The deck was swarming with people shouting, laughing, embracing each other against a noisy background of squeaking winches and competitive jabbering of porters. Awnings had been stretched overhead to provide shade, but heat rose from the planks in a suffocating waft of smells from tar to that morning's bacon and eggs. Alex almost bumped into his parents as they stopped, intimidated by the heat and press of people. Lydia merely turned to gaze out over the bobbing medley of small boats on a green oily sea, lost in her own thoughts.

"Alexander, I think it would be best for you to go over and enquire from the purser the number of Miss du Lessier's cabin," his father said decisively. "You will have a better chance of pushing through to his office alone. Besides, if your mother is going to choke in that dress, she had better do it near the gangway rather than in the midst of a crowd."

It was one of Austin's rare bursts of dry humour, and Alex wondered again at his light-hearted mood. Surely he was not also yearning to take another child under his wing. With a brief nod, Alex left them to shoulder his way through a criss-cross of people seeking their friends, porters hefting cabin trunks, crewmen attempting to perform their normal duties, and boys paging passengers. The purser looked harassed when Alex reached him, but soon answered his question by pointing to a group by the rail.

"You'll find Miss du Lessier over there, taking leave of some of her fellow-passengers, sir. They seem unwilling to go ashore."

The laughing group of young men clustered together in lively conversation, was a further reminder of that time Alex would never forget. They had stood together like that then, excited and eager for the great adventure of war. Yet he had been on the jetty, looking up at them, as the stretch of water between ship and shore had broadened, severing all connection between those who were going off to glory, and those who had been left behind. Alex crossed the deck now, the shadow of that sense of exclusion darkening his mood. If he had gone to battle, he would not now be dutifully meeting some obscure mourning girl who was certain to deaden life even further. In consequence, his hand on the nearest shoulder was impatient; his voice was curt.

"I was told I would find Miss du Lessier here."

A merry face turned his way. "I'll say she is!"

There was only one girl in the group, and Alex lost all interest in the young men who reminded him of those he had so reluctantly waved off to war. She was tall and svelte, her beautiful body clad in an amazing garment of deep violet crêpe de Chine which was swathed around the hips with pale-green satin, fastened by a giant silver tassel. Her bare arms, tanned a deep brown by the ocean sun, were ornamented with a number of silver snake-bracelets above the elbows. There was another around her left ankle, drawing attention to the most exciting legs Alex had ever seen. The skirt revealed a breathless amount of them, and it was a moment or two before his gaze returned to study her profile. Dark shining hair cut short and straight curved over her cheeks to hide her expression from him, but her voice was warm and merry as she held court surrounded by would-be knights.

With his heart hammering absurdly, and telling himself it was almost certainly a case of mistaken identity, he asked clearly, "Are you Miss du Lessier?"

The girl turned to him, and he felt a surge of heady excitement as large amber-coloured eyes heavily outlined with black looked him over with interest.

"Yes, I am. Who are you?"

In a daze, he put out his hand. "I'm Alex Beresford."

"*Cousin Alex*," she teased, a bubble of laughter in her voice. "What a delightful surprise." Turning her full attention on to him, she pushed aside his outstretched hand. "Take off that damned silly hat, and I'll greet you properly."

He took off the topee obediently, and she kissed him full on the mouth, in lingering fashion. There was a chorus of protest from those around them, but Alex stood in the aftermath of that kiss knowing he would cease counting twilights now the sun had risen so dazzlingly on his life.

Plucking the handkerchief from his breast pocket, the girl wiped her lipstick from his mouth as she smiled up at him. "You look even more attractive without that coffee-coloured monstrosity on your head. I notice all the local residents wear them. How quaint!"

He grinned with delight in her. "Mother has one at home for you. She'll insist that you wear it."

Her laughter was as uninhibited as everything about her. "Not me, sweetie. They went out with Dr Livingstone. I face the sun on equal terms."

"I'm sure the sun long ago acknowledged a truce," he murmured, admiring the golden shade of her skin. There was no doubt this girl would have her way even with Margery Beresford, and he could not wait to witness the confrontation. As he continued to gaze in appreciation, thanking the gods for such a sensational end to his run of bad luck, her eyebrows rose questioningly.

"Shall we go, or is there something we should do first?"

"We could start the greetings all over again," he suggested.

"Oh no, you don't," cried a voice beside him, reminding him that they were surrounded by other people on that ship. "We want our farewells first."

The girl turned to survey them all with her wide smile. "Sorry, boys, I have no intention of kissing you all goodbye. We shall be meeting up again in Singapore."

Some protested that they were going up-country to inaccessible places, others that they were travelling on within a week, but she shook her head, blew a kiss shoreward, and thanked them for their excellent company during the voyage. Then she turned back to Alex, and slipped her hand through the crook of his arm.

"Now I'm all yours, cousin dear."

Hoping that she meant it literally, he smiled down into her vivid face. "My parents and sister are over by the gangplank. I'll take you across and introduce you, then I'll see about your baggage."

The press of people had thinned, so that the three he had left waiting could now see them quite clearly. Alex studied them curiously as he led the new arrival toward what appeared to be three different figures. They were dressed in the same clothes, but their faces had changed colour and grown rigid. There was now a wax model in a green dress which threatened to choke her, another wax model with a dyed moustache and a coffee-coloured monstrosity on his head, and a third in a colourless, shapeless shift stretching almost to her ankles. They all seemed incapable of speaking.

"My mother and father," he explained to the girl beside him, in vague tones.

"Hallo," she greeted warmly. "It's Austin and Margery, isn't it? It's so generous of you to allow me to use part of your home as a studio while I write my novel. How fortunate I am to have you to introduce me to native contacts I shall need if I'm to genuinely convey the mystery of the East, with all its underlying passions and rituals. So many themes have been swimming around in my head during the voyage, that I can't wait to put them on paper." Turning to the third statue in the neat cream dress trimmed with baby-blue, she gave her wide, warm smile. "You must be Lydia. Thank you for your beautifully written letter. I didn't realise that you were still a schoolgirl, my dear, but I'm sure we can be friends, as you suggested." Including the whole group in her frank glance, she added, "I never use my full name, you know. It's so exquisitely *nice*. Please call me Thea." Her laughing amber eyes turned toward Alex, and she added softly, "As we are already kissing cousins, *we* may improve on that later."

★

64

The military ball promised to be a colourful extravagant affair. Sir Hartle had browbeaten his regimental friends into sending his godson an invitation, then informed Martin that he would escort Lady Weyford's niece to the function. Dreading the occasion, yet knowing there was no way of escaping it, Martin dressed in formal clothes to present himself at the Weyfords' sprawling house in the colony's most exclusive area, where they were to eat a light meal before setting out. He dined with the Weyfords once a week. Sir Hartle intended the evenings to be warm, friendly meetings designed to help his godson "pull himself together". To Martin, they seemed more like intense interviews for the vacant post of normal human being, as he was bombarded by queries on how he was progressing at the office, how he was fitting in with the routine at his shared bungalow, and how many friends he had made, to date. Feeling almost as if on trial by this distinguished judge, the dinners in his company brought out the very nervousness the older man deplored. Lady Weyford and the brittle, highly-strung Fay took a sadistic delight in baiting him, Martin felt, which produced evidence for their belief that there was no hope for him.

As he waited to be announced this evening, Martin told himself the coming hours must somehow be endured, and walked into the old-fashioned sitting room determined to remain cool and controlled, whatever happened. He need not have worried. After the usual preliminaries, Lady Weyford revealed that she had a fresh victim beside whom Martin was now quite insignificant. For once, he was interested in the matron's character-shredding, because it concerned the cousin from England the Beresfords had invited to Singapore. Martin had heard a little about a tragic bereavement being responsible for the young girl's visit, but his inhibitions regarding that family tended to make him walk away from conversations concerning them. His fear that they would be present at the ball was immediately realised when Lady Weyford expressed her deep regret that Dorothea du Lessier had accepted the invitation some military blunderer had been misguided enough to send her.

"In past years, the ball has been one of the most reliable events of the social calendar, Martin," she confided grimly. "When the guest list is extended to include such people, one wonders if the time has come to remove the date from one's engagement book."

Seeing his chance, Martin said, "If you would prefer not to attend, I shan't be in the least disappointed."

"Not attend!" she echoed in astonishment. "Whatever can you mean?"

"I thought you were unhappy because this girl has been invited," he explained, seeing hope fade.

"I am unhappy. However, we have a duty to introduce you this evening which we would not dream of neglecting, and you surely don't imagine that I would allow a creature of that ilk to keep me from an event I have graced for the past ten years."

"No doubt she'll leave early, Aunt Jane, when she realises that she is outclassed," Fay suggested soothingly, as the houseboy announced dinner by beating discreetly on a small brass gong with a felt-topped hammer.

Martin crossed to Lady Weyford, who insisted that ladies should be correctly led in to dinner, whatever the occasion. Tall and scraggy, he thought she resembled an ebony walking cane in the straight black lace evening gown, with her silver hair arranged in a flat knob on the top of her head. As he offered her his arm she continued her theme.

"The girl caused an uproar at the docks, they say."

Fay, in a stiff satin dress of yellow as acid as her tongue, had a wicked gleam in her eyes as she followed them, arm in arm with her uncle.

"Anything, from a coolies' brawl to a broken box of rotten fish, can cause an uproar at the docks. If I were the kind of girl who wished to create a sensation on arrival, I'd choose a more salubrious venue than a filthy crowded jetty."

"Margery Beresford is prostrate!" continued Lady Weyford. "The woman has been insisting that the girl is some kind of distant relative, yet they apparently knew very little about her. They believed her to be coming on a visit of indefinite length in order to recover from the death of her father, but she has arrived with the intention of *taking lodgings* at the Beresford house, and insulted Austin by offering him rent—can you believe it?—for the use of a bedroom, bathroom and a verandah while she works on a *novel*. Naturally, they have no idea what to do about her. She has made it abundantly clear that she is a law unto herself, and is wealthy enough to be as independent as she pleases. It's my firm opinion that the Beresfords are pandering to her only because they are afraid she will install herself in a hotel and cause them more embarrassment than ever."

"It's only a nine-day wonder," put in Fay, as the houseboy seated her aunt, then held her chair ready. "By taking so much interest in what the girl does, people are simply eating out of her hand. I'm bored by the whole affair."

Lady Weyford was determined that Martin should hear the full story, however, and continued it whilst drinking her soup.

"Her father was an Italian impresario—a distant relative of Tosti, if anything she says is to be believed—and was rarely at home. Far from mourning his death, the girl apparently hardly knew him. The identity of the mother is quite a revelation, Martin. *Anna du Lessier!*" With soup spoon poised above the bowl, she added, "In case the name means nothing to you, she is the author of a scandalous novel attacking the church and its attitude to divorce."

"The title of the book is *Girl in a Plate of Strawberries*, and the theme is quite equally meaningless. I read it when it was first published," he told the group around the table. "Flamboyant nonsense, claimed by advanced theorists to expose deep-seated concepts of morality as self-indulgent depravity. Bohemian sheep all said baa, and it has started a landslide of similar rubbish masquerading as brilliant novels."

The other three diners looked at him in amazement, and Martin was unsure whether it was due to the incomprehension of what he had said, or the fact that they could not believe he had uttered anything which could be considered intelligent conversation. They all decided to ignore it, anyway, and Lady Weyford continued as if there had been no interruption to her revelations.

"Miss du Lessier plainly hopes to emulate her mother. She told Mary Michaelson that she intends to tour the native quarters of Singapore in order to absorb what she calls 'atmosphere' for her book."

"Surely the Beresfords have advised her that she will never be allowed to do that," put in Martin, trying once more to participate in what was in danger of turning into a monologue.

"Clarrie Fitzpatrick dubbed her a positive hoyden," the elderly woman said with great firmness, the immediate change of direction indicating to Martin that his comments were not welcome. "Her clothes are vulgar and border on indecency, she uses language more suited to a trooper, and she *smokes*."

"A lot of girls smoke now, Aunt Jane," Fay told her. "It's a result of the war, you know. So many of them went to France and mixed with the troops, or they went to work in factories and as bus conductors. The old concepts about women vanished. The war did more for the female cause than the suffragette movement."

"Cecilia Tamworth declares their behaviour verged on the immoral," continued the well-bred voice throbbing with disapproval. "There on the deck, in full view of several hundred people, they embraced with complete lack of restraint. Two perfect strangers! Cecilia said he *took off his topee*, then practically *devoured* her."

Martin choked on his soup. It struck him as exquisitely funny that Lady Weyford should speak of a man removing his topee in public as if he had stripped naked.

"Are you all right?" queried the elderly lady sharply.

"Yes . . . thank you," he managed, eyes streaming and throat rasped by coughing.

"Oh dear, I did think you could manage *soup*," she complained testily, before returning to the juicier sacrificial lamb. "It has always been my private opinion that young Alexander Beresford is past redemption. The two older children succumbed to weakness of the constitution, but that boy takes after his grandfather."

"Oh come, my dear," interpolated Sir Hartle, signalling the house-boy to serve the fish. "He is a trifle wild, I grant you, but Justin Beresford was a liar and a cheat, running a brace of privateers and preying on other traders' vessels. The only good thing one can say about him is that he did the decent thing when discovered. You can't compare young Alexander with that bounder."

"He's only twenty-four," put in Fay. "Who knows how he might turn out later on, especially as it now seems clear Mrs Beresford's side of the family also has black sheep like this dreadful girl."

"How do you know she's dreadful?" asked Martin impulsively. "Have you met her?"

"Fay has heard what I have heard, Martin, which is more than enough on which to base an opinion," Lady Weyford declared with finality. "The girl has been reared in a Bohemian atmosphere, where she was allowed to do as she liked. Naturally, she copies the example set by her mother's disreputable literary friends. Clarrie Fitzpatrick says she calls the Beresfords by their first names, because she had always addressed her parents and their friends in that manner. So disrespect-ful! Margery is apparently making herself ill with worry. Having made such an issue over the girl being one of her own family, and insisting that her acquaintances must invite the girl everywhere, she now wishes she had never laid claim to her. One shouldn't have sympathy of course, because she really is a very foolish woman who has no one but herself to blame for this *bête noire*. Nevertheless, it must be very distressing for her to see her son so completely under the creature's influence. In addition, that sweet little Lydia has apparently lost all the vitality she once had."

Martin's heart lurched. What did that mean? Who had told Lady Weyford such a thing? Did everyone know and wonder why?

"Have you . . . have you visited the Beresfords recently?" he asked, with the dreaded stammer.

Lady Weyford's hands stilled in the midst of separating her sole fillet. "I never visit the Beresfords, Martin. They have been obliged to toil for their wealth. Ours has come by right of birth. We meet at social events, that is all. You should know that."

"You should also know what ails sweet little Lydia," put in Fay.

He almost dropped his fish knife. "I . . . why should I?"

A feline smile touched the girl's mouth. "The poor dear has a gentle sensitive nature which is easily upset by anything abnormal."

"I think the du Lessier creature is perfectly *sane*, dear," corrected her aunt, missing the point of the remark. "It is simply that her behaviour is quite uncontrolled, and she inclines toward eccentricity."

"You should get on well with her, Martin," was the next silky comment from Fay, who would never forgive him for being wealthy, young and totally uninterested in her.

"I doubt it," he managed to say, in tones returning to normal. "If she really intends to make a nuisance of herself by wandering into areas regarded by the native population as their private communities, I may end up parading her before Sir Frederick as a potential danger to ethnic relations."

At the end of the meal, the ladies retired to their rooms to prepare for the next part of the evening, and Sir Hartle took the opportunity to select a cigar while port was poured for him and for Martin. Whilst carrying out the delicate business of choosing one of the aromatic cigars from the box, he asked Martin how he was enjoying his work, and if he had made any friends yet amongst his colleagues.

Knowing that this was the start of the "trial" Martin answered carefully. "The work is fairly routine stuff, sir, but it certainly allows me every opportunity to explore some of those native communities Miss du Lessier is reputedly anxious to see. However, I'm not all that busy, so I sometimes help Dr McGregor. He knows the colony well, and I find his theories on its possible future very interesting."

"Hmm, do you?" Sir Hartle's heavy brows formed a straight line. "Not the kind of fellow to help you much, my boy. Queer cuss, by all accounts. Has a strong touch of the country about him, you know. Take my advice and steer clear of McGregor. Friendship with him will be a hindrance to your acceptance by those who matter out here."

Feeling it would be wise to change the subject, Martin then asked, "What are your views on the growing revolutionary movement in China, sir? There have been serious demonstrations in support of it in Hong Kong recently. With the large number of Chinese who have settled in Singapore, it seems likely that the pattern might be repeated here. Several of us in the department are concerned on that score."

"No need for that, I assure you," said Sir Hartle, puffing at the cigar to get it going. "Hong Kong is a vastly different kettle of fish. Ethnically Chinese, it is a damned sight too near the mainland for comfort. Here, we are surrounded by the Malay States. Nice easy-going people, the

Malays. You'll find out." He settled back to enjoy his cigar. "Ought to go up-country as soon as the opportunity offers, Martin. One of the most beautiful areas I have ever seen. Lush jungle, lazy waterways, brown smiling people, vivid birds, and animals galore. There are still tigers to be seen up there, you know, for those who know where to look." He exhaled cigar smoke reflectively. "Cunning beasts! I recall tiger shoots in India. The long line of elephants carrying marksmen in howdahs on their backs, and the beaters pushing through the long grass in a series of armed ranks, shouting as much to reassure each other as to frighten old stripes. Oh, and the maharajas! Splendid men who do everything with maximum pomp, covered in jewels. The Malay sultans can put on an impressive show, when called upon, but the Indian rulers are unrivalled when it comes to opulent magnificence." He drew on the cigar again, then blew a swirling cloud of smoke. "If you haven't experienced a tiger hunt, my boy, you haven't lived."

"I've experienced a manhunt," he said quietly. "It's run along the same lines, really, only without the jewels."

The glow of reverie left Sir Hartle's face abruptly, and he frowned again. "You think about such things too much. That's half your trouble, Martin."

"If you mean that I don't escape into make-believe often enough, you're probably right, sir, but I spent over a year in hospital with doctors who taught me to face facts without flinching."

Such reasoning did not please his godfather. "Maybe, but I brought you out here to forget all that."

"You're asking the impossible, then. I can no more forget killing men than you can forget killing tigers."

When the ladies joined them, they were in the process of destroying another reputation. Still testy with Martin, Sir Hartle concentrated on them as they made themselves comfortable in the car.

"Is that young Massingham you are discussing, my dear? Another young man who could not recognise good advice when it was offered."

"I saw Alice Van Leyden this morning with her mother and sister," said Fay. "She looked absolutely wretched, Uncle. I believe it's the first time she has set foot outside the house since Piers Massingham left. I don't know why they thought it necessary to imprison *her*. She didn't break the rules; he did."

Martin remained silent during the discussion, although he knew all about the Massingham affair. The fellow had lived in the bungalow he now occupied, his departure from the colony leaving the vacant rooms. A civil servant engaged to the daughter of a Dutch banker, Massingham had continued to maintain and visit his Chinese mistress, and the son he had had by her. When the deception had been discovered, he had been dismissed from his post and advised, at metaphorical gunpoint, to leave the colony with all speed. Facing disgrace in England, he had jumped ship at Penang, and it was generally believed that the Chinese woman had now gone up-country to join him.

"I did hear from Sir Matthew that Massingham had been spotted in Kuala Lumpur," Sir Hartle informed them. "He's probably trying to get work on one of the plantations. He should have inherited a sizeable fortune, but his family have cut him off without a penny, of course."

"Huh," sniffed Lady Weyford. "Another loose screw taking refuge from the consequences of his misdeeds up there amongst the rubber trees. He'll succeed in making a fortune. They always do. Take the case of Marmaduke Beresford."

That name caught Martin's wandering attention. He was about to ask if there was any connection with the shipping family when Sir Hartle turned to him, his good humour returning. He was a man never angry for long.

"I suggested only a while ago that you should make a trip up-country, my boy. Friends with young Alexander, aren't you? Get him to arrange a visit to his uncle's place. Better still, I'll suggest it to Austin. The family estate is one of the largest in the region. Hugely prosperous, of course. *Berondel* ships take the latex out, so there are no shipping costs going elsewhere. Marmaduke is a real character. Mad as a hatter! He has always been known to his friends as Duke Beresford. When he first went up to the estate, the aged Sultan thought he was the Duke *of* Beresford, and greeted him with great pomp and civility. The old rascal has never undeceived him, so the local people treat him almost on a par with the Sultan. Duke rules his rubber kingdom with great relish and his tongue in his cheek," he finished with a chuckle.

"I beg to differ, Hartle," put in Lady Weyford. "The man is a disgrace to society, besides being a great embarrassment to Austin and Margery. They have enough loose screws in their family, and are in danger of acquiring another, if this du Lessier girl really has Alexander under her spell, as reports say. I believe it would be a great mistake for Martin to become too closely associated with that family. They are the last people to help him take up a normal life. Quite the reverse, surely."

"Not at all, Lady Weyford," put in Martin, as casually as he could. "Perhaps we loose screws should all stick together."

There was an uncomfortable silence in the car, then Lady Weyford began a deliberate conversation with her niece on those she was likely to meet that evening. Sir Hartle sighed audibly and drummed his fingers on the top of his hat which he had placed on his knees. Wishing desperately that he could avoid the next few hours, which would entail watching Lydia Beresford in the arms of a succession of partners whilst he kept well away from her vicinity, Martin gazed from the window in growing gloom. At each side of the road water ran noisily through the deep monsoon drains, collected during a heavy afternoon shower. There was another in the offing; he could smell the dampness in the air. Behind the trees lining the road were the large stone residences of the wealthy Europeans and Chinese, the *kampongs* of the Malays, and the wooden hovels of the coolie class and lower-caste Indians.

The breeze contained more than the smell of rain: the pungent aroma of joss sticks, fried rice, stewed fish, curry, incense, ghee, the overpowering sweetness of frangipani blossoms, overripe mangoes and Chinese sweetmeats, the sweat of tropical humanity, and the stench of refuse. The combination was the unmistakable smell of the East. It was still alien to him. After six weeks in Singapore he had not even begun to like the colony. The heat sapped his strength, and the sultry nights alone in his room were a growing form of sexual torment centred around thoughts of Lydia. The European colonials were a breed with whom he could find no sense of rapport. The native races had to be treated with fairness and respect, but any attempt at close relationships meant being ordered to take passage home, like Piers Massingham.

Martin sank further into gloom. There was no place now that he could regard as home. The death of his father had changed everything. The old family house had been let to a stockbroker, and the East had been designated by Sir Hartle as the place to make a new start. Martin did not share his godfather's faith and, at that moment, felt that Piers Massingham had done very well out of the scandal. A rubber plantation miles from civilisation and others of his race, lush jungle, lazy waterways, brown smiling people, vivid birds, and tigers. Sir Hartle had painted an appealing picture.

As soon as they entered the ballroom, Martin's sense of unease increased dramatically. Not only did he immediately see Lydia Beresford looking across the polished length at him as she did in his nocturnal fantasies, he also found the strong military overtones disturbing. Men in uniform filled that elegant chandelier-hung hall, albeit in scarlet, blue or rifle-green rather than khaki, but the atmosphere of correctness and precision, straight backs, and clipped authoritative voices threatened to return him to past years, absent warriors. The excessive heat, despite doors flung open to the terrace, the swirling dazzle of colourful waltzing couples, the volume of a full regimental orchestra playing with early evening gusto, the waves of over-loud conversation, all combined to urge instant flight.

The preliminary signs of nervousness were starting, when Fay tugged his arm and hissed, "What a nerve! She's asking for trouble."

The blur of dancing pairs clarified to highlight Alex Beresford holding close in his arms a girl whose identity could not be in doubt. Willowy and supple, wearing a clinging silver lamé dress which was expertly draped from the shoulders to expose her tanned back as far as the waist, Dorothea du Lessier was creating a sensation. Half the assembled company was outraged, the young male half was thrilled. The virile shipping heir looked spellbound, as he circled the floor with someone who had certainly supplanted Martin as the latest kill to be picked at by society vultures. Taking in the sight of the daring gown, the array of jewelled slave-bangles on tanned arms, the scarlet finger-nails and lips, and the huge emerald worn on her brow in the manner of an Indian caste mark, Martin found he was neither outraged, thrilled nor spellbound by the girl. If he felt anything, it was wry amusement at the thought that, if the cavalier traits of Justin Beresford really had reappeared in his grandson, Alex had probably found the challenge he was seeking.

Although designated Fay's escort, it was an empty duty created for neatness on arrival. He had provided an arm for her to enter on. Now, he willingly stood aside whilst eager young officers and administrators lined up to write their names on her dance-card. His own card remained in his pocket. Nothing on earth would make him give a demonstration of neurotic inability to match thoughts with actions on that polished floor. In a well-tailored formal suit, stiff shirt and spotless white gloves, he looked quite acceptable to those surrounding him. Force him out there, with some luckless female grasped in his unsteady hands, and he would turn into an organ-grinder's monkey performing a pitiful un-coordinated prance that would make some guffaw and others go home immediately. Unfortunately, the usual alternative to dancing was also a risky proposition. An evening spent at the bar thinking about Lydia being pressed against a succession of shirt-fronts was liable to bring the same result. He very soon decided that, after introductions to those whom Sir Hartle and his wife felt were suitable people to aid his future in the East, he would retire to the terrace, find a seat in a secluded corner, and enjoy the peace while he chain-smoked until allowed to leave.

For the first half-hour, he fought his growing sense of confusion whilst attempting to conduct sensible conversations with advocates, doctors, bankers, financiers, colonels and diplomats. They were all friendly, knowledgeable colonists who spoke to him of the opportuni-ties open to him, or about his father's brilliant career which had ended so prematurely. Their wives addressed him in the soothing tones they would use to children or Chinese servants, and those with daughters looked relieved when Sir Hartle explained that his godson was not yet strong enough to enjoy dancing.

The ballroom was growing even more crowded; the volume of conversation rose accordingly. A number of subalterns, affected by wine and sultry temperatures, embarked on high-spirited versions of each dance which would earn them a reprimand in the morning. Martin began to see faces he had once known replace those now before him, and khaki replace the scarlet and blue. The old wartime tunes were echoing around the colonial walls, conjuring up scenes of troop-trains filled with singing volunteers on their way out, and carriages containing silent, hollow-eyed veterans on their way home. Panic sent him toward the doors leading to the terrace. He had done his duty; no one would miss him.

The terrace was wide and discreetly lit with ornamental Chinese lanterns. Their silken tassels swung in the slight breeze advancing before the rain which had been threatening for the past hour. Dismayed by the number of revellers already strolling the flagstones, Martin looked around for a place to hide. Despite his godfather's strictures about facing up to people, he had every intention of withdrawing into blessed solitude for as long as possible. At the far end of the terrace he saw the perfect spot, only to find on entering it a couple indulging in what he and his fellow-officers had termed "a military coup". Lucky fellow, he thought, backing out speedily. Then he caught sight of a flight of stone steps adorned at the foot by massive pillars supporting rampant heraldic beasts. Those beasts beckoned. Reaching the garden below the terrace he leaned back against one of the pillars with a sigh, to watch the alternate silver and black patterns cast by scudding clouds over the moon. They had hated nights like that. When attacking, the sudden brilliant moon-washed periods had been killing times. When being attacked, they . . .

Sudden movement beside him made him swing round with a cry, his hands lifting an imaginary rifle menacingly. The moonlight turned her into the semblance of a ghost. Her pale hair was silvered; the chiffon dress, robbed of its pastel shade, moved in the breeze as if ethereal. He stared at her, completely disarmed. She gazed back, eyes huge and full of fear for her own daring.

"Good heavens, I . . . I didn't expect to find *you* here, Martin!"

The eventual ridiculous lie, in a breathless voice, only emphasised her sense of guilt in deliberately seeking him out. Glancing around as if suspecting that she had been followed, her initial bravado vanished when she faced him again. Twisting her flimsy skirt in her hands, she said hesitantly. "It's . . . well, it's simply ages since you . . . since we . . . met."

"I know how long it is."

"Do you?" It was brittle and wobbly, indicative of her nervousness.

"I can count."

There was silence from her as the moonlight was doused by clouds. He wished it would remain dark. A man could imagine anything when unable to see reality. Then he wondered if he should slip away. The conversation could take any direction, and he had an obligation to prevent further friendship between them.

"Life at home has completely changed," she said with a rush. "Mummy and Daddy hardly speak without arguing. The house is just like a hotel—people calling all through the day—and Alex is so different I hardly know him." She paused, then added just as quickly, "It's all because of Thea. She's upset everyone at home and set the whole of Singapore talking. You must be the only man around who hasn't called to be introduced to her."

"Is that why you came out here after me; to arrange an introduction?"

The returning moonlight crystallised her, and the beauty of the sight touched him unbearably. He was being cruel to drive her away, when it was the last thing he really wanted.

Her twisting hands doubled their assault on the chiffon skirt. "You must know why I came out here."

"I wouldn't be asking, if I did."

Looking around in guilt again, she turned back to demand in a near whisper, "Is this part of it?"

"Part of what?" he queried, hating himself more every minute.

"Out there, beneath . . . beneath the frangipani. You *can't* have forgotten. Surely you can't have forgotten!"

Dear God, he had thought of little else. "No."

"Then . . . I don't understand," she cried softly. "You have deliberately ignored me . . . *for four whole weeks!* You've gone out of your way to avoid us on dozens of occasions, and when you couldn't, you said the minimum to my parents or Alex, and refused to utter one word to me. It was as if you thought I didn't exist. Oh Martin, what have I *done?* Tell me what I've done."

He realised the exchange was getting out of hand. She was making the situation worse with her emotional cross-questioning. There was one effective way of putting an end to it, and he dared not do that. The alternative was the *coup de grâce*.

"It should never have happened. I'm sorry, Lydia."

"*Sorry!* Is that all you have to say after you . . . after . . ."

"After what?" he challenged roughly. "Good God, is that why you followed me out here; for a repeat performance?"

Backing away, she retaliated in laboured sentences. "How could you think I wanted . . . that I would . . . ? When you kept pretending it hadn't happened by treating me so badly, I thought it might be because you were ill. *That*'s why I came out here."

"Why should I be ill?" he demanded savagely, as the night was again plunged into darkness by clouds.

Her voice came to him through the humid blackness. "Everyone knows . . . well, it's not normal for men to do what you did!"

Her choice of words blasted away the last of his restraint. The fantasies of his lonely nights since he had last held her were instant hectic reality. She grew limp against him, and almost folded when he thrust her away at arms' length after the kiss.

"Every time you chase after me in a dark garden, that's what you'll get . . . possibly more," he raged. "So if you merely want to enquire after my health, or ask whether or not I'm normal, write me a note, Miss Beresford. Better still, get your brother to invite me to a tennis party."

Like a flash of lightning, the moon appeared momentarily to illuminate the girl's stumbling progress up the flight of stone steps, much as his had been on the day they had first met. In that brief moment of brilliance, Martin saw a figure in shimmering silver emerge from the shadows at the top of the steps, and stand looking down at him.

Chapter 5

The scene Thea had unwittingly witnessed rasped the raw wound she had hoped the East would salve. Her original reason for seeking out a man Alex had described as a war casualty who had upset colonial equilibrium by filling a post which should have gone to a junior in line for promotion, was swept aside by a rush of bitterness too sharp to ignore. When he did not mount the steps to the terrace, she went down into the garden where he was no more than an indistinct figure, to confront him.

"Martin Linwood, I presume," she began in mocking tones, still hearing Lydia's broken voice pleading with him to tell her what she had done to deserve such treatment from him. "I came in search of you only to discover you're not worth that much distinction."

He gave no answer, which surprised her. They usually had such plausible excuses ready when caught out.

"Although no one else in that family appears to have identified little Lydia's condition, I recognised it right away. The subject of such secret guilty worship is usually a handsome cad, or a licentious middle-aged husband," she continued coldly. "I know you are not the latter, and what I saw of you in the ballroom established that you are hardly handsome. I can only think that you must instead be acting the rôle of battle-scarred hero to the hilt, and that's despicable."

Only when his silence continued did she have the strange suspicion that he was actually *unable* to speak. A shaft of moonlight through a break in the clouds illuminated his face momentarily; thin features, dark shocked eyes, tension in every line around a mouth working with emotion. She had seen so many like that, and her heart had bled for the waste of youth and intellect. Thrown from her line of attack, she found herself mounting a heartfelt defence instead.

"That girl has had the most incredibly sheltered upbringing. Margery has cocooned her from anything she regards as harmful, and that includes any hint of sexual awareness. If she has ever been kissed, which I doubt, it would have been no more than a peck on the cheek from a well-scrubbed youngster whose future could be destroyed by Austin and other colonial censors if he overstepped the line. Unbridled passion for older experienced men, or for anyone whom society condemns, is inevitable as a result. It is also volatile and dangerous," she emphasised to the man who was again no more than a shadow. "I don't know what has been going on between you two, but it's plainly time someone intervened to stop it. Don't you realise you're playing with fire by seducing that girl?"

His starched shirt crackled in the darkness as he made some movement, and his words almost burst from him in a sudden angry torrent.

"I suggest you return to the ballroom, Miss du Lessier. They have all come here tonight to find out if what they have heard about you is true. Go in and give them their money's worth, and to hell with your insufferable advice on something you could never comprehend."

No longer sure who was the real victim in the affair, and recognising the wounded creature showing its claws to another who was trying to prevent it hiding away until healed, Thea reached out in empathy to the man in shadow.

"The flow of advice has ceased, believe me. I had no notion that you were seriously involved with that child."

"Go away, damn you!"

Sensing the state of his mind, however, she was driven to remain with him "If you really wish to be rid of me, you go! I was so bored with most of the people in there, I have no intention of rejoining them just yet. I came in search of you because I felt you might be the one person I would enjoy talking to tonight."

"Somewhat inconsistent, aren't you? A moment ago I was the subject of your . . . your cynical forbearance."

"Oh, for pity's sake relax," she cried, stung into retaliation. "Shell-shocked men are two-a-penny in England. I've seen worse cases than you lurching through the streets of Bayswater. *They* have stopped feeling sorry for themselves and trying to hide their condition. When are you going to do the same?"

As he began moving away, she added swiftly, "Please stay. I don't give a damn if you start swearing at me, firing an imaginary machine-gun, throwing a fit, or whatever your particular variation is. Go ahead, and take as long as you like over it. When it's out of your system, I really would like to talk to you. That truly was the reason I sought you out this evening." As he halted on the lowest step, she continued quickly, "You've been in Singapore two months, that's all. You must surely be more *au fait* with the realities of the world than the youngsters who flocked around me in that ballroom, like fairground patrons eager to view the latest curiosity."

Without turning, he said bluntly, "Prior to coming East I spent a year in a mental hospital. I'm hardly *au fait* with the realities of the world."

"Of course you are," she declared. "Wouldn't you call that year

78

reality with a vengeance? I'm longing for a conversation with you. Most people out here do no more than *chat*. You must have noticed."

"Yes." It was quiet, hesitant.

"How do you stand intellectual starvation?"

He turned then, and said in a matter-of-fact tones devoid of any suggestion of self-pity, "When you've been to bedlam and back, you can stand most things."

Thea began to realise how she had underestimated this man she had begun by using as a whipping boy for her own lash. Moving to join him, she tried to compensate for her earlier hostility.

"Wouldn't you agree that it's indicative of our compatibility that we can come so far in a relationship without the absurd social necessity of formal introductions?"

"As the two greatest subjects of local tittle-tattle, at present, we needed no introductions. You can't assume compatibility on those grounds."

"Let's find others."

"There might be no others."

"I'll accept the findings and leave you alone, in that case." Attempting the next stage in gaining his trust, she said, "Shall we go up and find a quiet place to shelter from the rain which I am certain is coming?"

Without waiting for his consent she climbed the steps, holding her skirt clear of her feet and treading carefully in the darkness. He followed one step behind her. Most dancers had re-entered the ballroom to take supper, leaving vacant several sheltered arbours. Thea made for one at the far end of the terrace, confident that Martin would join her there. Settling on the seat, she looked up at him as he stood beneath a swinging lantern. It shed enough light for her to study him closely.

"You don't look old enough."

"For what?"

"To have been in uniform for all four years of the war."

"I volunteered with the rest of the Officer Corps of my school."

"The heroic sacrifice!" she snorted.

"We didn't think of it that way," he said stiffly.

"You should have," she countered with vigour. "Even at eighteen it must have been obvious to you all that there was a better way of serving your country than throwing up your studies, and going off to fight for a way of life destined to change anyway. A few less schoolboys in the trenches wouldn't have altered the course of the war."

"We'll never know whether or not you have a valid point," he observed evenly.

79

"What were you intending to read at university?"

"History and Classics."

"Now you're in some obscure department of the Civil Service out here. Why aren't you pursuing your university career?"

"I should have thought the answer to that was obvious," he said with a hint of impatience.

"Bedlam and back? What nonsense! Just because you sometimes jump at your own shadow and imagine Huns on the attack, it doesn't mean that your brain will no longer absorb facts. Not content with wasting your intellect once, you are set on doing it a second time. We're certainly not compatible on those grounds."

"I had no confidence that we would be." He leaned his right shoulder against the wall in a more relaxed manner than she had hoped for, as he asked, "Do you probe so blatantly into the life of everyone you meet?"

She smiled and shook her head. "Only those I consider worthy of the exercise."

After slight hesitation, he said, "You have all the matrons of Singapore against you."

"They'll grow accustomed to me, in time."

"That emerald on your forehead is a bit much."

"Not in the least. I studied my entire ensemble before leaving the house. It definitely reflected my mood."

"Ah," he said, as if enlightened.

"My father gave me the stone for my coming of age. He was Italian, and ridiculously generous."

"So was my mother."

"Generous?"

"An Italian."

"We have them then!" she declared in triumph.

"What?"

"Grounds for compatibility."

He nodded slowly. "I'll allow that. Do you speak Italian?"

"Fluently. Do you?"

"Of course."

Leaning back in her seat, Thea faced him frankly. "All the aspiring young colonials are against *you*, Martin, besides the old die-hards."

"So I understand."

"It doesn't bother you?"

His dark eyes glinted in the shifting lantern-light. "I've had the entire German army against me. Everyone else seems mild, in comparison. Even you, Miss du Lessier."

"Call me Thea," she told him absently, growing puzzled over the recent scene with Lydia. The man before her seemed supremely rational and intelligent now he had recovered from it. The adolescent girl's misguided hero-worship was easy enough to identify, but Martin Linwood was either as unstable as rumour claimed or he was giving her the same beguiling performance with which he captivated young Lydia. If the former were true, she would feel deep regret. If the latter, she would fight him tooth and claw on the girl's behalf. She knew from experience Lydia would never do it herself.

Martin brought her from speculation by asking, "Are you really intending to write a novel on the mysterious East?"

"Of course."

"Emulating your sensation-seeking mother?"

The comment took her unawares, and she asked sharply, "What do you know of her?"

"My father once attempted to prevent publication of a book she claimed was 'a frank and perceptive study of the hallucinatory powers of opium'. He denounced it as a vulgar tasteless halleluiah to drug-induced depravity, masquerading as a novel. His campaign failed. The book sold in its thousands, making Anna du Lessier the queen of a literary clique raising sows' ears to the level of silk purses. Very few aspiring aesthetes have the courage to confess that they see the sow's ear lest they be denounced as plebeian."

"Your father was Frere Linwood?" she asked, conscious of a sharp tingle in her spine. "My mother never forgave him."

"Why? She bested him, in more ways than one. He is dead; she is the darling of the literary shams."

Thea rose slowly to look more closely at him. Was it possible that he did not know? "You're very outspoken."

Straightening from his leaning position against the wall, he said pointedly, "The realities of the world, Thea. You assured me that I was more *au fait* with them than most."

More puzzled than ever by his enigmatic personality, she was driven to comment, "And you assured me that it was out of the question for you to handle more than a backwater job in Singapore. Who were you really trying to convince, Martin?"

He sidestepped that deftly. "My backwater job entails helping to keep the peace between the ethnic communities here. I've heard you have some notion of wandering wherever you fancy to look for 'atmosphere'. I must warn you that it would be inadvisable to the point of inviting danger. If I hear that you have ignored my words, you'll find our compatibility won't exclude you from the consequences. Your mother might get away with near criminal behaviour in London, but it's vastly different out here, I promise you."

The tingle in her spine increased as she challenged him. "Are you anxious to continue your father's campaign against the du Lessiers? We're not easily browbeaten, you know."

Before he could reply to that the rain arrived, sweeping across the terrace to reach even their secluded corner. Thea gave a cry, gathered up her skirt, and ran for the ballroom as the tropical downpour thundered down to dance over the flagstones and drench her to the skin in the short time it took to reach shelter. Together, they burst into an atmosphere of heat, noise and swirling movement to stand dazzled by the light from ten chandeliers. Thea's back was running with water, and her dress clung even closer to her body as the rain gathered at the hem to form a puddle at her feet. She turned her wet face up to smile at Martin, and was startled to discover that he had once more become the person she had seen first entering the ballroom that evening. Following his stony glance, she found Alex and Lydia standing with their parents no more than a few feet away. The girl's anguished look was no surprise, but she was taken aback at the anger on Alex's face. He was looking at them now with the pain of a betrayed lover. That he would become her lover eventually, she had few doubts, but his attitude was premature and unwelcome. It aroused her own annoyance, so that when he immediately came forward with a starched handkerchief from his breast pocket, she declined it sharply.

"I love being wet, sweetie. At home I used to take long walks for the pleasure of feeling the rain."

"Is that where you've been . . . for a long walk?" he ground out through tight lips.

"Good God," she exclaimed in deliberately loud tones, "is it another quaint custom out here to hold an inquest on why people get wet when it rains?"

Alex flushed a dull red, and she was instantly sorry that he had driven her to bait him. However, before anything could be done to aid the situation, their combined attention was taken by a blond lieutenant who came through the throng, sidestepping dancing couples in his determination to reach them. The man's face was alight with something verging on excitement, but it was the person beside Thea and Alex he greeted with a fierce handshake and a grip on his arm.

"*Martin Linwood!* I can hardly believe my eyes! I've waited three years for this meeting and it happens on the other side of the world by merest chance." His enthusiasm caused him to turn to include the entire Beresford family and Thea in his remarks. "I move on to

82

Shanghai in the morning, would you believe? It is the most incredible coincidence to meet this fellow here, of all places."

Facing Martin again, he told him, "I heard you'd received a 'Blighty' at the Somme. James Gilman told me. He was lost at Passchendaele, did you know? Long after we finally took it. Poor blighter trod on a mine that had surfaced after weeks of rain. When I was given leave I went to the hospital to see you, but you'd been discharged and sent back. I tried to find out which sector you were in, but organisation was in such a bally state no one knew where anyone was. Then Peter wrote to me out of the blue and told me you'd been with his regiment all along."

The young officer swung back to address them all again, his eyes glassy with emotion. "Your friend is an old school chum of mine, and one of the best. He put his own life on the line in order to free three men trapped beneath an overturned gun. One of those three was my young brother. They awarded Martin an MC for what he did, but no medal can express the debt my family owes him."

At that point he seemed overcome by emotion, and turned to grip Martin's hand once more. Only then did Thea realise that Alex had grown strangely rigid beside her, and glanced up at him. His expression as he gazed intently at the two men on her other side provided the greatest puzzle of the evening. There was something between Alex and Martin Linwood that had nothing whatever to do with her. Her tête-à-tête in the garden with the war hero had only intensified it.

They were all quiet on the way home. Alex longed to have Thea to himself, but his parents had ruled that they should travel as a family group. They had been quiet on the way to the ball, also, the only lively one having been Thea who chose to ignore the fact that she was the cause for the lack of gaiety in the others. By now, his family should have accepted that their unwelcome guest did not conform to the usual modes of dress or behaviour, yet they had been shocked when she had appeared for dinner in the daring gown he thought so perfectly suited to her unique personality. Most of the older ball-guests had shared his parents' opinion, but Alex had been the envy of every red-blooded man in that assembly. The knowledge had turned a routine event into a celebration of triumph as he watched those he had known for years trying to take Thea from him, and failing.

Most of his contemporaries romped through the sweltering predictable days, their every need catered for, contented with the sun-kissed simplicity of their lives. He, however, had counted those twilights, seeking the sunrise which would illuminate life with brilliance. Thea had recognised the yearning within him and responded wholeheartedly.

83

In this one girl was the promise of all he desired. She bloomed like a defiant exotic cactus-flower in the midst of a desert. She breathed excitement into every aspect of his life, stimulating his mind as well as his body. Since Thea had arrived, he had awoken each morning with a surge of energy. She had filled him with fresh confidence, a sense of inspiration, a ray of hope. Thea had completely captivated his senses and, in doing so, had somehow dissolved the bonds tying him to his family. They were not yet aware of the fact, but his own knowledge that they were no longer there was sufficient to make him enthusiastic for a future he had dreaded. He would be a shipper because he chose to be, not because his dead brother had placed a yoke around his neck.

Alex saw Thea as his salvation. His parents saw her as a threat. His father had already warned him about her liberated behaviour and the consequences of embarking on any kind of relationship with her. Reminders of his obligations toward his mother and sister had been a prelude to forbidding any kind of "fondling" or other "unmannerly gestures" under the Beresford roof. His father had then made an uncharacteristically crude reference to sexual practices between men and women, painting so disgusting a picture Alex had heatedly defended the implication that Thea was a harlot whom he intended to exploit. Understanding between them worsened even further.

Margery regarded the girl she had hoped to mother as a dual threat. Not only had she plainly taken Alex in thrall, she would sully Lydia's innocence with her unbridled language and behaviour. It was inevitable that she would prepare to fight for her children tooth and claw. Lydia appeared to have little feeling for Thea at all, so introverted had she grown lately. Alex ignored them all. He needed no one but his daring, darling girl. Her response to his kisses when they were alone, her wide-eyed glances across a room when they were not, her obvious rapport with his moods had all told him she was his. Then he had seen her run in from the garden with Martin Linwood, and jealousy had rioted through him.

Thea had slipped from the room without his seeing her leave. After twenty minutes had passed without sign of her, he had grown a little concerned, but nothing had prepared him for his feelings when the pair had burst in from the terrace, drenched to the skin and in strange accord for supposed strangers. If it had been any other man, Alex might not have given her cause to ridicule him. As it was, the old uneasiness over someone able to turn the tables on him had returned with a rush, instilling in him the absurd urge to snatch Thea from his side. What had happened then had been the cruellest twist of fate. After searching for three years, that confounded lieutenant had had to find his quarry at that instant, and proclaim his heroism. How could any man match up to that, in a woman's eyes?

Although Thea had been warm and wonderful afterward, the evening had never recovered for him. Taunted by that secret rendezvous in the garden, he nevertheless vowed he would not ask her about it and give her further grounds for gentle ridicule. Even so, as he now studied her across the dim interior of the car, all he could see was her expression, that half-smile, as she had tilted her face up to Martin Linwood. Fear began to gnaw at him. She had given him life. If she left him again, those twilights would gather to form eternal night.

"Did you know Martin Linwood in England?" asked Lydia, suddenly and so loudly Alex jumped.

"We hardly moved in the same circles there," Thea answered with a shake of her head.

"You've never been introduced to him, nor has he ever called at the house. How did you come to be so long in the garden with him you both got drenched?" The words smacked of accusation.

"My dear girl, it's possible to become drenched in less than thirty seconds, in this part of the world. I had heard so much about Martin from people unused to shell-shock cases, I decided to introduce myself and make my own judgement. When I saw him slip on to the terrace, I followed him out as soon as I was free."

"You mean you just walked up to him and began talking?"

Thea smiled. "We're the same people before a third person recites our names to each other, as we are afterward. I think it's absurd to ignore someone you are certain will interest you, simply because there have been no introductions."

"Did you find him as interesting as you expected?"

Thea considered a moment. "I found him enigmatic. That's always more stimulating than being merely interesting. They are all wrong, in my opinion. Far from being a dolt, he's a damned sight more intelligent than many I have met since my arrival. Sadly, the consensus of opinion is affecting his judgement of himself. Sir Hartle Weyford is more likely to destroy his godson than save him by persisting in keeping him here in a job any fairly competent youngster could handle."

Alex was about to comment on that when Thea turned to his mother, to say, "I'd like to invite him to the house occasionally. You have no objections, do you, Margery?"

He was dismayed at the reply. "Of course I have no objections, Dorothea. Whilst you are out here you must form your own set of friends, including any young men who interest you. You may invite Mr Linwood as often as you wish."

Lydia grew absorbed in the view outside her window, where the dark streets had been given a false beauty by flood water lying like giant sequins in any shallow depression. Alex wondered momentarily if his sister still retained a fancy for Martin Linwood despite his recent avoidance of the Beresford family. Maybe the emotional reunion of former comrades tonight had rekindled the faint hero-worship she had initially experienced. More to the point was his mother's sudden affability. Only a fool would not see the reason behind it. Thea had expressed interest in another man. Throw the pair together at every opportunity and a son might be wrested from her clutches. Small wonder she now had no objections to welcoming into her house a man she had once condemned as a threat to young virgins. That he might be a danger to Thea did not matter, apparently.

When they reached the house Margery gathered her chicks around her and conducted them upstairs in determined manner, leaving father and son together. Alex would have pleaded tiredness and retired, except that Austin suggested a nightcap in a manner that demanded acceptance. Settling in a chair in the room in which Martin had offered to help him out over the dragon affair, Alex was still unhappy with Thea's interest in him when his father raised a subject on which they had often argued, taking him by surprise.

"I have been giving some thoughts to Manila, Alexander. You are quite right to be concerned about our trading contracts there. The Refford consignments have now come to an end, as we were well aware they would, so it means that our ships will be returning with half-empty holds unless we pick up single cargo contracts each time. It's far too chancy." Settling into the chair opposite Alex, he sipped his whisky appreciatively. "There are too many rivals who can snap up occasional loads because they have their own men there, rather than an agent. Mendes is astute enough, but he serves many masters."

Alex was almost open-mouthed. He had been making that very point for months. It was why he had been so anxious to take up the Manila contracts shed by *Rochford-Kendal*. What had occurred to clear his father's obstinate blindness on the subject?

"Mendes is a damned sight too astute, sir," he commented boldly. "He serves best the masters who deal in lucrative sidelines not listed on the manifests."

Austin frowned over the top of his glass. "So you have impressed upon me several times, although I have always made my opinions perfectly clear to you. There will be no cargoes carried by *Berondel* which I am afraid to list openly. However, I am prepared to accept your recommendation to put in a tender for Merrydew's regular consignments of machine parts."

"You are?" he queried in astonishment.

"I've enquired into the integrity of the company more closely, and found it to be small but sound."

Alex had told his father those facts when the tender had been sought by the company, but his advice to offer terms so favourable they were certain to be accepted had been ignored. The question had not even been put to the Board. This sudden reversal was curious.

"Have you had words this evening which persuaded you, Father?" he asked, loosening his bow tie and undoing the top stud of his shirt in order to be more comfortable.

Austin, who was never less than immaculate and fully-clad no matter the occasion, continued to enjoy his whisky as if in the company of similar die-hards of tradition.

"Fletcher told me that *Eagle-Massey* recently outbid him on one of his regular contracts, which had come up for renewal. Said he was now looking for other prospects, no matter how small. My enquiries into the bona fides of Merrydew had proved satisfactory, so I have decided to let you have your way over the matter, my boy. First thing on Monday contact their Mr . . . what's his name again?"

"Thirsk. Malcolm Thirsk." Full of disbelief, Alex then asked, "Do you mean me to handle the affair from start to finish?"

"Not up to it?" queried his father dryly.

"Yes. Yes, of course I am," he protested. "Thank you, sir. I'll arrange a good deal, I promise."

"I'm sure you will." Tossing back the remainder of his nightcap, his father got to his feet. "Time to turn in, I think."

They left the room together, said goodnight to Ling, and started up the stairs in a mood of accord they had not experienced for months. At the head of the graceful curving flight their ways parted to different wings of the house, and Austin faced Alex with a curious smile lurking around beneath his dyed moustache.

"I have also been giving thought to another scheme you have been strongly advocating for some time. We must expand, I suppose, or be swallowed up by the giants." He put his hand on Alex's shoulder in a rare gesture of paternal affection. "I hope you'll take it as a sign of my trust in you that I have decided to let you have your way over Manila, at last. You have long begged to set up your own offices there and dispense with Mendes. I'm giving you your wish. You'll sail on *Sargasso* next Thursday to make your preliminary arrangements. When you come back to report to me, I'll then allow you six months' trial. If you

87

succeed, you may be our man in Manila for as long as you wish. Now, what have you to say to that, my boy?"

As Alex watched his father walk away he realised, with a sense of shock, that Austin Beresford was as shrewd and manipulative as any man when he had good reason to be. The business responsibility Alex had longed for, the chance of freedom from the family yoke, had just been granted with a smile and an encouraging pat on the shoulder. Yet, as he stood there facing an empty corridor, Alex saw the concession in real terms. The opportunity to prove himself was undoubtedly there; the implied freedom was an illusion. He was now firmly held in a cleft stick. His parents must be more afraid of Thea than he had imagined.

When Alex reached his room, Fong awoke from his doze on a chair just inside the door and got to his feet with a welcoming smile. There was no return smile from a man burning with a sense of impotency.

"You can cut along to bed," he told the boy absently, as he tugged off the close-fitting coat and abandoned the stiff shirt-front and bow tie.

"I no go yet," Fong assured him cheerfully. "You wanchee shower, be leddy for sleep."

"I'm not sleepy."

"I wait."

Alex rounded on him. "I don't want you to wait. I thought I made that clear."

The familiar stubborn expression settled on the round face. "I see you have shower, go bed. I takee launlee. Takee suit clean and pless."

Alex's stormy mood erupted. "I'm not going to bed yet, and you damn well know why, don't you?"

Strong disapproval joined the stubbornness of Fong's whole attitude, and the black eyes which could glow with merriment grew stony. Only a lifelong association which was less than parental yet more than domestic allowed the boy to say, "Velly bad thing you do. Old Master and Mem no likee. Miss Lylia no likee. Fong no likee. You have shower, go bed."

"Oh, for God's sake! I'm sick of being told what everyone else doesn't like. *I* like it. It's what *I* want to do. Take that old-maidish look off your face, Fong, I'm in no humour to stand for it. Now clear off!" When the Chinese made no move, he crossed the few feet to him. "If you've spoken about it to anyone, I'll flay you alive."

Fong was mortally offended by the suggestion that he would be disloyal to someone he had served for so many years. It was distressing loss of face, which brought tears to his eyes. Alex was so smitten by the evidence of pain he had caused a staunch ally, he ran his hand through his hair restlessly, muttering, "Forget I said that, old lad. I've just been faced with the knottiest problem I've ever had. I had to let fly at somebody, and you just happened to be there. Look, stay here if you must, but I do need to see Miss Thea if I'm to get any sleep tonight. I'm not doing anything bad, you know. It just seems that way."

Conscious of time passing, he crossed the room to the verandah and followed it around the house until he reached the point where a balustrade marked the end of it. Beyond, the sloping roof above the front entrance of the house rose up. Beyond that, the verandah began again and ran along the west wing of the house, where Thea's room was situated. Having done it several times before, Alex scrambled easily over the rise and fall of the roof, then vaulted the stone wall before hurrying past several empty guest rooms and rounding a corner. She was waiting for him; a shadow in a satin wrapper. Beneath it, he was certain she was naked, yet there was an unexpressed confidence in her each time they had met this way which told him it would be a mistake to see an invitation in the fact.

Tonight, he felt unequal to the challenge. The warmth of her body through the satin set inner voices urging him to escape the cleft stick by the most exciting means available to him. He soon discovered they were not available to him, when Thea drew back from his kiss and caught his errant hands in her firm grip.

"Easy, darling, easy," she cautioned softly.

"Impossible." He kissed her again, although his hands were still imprisoned. It was a lengthy salute, with variations on an original theme. Longing to hold her, Alex nevertheless derived a strange excitement from the suggestion of soft manacles around his wrists. She broke contact, leaving him in a heady state as she studied his face by the light from a star-spangled sky.

"These meetings may have to cease, Alex. We're going far too fast toward the point of no return. I don't want that."

"I do," he told her fervently.

"It would be disastrous. We have to slow down and think of your future."

Freeing himself, he drew her back into his arms, saying against her soft hair, "I can't think of anything but you. I love you, Thea. I daren't risk losing you."

"I have no intention of being lost," she assured him softly, "but I won't be held responsible for making you leap into a situation likely to disrupt the entire fabric of your life and give us both enormous obstacles to overcome. Is that what you really want?"

"What I really want is the freedom to love you," he said. "I want you in my arms all night, but it goes deeper than that. We think the same way. We find the same things amusing. You give me inspiration, because your daring augments mine. Why should we have to meet in secret like this, and pretend we're no more than distant cousins in public? What's so wrong in our loving each other? It's so ridiculous; so *unbearable*," he finished, bitterness over his father's actions adding heat to his words.

Turning from him to lean on the balustrade, she studied the starry eternity of night sky. "Don't ask me those questions, Alex, ask your family, your friends, the whole colonial brotherhood. They dictate the pace of our relationship, not me."

Stepping up behind her, he circled her body with his arms to draw her back against his chest.

"For the past two years I have tried to persuade Father to create a sub-office in Manila, so that we could dispense with our ageing Portuguese agent. He wouldn't hear of it. A few minutes ago he told me to go down there next week to find premises from which I can run the subsidiary on six months' trial. Before you came, I'd have jumped at the chance. Now every instinct urges me to refuse."

She turned swiftly in his arms. "That would be madness!"

"Would it? Believe me, it's not the compliment it appears to be. You must appreciate that, Thea. It's obvious why he's sending me now, surely."

"Of course it's obvious, but that's beside the point. You have your chance to escape the family bonds which damn near strangle you. No consideration should stand in your way of taking it."

It was a painful blow. "You're telling me to go away from you for six months."

Her fingers caressed his mouth in place of a kiss. "Six months apart, during which we can exchange letters, should prevent a catastrophe we should regret all our days. I'm in love with you, too, but I have things to do first. Please don't rush me into a total commitment now. I have a book to write; a defiance of my own to drive from my system. Go to Manila and set up your office, sweetie, but defy your parents' hopes by not forgetting me for one minute of those six months."

The embrace was more passionate than ever, and the open doors to her room were a severe test to his bruised self-confidence. Only the inner conviction that it would be a fatal mistake stopped him from taking her in to that bed as she responded in breathtaking manner. Yet she disarmed him totally when they broke apart, by saying, "It's not only this Manila business you're afraid of is it? It's Martin Linwood."

Robbed of words, he gazed down at her as she smiled.

"All through this evening men were making sheep's eyes or trying their luck with me, and you watched with smug pride. Yet, when I came in from the garden with that one particular man, there was something in your expression which was not exactly anger, jealousy or strange humiliation. Maybe it was a mixture of all three. Why, Alex?"

With his thoughts in confusion, he hedged. "You had been missing for a long time. I was anxious about you."

"Where Martin Linwood is concerned, it's Lydia you should feel anxious about, not me. Something is going on between that pair."

"What do you mean—*something is going on between them?*", he demanded loudly.

"Shh!" she warned, glancing along the verandah where several doors stood open to the night. "I'm not sure what his motives are, but Lydia's affliction is all too identifiable. They are heading for trouble, Alex, believe me. One way of trying to avert it is to throw them together as often as possible. Forbidden fruit is overwhelmingly tempting until there is a glut of it. That's why I told Margery I wanted to invite him here. She jumped to the comforting conclusion that I was taken with Martin myself, but I didn't expect you to see cupids linking my initials with his against a background of hearts and flowers, you idiot."

Alex could not treat it so lightly. "How do you know so much about it? What *is* going on? If that blighter is . . ."

"Calm down, darling! He's not planning to rape her. At least, I don't think he is."

"For God's sake, Thea!"

"Shh! I'm only teasing you," she admitted softly. "You're almost irresistible when you're roused." When he tried to prove her words, she held him at arms' length, however, saying with caressing gentleness, "Tell Austin you'll go to Manila, Alex. I'll still be here when you return, I promise. I also promise you Lydia will be perfectly safe. I have the affair under control even if they haven't."

Denied the fulfilment he sought, he had to ask sharply, "How is it that you know so much about what is going on between my sister and Linwood?"

Her face studied his in the hush of the tropical night. "I once went through what I believe Lydia is presently suffering. In my case, no one cared enough to attempt to save me from the inevitable consequences. I allowed the subject of my hero-worship to become my lover, and gave him anything he wanted." At his involuntary movement, she added, "If you can't take that on the chin, darling, you're not the man I thought you were."

As Alex gazed painfully back at her he realised he was not the man *he* thought he was.

Chapter 6

Thea sat outside the rooms she occupied, for which she had offered to pay and apparently insulted her hosts, enjoying the shade of the verandah. There was a pile of blank paper on the table before her. For the past two hours, she had been trying to defy the heat, the mosquitoes and the Beresfords in order to concentrate on her novel. The heat, the mosquitoes and the Beresfords continued to prevent her from making a start.

She missed Alex far more than she had expected to. The instant physical attraction she had felt on being met aboard by a muscular, good-looking young man with an impudent smile and a rakish air despite the obligatory topee, had deepened surprisingly swiftly into total rapport with someone who possessed a latent rebelliousness to match her own. It was proving very stimulating to coax and encourage a free spirit which had been so methodically crushed by his family. It was heady recognising in him all she wanted from life; a partner prepared to swim against the tide. Alex wanted excitement, new experiences, danger, even. He longed to use his body and mind to the full, to question and challenge, to kick out all the old inflexible rules and establish the right of the individual. The thrill of knowing that she was releasing the true man he was, was equal to that of recognising the spark of sexual response once more. This time, however, their shared passion was exhilarating, balanced and enduring.

He had sailed for Manila a week ago, unhappy over the parting. Distinctly shaken over the knowledge that she had had a former lover, he nevertheless had tried to persuade her to allow him to be her second before he left. God knew, she had been dangerously tempted. Prudence had told her that such haste to reach total commitment would spell disaster for him. Once they became lovers, there would be no turning back. He would want to share her room every night, running the risk of discovery and subsequent family wrath, or he would insist on a speedy marriage, with the same result. For his sake, she knew she must be the one controlling the affair. Yet, had it been entirely for his sake that she had resisted the temptation to surrender?

Leaving her chair, she wandered into the small sitting room adjoining the bedroom. An overhead fan provided slight relief from the humid air outside, and she dabbed at her forehead with a handkerchief soaked in cologne before sinking on to a *chaise-longue*. Then her mouth twisted

92

cynically: it was an action reminiscent of Anna du Lessier. How often had her mother reclined looking sapped of strength and *distraite*, surrounded by her followers sympathising with the state to which the demands of her work reduced her? For some years Thea had also been deluded by that pose of genius, until the cruel awakening.

In contrast to the Beresford children, Thea's life had suffered no restrictions whatever from the cradle onward. She had been blessed with health, wealth and freedom; also with an excellent nanny who had taken the place of parents she had rarely seen. Her youth had been spent in a succession of schools from which she had been dismissed as being immune to discipline. In consequence, friendships had been numerous but shortlived, which had enabled her to accept the loss of those she had liked and had given her the ability to socialise easily. Anna du Lessier had appeared as no more than an extravagant and dramatic woman prone to extremes of mood, who had no interest in her daughter. Thea had not minded that: she had had little interest in her mother. The man who had fathered her had rarely been in England, so she had had little interest in him, either. Ricardio Tosti had been known to the world as a feckless, handsome, intensely artistic man who had suffered from melancholia. When he had died six months ago at the age of forty-three, there had been no obvious cause and his Italian doctor had given the opinion that his patient's extreme sensitivity had left him unable to accept the horrors of the war which had ravaged the world for four years.

Thea thought the diagnosis rather fanciful, since her father had always lived in the greatest luxury, and had never been anywhere near any aspect of battle or those who took part in it. However, on one rare visit to England, he had sobbed openly at the discovery of a dead swan on the lake of their host's estate, so perhaps the carnage had depressed him beyond reason. It had left her mother untouched, however, so self-centred was she. Surrounded by her sycophantic Bohemian friends, she had continued writing dramatic tales peopled by artificial characters who performed all the human eccentricities formerly regarded as shocking and unmentionable. Many believed that Anna du Lessier truly campaigned for the misfits of society to be given sympathetic recognition, but it was a sad fact that the author of the bestselling *Girl in a Plate of Strawberries* wrote her risqué novels for the sole purpose of making money. The books were considered outspoken and brave: it was "the thing" to admire her and those who basked in her reflected notoriety. The volumes would almost certainly be considered worthless in a few years, and the next generation of readers would not even recognise her name. All the while they continued in

93

vogue, however, Anna du Lessier would pursue her selfish amoral path.

Lost in recollection, Thea forgot the white stone house in the heart of the tropics and returned to recollections of a Bayswater apartment on an afternoon when she had been alone amidst the draped Kashmir shawls, the ceramic pots surrounding a sunken pool filled with Chinese fish, and the copies, in pure untinted glass, of the Elgin Marbles. Whilst lying barefooted on the magenta carpet in a Grecian robe, she had glanced up from a book on Javanese fertility rituals to find herself being studied by a lean youth with eyes of a startlingly beautiful turquoise shade and a face that was dead white. As she had stared back, he had collapsed in a faint no more than a few feet from her. The mesmeric quality of that moment touched her again now, and the wound she believed healed began to tingle with awareness, as Dominic's aura worked its old remembered magic.

For two years she had adored him. His poems had made her weep with their sensitivity and subdued eroticism as she had sat spellbound at his feet, while he had read them in a voice her mother once described as heartbreakingly melodic. Anna du Lessier had launched Dominic Grant into her circle of artistic egotists, where he had speedily found that his own talent far exceeded that of those around him. Well caught in the web, he had agonised over the choice between toeing the du Lessier line as a sycophant, or courting poetic death by breaking from the charmed circle and attempting to build an individual reputation. The hesitant worshipping Thea had agonised with him. Time and again she had sat at his side in the apartment perfumed by Arabic spices, listening to his torrent of confused thoughts. Stretched on the rack of artistic yearning, his suffering had been so clearly revealed in those wonderful eyes that Thea's adoration had grown too intense to contain. His poems had then became reality; his love words addressed to her alone.

The loss of her virginity had been a rioting sublimation of her body and senses to appease the anguish of a personality which proceeded to dominate hers to the point of abandoning her separate life. From that day on, Thea du Lessier had become no more than a facet of Dominic Grant. As her worship intensified, the erotic interludes had grown more frequent. The girl in adolescent bondage had agreed to any demand, in the belief that the brilliant tortured artist could only gain solace through her sexual generosity.

The first great shock had been conscription. It had snatched him up, dressed him in khaki, and sent him away to face images and sounds which would surely destroy him. The black months of his absence had

94

deepened Thea's sense of commitment to the point of dedicated campaigning with other liberated females for an end to the war, at any cost, before there were no young men left sane or alive. When Dominic had arrived at the apartment on leave he had found a fiercely possessive and protective girl awaiting him. Yet he was no longer the same person. The turquoise eyes had witnessed depravity; the sensitive poet was obsessed by it. The wad of obscene verses he had brought from France with him were then hailed as the observations of a supreme artist. Immediately, he was placed on the pinnacle of poetic fame, needing the cloying services of Anna du Lessier no more. Neither did he need sexual solace from Thea, which had started a cruel cat and mouse game between them until she had begged him to tell her what she had done to cause him to shut her from his life.

That point in her memories always drove her to her feet with the pain of self-denigration generated by a past ungovernable passion. She believed that terrible afternoon would never be wiped from the recesses of her mind. Humiliation washed over her anew as she stared at Alex's mocking fan palms, seeing no more than a tear-stained girl on her knees clutching the khaki hem of a jacket in her desperation to prevent her love from walking away, as she cried, *"What have I done?"* A long list of her sins would have been less cruel than the careless information that she had done nothing.

The second great shock had been the discovery of her mother lying naked on the dais she used as a day-bed, whilst she anointed Dominic's body with aromatic oil from a jewelled jar. There had been an over-powering smell of incense or something similar in the room, and the lovers had moved almost hypnotically to complete their sensuous coupling. Thea had remained there to watch, as if hypnotised herself. Deep hatred for them both had been born that day. She had left the apartment to join a group of wealthy pacifist women who produced a news-sheet they distributed themselves from street corners. In their company she had matured and hardened, so that Dominic Grant's death in action a year later had not disturbed the numbness around her emotions.

That numbness might well have continued if one of the women in the group, which devoted itself to women's suffrage when the war ended, had not bought a copy of Anna du Lessier's latest novel *Domino*. Looking into it, Thea had found the names Dorothy and Domino had leapt at her from the pages to dissolve the numbness with the acid of betrayal. Her first vulnerable adventure into the realms of human love was there in minute detail. Everything she had done in the name of adoration, which only he could have revealed to the author, was set down in sensationally frank phrases. Her body was exposed to the world and ridiculed; her compassion was described, in mocking derisory fashion, as juvenile promiscuity. Dominic's virility was eulogised, and he became Eros enslaved by the one woman who caused him to kneel at her shrine, claiming her as his goddess. The novel was titillating, cruel, sadistic and ultimately shocking in its description of the young Domino's rape by his enemies leading to death by his own despairing hand. The book was selling in its thousands, hailed as Anna du Lessier's outcry against war and her finest work.

Thea had fled to an uncle by marriage, whose sister lived on the other side of the world. Even that did not seem far enough from her mother, but nevertheless, Thea convinced her host that the recent death of her father had depressed her so much she had to get right away. Doubly wealthy due to the terms of her father's will, Thea had bought a passage to Singapore and turned her back on England, intending never to return.

The long voyage had forced her to face the situation squarely, and she realised that running away was no solution. Slowly, the compulsion for revenge had been born. The most total form she could produce would be to devise a novel which would eclipse Anna du Lessier. By ruthlessly using her mother's friends in the publishing world, and exploiting the famous name to the limit, Thea resolved to write a grand novel of the East. Until now, the great stories had centred around conquest, plunder and exotic trade. She would conceive a human drama involving the people who inhabited the sweltering tropical areas to which she was travelling. The work would be honest, compassionate and pioneering. It would show up her mother's for the dross it was. Finding a purpose had been the commencement of the cure she had sought. Discovering Alex within the family she was joining had furthered it. The novel must bring completion, or she would never be free of that destructive episode of her young life.

To create a plot, Thea needed to gain atmosphere by visiting the ethnic quarters and speaking to the people who inhabited them about their lives and customs. Alex had told her it was out of the question. Austin and Margery had been horrified at the very mention of such plans, and Martin Linwood had practically threatened her with arrest if she attempted it. Nevertheless, she would have to go, and her thoughts had just revived the need to hit back at a woman who had not hesitated to sell her daughter's vulnerability for the highest price.

After a light tiffin in her room, Thea quietly left the house to find a passing rickshaw. There was one outside the main gate. The man who pulled it was dozing in the shade cast by trees. Waking him, she stepped between the shafts and settled on the warm seat giving him the name of a street she knew was in the Chinese quarter. He set off in the customary loping run, and she began to feel brighter than she had since Alex had sailed. In her large bag she had a camera with which she hoped to capture interesting people and scenes on film, to study at leisure when she finally began on her manuscript. Enthusiasm for the project bubbled up once more. The sights, sounds and smells which would make her work come to life were all around her. Descriptions would be easy enough. When she also had knowledge of the people, her novel would write itself.

On nearing the centre of Singapore, Thea came from her dreams very quickly. The European shops were still closed for the midday period. The native ones had shabby cotton blinds overhead to protect the goods inside from the destructive power of the sun. Bright shawls and brocaded silks would fade; ripe fruit would burst with the heat, and dried fish would curl up. The owners of these small shops relaxed in the doorways on charpoys or rush sleeping-mats, their maxim that what ought to be done today could always be left until tomorrow, encouraging lethargy. The East was not a part of the world where speed was popular. Thea, on the other hand, was brisk and full of eagerness now that she had made up her mind, so was not best pleased when the rickshaw rolled to a stop and the boy lowered the shafts for her to alight in the midst of the area favoured by shipping and mercantile companies. Near the harbour, its streets were lined with tall buildings of pale stone from which company flags fluttered, like vivid ribbons, on the crenellated façades.

"This isn't where I wanted to go," she told the boy in tones meant to indicate that she was not a person to be fooled.

He stood staring with a patient but implacable expression on a face covered with hollows and wrinkles, which poverty and hardship had put there. It was plain he intended to go no further, so Thea tried bribery with a handful of coins.

"This is twice the normal fare, which is virtual robbery, but it's yours when we arrive in the street I directed you to take me to," she told him tartly.

The bony figure in loose black tunic and trousers gazed back from beneath his conical hat as if she had not spoken. Black beady eyes sunken into folds of yellowish-brown flesh, seemed to contain an intelligence denied by his blank expression. The drawn-back emaciated jawbone left his teeth partially exposed, so that a gold filling flashed in the sunlight as he moved his head to avoid a persistent fly. Thea was left with no choice but to get out. Walking in the midday heat was madness.

No European male did it from choice; no female would attempt it, especially unescorted. However, as the Chinese took her money and ran off, Thea squared her shoulders and told herself she was an emancipated campaigner. Her work would not progress unless she was prepared to break outmoded taboos. Victorian women had braved the slums and underworld of London in their quest for social reforms. She prepared to follow their example by setting off briskly in the direction of the waterfront.

At first, there was shade from the brassy sun beneath the leafy branches of the trees bordering the street. Then, as the large buildings petered out to give way to the impressive flying roofs of wealthy Chinese merchants' homes, and on to narrower, dirtier areas of open-fronted shops and eating places, the overhead greenery was replaced by a canopy of tattered banners embroidered with black Chinese characters proclaiming ownership of the premises. Between the crowding walls of those buildings, whose upper floors overhung the streets, the heat was almost overpowering. Perspiration was running down Thea's temples by then, and the loose garments she wore stuck to her damp back. The strong odours produced by confined communal living made breathing unpleasant but, after walking for around fifteen minutes in such conditions, she reached the street known as the true centre of the Chinese quarter.

It was something of a setback to discover that she had been wrong about the native peoples of the island. They apparently shared the European habit of succumbing to lethargy when the sun rode high overhead, for there was no sign of Chinese women doing their marketing, or children running, careless and noisy with chatter, on feet which had never known shoes. The very narrow ramshackle lanes running off each side of the main street were empty save for the occasional scavenging dog. The roadside noodle stands were deserted. The smell of frying oil lingered in their giant blackened bowls, but there were no customers and no vendor turning the sizzling noodles with deft flicks of his wrist. Even open-sided eating places had been closed by the heat. Men lay open-mouthed in sleep along the benches. Some stretched out on the tables themselves; others were slumped across the oilcloth tops as if the meal just consumed had instantly drugged them. Cheap bowls littered the tables now covered with flies, and ants that had swarmed up the legs of the tables from the muck-laden stones beneath. In just one of such places, an ancient hunched figure sat with the sedateness of old age, alone in his wakefulness as he stared at the apparition of a lone white woman passing by, his watery soup forgotten in its bowl.

Thea halted to take a picture of this solitary diner, seeing the scene as particularly evocative. Then she took stock of her surroundings, now deep into the area she wished to study. There were still no women or children about to provide the domestic interest she sought. Another idea occurred to her. Along the route she had covered there had been several shops selling medicines, ointments and mysterious things in jars. Information on these Eastern apothecaries would be useful to a plot containing drama and ethnic cultures, she felt certain. Glancing about her, she decided there was a choice of continuing along the main street, or investigating one of several side alleys nearby. She decided on the latter, since she did not relish walking on knowing that the extra distance would have to be covered on the return. Those Victorian female stalwarts went up in her estimation even further, as she acknowledged that she was beginning to flag.

The narrow alley was even more dingy and odorous than ever, so she dabbed cologne on to a handkerchief in a vain attempt to refresh herself. Discomfort was forgotten, however, when she came upon a perfect example of what she was seeking. Taking out the camera, she filmed the narrow approach, the facade and the banner that proclaimed ownership of the curious premises. The entrance was no more than six feet wide; the interior lacked windows and was further darkened by piled wooden chests. On shelves lining the walls stood bottles of dark liquids, and jars containing mysterious objects floating in preserving fluid. From the ceiling hung bunches of leaves, grasses and twisted dried roots. Decorated bowls filled with coloured beans, fruits, nuts and seeds stood on top of a chest of drawers marked with identifying labels and pictures of relevant plants. Further into the shop stood a table bearing clouded bottles, wicker baskets, old European cigarette tins and cardboard boxes covered in bizarre labels.

Thea grew excited as she took it all in. What atmosphere! She stepped inside. At the far end of the shop hung a bead curtain in front of which were two simple stools. Could it be the waiting area, with the consulting room behind the curtain? A pungent musty odour of herbs and powders hung in the air, adding to the mystic quality of the place. Thea reached into her bag for the camera, then jumped nervously as a figure rose up from behind the chest of drawers like a silent jack-in-the-box. He was tall and surprisingly youthful in appearance, despite the usual black long gown and round black hat. Not a muscle of his broad face moved: his slanting black eyes were devoid of expression.

Undeterred, Thea smiled and approached the wooden chest in the manner of a potential customer. "Good afternoon. I'd very much like your help . . . but it isn't the usual kind of help you give. I'm looking for facts to help me with the novel I intend to write. A book," she added, in case he was uncertain of what she meant. Then, receiving no response from him, she went on, "I'm living in Singapore with some friends. They appear to know little about Eastern medicine, so it seems to be a subject worth exploring. Would you be prepared to tell me a little about your methods; the herbs you use? Naturally, I'd be willing to . . .'

He stopped her explanation with a tirade of incomprehensible words, accompanied by gestures which were very easy to translate. When she did not immediately leave the shop, he came round the chest in purposeful manner, still shouting angrily. His eyes were now immensely readable. Thea reacted with strong indignation.

"I merely want to ask a few questions, not probe into your professional secrets. There's no need to be so aggressive."

It did no good. Her arm was seized, and she was bundled across the room, through the doorway and into the alley. There, the man's hand shot out to knock her camera to the ground. It fell open exposing the film.

"Now just a minute," cried Thea furiously. "That's an expensive . . ."

There was no point in finishing the sentence. The apothecary had whisked back into his premises, and a heavy slatted metal shutter dropped with a rattle only inches from her face, closing the tiny shop from her view. Shaken by the swiftness of her defeat, she stood for several minutes glowering at the shutter whilst attempting to regain control of her temper. It took longer in the tropics, where even the smallest irritations grew to inflammatory proportions when the victim was already trying to fight the heat, the insects and the longing for the temperate climes of a distant homeland. Too late, she wondered if it would have been more prudent to take an interpreter, although all the Chinese she had encountered so far understood English well enough, even if they occasionally chose to pretend they did not. All the same, there had surely been no justification for such a violent reaction to her approach.

Bending to pick up the camera she realised how hot and weary she had grown, and decided to abandon her research for the day. Only then did she face the fact that she had walked a great distance, which now had to be retraced on foot until she regained the mercantile area. Her heart sank. The Victorian do-gooders should have tried it in temperatures like this, she decided. Maybe their results would not have been quite so praiseworthy!

She had not travelled far in what she hoped was the right direction when, rounding a corner, she came upon a crowd blocking the lane completely. Forced to halt, she looked at the scene with curiosity. A crude ramp, made from bamboos lashed tightly together, ran from the street to a tiny window in the third floor of a poverty-ridden dwelling. The clustering Chinese gazed upward with an air of expectation amounting almost to awe. Casting aside her irritability, Thea moved forward to observe the mysterious activity. Hardly had she reached the edge of the crowd than movement occurred at the high window. A long box, lashed around with rope and controlled by some unseen person in the upstairs room, began to emerge through the aperture. Cursing the inability to take a photograph, Thea realised she must have come upon a family in the process of moving house. This was local colour such as she had sought, and she pressed closer in her eagerness to observe the contents of such meagre homes as they reached street level.

After some precarious manoeuvring by the hands of the hidden residents, the box was swung round to rest on the ramp. Next minute, it raced down the flimsy swaying construction to arrive in the midst of the grouped observers with a resounding thump. Curious to examine the contents closely, Thea decided she would have to push her way to the centre of the mob filling the lane. However, at that point, they began to fan out making it easy for her to see the handcart on to which several men were now settling the open box. Moving forward, Thea peered into the depth. The scene turned upside down, then began to spin sickeningly around her as she groped for the nearby wall to support her. Inside the box were the dead bodies of a young woman and a newborn child.

For several moments, Thea fought rising sickness. Shaking with sudden chill, she leaned back against the wall and closed her eyes against the sight. Yet she still saw those two bodies which had been ejected from a window like so much baggage. The shivering in her limbs extended to her face, setting her teeth chattering. She opened her eyes, looking wildly around for somewhere to run. Instead, she saw two men approaching her swiftly. One was dressed in a crumpled linen suit and carried a black bag in his hand; the other wore the usual uniform of starched white jacket and trousers. Their expressions, beneath their coffee-coloured topees, were darker than the band around the turban of the giant Sikh policeman who accompanied them.

"*Thea!* What, in God's name, are you doing here?"

Concealing the relief she felt, she managed to reply, "I could ask the same of you, Martin."

His eyes narrowed angrily. "Don't tell me you're alone."

"Yes, I am. Why not?"

"*Why not?*" he roared. "It's asking for trouble, that's why not. There are two of us, but even so we wouldn't dream of coming without a police escort. He makes the visit official, and we are accepted. What the hell are you up to, you little fool? Come on, out with it!"

Regaining her poise quickly, she countered his astonishing aggression with some of her own. "Don't use that officious manner with me! You're no longer Captain Linwood, and I am not one of your subordinates."

"By God, if you were, I'd have you pilloried for disobedience, if not for stupidity. I warned you against this! I threatened you with official reprisals if you attempted this ridiculous nonsense. Haven't you any spark of intelligence, any grain of . . ."

"All right, Martin, I think you have said more than enough to this young woman," put in the man beside him with calm authority, laying a hand on his arm and gripping it. "Perhaps we should end the castigation and instead offer her our assistance." With a frown he asked Thea, "Are you all right? You look just about done in."

"I'm fine," she assured him, sobered by the violent loss of temper by a man she had once told he could not shock her with excessive behaviour caused by his mental wounds. Yet she was shocked by the evident frailty of his stability. He stood silently now, letting his companion handle the situation.

"I'm George McGregor, and the only Thea I know of in this colony who would go out in the streets dressed like a Cantonese amah, is the daughter of Anna du Lessier," he said with a wry twist to his mouth. "My dear Miss du Lessier, you are not only trespassing on the one part of this island they can truly call their own, you are trespassing upon their customs. I will ascribe your behaviour to thoughtlessness; they will regard it as western arrogance and mockery. Martin is basically correct. You have exposed yourself to risk if not to actual danger this afternoon. It's fortunate that we happen to be here at the right time."

Sobering further, Thea attempted to vindicate herself. "This loose cotton suit I'm wearing is my solution to keeping cool in deadly temperatures. Of course I'm not insulting these people. It's more a compliment to their good sense in wearing suitable clothing instead of trussing themselves up in corsets and tight bodices, like European women." At his apparent lack of understanding, she elaborated, "I am well known as an individualist, Mr McGregor."

"Not by the Chinese, unfortunately."

After a moment, she gave in gracefully. "Point made. I'm sorry if I have upset anyone."

The man smiled, which made his craggy face look much younger. "You have certainly upset Martin." Casting a glance at them both, he added speculatively, "Not for the first time, I suspect."

"Ask him," she countered, unwilling to continue the subject.

He nodded. "Right, I will. Meanwhile, what *are* you doing here, Thea? Did you lose your way?"

"No." She liked his use of her first name, and confided in him without hesitation. "I came to research facts for a novel I intend to write."

"The research is over for today," put in Martin firmly, but with more control now. "You are leaving with us . . . *now*. I want no arguments from you or from George."

McGregor laughed softly. "We'll come quietly, never fear." Taking Thea's arm, he murmured, "It's Martin's responsibility to ensure that there's no trouble in these areas. I'm just the humble medicine-man. Come along, we have a car waiting at the end of the street."

It was the best news she had heard that afternoon, but would not let them know that. Going with them, escorted by the armed Indian, the shock of what she had just witnessed receded enough to allow her to question her companions.

"What brought you here? Had it anything to do with that bizarre scene I have just witnessed?"

"Dr McGregor is with the Health Department," Martin told her, calmer but still aloof. "Epidemics spread very quickly in places like this, so he has to ensure no body is buried before someone has checked the cause of death. They sometimes get away with it."

"Is that why they were sending the body down from the window? An attempt to avoid you?"

George McGregor shook his head. "To dodge the devils waiting by the door. They are reputed to lurk outside houses where a death has occurred, in order to seize the spirit of the departed one and make away with it. The relatives fool them by sending the body out through the window."

"But it's so . . . so irreverent!" she protested, as they reached the car where the syce opened the door for her.

"Not at all," he assured her, climbing in to sit beside her. "The body is dead and no longer of any importance. The spirit, however, must be protected from devils and sent on, fully endowed with symbolic paper wealth and goods, to the paradise of after-life." His appealing smile lit his face again. "They cheat the devils, but not me. At least, today they didn't. We have no idea how many burials they manage to keep secret."

Intensely interested, Thea asked, "Surely it's in their own interest to prevent epidemics?"

"Sure, but they resent our interference in their ceremonies and religious rituals. It's natural enough. Don't you think we'd feel the same if they started wandering freely in our churches to observe what we get up to? However, as we have declared ourselves responsible for this island colony, it's up to us to keep it pleasant and free from infection. We are aware that many old people die and are interred before we ever hear of it but, when death is sudden, or the victim is young, we have a public duty to check on the cause."

Once Martin had settled in the car, the driver set off slowly through the maze of thoroughfares. Thea then asked what had killed the young woman and child she had just seen.

"They had been poisoned," the medical man told her.

"Murdered?" she cried, aghast.

"No, no." His smile teased her, this time. "Sorry, no spice for your novel, Thea. It was food poisoning. A very common killer out here. Overripe fruit, meat which has become tainted, water polluted by germs—any one of those causes. Too sordid for an aspiring author, I imagine."

"Don't make fun of me, George," she warned. "I shan't hesitate to retaliate."

"Retaliation from you could be enjoyable," he ventured, "but to show you how seriously I regard your project, I'll undertake to help with your research."

Thea angled toward him, turning her back on Martin, who had grown very quiet. "How can you help?" she asked curiously.

"I'll introduce you to some friends of mine. They'll give you all the colour and Eastern flavour you need, preventing you from repeating today's foolishness." He tried to smother his amusement as he said, "You'll find they're individualists, also. I confess to anticipating the meeting with considerable relish."

She treated him to a wide friendly smile. "I suspect that you are still teasing me."

"Perish the thought, my dear. I'll arrange a time to suit them, then contact you."

"Fine. I'm staying with the Beresfords."

"So I heard. I also heard that you have poor young Alex so bewitched, his parents have been compelled to send him out of the country in an attempt to save him from your clutches."

"That's not in the least amusing," she snapped in swift anger.

The thick eyebrows rose in surprise. "Ah . . . the lady has hidden depths!"

"I'm disappointed that you join the rest of the colony in classing him as an irresponsible boy, that's all. You obviously have hidden shallows."

He laughed so heartily and enjoyably that her anger melted as swiftly as it had arisen. When he was able, he said, "What a blessing you chose to come to Singapore to write your book, and not some other place like Tahiti. I think you'll shake this colony until its dry old bones rattle."

They took her back to the Beresford house, for which she was very grateful, and George McGregor promised to contact her as soon as he could speak to his rather mysterious friends. Martin had to climb from the car to allow Thea to alight, and she smiled up at him as he stood by the open door.

"Are you still angry with me?"

"Would it have any effect on you if I were?"

"George has found it easy to forgive me."

"He didn't tell you not to go there."

Remembering the meeting during which he had warned her, she saw her opportunity to put into practice her plan to throw the troubled lovers together.

"To show how repentant I am, I'll entertain you to tea tomorrow."

"Where?"

"Here, of course."

"No, thanks."

"The next day, then?"

"Sorry."

Suspecting that he guessed what she was attempting to do, she decided further persuasion was needed. "I thought we could tell each other about our exotic parents—in Italian, naturally. Wouldn't that be fun?"

His hostile eyes darkened further. "They're both dead. Where's the fun in that?"

Determined not to be routed, she then said, "We agreed that we were compatible, didn't we? Life's so dull now Alex is in Manila, and I'm desperate to talk to someone intelligent."

"I would have suggested you conduct a conversation with your own reflection, but after this afternoon it's no longer sound advice."

She drew in her breath. "My God, you *are* angry, aren't you?"

"Wait until young Beresford gets back and hears how dull you have found life without him at all those parties and soirées, in company with just about every bachelor in Singapore. It might then dawn on you that being an individualist is a convenient cover for arrant selfishness. I have no wish to have tea with you here, Miss du Lessier, on any day you might suggest, and I advise you to get your own affairs straightened out before attempting to do it for others."

Having said that, he climbed back into the car, slammed the door, and told the syce to drive off. Thea was left to go up the steps and into the house deep in thought. In the hallway she came face to face with Lydia, pale and with daggers obviously drawn.

"Was that Martin Linwood I saw?" she asked, in a voice Thea could almost recognise as her own when speaking of Dominic.

"Yes . . . in an extremely bad mood."

"What did you say to upset him?"

"I asked him to come here to tea one day this week. He seemed to think I was interfering in his affairs. I can't think why. I was simply being friendly."

"He's not like other people, you know."

"Oh?" Thea commented casually. "Why not?"

"He's shell-shocked."

"So are hundreds of other men. What's so different about Martin?"

"When is he coming?"

"He's not. He made no excuses, just said no and meant it."

The girl's eager look faded, and Thea pursued the subject further.

"Lydia, it wasn't just that he was in a bad mood. I have the impression that he and Alex are not on the best of terms, which forces him to hold aloof from this family. Do you know anything about it?"

For a while Thea thought no answer would be offered, then the girl walked out on to the broad stone area at the head of the steps. There, she gazed over toward the gardens and said with quiet ferocity, "Alex was an absolute pig to Martin. I've never forgiven him."

Thea moved out to stand beside her. "That's a very damning accusation to make of your brother. Won't you explain it?"

Still facing the garden, Lydia said, "Sir Hartle and Daddy forced him to come to our tennis party. Alex was beastly. He told all his friends that Martin was . . . was . . ." She swung round emotionally. "They all stared at him when he arrived. It was *terrible*. Alex made him play a stupid game of three-a-side, even though the poor man looked absolutely ill. Then Mummy and Daddy made him so nervous with their questions he fell over the small table and spilt the sandwiches. It seemed so cruel," she ended thickly.

Thea frowned. Could she really be telling the truth, or was it a dramatised account of something quite harmless? "That sounds very unlike Alex. Why on earth would he behave in such a heartless way?"

"Because Daddy had been forced to invite Martin in return for Sir Hartle's help in preventing Alex from being expelled from the Turf Club. He's always doing outrageous things to shock and upset people, and Daddy always has to try and soothe them. Alex and Daddy had a hectic scene over it just before the tennis party."

"So what? Alex is too mature to vent his anger on a shell-shocked guest, who played no part in the affair in question," reasoned Thea, still puzzled.

"All I know is that even before Martin arrived, Alex was telling everyone his MC was worthless because every officer was given one just to compel him to return to the trenches after leave, and carry on fighting."

Unable to equate such behaviour with the Alex she knew and loved, Thea probed a little further as a nebulous theory occurred to her.

"Lydia, why did Alex never volunteer in the war?"

"He almost did, until Mummy and Daddy made him see that he couldn't."

"Couldn't? Why was that?"

"He was needed here, of course."

With a mixture of thoughts slowly settling into places that made sense, Thea said quietly, "They've sent him away now, however."

"That's because . . ." She broke off abruptly.

"Because they think I have designs on him? I have."

As the young girl's expression was confused, Thea took a chance. "I'm not your rival with Martin. I invited him to tea for your sake, not mine."

Lydia's cheeks grew faintly pink. "Why would you do that?"

"Because it's clear to me that he attracts you."

Further confused by such frankness, the other girl tried to assume nonchalance. "He's lost his entire family, poor man, and Singapore must seem very strange to someone who . . . well, who's suffering from the war. I'm trying to be his friend, that's all."

"Just so long as you realise that's all you can ever be to him, Lydia."

The blush deepened dramatically. "I don't know what you mean."

"Yes, I think you do," she contradicted gently. "Don't make the mistake of seeing him as a romantic wounded hero, and yourself as the only person in Singapore who can help him. His wounds are mental and unpredictable, so I doubt if he even understands himself yet. Trembling hands and hesitant sentences might arouse your compassion, dear girl, but the effects of shell shock can be quite devastating, at times. He is well aware of that, and is attempting to spare you the distress of witnessing the full extent of his war legacy. By all means be his friend, but don't demand more of him than he feels able to give."

It was not at all what Lydia wanted to hear. Adopting a cool attitude, she said, "I really can't see what all this has to do with you. I thought you came here to write a book."

"I did, but I can't stand by and watch you make the mistake I once made. It brings little happiness and quite devastating pain. In this instance, I think both you and Martin would suffer equally." She began to turn into the house. "If you ever want to talk to someone about it, you know where to find me."

Thea was pensive as she made her way upstairs. Her first impressions of this colony had been wrong. Far from being simplistic to the point of boredom, the residents appeared to have deep, devious emotions battened down tightly beneath their starched suits and correct topees. What would it take to bring them all to the surface, and what would be the outcome? As she entered her own rooms, it occurred to her that the European inhabitants here had customs and rituals every bit as bizarre as those she had witnessed in the Chinese quarter that afternoon.

Chapter 7

Having carefully planned his strategy during the voyage to Manila, Alex lost no time in implementing it once he arrived. Mendes, who had acted for *Berondel* for some years, occupied a suite of offices so impressive it was immediately clear that he must have major clients whose business brought rich percentages his way. A man whose bland expression hid a devious personality, the Portuguese was unperturbed by the information Alex gave him.

"I am devastated that you no longer entrust to me your much valued business, Mr Beresford," he said, with perfect equanimity.

Smiling inwardly, Alex replied straightfaced, "Believe me, I can only bring myself to sever the bond between *Berondel* and Alfredo Mendes because I'm assured that you'll manage to struggle along somehow."

"Struggle? Ah, yes . . . perhaps," came the melancholy comment. "One must hope that when a bond is broken, someday another might be forged to partially replace that loss." Standing to signify that he was prepared to usher Alex from his office, his sallow face assumed a mournful expression. "Is it too much to request that you do not put me completely out of business?"

The smile could no longer be repressed as Alex shook the man's hand. "Goodbye, Mendes. I'll have a damned good try, but whoever else you deal with must have either a fleet of vessels triple the size of ours, or he's running some pretty close cargoes. I'd watch him, if I were you. He's a bigger threat to you than our sub-office will ever be."

With that relationship severed, it was essential to set up the new office with all speed. The *Berondel* premises in Singapore had been owned by the company for many years, but Alex felt that the dignified ultra-respectable image was not what he wanted for his new office. Now he had finally been given his chance to express a more vigorous enterprising side of the family line, he intended to make changes to that end. Before going further, he made a tour of the offices of other lines in Manila, browsing over advertising schedules or chatting to junior clerks on the advantages of cruises he had no intention of making, whilst studying the style of the premises. As in Singapore, he found they had impressive costly furnishings and fittings which suggested a modern, affluent company. For once, this evidence brought no angry frustration. He was out on his own now, with freedom to act without consulting his father, and he vowed to make the *Berondel* sub-office rival that of any other line.

Enthusiasm acted as a spur to seek the vacant building which could be turned into a smart, impressive suite of offices. In a port like Manila it was not easy to find, naturally. For ten days he pestered land agents and inspected any number of addresses in the vain hope of finding exactly what he wanted. Ideally, the new office should be near the docks, yet central to the commercial area where business was conducted. After a week, he was forced to consider property on the outskirts of the city, growing desperate because he could do nothing until he had fixed a location. Several sites were large enough, but he firmly resisted signing ownership because he knew the distance from the centre of Manila would deter clients despite any amount of tempting advertising. They wanted to conduct their business in luxurious surroundings, with the smell of salt spray in their nostrils.

By the tenth day, he was viewing places within the city which he had initially declined to inspect because the size of the rooms was too cramped, or because they were sited in insalubrious streets. No matter how impressive the interior, he knew clients could be unfavourably influenced by the address.

It was when leaving one such street accompanied by an effusively persuasive Spaniard who extolled the virtues of the slum he had just turned down, that Alex spotted a large three-storey private residence standing back from the road which was very clearly vacant. Halting the taxi, he sat considering the possibility of converting the place into a suite of offices. From outside it looked spacious enough, although he knew it would be fatal to grow too enthusiastic before looking inside.

Gazing speculatively at the white stone façade, he said, "If you had something like that to show me, Cortez, it would interest me enough to consider a purchase. *That* is more the kind of place I'm after, not what you've just had the temerity to offer."

"But such a place is very expensive, Señor Beresford," the Spaniard told him. "More than the sum you mentioned. That is why I did not consider this address for you. Yes, very expensive."

Alex swung to face him. "You are handling the sale of this house?"

Moist black eyes registered reproach. "Who else but Cortez would handle such a desirable property? A prime position, elegant rooms, gracious architecture and a most impressive approach to the entrance, would you not agree? Alas, very much money indeed is needed to secure such a fine house right in the best part of Manila."

Excited, Alex asked, "How much does the owner want for it?"

Cortez was offended by such directness. "It is necessary to see inside this exceptional property to correctly assess its inestimable value. Only yesterday was I given the privilege of disposing of it and I assure you, Señor, I have a list of gentlemen anxious to acquire it."

"Have you?" responded Alex smartly. "Then my name tops the list. I'm on the spot and want to see around this house now."

With a sunny smile the agent produced a key from his pocket. "I already have an appointment at noon to show another Englishman this prime residence. However, if you insist on inspecting it now, I can hardly refuse. A great deal of money, Señor, as I said . . . but you twist my arm." Leaning forward to open the door, he added, "Just to step inside will convince you of why I did not immediately mention it to you. My client at noon has put no limit on his price, I warn you."

"Forget your other client, for the moment," Alex said tartly, climbing from the car. "If these premises are as good as you suggest, you can cancel your noon appointment. *Berondel* can match any price, I assure you."

Before descending for dinner Alex wrote a long triumphant letter to Thea, telling her about the coup he had brought off that morning. That he wrote to her rather than to his father underlined the fact that he knew she would receive the news with an open heart and mind, being glad for him without reservations. He certainly had no intention of informing his father of each step he took. Better to present a *fait accompli* on returning to Singapore, then be prepared to defend it.

He missed Thea very badly. Sensing in his heart that she was not yet as totally committed to him as he was to her, the thought of other men moving in to woo her in his absence caused him great torment. Discovering that she had had a lover in England had been a painful blow initially, yet she was a girl of such a vital passionate nature he later realised she could hardly have remained a virgin until meeting him. All the same, he had not questioned her on the subject. That would have been rubbing salt in his wound. From her reluctance to elaborate on her confession, Alex had deduced that she had sustained wounds of her own. It caused him deep anger to think of anyone treating her cruelly. He vowed no other man would hurt her, but knew she was probably right in saying that to rush into marriage with him would be unwise. Yet the reason she had given—his family's opposition to her and the risk to his future—would always be a stumbling block, and he could not help feeling that it was more for reasons of her own that she had insisted on delaying what he wanted with increasing urgency. Ten days in Manila without her had seemed an age. How would he endure six months here after setting up the new office?

The prospect of so long apart from the girl he loved so passionately, suddenly overshadowed his sense of well-being and satisfaction over the speedy closure of the morning's deal to purchase the gracious old house for *Berondel*. To counter his sense of loneliness, he sauntered into the hotel bar before dining for a drink or two. Even after three he was still filled with longing for Thea, and was brought back to his present surroundings abruptly when a man's voice beside him asked if he was addressing Alex Beresford.

He turned to see a tall, very muscular blond dressed in the usual tropical evening attire, drink in hand, regarding him with an intensity he found strangely disconcerting. It was surprising that a total stranger should know his name, and that he was presently in Manila where he was relatively unknown by the residents. He rose from the bar stool. Tall and athletic himself, Alex nevertheless felt almost a lightweight beside this compelling figure.

"Yes, I'm Beresford," he admitted, "but you have me at a disadvantage, I'm afraid."

An easy, assured smile added to the man's impressive good looks, yet there was no warmth in his eyes as he offered his hand. "Randal Forster. Import-exports."

Alex shook the hand, finding the man's grip unpleasantly strong. "How do you do. My word, news travels fast in Manila. The *Berondel* sub-office is hardly established, as yet, but I'll be glad to discuss business with you, Mr Forster. What are you drinking?"

The easy smile widened. "Sorry, old lad, but your sub-office is still non-existent. Cortez received a hefty deposit from me for those vacant premises at nine this morning. Sad, but there it is. The early bird, and so on." Tossing back the contents of his glass, he added, "I'm sure you'll find somewhere equally suitable for your little office."

Alex frowned, curiously disturbed by this man's whole approach. "I'm not sure I follow what you're saying."

"Let me put it a little more clearly, in that case," came the smooth response. "Magnolia Place is the chosen site for my new distribution base in Manila. It's a prime situation which I naturally snapped up the moment it became available."

An unusual brand of anger ignited in Alex at the arrogant attitude of someone he had believed wished to become a *Berondel* client a moment ago. With three swift drinks to aid his aggression, he stood his ground.

"Perhaps I should express myself more clearly, also, Forster. At eleven-thirty this morning I signed a deed of purchase for Magnolia Place, and backed it with a draft on the company's bank for the full purchase price. Are you telling me that you signed a similar document two and a half hours earlier?"

"Not worth the paper it's written on, old sport," the other told him in casual tones, which had now acquired a slight edge. "Cancel that bank draft pronto, is my advice."

With that, the man began to turn away. Alex stepped round to confront him determinedly. 'Just a moment! Let's have a little clarification on this subject before you walk off. All I have heard from you is that you gave Cortez a hefty deposit at nine this morning. Is that all you did?"

Forster's eyes grew coldly speculative. "It secured the property. Cortez knew that quite well. He and I have had any number of dealings, Beresford, so he should have known better than to lead you up the garden path, the sly old sod. Never trust a dago, old lad. The only thing they understand is a boot up the backside."

Conscious that interested eyes were watching their exchange, Alex was nevertheless obliged to raise his voice above the sound of the Eurasian cabaret girl who had begun to sing in the adjacent restaurant.

"Perhaps you should take your own advice and give him one because, sly old sod or not, unless you have signed a deed of sale for that property and backed it with a banker's draft for the full amount, your hefty deposit gained you nothing from Cortez." He tried to smile, but did not succeed as he added, "If you've been in the habit of conducting business with the man, I'm surprised you still recommend others never to trust 'a dago' when you apparently have such great faith in his loyalty to you." Disliking the attention they were commanding from the male occupants of the bar, Alex tried to neutralise the animosity which was dangerous in the business world. "Look, I offered you a drink just now. Let's sit down with one and clear the air, shall we?"

Forster remained where he was, one businessman who apparently feared no emnity from his rivals. "I heard that you were no more than a mere whipper-snapper dominated by old man Beresford," he said coolly. "You're biting off more than you can chew here, old lad. I very strongly advise you to tear up that deed of sale and look elsewhere for your little sub-office. You've been let off the leash by papa for the first time, and you're liable to come a big cropper unless you listen to the voice of experience. I need that place. For the amount of business *Berondel* is likely to handle here in Manila, a couple of small rooms near the docks would be more than ample. My business is conducted throughout Asia, on a scale which makes yours appear little better than chicken-feed." His disconcertingly charming smile appeared again. "Once I'm established in Magnolia Place, I can put a nice little bit of trade your way, you know. With my network of connections, I could do your little old-fashioned line a few favours."

Having told his father on many occasions that *Berondel* was old-fashioned, Alex was immoderately annoyed to hear this man describe it thus, and leapt to the company's defence fiercely.

"I suggest that you use your network of connections to help find other premises for your distribution centre . . . unless, of course, you can produce a legal document proving purchase of Magnolia Place, which I bought this morning. *Berondel* is expanding, Forster, and will soon be a line to be reckoned with—even by men whose business is conducted throughout Asia. We don't need your favours, *old lad*. My father is known and respected by the business community here in the East. Nothing a man like you can do would add to *Berondel*'s standing, believe me."

Randal Forster smiled again, apparently unruffled by the outburst. "Really, old sport, there's no need to get hot under the collar over a little commercial hard-bargaining. Still wet behind the ears, as I'd been told. You hold your ground well, but you really must learn a little more finesse. Must remain gentlemen, you know, even when we hold the winning hand. I'll be watching Magnolia Place. See how you measure up there, and so forth. Well, chin chin!"

Soon, his broad back was lost in a sea of men clad in similar white jackets. Alex stood feeling more uneasy than victorious. There was something about Randal Forster which suggested he was not nearly as urbane as he pretended; something almost *unwholesome* in the man's clean handsomeness. Shrugging off the strange feeling of having been touched by malice, Alex ordered another stengah and downed it in one gulp. Even when he began a solitary meal to the sound of the Eurasian girl's sultry love songs, his thoughts of Thea continued to be marred by the unpleasantness of that encounter with Randal Forster. The man had got under his skin, even though Alex had won the day over Magnolia Place. He determined to make enquiries amongst his friends when he returned to Singapore. Some of them must surely have come across Forster and his apparent big business deals.

As Martin waited for George to collect him in the ramshackle car that had once been a Singapore taxi, he regretted having allowed his friend to talk him into visiting the people who had offered to help Thea with local colour for her novel. He usually welcomed any opportunity to avoid Damien Lang's revels with his wild cronies on Saturdays, and would have anticipated the day with pleasure if Thea had not been going with them. After their encounter in the Chinese quarter, George had made an issue over the way Martin had treated the girl, probing for an explanation of his animosity. Since he could not reveal the true cause, he had replied that he thought her vain and superficial—like her mother—with as few morals. George had challenged him to discover more about her before passing such harsh judgement, claiming that he would have the perfect opportunity on this visit to a mysterious place on a hilltop along the wilder coast of Singapore. Regretting the need for Thea's presence, Martin nevertheless told himself he would have no fear of meeting Lydia on the day's jaunt; that, in itself, was enough cause to relax and enjoy a day out. If the du Lessier girl attempted to reopen the subject of his feelings for Alex's sister, he would silence her in no uncertain terms. She was welcome to drive young Beresford crazy, but Martin would not allow her to interfere in his own life.

The ancient blue car soon rattled up the driveway and halted with a bang at the foot of the steps. Thea waved gaily from the passenger seat, calling out a greeting.

"Hallo, Martin. Isn't this motor too quaint for words? Come on. Get in for the experience of a lifetime."

Taking up his jacket from the back of a chair, Martin went over to where the vehicle stood spluttering and shuddering. George was grinning with pleasure at having Thea beside him, as well he might. Dressed in a shift of ivory cotton patterned with huge red and black poppies, her upcurved mouth was as vivid as the dress.

"What fun this is going to be," she declared. "I'm so glad you're coming, too. I'm sure we'll find his friends fascinating." Pushing open the small door to reveal the full glory of long legs exposed by the short dress, she invited him to climb in. "Are you going to squeeze in beside me, or recline in solitary splendour on the back seat?"

In no mood for her bubbling gaiety, he murmured, "It's a little too hot for squeezing. I'll go for the solitary splendour." Climbing up to edge past her, he dropped his jacket on to the shabby leather and sat beside it. "George wouldn't thank me for ruining his chances, either."

"Cheeky blighter," chuckled the driver. "I've my work cut out coping with one precocious lady, much less two."

They set off somewhat jerkily at little more than the pace of a rickshaw, and Martin soon realised Thea's description of "the experience of a lifetime" was not altogether exaggerated. Every lump in the road was transmitted through the ancient machine to the bones of the occupants, but there was a certain strange sense of grandeur in travelling within the long open interior resembling a nobleman's landau with the top folded back, while the world passed one by on bicycles, in rickshaws, or in smooth, sleek, fast machines driven by uniformed servants. Lounging in the roomy seat, Martin rested his head against the leather and gazed up at the foliage passing overhead. He was reminded of boyhood drives beside his brother Giles, returning lethargic and greatly contented after family outings. They would lie back, as he was presently doing, and watch the canopy of elms lining the approach to Larkswood Court, hardly able to stay awake, while their parents chatted softly on the opposite seat.

The memory of those voices returned strongly; his mother's sweet and attractively accented, his father's deep and assured. That assurance had died with Rosina Linwood: the spirit of an entire family had died with her. Although broken by the loss of their mother, school had helped the two boys through that terrible period. Nothing had helped Frere Linwood, and he had thrown himself into his work in defiance of all advice from his doctor. In that moment, Martin suddenly understood something his youth had prevented. Lonely days, tortured nights. Yearning for something unattainable. How much worse for a man who had once possessed the prize, then had it taken from him. Add the sudden destruction of the fruits of such a union—one blown to pieces, the other deprived of his senses—and what man would care two pins for health and continuing existence? Straightening in his seat, Martin studied the shapely back of the girl ahead. Perhaps she was right to live as if she did not give a damn for anyone.

Thea turned at that moment and caught him watching her. "You look beautifully relaxed. Is there a truce between us today?"

He nodded lazily.

Her ready smile washed over him. "Good. You're so much more stimulating when approachable."

"Stimulating? I'm flattered."

"Nonsese! Any man who intended to read History and Classics at University, and who speaks fluent Italian, must have an excellent brain."

He moved his head in a negative. "This man never went to Oxford, despite his good intentions, and he was bilingual from birth."

Waving that aside, she asked him in excellent Italian, "Tell me about your mother."

He must have been more relaxed than he imagined, because he found himself responding in the same language, and speaking of someone he had rarely mentioned since the day his housemaster had broken the shocking news to himself and Giles. When he finally finished speaking, Thea nodded.

"That confirms all I have heard about her."

"From whom?" he asked curiously.

"My own mother."

Frowning, he asked, "What could she have known of someone she would never conceivably have met?"

Thea's amber eyes regarded him shrewdly for a moment or two. "She certainly met your father, didn't she?"

"Only on the battlefield."

"That's a curious way of putting it."

"I don't think so. Father fought very hard to stop publication of that book. I'd go so far as to say there was deep emnity between them."

"Would you?" she mused slowly.

Puzzled by her strange attitude, he then asked, "Was your father really related to Sir Paulo Tosti, as everyone in Singapore claims?"

Laughing, she nodded. "About as distantly as I am related to the Beresfords."

"Why have you adopted your mother's name?"

Her laughter faded. "When I was born she decided that I would derive greater benefit from being known as her daughter rather than his."

"She was right, wasn't she?"

"You have more intelligence than to make that comment," she said sharply. "I'm always prejudged on her reputation. People read into my every action a motivation based on their scant knowledge of her. You do. You dislike me because you dislike her. You have convinced yourself that I'm shallow, promiscuous and self-centred. You imagine that my desire to write a novel is an affectation, and my interest in ethnic cultures merely a pose."

For a moment he studied the face so arrestingly framed by short glossy hair, the angry eyes artificially enlarged with black pencilling, the reddened mouth, and the eye-catching dress which matched her personality so well. Then he caught himself smiling at her.

"I thought we had a truce today."

Surrender was immediate. "Yes, sorry . . . but you haven't denied my words."

His smile deepened. "Prove me wrong, Miss."

She gave a delighted gurgling laugh. "I told you you were stimulating when the barriers were down."

"Don't forget the poor old driver," interpolated their friend at the wheel. "I don't understand all that fiery Italiano stuff, and I'm beginning to feel ever so slightly *de trop*. Can we get back to basics?"

"Poor George," soothed Thea in English. "I'll concentrate on you exclusively until we get there. Is there much further to go?"

Martin was not overanxious to reach their destination. He was enjoying the quality of the morning far more than he had expected. Resting back once more against the leather, he took pleasure in the passing scene. The civilised part of Singapore had been left behind. The road they now travelled was little more than a track cutting through jungle. Where it undulated it was possible to see a vast spread of dark-green stretching out all around them. There was a hill away to their right, rising from the dense growth. Martin supposed the high ground to be their destination, for George had said his friends' home was on a hill. There appeared to be some distance yet to go, so he stretched contentedly, lit a cigarette, and gazed from the car through half-closed eyes at it rattled and shook over the red earth track.

Martin supposed that most of his colleagues would not care for the sensation of total isolation created by the impenetrable jungle, yet he found it attractive. A man could find peace in a house on a hill surrounded by trees. No people to stare and find fault. No risk of clumsy behaviour. No feelings of inadequacy because those attempting to become friends still seemed like strangers. How wonderful it would be living on a pinnacle which rose from a lush green carpet.

The track narrowed further, and began to curve toward the hill. Bumping and coughing, the old car took the pitted surface at little more than a walking pace. Taking one or two painful cracks on the head, Martin decided it would be as well to sit forward and avoid the risk of being knocked unconscious. After the sweltering atmosphere induced by the encroaching jungle, there seemed to be a fresh scent to tease at his nostrils. It took him several minutes to identify it. The sea! Beyond the high ground must run the coast.

The car halted abruptly with a loud backfire. George turned off the engine and flexed his stiff shoulders beneath his damp shirt.

"Everyone out!" he cried.

"Here?" queried Thea, in dismay. "Has it broken down?"

"My dear young lady, this car has never broken down," its affronted owner told her. "We must walk about a hundred yards, where a surprise awaits you. Come on, lazy tykes, out with you!"

They climbed from the vehicle that looked so incongruous in these surroundings, and Martin asked, "Are you quite happy leaving it here?"

"Who's likely to take it; snakes and lizards? The people around here know me and wouldn't dream of touching anything of mine."

Thea looked in amazement. "There are people here?"

He nodded. "In this jungle are several Malay *kampongs*. The occupants will all be aware of our presence here today, believe me. You could leave anything you liked in the car and it would be there when we came back." Waving an arm to indicate the direction they must take, he walked off with long strides.

After exchanging wry glances, Martin and Thea set off after him. Next minute, they were attacked by hordes of hungry mosquitoes which emerged from the trees to settle on any area of exposed flesh like a tormenting cloud. Cursing, and slapping their limbs to kill the pests as they fed, they were assured by their guide that once they reached the top of the hill all would be well.

Thea looked at Martin fearfully, asking in a low voice, "How do we reach the top, do you suppose?"

He grinned. "On our hands and knees if it really is as steep as it looks. Don't ask me to carry you when the going gets rough. George is the one who has fallen for your charms, not me. I leave that honour and delight to him."

The honour and delight, if it was such, fell to two sturdy Chinese. The surprise awaiting them comprised three sedan-chairs in which they were to be borne up the winding track leading to the home of their mysterious hosts. Martin climbed into the third of these curious conveyances, filled with fanciful notions of bygone days. When he was seated inside the cage-like bamboo interior, his bearers put their shoulders beneath the long pliant poles and lifted him from the ground. It was a unique experience, and Martin felt that he was lost somewhere in another beckoning world during that journey up a track which had been cut in the side of the hill. On his right there rose a sheer wall of red earth, but on his left the scene was ever-changing the higher they climbed.

He soon grew accustomed to the bouncing motion and, after the first five minutes, no longer kept his gaze on the two chairs ahead. The dense jungle at the foot of the hill thinned into a mere straggle of trees, in which the brilliant plumage of birds could be glimpsed, as they flew up disturbed by the passage of the procession. They called warnings to each other in harsh or unbearably beautiful notes, which were magnified by the surrounding hush, and Martin's senses grew charmed by all he heard and saw. The track was tortuous so that he could not tell what might lie beyond each bend, and he leaned forward eagerly in the fragile cage. Mosquito bites forgotten, he almost sighed with pleasure when a fresh curve in the track revealed glimpses of the vivid blue-green sea below. Then there were blossoms to add colour and perfume to his enchantment as the higher levels replaced trees with shrubs, rioting in oranges, yellows, scarlet and white, as well as many shades of pink.

It was now possible to see the sparkling water rippling out from the coastline directly below them, and to trace the indented outline of

Singapore Island as it stretched westward. In the distance lay a group of green offshore islands, around which the waves broke like white frills around a dark hem. The air was now sweet, fresh and tangy as the warm breeze from the sea fanned Martin's face. He had been so lost in the unfolding beauty, arrival at the summit took him unawares. Yet the greatest delight of all lay there, for he appeared to have entered an Oriental paradise.

The house was large and set on three different levels, with several graceful green pagoda roofs in concave curves outlined with red. Segmented doors were folded back to allow air through the rooms. From within came the faint sound of tinkling bells disturbed by the breeze which, together with the music from numerous fountains, provided a mesmeric symphony. The gardens were truly Chinese, filled with miniature pagodas, pools, twisting paths, ornamental bridges, and vivid dwarf shrubs. The pools shimmered with gold and silver fish gliding through their sun-dappled shallows. Golden pheasants picked their elegant way through the shrubs, their iridescent plumage glowing as they crossed unshaded areas or settled alongside layered azaleas, their long striped tails becoming invisible against the chequered light and shade of the earth. In the trees the usual rainbow of birds moved, but there were also small monkeys with long white silky fur and bright eyes circled with black, as if they wore spectacles. They studied the guests with speculative glances, but prudence told them to remain in the canopy of branches.

Martin climbed slowly from his sedan-chair. A curious trance-like sensation washed over him as he stood in the balmy warmth of the most peaceful atmosphere he had ever known. When a hand lightly touched his arm, he went forward as if motivated by another power, following the man and girl over an arched bridge and up a crescent of steps to a terrace in mosaic stonework. A servant in loose blue coat and black trousers had appeared from within the house. His deeply wrinkled face and grey beard suggested that he was several centuries old, a fantasy Martin thought quite in keeping with the atmosphere. Bowing, the old man led the visitors inside. They followed without exchanging a word. The loud echo of their footsteps on polished marble floors seemed to verge on sacrilege as they passed through rooms filled with jade, ivory, silken hangings, and very dark furniture heavily carved and decorated with inlaid mother-of-pearl. Utterly bemused, Martin realised he was seeing the ancient face of the Orient now. To think he had almost refused the invitation!

The servant halted, bowed, then backed away to the left leaving the visitors facing two elderly men in black brocade long gowns, with the usual black hat on greying heads. Their hands were tucked into the sleeves of the gowns as they solemnly bowed by way of greeting, and it did not seem at all awkward for any of them to return the gesture instead of offering their hands to shake. Martin was then taken by surprise when George broke the formal mood by laughing vigorously and stepping forward to take each frail man in turn by the shoulders, breaking into a flow of Chinese dialect as if it were his mother tongue. His friend turned back to them then, his expression full of relish at the obvious success of his plan. "Sing Kong Wok and Sing Lee Ho are deeply gratified by your dual expressions of wonderment," he told them with a grin. "It is the greatest compliment to their consequence and aesthetic good taste to witness your appreciation of all you have seen here." Drawing Thea forward, he said to the pair so alike they could have been twins, "My revered friends, may I present Miss du Lessier, whose purpose in visiting Singapore is to write a book containing a truth which will never have been written before?"

The brothers bowed again, one saying in good English, "We are honoured that you have made such a journey to visit us, Miss du Lessier. We are humbled in the presence of so notable a scholar."

Thea flushed. "No, really, I . . ."

She was halted by a nudge on the foot from George, and then simply mumbled a phrase of thanks for their hospitality. Martin was drawn forward, to be introduced as a warrior of great courage, who now worked for the colonial department dedicated to ethnic affairs.

Elaborating a little on Thea's vote of thanks, he ended by declaring, "This hill is the nearest place to heaven I have yet found."

"Thank you, Mr Linwood," said the spokesman of the two. "My brother and I are happy that you are at peace here."

It seemed a curious comment, and Martin wondered if George had told them anything of his medical history. There was little time for speculation, however, for their hosts then led them into an adjacent salon, where the Chinese custom of offering guests refreshment before embarking on serious conversation was observed. The sumptuousness was continued in a room with one side open to the sea, giving an impression of hanging on a cliff edge with a sheer drop to the sparkling straits below. A table was set with Oriental delicacies in bowls of matching design. Plates of tiny biscuits and cakes grouped at one end, and a huge layered stand bearing fruit which scented the air had been placed in the centre. When they were all seated, a servant appeared with hot fragrant towels for their hands and finger bowls filled with aromatic water scattered with flower petals.

Casting Thea an expressive glance, Martin then followed George's lead in protocol. Sampling just a small amount from the sweet or tangy dishes, he worked his way through shellfish, pork, finely chopped vegetables, egg and noodles, miniature stuffed dumplings, poultry, and several substances he could not identify. Amazingly, each flavour complemented the others, and all were delicious when washed down with a sweet refreshing drink sipped from tiny porcelain cups without handles. He declined the cakes, although Thea found them irresistible, and finished his meal with mango dipped in ginger. The entire experience of eating with an ocean spread at his feet strengthened that feeling of nearness to heaven, and he participated in the light conversation without once remembering that he could be clumsy and nervous in such situations.

The Chinese men ate nothing, and Martin could only suppose there was an ethnic reason for it, because George accepted the fact without comment or surprise. Only when the meal was finished, and they all returned to sit on polished upright chairs in the room where introductions had taken place, did Martin discover the truth about the two men who were such generous and courteous hosts. In explaining their close association with the Scottish doctor an astonishing story emerged. As young men, the Sing brothers had been wealthy and influential members at the court of their local mandarin. Distinction and further riches had been their promised future, until an advancing warlord had overrun their province and punished them in symbolic fashion. For some years they had languished in prison as paupers, until a new warlord had ousted the first. The brothers had been allowed to escape. They had made their way first to Hong Kong, then on to Singapore where they had amassed a fortune from silk.

"We could not fulfil our rightful roles at the court of a mandarin," Kong Wok quietly explained, "so we accumulated enough wealth to fashion our own court high on a hill, where it is impossible for any man to be made lowly. I am no longer able to see the beauty surrounding me, but it is possible for me to experience it through other eyes. My brother can no longer create beautiful things, but his knowledge guides me so that I may do so. He is my eyes; I am his hands."

With a prickling at the back of his neck Martin suddenly realised the terrible truth. Kong Wok was blind, and his brother still had his arms buried in the voluminous sleeves of his gown. The warlord had lopped off the hands of one, and put out the eyes of the other.

"Ten years ago, we were struck down by a fearsome plague which attacked many Chinese in Singapore," Lee Ho then continued. "Doctor McGregor had recently set up practice here, and we defied tradition by asking him to treat us. We lived. Our gratitude is too great to be experienced in our lifetime. If we can offer any assistance to his friends, we shall be showing but an infinitesimal part of it. Please, Miss du Lessier, tell us how we may be of service to you."

Thea appeared to be lost for words, for once, so Martin caught himself stepping into the breach on her behalf. "As a keen historian, sir, I can think of no greater pleasure than to hear you speak of your early days at the court of a mandarin. I am certain Miss du Lessier would find your account of infinite value."

"Oh yes, yes," she agreed eagerly, "so long as it would not upset you to recall that time."

It seemed they could not have made a wiser request, and the afternoon passed like a glimpse into a history book for Martin. Only when George warned that they must take their leave, did he realise that he had monopolised the conversation in his fascination with all the brothers had told them. His reluctance to leave was so apparent his hosts urged him to visit them whenever he could, adding that they rarely had the great boon of conversation with a man of such intellect.

The sedan-chairs were waiting to transport them downward, and Martin made the journey in a state of deep regret. By the time they reached the foot of the hill, he was beginning to wonder if he had been wandering in mental fantasies again, so bizarre did it all seem as they covered the short distance back to the car, assaulted by mosquitoes once more.

His companions were vastly more prosaic than he about the visit. George was highly amused over the surprise he had sprung upon them, and Thea appeared more struck by Martin's knowledge of ancient China than with ideas for her novel.

"Now, more than ever, do I insist that you're wasting your life by stagnating in that office," she told him forcefully. "George, you must agree. Weren't you astonished at the way he talked about success-ive dynasties, and the various conquerors who have influenced the development of China?"

"Not really," came the good-humoured reply. "I can assess Martin in a way you never will."

"What does that mean?" she asked, slapping at a cluster of insects sucking at her left calf.

He grinned. "It means that I'm simply another male."

"What of your novel, Thea?" put in Martin in an attempt to end the subject. "Are you going to use that wonderful account of court intrigue for a dynastic saga of old China?"

"Good heavens, no," she told him as they reached the car. "Thank goodness we can get away from these mosquitoes. How can it be so blissful at the top of a hill and so pestilent at the foot?"

As they climbed in to settle in the seats they had occupied before, Martin pursued his theme. "This visit was arranged for your benefit, you know. You said you wanted 'atmosphere'. It was there with a vengeance. Didn't you learn anything to help with this great Eastern drama of yours?"

Turning to look at him over her shoulder as the car began to reverse along the track, she said, "Of course I did. My story is to be an account of contemporary life out here. The details of butchery and betrayal were hair-raising, especially when one finally realised that both those men had been maimed, but what I found so fascinating was the entire concept of that place and its owners. Down in the Chinese quarter I saw poverty and squalor. Today I saw the real face of China. You, George, and a whole department are more concerned about the underprivileged of their race than they are. Ousted from what they considered to be their rightful place in the hierarchy, they have created it for themselves on a hill which places them higher, both geographically and symbolically, than their fellows. It made me realise that if our administration were to end, and you all packed up to return home, the system would return to the one those men knew when they were young. The Oriental way of thinking hasn't changed for centuries. Don't you think that will make a better story than the picaresque one you suggested?"

Martin remained silent. Her concept disturbed his mood. Where he had seen romance, her bold gaze had merely detected self-indulgence. The legendary splendour and depravity of one of the oldest cultures in the world had been translated into an example of undesirable social inequality by her. Her novel, if it were ever written, would lack lyricism, colour and imagination. No doubt she intended to fill her pages with the libidinous ingredients used so freely by Anna du Lessier. He gazed morosely from the car during the long backward journey made necessary by lack of space to turn, knowing that Thea had spoiled the afternoon for him by her lack of sensitivity.

When the track finally widened, and George completed the noisy manoeuvre in a series of backward and forward movements, the girl, apparently unaware of her destructive powers, said warmly. "Those old men are touchingly indebted to your medical skill. What was the terrible plague from which you saved them?"

He laughed heartily. "Measles, my dear. There was an outbreak amongst the European children, and Chinese appear to have no resistance to it, at all."

"You fraud!" she declared, in amusement. "I imagined that you had discovered a miracle cure from some obscure and terrible tropical disease."

"It was a miracle, as far as they were concerned," he assured her. "Confess, now! If I gave you a lotion which would stop mosquitoes from biting you, wouldn't you look upon me as a saviour of no mean kind?"

"You haven't such a lotion, have you?" she pleaded, scratching her swollen leg.

"I'm working on it. When I find the correct formula, it'll make my fortune. I'll have a place on a hill like theirs." Glancing lightly at her, he asked, "How about sharing it with me?"

"No, thanks. I'm not that much of an individualist."

They sat laughing together, but Martin looked back at the hill, outlined now by the sinking sun, and knew that if he had a house up there he would never come down from it.

In George McGregor's car it was impossible to arrive anywhere quietly, so they drew up outside the Beresford house with the usual backfire and hiss of escaping exhaust. To Martin's dismay, the noise drew someone from the garden to the front entrance. Lydia stopped a few feet away from them, twisting a small head of frangipani blooms in her hands. She gazed at Martin with an echo of his own instant yearning, as they climbed from the car. The cool green of her cotton dress enhanced the youthful smoothness of her skin, and her pale hair drawn back from her face by a band of matching ribbon. She looked so serene, so untouched by the maladies of life, so unbearably beckoning to a man still under the spell of that other world he had glimpsed this afternoon. He could think of nothing other than the delight of sharing it with her, high on a hill where no one would intrude upon their idyll.

"Hallo," greeted Thea gaily. "We've had the most diverting day. You'll hardly believe what I have to tell you." Dragging George forward, she added, "This is Dr McGregor, who owns this abominable machine."

When the pair had shaken hands, Thea said, "Come in for a sundowner before you drive off. It's the least reward I can offer you both."

George nodded, smiling. "Thanks, we'd love to."

"Sorry, I have to get back," Martin announced, in a rush.

"Nonsense," said Thea, slipping her hand through the crook of his arm. "Singapore night life doesn't start until well past nine. You've plenty of time."

Already irritated by the discord she had introduced into the bewitching quality of his day, her typical arrogance was the last straw. Breaking contact swiftly, he rounded on her.

"The visit today was arranged by George for your sole benefit. You've been delivered safely home, and it's now over. What I do now is my affair. Stop being so damned high-handed."

Her darkened eyebrows rose. "I only offered you a drink."

"I know what you're up to," he countered, further annoyed by her assumed innocence. "I know exactly what you're doing."

"Come on, Martin," said George encouragingly. "One drink won't take too much of your time, and it'll round off the day very nicely." Aiming a smile at Lydia, he went on, "It will have to be extremely informal, Miss Beresford. Neither Martin nor I have more than crumpled jackets to add to what we're presently wearing."

She answered with quiet composure. "It's quite all right. Come as you are now. Alex and his friends often do so after polo."

She led the way around the house to the verandah where Martin had had tea with her and her brother on that fatal afternoon. Memories of that occasion did not help his sensation of being trapped. He felt he was being controlled by those around him. They mounted the steps, and one boy went off to fetch drinks while the other began lighting lanterns with a taper. They all elected to remain standing after the long car journey, and Thea engaged George in deep conversation. That left Martin to face Lydia in comparative isolation.

"Wherever have you been all this time?" she asked, studying his face with disconcerting scrutiny.

Finding her proximity a problem, he was confused over the question. "My job takes up a lot of my time, so I don't socialise much."

"I meant, where have you been today. Some distance, I imagine. Thea left here ages ago."

"Oh . . . yes. A house . . . on a hill," he told her jerkily. "On the far side of the island. Through rather a lot of jungle."

"Wasn't it dangerous?"

He shook his head, deploring the way his wits and confidence flew in her presence. "Not in the least."

"I suppose very little seems dangerous after the things you've done," she said fervently.

"Only standing here next to you." It was out before he knew, and he cursed his runaway tongue.

The boy arrived carrying drinks in frosted glasses, with ice-cubes clinking against their sides. Martin took one and tossed it back in a single draught. The action brought a speculative glance from George. He glowered back at his friend, holding him partially responsible for this predicament.

"Why are you always so angry, Martin?"

The soft question from the girl in mint-green beside him, drew his attention back to her. The glower remained. "I'm not always angry."

"Yes, you are. You shouted at Thea a moment ago, and looked at her daggers drawn. You're doing it again now."

"Am I?"

She nodded. "Have you really another engagement, or were you just making an excuse not to come in?"

He refused to answer that, feeling that she had now joined the plot to trap him. Taking another drink from the tray offered by an observant boy, he swallowed that as swiftly as the first.

"I think you were just making an excuse," she accused hesitantly. "It wasn't because of me, was it?"

"Of course it was," he told her savagely.

With her colour deepening, she took her courage in both hands. "I'm sorry I ran away from you at the ball, and I'm sorry for the things I said to you. You must have thought me very silly, and I quite understand why you didn't want to meet me again."

It was the wrong time and place for such a conversation. Beguiling lantern-light, the headiness of the sultry evening air, and two swift stengahs gave birth to the familiar rush of desire for this girl who offered him the jewel qualities that had been lost from his life long ago. He tried to counter it with aggression.

"You live in a world of make-believe, where people are either good and kind, or utterly wicked. They're not. Each of us has virtues, and a hell of a lot of vices. The men you usually mix with can control theirs. I can't. If you persist in chasing me, it'll be disastrous for us both."

To his surprise, she stood her ground, but her cheeks turned the violent red of a full blush as she said, "I'm not chasing you, Martin, I'm trying to be your friend."

"We can't be friends. Surely I've demonstrated that on more than one occasion."

"Then we'll be anything you want to be," she promised softly, "but please don't be angry with me any longer."

Totally disarmed, he gazed at her with growing hunger, saying eventually, "I'm not angry with you, but myself. I'm the one who should apologise for that business at the ball." Sighing, he went on, "I was ill for a long while before coming out here to Singapore, and it seems that I'm not ready to . . . to behave myself with a girl like you. I shouted at Thea, because she's always trying to force me to do things I don't want to do. I suppose I feel the same about you, only in a different way."

Her blue eyes appealed to him. "You're wrong. I truly don't want you to do anything against your will."

"I know that, but you do it by just being you," he told her clumsily.

"How?" she asked in concern. "Tell me, and I'll try to stop."

Feeling that he was liable to launch into a highly erotic explanation of that last remark if she continued looking at him the way she was, he desperately tried to change the subject, before his sexual response to her turned into an appalling display which would leave no one in any doubt about his thoughts.

"I was already annoyed with Thea when we arrived. She took such a flippant view of the place and people we visited today. She seems incapable of taking anything seriously, and treats both the ethnic delights and the contrasting squalor of this colony with her usual disparagement. I wonder if she really cares deeply about anything . . . or anyone."

"Yes . . . Alex," Lydia said with a sigh. "She told me as much."

"Then why has she been seen all over Singapore with a succession of escorts all the time he's been away?"

"Just to get away from the house. She doesn't get on very well with my parents, but it's mainly her fault. She goes out of her way to do things that make them angry." She smiled, turning his heart over with the suggestion of its intimacy. "She does it to other people, too, you see, so don't think you're unusual."

"What about your brother?" he asked quickly, trying to calm down. "Does she make him angry?"

"No, not Alex. I've never known him to be so full of life and laughter as he's been since she arrived. They're two of a kind really, aren't they?"

"I suppose so."

"Tell me about the place you went to this afternoon, Martin," she invited. "The house on a hill, in the middle of jungle."

Thankfully, as he visualised it all again, his enthusiasm was directed into a description of the journey in sedan-chairs rather than in appreciation of Lydia's golden body. When he began to eulogise on the exotic ornamental gardens, he was delighted by her obvious interest and wonderment.

"I had no idea there was such a place on this island. It sounds like something from the pages of a novel," she declared.

"It's not the kind of place your family or friends would know about or, if they did, probably wouldn't visit," he told her thoughtfully.

Touching his arm lightly, she smiled up at him. "I'd so love to see it for myself. Would you take me there one day? Would you, please?" Turning desperately from the eager invitation of her words, he grabbed a third drink. In the midst of draining the glass, the doorway leading from the house was suddenly filled by two figures. Margery wore a dinner gown of puce crêpe-de-Chine, and Austin looked immaculate in evening clothes. They surveyed the scene on the verandah with disbelief. That two men in crumpled trousers, and shirts with sleeves rolled up above the elbows, waited on by Ling with sundowners, could possibly be there in company with their liberated guest and an unbecomingly flushed daughter was a fact so unwelcome it kept them silent.

Not so Thea, who caught sight of them and smiled. "Heavens, is it that late already? The time has just *flown*."

Margery recovered enough to say, "I naturally believed you were in your room dressing for dinner, Lydia. Why have you not done so?"

With her colour still high, the girl replied, "Thea invited her friends in for a drink after their long drive. I have been helping her to entertain them."

Her mother's expression did not relax. "I'm sure they will now excuse you, dear."

It brought forth a surprising defiance. "Mr Linwood is in the middle of telling me about his interesting trip this afternoon, Mummy."

Intervening in what threatened to become an embarrassing scene, Thea calmly drew George forward. "I understand that you and Dr McGregor are unacquainted, even though you have all lived in the colony for years. What a sad state of affairs! Let me remedy it by introducing you now." Turning to George she said, "Margery is the sister of my mother's brother's wife, you know. She and Austin have been extremely kind and long-suffering toward me." Swinging back to face the Beresfords, she smiled. "George is a fascinating man. He's a colleague of Martin's, attached to the Civil Service, and has been claimed on this island as a miracle-healer. His knowledge of the East and its indigenous races is quite astonishing."

"Glad to meet you at last, Beresford." George stepped forward with his hand outstretched. After several moments, the immaculately-dressed Austin shook it rather stiffly. Margery merely gave a half nod in reply to his greeting. Their frigid attitude did not deter him, however.

"I apologise for our somewhat dishevelled state," he said easily, "but your daughter assured us that her brother and his friends often gather here informally after polo."

"Indeed," commented Austin so tonelessly it was impossible to guess whether the single word was meant to convey agreement or surprise that Lydia should have said such a thing.

"I own an old convertible. It's spacious and comfortable, but as

129

unpredictable as an old maid to handle," George continued blithely. "It's pointless togging myself up for a trip in her, for it's a basin of faggots to a tenner I'll have to dive under the bonnet with a spanner somewhere along the route."

Austin regarded him with distaste. "I'm surprised that you do not employ a syce, Doctor, as we do."

"It's such a pity Alex is away," said Thea swiftly. "He'd have enjoyed coming with us today. George's friends have the most perfect small-scale version of ancient China you could imagine. Sitting on a hill on the south-west coast, the house has a breathtaking view and is surrounded by a fantasy of pools, bridges and pagodas filled with roaming pheasants and monkeys."

"Indeed," said Austin again, with equal lack of tone.

"You took Dorothea to such a place, Doctor?" cried Margery accusingly.

George nodded. "She wanted information for her book. The Sing brothers are very old friends of mine who expressed great willingness to give her any help they could offer."

"The Sing brothers?" queried Austin. "You surely cannot mean the Chinese pair who made a fortune from silk."

"The most wonderful old men," supplied Thea enthusiastically. "They still live in the past."

"That is a complete untruth, Dorothea," he contradicted sharply. "Kong Wok and Lee Ho are modern enough to exploit their country-men by paying starvation wages for long hours of work in factories that should have been pulled down long before they were. Your 'wonderful old men' acquired their enormous wealth by the most ruthless and inhumane means."

Thea turned to George with a frown. "Is that true?"

"In essence, I suppose it is."

"Mmm, I commented on their lack of interest in the poverty and squalor to be found here. I was more perceptive than I guessed."

"Take the theme a little further, my dear," George urged. "Without that work, many people would have gone under. Starvation wages are better than no wages at all, aren't they?"

Her smile was rueful. "No socialist would agree with that."

"He might, if he had been treated as they were by their own countrymen," put in Martin with force. "Suffering tends to change a man's outlook on what is right and wrong, Thea. He reaches a point when self becomes uppermost, and the rest of the world is left to fight its own battles." He turned to Austin. "When someone has had his hands sliced off, or his eyes put out by his own people, I imagine the victim feels he is extremely tolerant to pay some of them to do the work his mutilations prevent him from doing."

The dinner-suited shipper shook his head. "No, Linwood. Inhumanity can never be excused on those grounds. *Do unto others as you would have them do unto you.*"

After three swift stengahs, Martin was driven to retaliate. "If someone cut off your hands, would you ask him in for a drink? Put your piece of idealistic theorising to some men I've known, and I wouldn't vouch for your safety."

"Quite probably, young man," came the response heavy with inference. "Your godfather has told us a little of those with whom you mixed prior to coming out here." He fixed Lydia with a stern look. "Do as your mother asked, and go upstairs to dress for dinner as you should have done half an hour ago."

Martin pretended to be unaware of the agonised look the girl threw him before walking away with as much dignity as she could muster. He felt suddenly very tired. It had been a long day; one which had sprung too many surprises on his senses. All he wanted now was to be alone. George was making a tactful parting speech as Margery went in pursuit of her errant daughter. Small wonder Lydia was unequal to her own emotions, Martin thought wearily. An unexpected flame of anger leapt in him as he imagined the possessive mother now going upstairs, to turn a drink with two casually dressed men into a shameful and brazen episode. By the time Margery had finished, that poor little girl would believe she had practically stripped naked and invited violation from a pair of hardened libertines on her own verandah.

Following George down the steps to the garden, Martin told himself yet again that coming to Singapore was a terrible mistake. The people here were either totally out of touch with the rest of the world, or too eager to discover and conquer it. He thought of Piers Massingham, who had been rejected by them and found peace amid lush jungle, lazy waterways, brown smiling people, vivid birds and tigers. Lucky devil! He had escaped.

Reaching the car, Martin pulled his jacket from the back and said that he would walk the short distance to his bungalow.

"I think I need to recover from Austin Beresford's brand of social manners before facing those of the fun-loving fellow who shares my quarters," he explained, with a sigh. "I made a fool of myself in there, but he touched me on the raw." Putting a finger through the loop in the back of his jacket, he slung the garment across his shoulder and lifted the other hand in a gesture of farewell to his friend sitting behind the wheel. "I'm glad I came today, George. Visiting the Sings was a rare and exciting experience. I mean to take up their invitation to go again."

"I'm glad. They'll enjoy it as much as you will."

George moved off down the drive in a cloud of dust. Martin set off in his wake, waving his free hand across his face to disperse the fumes floating in the still night air. The heaviness of the dusk matched the heaviness of his spirits as he faced returning to a bungalow probably filled with Damien Lang's noisy crowd. More than anything, he longed to go back to the house and Lydia. Coming to a halt in the driveway, he turned to look up at the lighted windows on the first floor. She was up there somewhere, longing for him almost as much as he longed for her.

Sighing heavily, he wondered if Thea might have been right in her determination to throw them together. Perhaps, if they could be together often enough under normal circumstances, the whole thing might cool down. If he had permission to court her in the accepted manner, with invitations to tea or dinner with her family, and parties in the company of others, maybe the overwhelming desire to possess her would diminish. Brief stolen moments in dark gardens only created the danger he was trying to avoid. Alternatively, he could allow himself to seduce her, then take her off up-country like the enigmatic Piers Massingham and his mistress, to live in blissful seclusion whilst she made him forget horror and death and shattered minds. In a jungle retreat, he would surely gradually learn to love her more gently. Isolated from watching eyes, wagging tongues, smirking faces, his nervous clumsiness would vanish. Lydia had never deplored it. At their first disastrous meeting, she had shown no distaste or distress over his fumbling progress, or smashed teacups; gentleness and understanding in the face of general revulsion. With her, he could surely rebuild his life in the only way open to him now. If he had Lydia and solitude, he could be a different man.

The visions faded as he stared at the anonymous windows. Piers Massingham lived in exotic contentment with his Chinese love. It would be vastly different if the girl were European. An illicit alliance would never be permitted by this society. Seducing Lydia would lead to himself being hounded from Singapore alone, whilst his love was shipped off to England to bear any possible consequences of her downfall in secret. The only way to make his dream reality would be to take her up-country as his wife. That, he knew, was impossible. The Beresfords would never allow a twitching stuttering misfit to partner their beautiful daughter in anything, much less marriage.

As he stood gazing miserably at the house where his girl was imprisoned, sudden bright light on his face dazzled him. The sound of a car approaching suggested that George had returned for some reason. However, it was not his friend who spoke as the taxi drew alongside and stopped.

"Hallo, Linwood. What on earth are you doing hanging around in our garden?"

Confusion at seeing someone no one appeared to be expecting, plus a sense of guilt over thoughts the man must have guessed if the suspicion in his tone was any guide, Martin stumbled over his words.

"I thought you'd gone . . . were away . . . in Manila."

"Just as well I'm home, perhaps," came the crisp reply. "Have you been visiting my family?"

"Not exactly."

"What do you mean by that?"

"We had sundowners. I'm going back," he said heavily, knowing he could delay his return to that bungalow no longer.

"Have you forgotten the way out?"

At the end of a mentally exhausting day, Martin was unequal to Alex Beresford's curious aggression. He was certain to make a fool of himself once more. Starting to move off, he said, "I remember the way out, and I'll now follow it. Goodnight." Ten yards beyond the car, he added softly, "Welcome home. At least you still have one, you lucky devil!"

Chapter 8

Dinner was delayed an hour due to Alex's unexpected return from Manila. He spent most of those sixty minutes in his room taking a shower, shaving, and dressing for the meal. He had walked in to find his parents edgy and distinctly unwelcoming. His mother had castigated him for not letting her know of his intended arrival; his father had added his stricture on that as well as making no secret of his opinion of a son who had been sent to do a job requiring at least six weeks, but had returned after only three.

Alex had raced along to Thea's room on going upstairs, but Ah Toy had told him, through a modest opening in the doorway, that her mistress was in the bath. Walking disconsolately back to his own room, he was reminded of Martin Linwood as he passed Lydia's door. What had the fellow been doing lurking near the shrubbery in the darkness? His story about sundowners hardly rung true. He had been dressed in the most casual fashion, yet his parents had been correctly garbed for dinner when he had entered the house a few moments later. Could Linwood be the reason for their frostiness? Was whatever was going on between him and Lydia, still going on? He sighed as he reached his door. What a homecoming!

Fong was delighted to see him, and soon cast some light on the situation.

"Missy Dorotee bling flend on velandah for G and T, but Old Master no likee flend and no likee no ploper suit for evening. He no likee Missy Lylia with flend. Mem no likee. Missy Lylia go loom, plentee cly. Missy Dorotee angly make Missy Lylia cly. She no likee."

From that information, Alex deduced that Thea had invited Martin to the house in order to throw him and Lydia together, as she had vowed to do, and the whole affair had turned into a disaster. Everywhere Linwood went, he appeared to induce disaster. Perhaps Thea would now see her error in meddling. He had plans which would leave her little time for it, anyway.

His immediate plan was to take her to bed, when he hurried downstairs to join the family and she, dressed in an emerald silk sari with a many-tiered collarette around her throat, walked straight across to him and boldly kissed him full on the mouth and said how delighted she was to see him again. That plan had to be shelved, of course, and her deliberate defiance of his parents increased the sharp frostiness of that tropical evening. With Lydia silent and rather red around the eyes, his parents stiff and unapproachable, and Thea plainly in her most sparkling militant mood, the meal resembled a skirmish rather than a convivial gathering.

Eager to tell his father details of his trip, determined to get to the bottom of the link between his sister and the man who kept crossing their path in the most unsettling manner, and longing to have Thea in his arms again, Alex knew he must tackle the first of the three desires as soon as the difficult meal ended and coffee had been served. When they all ritually filed into the sitting room where coffee was dispensed by Ling, and his mother asked Lydia to play some of her favourite pieces on the piano, Alex suggested to Austin that they walk through to the verandah for a smoke.

"I'm most anxious to outline the details of my trip," he confessed.

"Very well," was the unpromising reply. "I suppose the matter will have to be discussed."

They walked out to find a wind had risen before oncoming rain. Ling had lowered the blinds and fastened them down. They rattled and cracked like the sails of an old clipper in a lively breeze, and the lanterns swung to flicker light over the polished floor.

"Monsoon," observed Austin, taking a cigar from the box Ling proffered. "It's been threatening all day."

"Sir," Alex began, as soon as he had lit his own cigarette, "I can give you a brief outline of the scheme I have set in motion, but the costings and proposed schedules are upstairs in my room and need detailed explanation which can't be covered tonight. I thought we might get down to it tomorrow, before tiffin. I've drawn up a provisional time-table of the availability of specific cargoes which is, naturally, subject to the success of crops etcetera." Growing enthusiastic despite the earlier depression of the evening, he added, "Believe me, Father, we're on to a good thing out there."

Pausing in the lengthy business of setting his cigar alight satisfactorily, Austin cast him a dour look. "What is that somewhat inelegant expression intended to convey?"

Alex smiled confidently. "Not what you plainly imagine. I've organised or decided nothing to which you could have any objection. All the deals I have made are with bona fide traders, I assure you."

"I hope I misheard that last remark, Alexander."

"I don't understand you, sir," he said, denied the full flood of his narrative.

"You spoke of deals you have made."

"Rather acute ones, if I may say so without sounding too smug."

His cigar forgotten in his hand, Austin stared at him. "You have proposed and accepted terms; signed documents committing *Berondel* to such terms?"

Alex nodded. "Of course. Isn't that why I was sent to Manila?"

"You were sent to investigate the possibilities of setting up our own offices out there. *To investigate the possibilities*."

"I did," he affirmed, the first warning signs beginning to indicate something he could hardly believe. "The plan is an excellent one certain to increase our profits considerably, besides extending our present routes. I found premises equidistant from the wharves and the mercantile centre. The interior needs some attention, but the rooms are a good size with the two upper floors served by a most impressive staircase. I put the decorating and maintenance in hand before I left. An extremely capable Eurasian called Bannister, whom I've engaged as my chief cook and bottle-washer, will oversee the work and instal the office furniture I chose. That was a trifle pricey, I'm afraid, but I thought it important to give an impression of affluence." Continuing courageously, although he now suspected that he was on a sinking ship, he forced a confident smile. "I pulled a fast one by inspecting the offices of our competitors in the guise of a prospective client, and made a note of their expensive decor. There was no option but to match it. First impressions are vitally important, and we wouldn't stand a hope of attracting new clients, or of luring some from our rivals, if we operated from dingy, old-fashioned offices, don't you agree, sir?"

Against the noise of flapping blinds, his father said, "I should have realised what folly it would be to give you your head. In three short weeks you have provided more than enough justification for my intention to retain full control of *Berondel* until you convince me that you are fit to fill my shoes. I gave you an inch; you have seized a mile."

"All right," Alex conceded, trying to reason with an implacable nature, "perhaps I have. I was on the spot for the first time, and I didn't see the sense in making mere observations when the opportunities to act were staring me in the face. If I had waited to gain your approval, it might have been too late."

"And you might never have gained it. That's what you really mean, isn't it?"

"Yes . . . if you want the truth," he admitted.

Austin crushed his half-finished cigar in the ashtray, and stood trying to hold on to his temper. "So you own to being aware that what you engaged in in Manila was likely to meet with opposition from me?"

"Yes," he agreed, taking the bull by the horns. "But your opposition would have been mounted against the fact that I had used my own initiative, not against the virtue of any decision I made. You haven't yet seen my figures, the trade schedules, or my proposals for expansion into exciting new areas, so how can you claim justification for retaining control of the damned line? What *you* are really saying is that whatever I do is going to be wrong in your book." He let out an explosive sigh. "Those three weeks were a total waste of time. I knew you had an ulterior motive in sending me away after denying my requests so often, but I mistakenly believed that you would be forced to accept my ability to make a useful contribution to a company you like to remind me I shall one day have to control. I tell you now, Father, you may lay your fears to rest. I don't want *Berondel*. It's staid, unimaginative and on its way to extinction because you are choking the life out of it."

Looking surprisingly shaken, Austin, said, "There is no need for drama, my boy. My scepticism is born of the suddenness of your return today. Three weeks does not, in my experience, seem sufficient time in which to achieve the acquisition of suitable offices, reliable employees to staff them, and a miraculous list of new clients which Mendes, apparently, knew nothing of."

"That was only because you're so cautious," Alex countered hotly. "You check everything a dozen times, then ponder on it for days before even considering putting it before the board. They then sink their chins into their grey beards and ruminate until the impatient client presses for a decision, or until they realise that some other line has been carrying the merchandise for several months in our stead. In Manila I made swift decisions . . . and I loosened the purse strings," he added knowing he had nothing to lose by the confession.

"You have no authority over payments which are not backed by my signature," his father said in alarm.

Alex stubbed out his cigarette and, unusually for him, lit another immediately. "Don't worry. I only wrote one actual draft on our bank." His mouth twisted. "*Berondel* has such an impeccably honest reputation, I got all I wanted on trust. If you explain that your headstrong son overstepped his authority, I'm sure you'll be able to return everything without much difficulty . . . and I already know of a man anxious to acquire the premises."

Austin appeared to be in the throes of a dilemma. Keeping his gaze on his son, he thrust his hands into his pockets, withdrew them, stroked his chin thoughtfully, then took up his goblet of brandy Ling had left on the table with his usual efficiency. Letting out a faint sigh, he then sipped reflectively, still studying Alex. Finally, he spoke. It was on a new subject and was uncharacteristically frank.

"Your mother and I have been under a great deal of stress recently. This evening is another example of how Dorothea is disrupting the tranquillity of family life. With her usual warm generosity toward young people, your mother encouraged Dorothea to make her own friends and bring them to the house whenever she wished. It was a mistake. I regret to tell you that the young woman we so willingly took into our home has brought us little but embarrassment and distress. Our long-standing friends have been affronted, our peace has been shattered, and our home has been used with deplorable thoughtlessness to entertain a procession of young men, some of whom we have previously declined to know because of their undesirable reputations. Your poor mother is burdened by the responsibility for an unmarried young woman placed in her charge by her brother in England—a young woman who is so unrestrained she will heed no one—and lives in the fear that Dorothea will expose herself to the greatest risk imaginable by disregarding advice. The effect on Lydia you must surely have seen for yourself this evening. We descended for dinner to discover your sister on the verandah, where she had been inveigled into entertaining, in the most unorthodox manner, that unstable youngster Linwood and, of all people, George McGregor! The pair, well flushed with alcohol, were regaling Lydia with tales of their visit to the Sing brothers. Yes, the Sing brothers! McGregor had apparently taken Dorothea there this afternoon in her quest for information for this . . . this novel!"

So Martin had not been invited alone. Why had he not left with the other man? Fighting the desire to leap to Thea's defence, Alex determinedly pursued the main problem. "Are we leaving the subject of Manila up in the air? I think I am at least entitled to know what action you intend to take, after working damned hard for three weeks over there."

After a fresh series of uneasy gestures, Austin said, "Your mother and I are aware of how . . . how impressed you were by Dorothea when she first arrived in our midst. It saddened us, but in the wisdom of our greater years we perceived that your youthful energies should, perhaps, have been allowed a more productive outlet. Deterioration of our situation in Manila provided a timely solution, whilst offering you the opportunity to escape Dorothea's influence and see her in a saner perspective. When you arrived just before dinner tonight—it would seem quite deliberately without warning—I had the greatest misgivings. Tell me the truth, Alexander. Did you act with haste and lack of judgement out there in order to return to that young woman? Have you been fool enough to surrender integrity for the chance to resume your misguided admiration for a female who is greatly adept at winding impressionable youngsters around her finger?"

Alex crushed out the second cigarette with unnecessary force. "Hasn't the wisdom of your greater years suggested to you that an impressionable youngster might still have enough sense to know that making a complete ass of himself, when presented with the first real opportunity to prove his worth, would endear him to no female whatever?"

"I see. You did not hurry back to resume your misguided attentions to Dorothea?"

"Yes, certainly I did . . . but not before I made first-rate arrangements for *Berondel* in Manila."

His father plainly did not know how to deal with that statement. To cover the moment, he poured himself a second brandy from the decanter left by Ling, then made a gesture toward contrition by recharging his son's glass. The two sipped their drinks in a silence broken only by the frenzied flapping of the blinds as the monsoon finally arrived. The almost immediate thunder of rain made further conversation impossible, save in raised voices. Austin had to end hostilities for that evening in as dignified a manner as he could muster.

"You may show me your plans and estimates in the morning. If they are as good as you suggest, I shall send you back to Manila immediately."

Feeling that he had conducted the interview rather well, Alex said caustically, "I expected that, naturally. I'm rather tired so I'll turn in now. Goodnight, sir."

Thea appeared to have made the same decision, for she was not in the sitting room with his mother and sister. They were both subdued as he exchanged a few words with them before kissing Margery's cheek, and patting Lydia on the shoulder as he said goodnight. Up in his room, he found Fong stony eyed and stiff with disapproval. A glance over the shoulder of the Chinese servant revealed the cause. His pulse quickened.

Pushing past Fong to reach her, he said exultantly, "You crazy, beautiful creature! How dared you kiss me so thoroughly in front of them all the minute I walked in?"

Her smile was wide and wonderful to his starved eyes. "If you were only half as daring, you'd have pushed past Ah Toy and kissed me in my bath. I was fearfully disappointed in you when she told me you'd meekly walked away."

He laughed. "The news would have been all around the house in two minutes flat."

"So what? I hadn't seen you for three weeks."

The challenge was irresistible. He met it with assumed dismay. "You weren't really disappointed in me, were you?"

"Of course. I thought you were known as Mad Alex."

"You would have liked to be kissed in the bath?"

"Madly," she affirmed. "But you're plainly too much of a gentleman for that. It comes of wearing coffee-coloured monstrosities on your head."

"Oh, it does, does it?" he demanded, moving into action with relish. "We'll see about that." Seizing her by the wrist, he headed for the verandah doors, thrust them open, and stepped out to run with her toward the staircase used by Fong. Drenched in an instant by the thundering sheets of monsoon rain, he dragged her down the wooden steps to the garden directly below. Once there, he pulled her against him to kiss her fiercely. It was a form of wildness he had never before practised, and it was heady. He continued to kiss her, over and over, revelling in the sense of power such defiance of the elements and plain commonsense gave him.

Pulling away from him, she cried, "Crazy idiot!"

She looked even more exciting with her hair clinging like a black bathing cap, and her breasts beautifully outlined by the saturated silk dress. "I love you," he yelled back. "I love you to distraction."

The rain beat relentlessly down on them, and that sense of elated freedom he always felt when yielding to impulse was there in full measure, as he cried, "Do you still claim that I'm not daring enough because I'm too much of a gentleman?"

"You were earlier this evening."

"Right," he cried and before she knew it, he lifted her in his arms and headed toward the small ornamental pool encircled by the driveway. Stepping into it, he sat down still holding her, so that the tepid water lapped around their waists and water lilies added pink and white floral adornment to their evening clothes. There was enough light from the lamp above the door to illuminate Thea's disbelieving expression before she began to laugh, tipping back her head with pure delight.

"I'll kiss you in this bath," he bellowed above the tumult around them. "In fact, I'll do more than that before I'm through with you tonight."

Bending to kiss her, he overbalanced and rolled over so that they both received a complete ducking. When they came up spluttering, they exchanged one look then clutched each other in uncontrollable joy. Alex had never felt so marvellous. After three weeks, he was back with the girl he had missed so badly he had felt only half alive.

Fong was still decidedly disapproving as he helped Alex to dry himself and put on a casual shirt and grey flannels. He had undoubtedly witnessed the frolic in the garden, and reached the conclusion that the girl who had upset the calm running of the household was a mischievous spirit sent to steal away the wits of the young man he had tended since boyhood. In essence, his reasoning was correct. Alex was decidedly light-headed as he quietly made his way downstairs to a small back room used mainly by his mother when writing letters for her various committees. Ling had been requested to bring coffee and a large quantity of sandwiches to the room. Alex was ravenous. Happiness induced hunger of varying kinds. The room contained the peculiar musty smell induced by rain in the tropics, and he pulled on the light pullover he had draped around his shoulders to counteract the chill. Thea came in a few moments later, and commented immediately.

"Gracious, you must be *sweltering* in that woolly thing."

He grinned. "I needed something to keep me warm until you arrived. Now you're here, Miss . . ."

He kissed her more comprehensively than he had done so far that evening, the conditions now being far more suited to real ardour. She responded with equal pleasure until he grew too demanding.

Arching back within his arms, she said huskily, "This may not be a bedroom, darling, but your thoughts appear to be running along those lines. I suggest you tackle the sandwiches rather than me."

With great reluctance he did as she said, whilst she wisely sat with a reasonable gap between their chairs. He made inroads into the plate of sandwiches, and Thea enjoyed her coffee as she sat with her legs hooked over the arm of her chair. In a garment resembling a stage costume from the *Arabian Nights*, yet which managed to cover her from neck to ankles, she looked fatally alluring as she questioned him about his trip.

"If it was so successful, why did Austin look ready to emulate your grandfather all through dinner? Darling, what went on between you two while poor Lydia played 'Mother's favourite pieces'?"

The remark diverted his thoughts. "I could ask what went on this afternoon between my sister and Linwood to make her so wretched!"

"Nothing went on between them. That's what made her so wretched."

In mid-bite, he lowered the sandwich again. "That's not clever, Thea."

"Sorry, but it's true Lydia is crazy about him in a very emotional way. He's as crazy about her in, I suspect, a much more physical fashion. He's afraid of her innocence; she's excited by his maturity. It's making them both desperately unhappy, but he doesn't trust himself enough to follow my advice. You had better act to avert disaster."

Disturbed by what she said, he frowned. "I don't see how *I* can take up the subject with Lydia. It's the sort of thing a girl can only talk about to another female, surely. What about Mother?"

"Really, Alex," she said in exasperation. "If the poor girl so much as breathed a *hint* of what she felt to Margery, she'd be sent to a convent, and Martin would be given the Piers Massingham treatment. Just for being in company with two men who were not correctly dressed for dinner when the sun went down today, Lydia was ordered upstairs like a recalcitrant child. To be treated that way in the presence of the man she worships would have been as painful as having her skin peeled off, layer by layer. I know, Alex," she told him with deep feeling. "Believe me, I know. The only good thing about the affair is that your parents are so convinced of Lydia's virtue, they haven't spotted the truth. If they ever do, Martin is a condemned man. It's up to you to tackle him about the situation."

"My only advice to him would be that he should return to England on the first available sailing," Alex told her crisply.

She studied him for a moment or two, then nodded. "I thought it might be. Would you offer that pearl of wisdom in order to protect your sister's honour, or merely to rid yourself of someone who appears to be a constant thorn in your side?"

Countering her taunt, he said, "He doesn't fit in here. You must see that."

"I think even he sees that," she responded caustically. "Alex, why do you hate him so much?"

"I don't hate him," he denied swiftly. Then, at her raised eyebrows, repeated it. "I don't hate him."

"He affects you more than any other man you know. There must be a reason."

He leaned back in his chair, feasting his hungry eyes on her loveliness while he considered his reply. Finally, he decided on the truth.

"He did the one thing in my life I burned to do, yet didn't. I envy him that experience more than I can say."

"He gave up half his mind for the experience! Do you envy him that?" she cried.

"Of course not."

"What, then?"

"The fact that he has faced mortality and survived," he was driven to confess. "According to that schoolfriend of his, Linwood even courted death to save the lives of three others. He's made his contribution to mankind, even if he never does another worthwhile thing in his life. I admire that more than any words can express." He sat forward to emphasise his next comment. "What have I done? Roistered around this island with other wealthy youngsters, and counted twilights as I sat making no mark on the world whatever."

She rose to face him frankly. "Don't take it out on Martin, Alex. I don't agree that it would have been to your credit to join the mass sacrifice of young men in the war, but it was something *you* desperately wanted to do. Through a misguided sense of family obligation, an inborn loyalty that overruled your own desires, you surrendered to their selfish demands on you. In doing so, you also surrendered your role as an individual. For the past six years, you've been paying a higher and higher price for that with every one of those twilights which haunt you, and the longer you continue doing so, the less likely your hope of breaking free."

He rose swiftly, eager to vindicate himself. "All that is very easy for someone like you to say. No one has ever thwarted your greatest desire, demanded from you something you find almost impossible to refuse. When a woman who has suffered deep grief over the loss of her other two children clings to you in a frenzy of distress because you intend to go, you'll find it's not that easy to follow your own star. When a man who has sacrificed his own youthful hopes and dreams in order to atone for his father's crime against society, then sees his one surviving son preparing to risk his life and begs him to stay and make his own sacrifice worthwhile, there is an emotion which rises to swamp self-interest. You've always been a free spirit; you've never been torn apart by conflicting loyalties," he pointed out quietly. "Don't condemn, Thea, until you've faced the same pressures and successfully overcome them."

She put her hands up to gently cup his face as she nodded slowly. "You're right, darling. My greatest fault is my tendency to philosophise on situations I have never experienced. Forgive me?"

Pulling her into his arms, he showed her how easy it was to forgive her, and they both enjoyed the interlude. Then she drew away to smile up at him.

"You have no reason to envy Martin, my dear. You might not possess a medal, or the legacy of shell shock to prove it, but your courage and sense of duty is equal to his. All the same, Alex, you'll have to choose between them and me when it comes to the point. That's their condition on our future, not mine."

"I chose you the moment I first saw you," he told her fervently. "Thea, marry me soon and put an end to all this nonsense. Come to Manila with me as my wife. I want you so badly, I'll never endure six months without you."

Her expression held a hint of sadness as she said, "Darling, I asked you not to rush me. I love you; I want you badly, too, but I came to Singapore to write a novel and I have to do it before clouding my resolution with the consequences of becoming your wife."

"Why?" he cried in frustration. "Why, in God's name, is this urge to write a book so vital to you?"

"For the same reason your father feels the need to redeem the Beresford name. It's something I have to do. Understand, darling. Please understand."

During the next few days, Alex indulged in a great deal of soul-searching. His father had studied the papers outlining business proposals for the Manila office and, with one or two minor reservations, reluctantly approved them. Alex knew it was less a sign of confidence in his ability than a means of keeping him in Manila for the next six months, so he considered the project only in terms of his future hopes. Six months apart from Thea would be purgatory, yet they would constitute the initial break from the family which would soften the final severance from them. That being so, was there some way he could persuade Thea to go with him? The book she insisted on writing could as well be conceived there as in Singapore, surely. The Eastern influence was there in Manila. She had asked him to understand her reasons, but he found it difficult in the face of his own longing for her, and the problem of his impending return to the new sub-office lay heavily on his spirits.

After several days without reaching any solution, a new complication threw him completely off balance. It began as a nebulous thought flitting momentarily through sessions of troubled reasoning, then suddenly crystallised to produce an astounding truth. He had no wish to run the new office in Manila. His brother Charles should have inherited *Berondel*. If he had lived, Alex would never have chosen to join him in the family firm. His heart had never been in shipping: his buccaneering spirit yearned for action, excitement, exploration. If the pattern of his life was about to change, then let it change completely. The ending of his family tie might as well be a swift agonising wrench, as a slow tormenting severance which would leave them all permanently maimed.

Possessed by inner excitement, he then feverishly considered the most momentous decision of his life. His bank balance was permanently low because he spent money as fast as he acquired it, but he had a few investments which were secure until he reached the age of twenty-five. He could take out a loan against those shares to enable him to establish himself in whichever career he chose. The knowledge that he was about to make his bid for freedom, at last, allowed him to consider seriously what he had hitherto only dreamed of when frustrated. Action, excitement, exploration all added up to one thing, so far as he concerned. Flying! Aviation would repeat those old seafaring feats and thrills his great-grandfather had known. Aircraft would fly faster and cover longer and longer routes. Men would pit their skill and daring against each other in the race to claim the world. Shipping had become staid and dependable, suited to men like his father. Vessels had grown solid and cumbersome. Young men now turned to the skies for glamour and daring. The element of risk beckoned irresistibly. Aviators were fresh-faced, keen, virile and as unlike the Austin Beresfords of the world as it was possible to be. Aircraft designers were creating machines that were sleeker and more versatile with every model. The idea of actually following that particular star put him in a ferment of anticipation as he considered the plan from every angle.

It would mean going to England and finding somewhere to live while he set about persuading an aviation company to employ him whilst he learned to fly. Within a year, he could withdraw his investments and pay back the loan. With what remained, plus his salary, he would have more than enough to enable him to buy a home. It all sounded very feasible, and answered that ache of restrained freedom in every possible way. As the day of his proposed return to Manila loomed, he avoided all thought of the reaction from his family to his news. The announcement would have to be made soon, and he would have to ride out the storm it would create with the knowledge that he was now entitled to his own life.

Only after several days of concentrated planning during which he began the mental metamorphosis from shipper to aviator, did he remember Thea's book. It could not be so important to her that she would refuse to return to England with him, especially as he was taking this tremendous step in response to her own ruling that he must choose between his family and her. Amputating himself completely from *Berondel* was the only way of doing that. Surely she would recognise his declaration of devotion, and respond. Yet he hesitated to put such reasoning to the test, and it added to the fever in his brain as the days passed to bring the moment of truth nearer and nearer. The twilights took on a new significance as he counted them off, and braced himself to ask Thea the question he knew would set the seal on his hope of future happiness.

Chapter 9

It was one of those rare occasions when Martin and George were in their adjoining offices for the entire day. They were working on a report on their findings concerning a proposed development of an area of jungle in which several Malay *kampongs* were situated. Malay leaders were objecting to plans they claimed would destroy the peaceful and unobtrusive settlements of their people. They did not understand the need for more roads through unspoiled parts of the island, protesting that such easy access would bring factories, large houses, and luxury hotels of which there were already enough to satisfy the wealthy traders and settlers.

Plans had been drawn up by civil engineers, and the colonial administration was eager to implement them. However, as the area contained not only Malay *kampongs* but also a considerable stretch of swampland, George had been sent to investigate possible health risks of mosquito-infested areas close to the proposed development. Martin had been told to visit the *kampongs* as a sign that interest was being shown in the protests from ethnic leaders. Knowing full well that he had been given the task because it was no more than an empty gesture, and because no other man in his department wished to enter the daunting and uncongenial section of the island, Martin had followed George through humid venomous jungle, vowing to submit a lengthy complicated report of his visit. It was this he was compiling on a day of particularly high temperatures, when even the overhead fans did no more than swirl hot air around the suffocating confines of the office.

Apart from the oppressiveness of the day and an almost vindictive desire to call his department's bluff by taking his job very seriously, Martin was in a rebellious mood as he covered page after page with the kind of prose he had learned to use in the Army, when wishing to confound those at headquarters who conducted the war without actually participating in the fighting.

He had spent the previous evening with the Weyfords—his weekly penance—and it was that which now created the rebellion affecting his every action today. The bright promise of further acquaintance with the Sing brothers could only be fulfilled by buying a car of his own. It was his only means of reaching the foot of the hill on which their magnificent atmospheric home sprawled. To buy a car, Martin needed Sir Hartle's consent to the withdrawal of funds. It was the first time the terms of his father's will had made any impact on Martin, so he had broached the matter with his godfather in complete confidence that his agreement was no more than a formality. He had been thunderstruck by the judge's response.

As disapproving and tetchy as Austin Beresford had been over the meeting with the Chinese brothers, Sir Hartle had flatly refused to authorise the release of money for the purchase of a car so that further meetings could take place. He had explained that it was not so much the idea of Martin driving his own vehicle to which he objected, as the purpose for which he wanted it. A long lecture had followed, enumerating the errors of pursuing the path Martin appeared to be taking. Sir Hartle had been made aware that his godson avoided social gatherings whenever he could, frequently excusing himself on the grounds of being too busy when everyone knew that he was the most junior member of his department, who had few responsibilities. Sir Hartle had also heard that, despite the praiseworthy attempts of the younger colonial element to take him into their lively circle, Martin still resisted any form of integration with those who mattered in Singapore.

"From all reports, it appears that the only place you frequent is the Swimming Club. For all the hours you spend there, you still decline to form friendships with the other members," the elderly man had said in rebuke. "It won't do, Martin, it won't do at all. I have made considerable efforts to help you, at the risk, I might add, of straining the excellent terms of acquaintanceship I have with some very important people out here. I introduced you to the Fortnums, the Rosedales and the Beresfords, all families with youngsters your own age, yet you stubbornly decline to pursue that initial contact."

After some moments of agitated puffing at his cigar, the perplexed and responsible man had continued his theme. "Can you wonder that I feel unable to approve the purchase of a motor-car? My boy, I am as uneasy over the charge your father laid upon me as you are, but I am honour bound to manage your inheritance until the medical men are willing to give notice as to your fitness to do so. It's my experienced opinion that you will not gain this by associating with men like the Sing brothers, or with that strange character George McGregor, who spends more time with the native races than with his own countrymen. No, Martin, that will not do, you know."

Sitting heavily and mopping his brow with his handkerchief, Sir Hartle had then tried to soften the blow. "When judging difficult cases, I sometimes propose a 'bargain' with the accused. In return for a solemn promise to mend his ways, I offer slight leniency. Let us do that now, my boy. Make a determined effort to pull yourself together, accept

147

invitations, form suitable friendships with youngsters who will have a helpful and stabilising influence on your new start out here, and I'll reconsider the purchase of a motor-car. Come to me again in three months' time, and we'll assess the situation."

That ultimatum had sent Martin to bed in a black mood. George provided the only brand of friendship he wanted, and the Sing brothers had offered such an attractive outlet for his major interest, denial of it now seemed particularly frustrating. He had already approached taxi-drivers, and found none who would take him that far across the island through jungle known to be hostile in so many ways. The only solution was to have his own car, yet how could he consider Sir Hartle's so-called "bargain" when compliance would mean encountering Lydia wherever he went?

It was hardly surprising that he felt the need to hit out at someone, and used the report he was compiling as the means of doing so. With his clothes sticking to his damp body and his thoughts inflamed by a sense of injustice, there was no sound in his office save the scratching of nib on paper as he faithfully recorded every word of every conversation he had had, through an interpreter, with the gentle unhappy people of the *kampongs* threatened by the proposed development. Admittedly, the settlements had been little more than collections of attap huts, with children and livestock running freely about the jungle clearing, but they were as much home to these people as Larkswood Court had once been to him. Thought of that large estate in Kent halted his racing nib. The ink dried on the page as a fresh sense of despair washed over Martin. He belonged nowhere; he felt rapport with no one on this island colony save George. What could he do? He was in a trap, yet escape from it offered nothing but a terrible void he did not yet feel strong enough to tackle. The doctors at the hospital had told him to approach his future one step at a time: he must, therefore, give Sir Hartle's proposed new start a fair trial before condemning it as a failure.

While the fan circled endlessly over his head until he felt he was spinning with it and getting nowhere, desperation drove him to do something from which he had shied before. Getting to his feet, he crossed the room to the doorway leading to the next office, and stood for a few seconds watching George copying facts from one of the large medical books on his desk.

"Shall I be interrupting a vital train of thought if I beg a few minutes of your time?" he asked eventually.

The other man looked up. "My trains of thought are more often than not uncoupled carriages left standing in sidings." Leaning back and stretching sluggishly, he added, "That simile describes the extent of my success with my seniors. What I consider to be an express invariably meets with signals of opposition, and points of objection until it is broken apart and distributed in small, ineffective parts to lines with old buffers at the end of them." He gave his attractive smile. "How's that for a piece of effective prose? Do you think the delectable Miss du Lessier would like it for her novel?"

Unwilling to be side-tracked now he had plucked up the requisite nerve, Martin asked, "Can I talk to you confidentially—as a doctor?"

Lowering his arms from their overhead stretch, George changed his approach rapidly. "Feeling ill?"

He shook his head. "Just the reverse, actually."

"You look a bad advertisement for the condition, if I may say. 'Bursting with health' is not a phrase I would ever use in connection with you, old lad."

"I'm bursting with something else," he confessed in a rush, to get over the initial embarrassment. "It's driving me nearly nuts."

George began to laugh, gently at first, then with growing vigour. "If you mean what I think you mean, it's not a doctor you need, it's the address of a safe brothel."

Half inclined to walk out at that point, Martin told himself he must continue now he had embarked on the problem. Swallowing hard, he said, "I've been there . . . been to several different ones. I can't . . . I mean, it's no use. Just a waste of time."

The laughter subsided as George took in the implication of those words, and Martin's tone of desperation. "I don't understand. Are you saying you're impotent?"

"No. At least, for twelve months, I thought I was. Now I know I'm not, it's a worse worry than the first."

Putting out a hand, the medical man said, "Come in and sit down. If you close the door behind you, we won't be overheard by any of those damned messengers forever flitting in and out. They pretend not to understand any but the most basic English, but they know more of what goes on here than any civil servant."

Too restless to sit, Martin faced his friend while forcing out facts he regretted having to confide in anyone at all. It was a subject about which most men could joke, brag or claim to be an expert, yet shrank from speaking honestly if it was in any way self-demeaning. However, twelve months in a mental ward had taught Martin the ability to lay bare his shortcomings to another. He did so now without sparing himself as he told of an anonymous girl who had brought such a violent return of sexual drive.

"The minute I set eyes on her, I was like a stag in the rutting season,"

149

he admitted tensely. "It was in the presence of a crowd and if they weren't aware of what had happened, they must have been blind. I hardly remember leaving the damned place. I reached my bungalow in time to have the worst attack since leaving hospital. Our next meeting was something I couldn't avoid, much as I tried. Same thing happened, and when we were alone in her garden I . . . well, I damn near had her flat on her back."

"What was her reaction to that?"

"How the hell do I know?" he snapped, finding the entire conversation a strain. "Shocked, I suppose . . . but if you're thinking she worked me around to it, you're way off course."

"She was totally resistant to you?"

"Not exactly." He pushed his hand through his hair in his agitation. "Look, George, this girl is a sweet young English virgin, unaware of what she can do to a man."

"Come off it," put in George caustically.

"Unbelievable though it sounds, it's true," he insisted.

"Yes, I suppose there are one or two on this island who might conceivably be that innocent of life, and, remembering the way you turned on Thea last week when she forced you to stay for a drink at the Beresford house, I think I have the identity of your *femme fatale*."

"This isn't funny, damn you," Martin cried, furious in a flash, "and if you speak one word of this to anyone, I'll break your neck."

"Calm down! We'll get nowhere if you fly off the handle for no reason." The instruction was sharp and commanding as George rose to his feet and rounded the desk to perch on the corner of it. Then he said in quieter manner, "Let's probe a little deeper. For twelve months you had no response, you said. Was that the period you were in hospital?" At Martin's nod, he went on, "Before that, you were as randy as the next man?"

"I visited French brothels, if that's what you mean. We all went. It was one way of getting things into perspective. There was also a girl in Paris during one leave—a nice girl who was just very lonely." He suddenly recalled her very clearly. She had been blonde and young, like Lydia, but she had seen too much of life rather than too little. "I liked her a lot, but I never saw her again."

"Had you planned to meet?"

"Yes, but with the fatalism of most soldiers and their girls during a war. I was blown up and shipped home. That's the end of the story."

"Have you thought a lot about her since?"

Martin sighed briefly. "No. She was a lovely, compassionate, vital human being who gave me all a girl can give, yet I've not thought of her once until this moment. Isn't that terrible?"

George frowned. "Not really. It's what men have done since the world began. Don't start those kind of recriminations to complicate the problem. I see, so everything was fine until you were wounded. What had the neurologists to say on the subject?"

Now they were on purely medical grounds, Martin felt less self-conscious and spoke more freely. "They assured me that the state was only temporary. Actually, I wasn't in the least bothered. When you don't want something, it doesn't upset you not to have it."

His friend gave a faint smile. "A blissful state, I agree."

"I didn't expect it to come back with a great whizz-bang in the presence of a crowd of youngsters, who had been warned that I was slightly dulally," he continued heavily, remembering that tennis party with sharp pain. "I felt more exposed than an unarmed man crossing no-man's-land in bright moonlight."

"Poor bastard," said George sympathetically. "It was this one girl, was it? Well, she's . . . she's . . ." He broke off to look frankly at Martin. "Good God, man, Lydia Beresford is hardly the world's greatest vamp. I'll admit she's pretty . . . very . . . but whatever was it that created such a reaction in you?"

"Whatever it was, I wanted it." Growing diffident once more, he added, "I still want it every time I see her. Now you know why I snapped at Thea for trying to drag me inside for a drink. She damn well knows how I feel."

"Christ, how did that happen?" exclaimed George.

Martin moved away to the window to avoid his friend's scrutiny. "At the Military Ball, Lydia followed me outside into the grounds. I couldn't keep my hands off her, and it appeared our Miss du Lessier had a ringside seat for the entire performance."

George whistled softly. "I knew that young woman would cause havoc out here."

Martin swung round. "She thinks that throwing us together as often as possible is the answer."

"She's right."

"Oh, come on! On three separate occasions now, Lydia has only been saved by the bell. One night, that bell won't ring."

"Then you'll have to defuse the situation some other way, old lad."

"I've been trying, haven't I?" he raged. "I've visited practically every clean brothel in Singapore, and stumbled out with laughter ringing in my ears. Whores leave me cold!"

"The only thing to do, in that case, is to pretend Lydia is a whore, and the girls at the brothel are sweet English virgins. That ought to do the trick."

With the familiar shakes taking hold of him, Martin stared at the man in whom he had so reluctantly confided. "My God, you think this is one big roaring joke, don't you?"

George straightened up immediately and crossed to him. "No, I swear the opposite is true. Neurology is way out of my territory, so my reasoning is that of a layman. I don't know what goes on inside that head of yours any more than you do. Forgive me. I'm simply throwing ideas at you in the hope that one of them proves to be of help." Putting a hand on Martin's arm, he said quietly, "Look lad, I'm in the brotherhood too, you know. They all think I'm *more* than slightly dulally when I foam at the mouth and twitch."

Martin thought that over for a few moments as the shaking subsided. Then he nodded. "Sorry. I should never have bothered you with this, but I had to speak to someone. Sir Hartle is reading the Riot Act because I hide myself away, yet I can go nowhere, it seems, without encountering the Beresfords. I'm at my wits' end, George. It can't be normal to be so violently attracted to one girl, yet be unable to perform with any other."

"You're not exactly a normal chap, are you? No, don't look at me like that. What I'm getting at is the fact that you have seen and experienced things many men have not. Your outlook and reactions are certain to be different now. For example, the heated and pertinent response to Austin Beresford's maxim about doing unto others what you hope they'll do unto you. You have had proof that it doesn't work that way."

"Maybe, but it doesn't give me the right to violate a decent young girl."

"Of course not, but are you so certain it will come to that?"

"Not certain; just afraid that it might."

George was silent while he took up a packet of cigarettes from the desk, offered one to Martin, then lit it and his own. He drew on it and exhaled the smoke before saying, "As I already said, this is completely out of my field, so I suggest that you write to the neurologist you had in England and ask for his views on the problem. Meanwhile, all I can offer is a piece of basic medical theory. Have you raped girls before?"

Martin scowled. "Of course I bloody well haven't."

"Then I can see no reason why you should do so now. Stop the senseless visits to brothels. Why pay out money and get nothing in return?" He gave Martin a sidelong glance. "Do they *really* arouse nothing at all in you?"

He shook his head, tapping the ash from his cigarette with an

152

unsteady finger. "Only embarrassment, and a slight sense of revulsion over the things they offer to do in their desperation to succeed."

"Well, well, the East is full of surprises," George commented with a sympathetic grin. "I truly believe you should give Thea's theory a trial. Meet Lydia as often as you can, although it might be circumspect to steer clear of moonlit gardens with no one else around. Avoiding her, holding yourself under tight control when you can't, makes the situation far too inflammable. Try concentrating on her personality rather than her body, if you can. If you can't, at least kick out the notion that holding her hand will lead to your pulling her into your bed." Punching Martin's shoulder gently, he grinned again. "Go on out and cuddle the girl if you feel like it. It'll do you both no end of good." Pulling out his handkerchief and wiping the back of his neck with it, he went on, "Mind you, if you could only concentrate your wicked thoughts on our Miss du Lessier, you'd be able to get what you wanted without fear of the consequences. At worst, you'd get a box on the ears when it was over, followed by an invitation to do it again the next day."

Martin enjoyed his cigarette for a while, relieved that the *bête noire* had been temporarily quietened. Then he smiled at George. "I suspect the box on the ears would come before I even began, and the invitation would be to vanish before something more painful followed." He poked a finger at George's chest in warning. "Watch out! I've lived for a year amongst those whose behaviour was stripped down layer by layer to reveal the most basic of impulses. I know what I'm talking about."

"Do you?" countered George good-naturedly. "It's a pity you're not so bloody clever about your own basic impulses. You wouldn't then come bothering me for advice."

Thea du Lessier was apparently a subject occupying the thoughts of Damien Lang, Martin discovered as he relaxed that afternoon for tea with the man who shared his bungalow.

"That girl has been like a dose of salts in the Beresford house," Lang commented coarsely. "Fizz and bubble in a sluggish constitution are sure to bring about a violent reaction. Old man Beresford is now fighting not only his son, but the unwelcome inamorata. Mother Margery is trying to gather her remaining chicks beneath her ample plumage to protect them from the plundering she-wolf, and the grapevine says Little Bo Peep is just beginning to discover there are rams as well as ewes in her flock."

Annoyed by his sneering tone, Martin asked, "Can't anyone do anything in this colony without the rest holding a post-mortem?"

"Not a hope," came the amused reply. "Good thing you can't hear what's being said about you, old sport."

Martin continued with his tea. "I daresay I could stand it."

"Of course, the family tries to exercise some kind of control over their guest but, as the saying goes, you can't keep a good girl down —although there are any number of men who aim to try," he finished with a knowing wink.

"Not with Alex back on the island."

"Lucky dog! However, word has it that he runs the risk of being cut off without the proverbial shilling if he has any idea of taking the affair beyond the restrictions set by his elders. Bets on the outcome are about even, at the moment, but du Lessier is reputed to be a match for anyone and it will really depend on how much she wants Mad Alex."

Glancing up as he took another sandwich from the stand beside his chair, Martin asked, "Why do you call him that?"

Lang's smile deepened as he shifted his position so that he was draped elegantly over the arm of his chair, head against the piled cushions.

"You don't know why? I thought you and he were chums." His dark sidelong glance was bright with speculation. "Oh ho, is it really baby sister who interests you? I suppose she's the sugary-sweet compassionate type who would appeal to a chap with your background."

"I asked you a question."

"Mad Alex? Dear boy, he has inherited the Beresford lunacy, without a doubt. Has a lemming-like drive to kill himself by indulging in daring and immensely juvenile pranks. Old Beresford should have allowed him to go to the war, after all. It would have saved him the embarrassment of his son's bizarre attempts to prove his manhood by committing suicide."

That was one of Lang's provocative remarks Martin could not ignore, as he usually did. "Why didn't you go to war, Lang? I have been meaning to ask you."

His companion remained characteristically unruffled. "Ears, old sport. Deaf as a post, at times. I would never have heard the other blighters shout 'Over the top!' and stayed where I was. Some dedicated hero like you would have shot me as a coward then." He threw Martin a quizzical glance. "Did you ever have to do that, Linwood?"

Martin looked back at him steadily. "The only men I ever shot were brave ones in the opposing army."

"Some of our number went, naturally," the other man continued in his usual lazy drawl. "Fired with patriotism and thinking it was the greatest adventure of all time. Can't ask them if it was. None of them came back." He bit into a cake, then waved it at Martin to emphasise his point. "Good thing some of us stayed here to keep the flag flying and the Empire intact. The Beresfords, and other shipping companies, loaned vessels for mercantile purposes. Output of rubber was greatly increased, naturally, to say nothing of coconut and palm oils. Then we mustn't forget the jolly old pineapples. Tins of fruit for our gallant lads at the Front, you know. Did any of it reach you, Linwood?"

Martin shook his head. "Not that I remember."

"Pity. We all worked bally hard, I can tell you. Punishing in this climate. Wars can't be won without the men behind the men behind the guns."

Martin leaned back against his cushions, smiling faintly at his handsome neighbour. "It wasn't necessary to mount such an impassioned self-defence. The ears sufficed."

Lang returned cool scrutiny with some of his own, then gave a short deprecatory laugh. "You're a damned queer cuss, Linwood. I can never quite decide whether you really are as simple as the story goes, or so bally deep you have us all fooled."

Martin continued to eat his tea, enjoying the peacefulness of silence from his companion which allowed him to hear the liquid call of golden orioles in the surrounding trees. There were delights to be found in Singapore. He loved the early mornings when foliage was damp from the watering of the *kebun*, and the smell of wet, warm earth was mixed with heavy perfume from exotic blossoms. There was a certain pleasant anticipation in the rising of a warm breeze and the scent of approaching rain after a sweltering day. The taste of unusual plump fruits for breakfast, eaten on a verandah open to the lushness of tropical greenery, was particularly enjoyable, and nights when the moon was so huge it seemed to fill the whole of his window contained a magic both tormenting and sharply thrilling. Singapore without people would be a far more acceptable place, he decided. Then he immediately revised that decision to allow a few humans into his ideal. George would provide perfect companionship. Lydia would provide perfect everything else. Add the Sing brothers to feed his desire for intellectual discussion, and a new start in this colony might be very satisfying.

Thought of the Sing brothers set him brooding about Sir Hartle's conditions for releasing money for a car, and it seemed almost providential when Lang rose from his draped position, stretched gracefully, and said, "You won't get any dinner tonight, old sport. I've given Wah the evening off. Five of us are having a bite to eat, and some fun afterward. Why don't you join us?"

On the verge of a customary refusal, he realised that the evening might go some way to representing a willingness to mix. "Thanks," he murmured. "What kind of fun afterward?"

"Right first time, Linwood," came the reply accompanied by a broad wink. "My friend knows of a new place, which caters for men with the most eccentric of tastes. You'll be all right, old sport."

Martin's heart sank. Another painted girl with a thrusting much-abused body. Another humiliating retreat after putting twice the normal sum on the tawdry dressing table. This was the price he had to pay for a car.

When they all met up at seven that evening, Martin found Lang's friends were of a similar type. Two had spent all their lives in the colony, yet were more rigidly British in their outlook than Martin. The third was a man of around twenty-eight who had come to the East after the war to take an administrative post, as Martin had. Also an ex-officer, he appeared never to have left his native shores throughout the four years of conflict. Martin felt no resentment of him, he just admired the man's ingenuity in successfully accomplishing what he and most of the others would like to have done. The fourth in the group was a coffee-planter's son who had fallen foul of the authorities in Kenya, and subsequently decided to try his luck with rubber in the Malay States. When that had also failed, he had drifted down to Singapore and started an import-export agency, which was now a flourishing concern. Randal Forster wore an air of wealthy confidence. He was not only the owner of the sleek motor in the driveway, he was the friend Lang had promised would fix Martin up with a girl of extraordinary talent that evening.

They all roared off in the open tourer to a good hotel, where they were served with a first-class dinner and half a dozen bottles of wine for a remarkably small charge because Forster claimed friendship with the under-manager. Martin found that first part of the evening more enjoyable than he had expected. The high spirits of his companions reminded him of officers' mess frivolity, and an excess of wine loosened his tongue to such a degree he was able to match some of their hilariously vulgar stories with some of his own. They all roared with laughter, and Lang slapped him on the back encouragingly.

In this mood of youthful exuberance they all piled into the car again, and headed in a direction Martin knew led to that part of the city which housed the more sinister personalities invariably found in heat-ridden crossroads of the world. Armenian pedlars of pornography, Turkish traders in hashish, Siamese outcasts from monasteries, Egyptian pimps who provided beautiful boys for those with illegal tastes; all these thrived and dealt in the darker merchandise of life behind discreet shop fronts or garishly-painted workshops. In the back rooms of this area, the scene was vastly different. Although a relative newcomer, Martin knew of this sector and its secrets, because his department was forever attempting to stamp out the vicious trade. As fast as men were caught and imprisoned, others moved in to take their places. Crime and vice were on the increase in the colony, expanding with it to cater for the growing population.

Feeling decidedly inebriated by then, Martin was driven to warn his companions of their folly. Struggling up from his recumbent position on the back seat, he said thickly, "I think I should tell you this area is out of bounds to Europeans."

A hand pushed his head roughly down again, and someone shouted, "This isn't a bally schoolboys' outing, Linwood. Nor is it the Western Front. Just shut up, there's a good chap."

It seemed sensible advice, so he rather muzzily did as he was told and followed the others into a narrow alley when they all eventually clambered from the car. Their destination appeared to lie through the interior of a shack at the end of it. By the dim light inside, Martin deduced that they were in a carpenter's workshop. Around the small confines stood half-finished chunks of carving, beautiful chests, pieces of elegant furniture such as graced the houses of wealthy merchants and colonial servants, and heavily carved lampstands. The smell of aromatic camphorwood was pleasant in his nostrils as he gazed around the deserted place. However, when Forster pushed open a door in the further end of the shack, an entirely different smell filtered through. Stifling heat, heavy perfume, and the unmistakable pungence of joss sticks.

By the time Martin entered a large circular room heavily embellished with gilt, and decorated in the vivid colours beloved by the people of the East, he had realised that the extensive apartments behind the carpenter's shop were those of a Chinese love-palace, as they were erroneously named. Forster was greeted by a large Eurasian who appeared to know him well, and the group was conducted to a table of dark wood which stood in an alcove framed by gold-fringed curtains that could be drawn around it for privacy. Soon after they were seated, a girl appeared through a clinking bead curtain and went to the bar for instructions. The Eurasian nodded toward the six Englishmen as he poured drinks, and the girl glanced across at their table. Martin gazed at her. She was small, but had the most beautifully formed body he had ever seen. Every inch of it was outlined by a tight-fitting scarlet cheongsam, slit to the thigh on both sides. Her face appeared to be a perfect oval, with slanted eyes heavily outlined in black. Her mouth was, in truth, the rosebud that enraptured poets forever extolled. The multi-racial collection of men and their painted partners at the other tables were too engrossed to notice her, but Martin could not drag his disbelieving gaze from her, as she put six glasses on a tray to carry across to them.

"There are plenty more like her in the rooms beyond the bead curtain," said a voice in his ear. "You can have them singly, or two or three at a time."

He turned to find Forster smiling at him, his face demon-like in the light thrown from red lanterns on the walls. Martin realised that he, too, must resemble an inhabitant of hell sitting there.

"Tonight is your introduction to Ammul," Forster went on. "Now he knows you are a friend of mine, you'll have no trouble whatever getting what you want. If your tastes run to extremes not already available here, Ammul will scour Singapore to find it for you." He gave a knowing wink. "Mind you, it'll cost a little extra, so you'd better think up a good story for your godfather. He might not consider this a good idea, in your state."

With the mood of enjoyment slipping away fast, Martin turned as the girl arrived beside him with the drinks. It was a shock to discover that she was no more than a child; a human doll whose eyes stared at him with the same blank expression as those of her toy counterparts, while her lips smiled automatically.

"By God, she's no older than twelve!" he said, turning back to his companions.

The ex-officer smiled at him, "She has forgotten more than most females hope to discover, take my word for it."

Looking at Forster, Martin said, "Are you aware that I work for the department dedicated to closing down places like this?"

His eyes narrowed as he nodded. "It's always sound policy to have friends in the right places, old boy. Why do you think I extended the privilege of an introduction to Ammul? You wouldn't be stupid enough to bite the hand that feeds you."

"Are all his girls as young as this one?"

"Any colour, any shape, any size. It's Ammul's slogan."

Feeling slightly sick, Martin said emphatically, "I don't need your bloody introductions, Forster, and you certainly won't get any favours from me in respect of this place."

"Shut up, Linwood," hissed Damien Lang from the far end of the table. "You're beginning to shout, and that's dangerous in a place like this."

"Very dangerous," Forster impressed on him. "Your presence here has been noted, believe me, and these people have long memories.

Drink up, and stop thinking about King and Country, for once. We're here to enjoy ourselves."

Martin said no more. After all, he had seen the tragedy of women stripped and raped by gangs of drunken troops. He had seen nuns after they had been abused and humiliated. Why care about child prostitutes? They were, at least, paid for their services, and certainly received better food and care than their sisters in ramshackle hovels outside. The evening had turned sour, however, and the crowning moment of disgust was when he entered a room containing a bed covered with purple silk sheets, led by a girl wearing a costume resembling a white Persian kitten, who had been especially selected for him by the others. Once the door closed behind them, the girl changed into a veritable tigress. The tussle lasted longer than usual, because he dreaded the news of his inability being passed on to Lang. Groping his way through the ordeal, he fought the nausea her astonishing actions induced in him, and tried to suggest that he found her entirely unsatisfactory. He succeeded too well. The girl grew distraught and burst into tears, begging him not to report her to Ammul. As he struggled back into his clothes, he realised that the drink he had been given by the owner of the place had contained more than simple alcohol. The room was starting to swim around him, and the heat was suffocating. He must have passed out, because he was lying on the floor with the girl anxiously patting his cheeks when he regained conscious thought.

After paying the girl, who would have to pass the money on to Ammul, he left the room in a confused state and stood for a moment or two in the corridor, leaning against the wall. Despite his confusion and slight blurring of his vision, he nevertheless easily recognised the man who slipped from one of the rooms and left swiftly by a rear door. Shock kept him where he was for some time afterward as he told himself Lydia's father had been that man. A much-respected businessman with positions on boards and committees, a man of wealth and influence who had a wife and family, a man of conservative tastes and with a strict moral code, frequented a brothel offering partners younger than his own daughter? No, it was a mad, disgusting, inconceivable idea. Yet he knew it was Austin Beresford he had seen.

The discovery still obsessed him when his companions, now minus Forster, gathered once more in the outer room, well pleased with themselves and eager for further diversions. Cramming into the motor again, they set off with a roar into the noisy, garish atmosphere of a Singapore evening. Martin had lost all trace of time when the car pulled up with a squeal of brakes on a small jetty, where a paddle steamer dressed overall with Chinese lanterns and bunting was preparing to pull away from the shore. His companions scrambled from their seats shouting instructions to hold the gangplank, and Martin found himself being hauled along in their midst to the sound of cheers from the laughing young people aboard, who spurred them on. No sooner were they on deck than the boat moved off, with a great thrashing of water that added to the uproar of gaiety beating against his ears. It did not take long for Martin to guess they had joined a private party to which none of his group had actually been invited.

Instinctively backing away from noise and crowds he sought a dark narrow passage alongside the wheelhouse, and stood leaning against it hoping to steady his racing pulse and swimming head. Even so, the shore which was growing further and further distant was dancing up and down, despite a flat sea. The tall centres of commerce, the graceful banking houses, the elegant hotels with their palm-secluded gardens were all shifting dizzily before his eyes, and the cranes, winches and godowns of the mercantile docks swayed back and forth as the steamer glided past them. Sick and depressed, he closed his eyes against the glittering shoreline. All he could then see was that tall spare man with a harsh face and very brown moustache coming furtively from that room to return home, where he would fondle and kiss goodnight a daughter he professed to cherish. George had once told him to forget his own weakness and look for those in the people around him, but this was one Martin would rather not have seen.

The evening celebrated the official engagement of an eminent banker's son to the daughter of a planter. In the eyes of the majority the marriage would constitute more a business merger than a love-match. That view did not prevent practically every affluent youngster presently in Singapore from accepting an invitation to the floating party, where champagne would flow and dancing to a ten-piece band would continue until morning. Lydia had been gently forbidden to go by her parents, and Alex would have preferred to spend the evening alone with Thea if she had not been avid to attend a function she claimed would give her ideas for her novel, which had finally been started. Reluctantly, he had agreed to escort her and now stood watching as she danced a two-step with a bronzed young planter wearing a white dinner jacket, who was studying her ravenously after long months up-country with no white women save the listless wives of colleagues. Who could blame the fellow? Thea looked sensational tonight in a dress which had brought a gasp from everyone on first sight of her. It had even caused their hosts to refuse her access to the steamer, until they realised who she was. In an audacious and flagrant defiance of attitudes, the girl he loved had chosen to attend the party dressed in a Chinese cheongsam of white pure silk delicately embroidered with black and silver dragons. It hugged her slender body from the high upstanding collar to mid-thigh, where a long slit in the right seam gave her freedom of movement and revealed more of her leg than European fashions allowed. With her short black hair dressed in Chinese style, and long jet spears hanging from her ears, Thea exactly resembled one of the high-born daughters of influential Chinese on the island, who were occasionally to be glimpsed on a rare outing from domestic confinement comparable to that of the strictest convent. The effect was stunning, and typical of the girl she was, but her display of individuality also brought trouble.

There had been a major confrontation before they set out. Margery had been upset to the point of ending in tears, and his father had gone beyond his usual restrained disapproval to openly forbid Thea to attend the party in such a costume. When she had pointed out, reasonably enough, that his protest was not inspired by the dress itself but by what it represented which was exactly the point she was making by wearing it, Austin had then forbidden Alex to escort her unless she dressed in something more suitable. Knowing Thea would go unescorted, if necessary, and seeing his opportunity to ease into his proposed break from their authority, he had said that he supported her right to wear whatever she wished so long as it did not exceed the borders of decency. Angry words had flown back and forth until Alex had taken Thea's arm and walked out, putting his father's excessive aggression down to the fact that he had had an early dinner and returned to his office for an hour or two to work on some legal documents. Austin had been returning from this session as he and Thea were about to leave the house.

Alex looked at his watch. They had been at sea no more than an hour. Thoroughly bored, he continued to study Thea and the voracious planter through half-closed eyes. The guests were the same young people who attended every party in Singapore. They had surely said all they could say to each other long ago. All he could see of the shore was the occasional flickering lamp on a sampan, and the faint outline of palms against the skyline. They were cruising along quiet stretches of the coast now, and he was trapped on that damned boat where Thea was being pawed and ogled by every man present, until the engaged couple decided enough was enough. Turning his back to the awning-covered stern, he leaned on the rail knowing he must tell her tonight about his plan to go to England. The sound of laughter and music was snatched away by the breeze, leaving only the throbbing pulse of the pistons and the surge of water threshed by the paddle-blades as he stared out across the dark sea. The odours of salt spray, engine oil, sisal ropes, tar and ancient weathered wood mingled with the appetising waft from food being prepared for a buffet on which no expense had been spared. He would be leaving all this behind; leaving the only life he had known to venture into strange and exciting territory. He could not wait, but what if she refused to go with him?

"O, what can ail thee, knight-at-arms?" quoted a teasing voice beside him, and he turned to find Thea holding two glasses of champagne and looking at him with the frankness which constantly challenged him.

"Shouldn't you be reciting the words of a Chinese poet, rather than Keats?"

Her golden-brown eyes glowed with amusement as she offered him a glass of the chilled sparkling wine. "Darling, the one thing I love above all else about you is the inbred colonial caution you can't quite shake off. Admit it, sweetie, you enjoy having everyone here knowing you're my lover."

"I'm not, though, am I?"

She kissed him lightly on the mouth. "Sweetie, even I have enough manners not to seduce my hosts' son beneath their own roof. What I want for you is freedom, not an exchange of captivities."

Slipping his free arm around her and keeping her close, he said, "What I want for us both, is an exciting future and a lasting marriage. Darling, I'm not going back to Manila next week. It wouldn't be a true break from the family because Father would still control *Berondel* one hundred percent. Besides, it isn't what I really want. Now wait and listen," he cautioned as she began to look concerned. "I've worked it all out very carefully before giving you even a hint of my plans, but I can't leave it much longer before breaking the news at home. It'll cause an unprecedented scene, and I don't think you should be present when it happens despite the fact that you figure prominently in my plans."

"Alex, for God's sake get to the point," she exclaimed.

Eagerly, he launched into the details of his intention to enter the world of aviation in the homeland of which he knew so little. Thea listened intently, her warm gaze unwavering as he outlined his project for the future and his sincere promise that their life together would be as exciting and adventurous as he could make it."

"I'll have to make the announcement before next Wednesday, when I'm supposed to leave for Manila," he told her. "We'll sail as soon as possible after that. I've no wish to prolong the agony all this is certain to cause and, since my mind is made up, it would be unfair to them to hang around causing further tittle-tattle among their so-called friends." He drank the champagne swiftly, feeling that he needed Dutch courage before asking her verdict. "Well, what do you think?"

Her expression of approval and admiration was all he had hoped it would be. "It's perfect, darling. Absolutely perfect! I'm so very thrilled that you're finally going to fulfil your yearning for life in a field for which you're so exactly suited."

The fervour of his kiss betrayed the extent of his relief at her response. The night was suddenly lit with stars so bright, he felt he was already flying up there amongst them.

Thea drew away, laughing. "Cool off, darling! I also have enough manners not to seduce you in the middle of someone's engagement party. You may have to hire a room in a seedy hotel for the purpose before you leave."

The stars began to dim. "What does that mean, Thea?"

"I shall have to stay here until the book's finished, of course."

He stared at her. "You don't mean that."

"Alex, you surely took that into account when you made your plans. I told you it was something I had to do."

"You told me I had to break with my family before you'd think about marriage. You told me I had to choose between them and you."

"Yes, darling, I did," she told him urgently, "but surely you're taking this wonderful step for your own sake and for that of your entire future, not because I placed conditions on my commitment." Taking both his arms from around her waist, she held his hands captive. "Alex, you have a right to your own life; a right to do whatever you long to do. Tell your people in the morning; go the day after. As soon as my novel is finished, I'll join you. You'll need breathing space in which to establish yourself before taking on a wife. Sweetie, the important thing is for you to feel *free*. Our love is merely an exciting extra."

"To me it's an exciting everything," he told her bitterly. "I mistakenly believed that you were telling me you felt as I do when you issued your ultimatum. I'm offering to throw up all I've ever known and launch out into an exciting but chancy future, for your sake, and that apparently still isn't enough for you. What do you want, Thea? What more must I do before you're satisfied with me?"

"Wait for me a little longer," she responded fiercely. "We all have our own need to break free of the bonds around us. Allow me that freedom, too."

"You already have more freedom than anyone I know," he said. "Look at you now—defying convention simply because it's there to be flouted. You speak your mind under the pretext of modern emancipation; you break rules with blithe disregard for whom you offend. You use your body to tease men until they make fools of themselves, then tell them they must wait for what you've promised them. I'd call that a hell of a lot of freedom."

"Ha!" she cried angrily. "Now we have the true colonial in the coffee-coloured topee speaking."

"No, Thea," he cried, "it's a man who loves you to desperation, who's trying to understand what you're doing to him. Are you refusing to come with me because *he* is still in England . . . your former lover?" he forced himself to ask.

She shook her head. "He was killed in action."

"So it's just this ridiculous desire to write a bestselling novel that is coming between us, is it?" he demanded hotly.

"No, Alex, you're the only thing coming between us," she flamed. "I'm going to enjoy the rest of this party before having to return to the situation we left earlier this evening. You Beresfords really are *unbelievable!*"

Alex was left standing by the rail as she rejoined a merry group heading for the buffet, now spread in a tempting display to delight eye and appetite. Turning to face the sea, he gripped the rail tightly. What a fool he had been to believe she really cared for him, to think that offering his life to her on a plate would earn her love. While he had been in Manila she had dined and danced with all the bachelors in the colony, if the stories he had heard were to be believed. No suggestion of pining for him, as he had for her during their parting. What a fool he was to imagine a girl with her liberated personality would consider marriage with him, or anyone else. He should have seduced her long ago, instead of respecting her pleas not to rush her into bed. Doubtless, the lover killed in action had been more astute and taken her by force.

Sick with the pain of rejection, he considered the plan he had thought so exciting and found it no longer beckoned him. Without Thea, nothing made sense. Going to England alone spelled isolation and unhappiness. Yet could he remain in Singapore, seeing her every day and still wanting her despite her heartlessness? He had metaphorically severed his ties with *Berondel*, and all the confines of colonial life already, which left him in limbo, unable to continue his present path, but not yet treading the new, now less attractive one. As he stood staring down at the sea, lost in uncertainty, time passed him by until he grew aware of two people nearby indulging in a sexual tussle. Still abstracted, he returned to his study of the distance until a voice called to him softly.

"Lost your girl, I see, Beresford."

Glancing back at the pair, he discovered them to be Damien Lang and Lady Weyford's niece, Fay Christie. He did not care for either one and was about to ignore them when the obnoxious Lang nodded his head in the direction of the bow.

"I've had my suspicions about that blighter all along. Shell shock is a damned convenient excuse for bad behaviour, if you ask me, but the fair sex fall for it every time."

Alex hardly noticed the other two drift away as he stared at the couple isolated in the bow, heads practically touching, aware of nothing but each other. They created an attractive picture—a slender pliant girl whose hands moved with expressive grace, and a tall rangy man whose nervous vitality was betrayed by the manner in which he jabbed a finger at the rail to emphasise his words. They appeared to be arguing intently, until he made to move away. She put a restraining hand on his arm; spoke an urgent plea as she gazed up into his face. Then he slowly surrendered, to remain at her side. The squat vessel was now pushing past brown-sailed junks with their painted eyes on the prow, past hooded sampans low in the water from the weight of three generations housed within, past *tongkangs* loaded with rice or coal, and past all manner of ships including those of the *Berondel Line*. The man and girl in the bow saw none of them, so engrossed were they in each other. Alex grew cold as he watched them. Was Martin Linwood the reason for Thea's refusal to leave Singapore?

"Ah, Alex, old boy, there you are! Bin looking all over the bally ole tub for you." A figure lurched into his line of vision, cutting off his view of the man and girl who had both so unsettled his life. "This's a damned flat affair, 'f you don't mind my saying. Let's liven it up, eh?"

Ferdy Hancock's brand of nonsense was the last thing Alex wanted right then. "You've had too much bubbly. Go off and sober up somewhere, or you'll never last the night out," he recommended sharply. "Go on, clear off, Ferdy!"

"Ah, ah, ah," chided his inebriated friend, staying where he was beside Alex. "*You* haven't had 'nough bubbly, ole chap. Never known you stay sober at a party. S'why the affair's so flat. Knew there must be a reason for it."

"Clear off," Alex repeated, turning back to stare miserably at water being churned into white foaming froth by the powerful blades of the paddle. Why did Martin Linwood continue to hold her interest? Was it only for Lydia's sake? He recalled how they had run in from the rain at the Military Ball, in such accord. Had he overlooked what was staring him in the face?

"S'matter with you?" Ferdy's face was thrust in front of his as his friend's unsteadiness threw him against the rail. "Not been the same ole Alex since Theah came. S'trouble with girls. Make a fellow damned *dull*. Always do. Never fail. C'mon, have some bubbly. Liven things up, eh? Know you can do it, ole bean. What say you climb the rigging. Jus'like your dear old grandad. Eh, what say?'' Ferdy poked him in the ribs to gain some response. "I'll lay a wager you can't climb the rigging, I will.''

Alex edged away from him moodily. "It's a paddle steamer, you fool.''

"Climb the paddle, then. Wager you can't climb the paddle.'' The absurd challenge prompted a bout of drunken giggling. "Climb the paddle. Even ole Alex can't do that!''

Alex continued to stare at the water churning noisily below him as the blades thrust through the sea. As he watched, he grew aware of the steady deep pulse of the pistons that turned the great paddle wheels as the bows cut through the dark sea. Almost level with the deck on which he stood rose the massive black curve of the paddle guard. No more than a few feet away, on the other side of the bulwark, the blades were slicing through the water and rising from it covered in seaweed. Beneath that guard were blades so powerful they could slice through almost anything.

He leaned over the bulwark and studied the guard. It was broad—so broad it was impossible to see the outer edge of it in the darkness. Nor was it possible to gain an accurate idea of its exact curve. Anything falling into the sea behind that wheel would be swept away from the boat by the boiling surge of water; anything falling in front of it would be mangled by the blades as they passed over it. Alex glanced once more at the bows. Martin was shaking his head gently as Thea stood laughing up at him.

"All right, Ferdy,'' he said swiftly, "let's liven up this damned party. "I'll not only climb the paddle, I'll drink a whole bottle of bubbly while I'm doing it.''

His friend began shouting for someone to bring the champagne, and the attention of those nearby was soon caught by the activity. Alex stripped off his dinner jacket, then his shoes and socks. The news spread to more of the revellers, and they crowded around him, some telling him not to be a fool, others egging him on to perform a feat so risky they were drunk on the excitement of the prospect. Pushing away a few restraining hands, Alex stared just once more at the white foam directly below. One slip out there and . . . Another glance at the bow destroyed the last remnants of caution. The pair were totally oblivious of what was happening.

Taking the bottle of champagne from Ferdy, Alex climbed over the bulwark until he was standing on the paddle guard with one hand on the rail, where spectators were jostling for a good view. There was a shout from above, and Alex glanced at the wheelhouse to see the captain gesticulating violently that he should return to the deck.

For answer, Alex held the champagne aloft. "Cheers, skipper!"

When he turned back to face the sea it seemed blacker than before, and immensely lonely out there. For a moment only he hesitated, then knew he had no choice but to go on. Letting go the handrail, he took his first step forward. Beneath his bare feet the metal shuddered from the motion of the blades it protected, and he realised the guard was slippery with salt spray. It grew colder as he moved away from the waist of the ship, and he shivered with the chill of excitement. The element of risk, the sense of challenge now had him firmly in their grip. It was still impossible to determine the full width of the guard ahead of him as he took another step. The vibration beneath his feet increased: he could hear nothing but the deafening sound of rotating machinery and rushing water as he inched forward. He forgot those behind him watching as he was whipped by flying spray, tugged at by the wind, shaken by the immense power over which he was walking.

It was difficult to keep his balance with nothing ahead on which to fix his glance. Ahead, and on each side, there was blackness to match that of the metal beneath his feet. Yet, as he moved gradually forward, arms outstretched to counter the effects of the breeze and the shaking of the surface across which he was walking, the darkness became patchy to reveal the outer edge of the guard overhanging a slightly paler sea.

Soon, he was there, right at the edge, and that was the most dangerous moment of all because he had to turn his back on the sea to face those awaiting his return. For the space of a second he looked down to where he could now see the blades thumping into the water one after the other with relentless power. Then he began to pivot, slowly and carefully, on the balls of his feet until he could see the lanterns, the white bulwark, and the mass of pale faces staring out at him.

Why go back? a voice whispered to him. *Isn't it better out here where no man can rival you?* It was at that moment that he spotted a figure in white silk standing right beside the wheelhouse, watching as silently as those crowding around her. With great deliberation he put the bottle of champagne to his mouth, tipped back his head, and began to drink. Only when the bottle ceased to gush liquid into his convulsive throat did he straighten up again. Staring at the ship there appeared to be twice as many faces looking at him now.

The unsteadiness of the metal beneath him seemed to have increased, and there was a moaning, groaning noise below which surely he had not noticed before. It had turned colder, and that sense of isolation was now almost frightening. When he put one foot experimentally forward he felt amazingly giddy. The nearest handhold looked a long way away. The blackness around him had closed in. His feet were now icy and numb, so that he was not even certain he was still on the metal guard. He took another cautious step forward, wobbled frantically, and threw out his arms to seek steadiness. His dulled senses heard a gasp rise up from the watching faces, and he caught himself grinning drunkenly. That put the wind up the faint-hearted fools!

After risking another step, he realised that he still had the empty bottle in his hand. He dropped it, and it rattled down the curving guard to vanish into the darkness way below. It was a long way down there; a long way to that foaming turbulent water. He tried to concentrate on those watching him, but their images were jiggling up and down. His senses swam, but he knew he could do it; knew he could reach their outstretched hands. There was nothing he could not do to show her that he really was free and master of his own destiny. So, despite his numbed feet and the effects of the champagne, he successfully edged closer and closer to safety until he gripped the handrail with one shaking outstretched hand. There, he glanced up to see Thea's large amber eyes gazing at him with the fire of excitement in them. He tried to speak to her, but the lump of elation in his throat prevented words from forming.

Then he realised that Martin Linwood was beside her, watching him with an unreadable expression, and what he had done suddenly became an empty deed. The sense of triumph faded, as he saw the feat as no more than a pathetic attempt to match up to a man who had no further need to prove himself. Crushed by that thought, he flung out his other hand to pull himself in. He was too careless. His foot slipped on the wet metal; he fell sideways trying desperately to retain his hold on the rail. The strain on his chilled fingers was too great, and he clawed wildly at the paddle guard for a handhold. Slowly, amid the sound of screams, he began to slide downward over the curving metal toward the churning water below.

He was tossed and pummelled by the turbulence; dragged down, down into blackness that roared in his ears. There was pain in lungs fighting to take in air, and his heartbeat thundered in his torso as a result of the punishment to his body. The instinct of a prime swimmer led him to rely on natural buoyancy, so he wasted no precious oxygen or energy in struggling. It would be needed when he surfaced. A lifetime seemed to pass before he saw the stars overhead, and the lights of the steamer that was still pushing its way through the sea. Gasping, he trod water while fighting the effects of champagne and lack of oxygen. The decks of the ship were still lined with people, and the white circle of a lifebelt bobbed in the waves between himself and the vessel.

When he considered himself able to make the effort, Alex struck out for it in a slow easy crawl. Sobered by the ducking, he remembered the reason for his escapade and felt deeply depressed. It would achieve nothing but public confirmation of his immaturity or inherited eccentricity. Better take Thea's advice to cut and run—without her, that much she had made clear. Yet she had looked at him with glowing excitement as he had almost made it back to her on that paddle guard. What did she really want of him? Did she know the answer herself?

To his astonishment, someone was already clinging to the lifebelt. The thin pale face was twisted by a grimace of pain. As Alex grasped the hard white surface facing him, Martin gasped, "I've got the bally cramp. Sorry."

As they rose and fell with the violence of the wash from the steamer, Alex stared at him across the circular buoy by the light from the moon.

"What the hell are you doing here?"

"Came in after you. Pure instinct. Forgot you swam like a fish," came his jerky reply.

"Can't you?" Alex demanded.

"Not bloody likely. I must have been drunker than I thought."

All at once, Alex sensed the echo of a far-off experience he had never had. *This* was camaraderie. *This* was danger shared, no matter the risk to oneself. *This* was the bond which had existed between young men whose lives had been in each other's hands, no matter what personal differences they had. This, then, was what he so envied the man now facing him across a small circle keeping them both afloat.

Chapter 10

That Saturday evening was doomed from the outset. The host family was deeply divided, and none of the guests had wanted to attend the dinner party. Those conditions did not augur well for a gathering which Austin and Margery had felt obliged to arrange in order to thank a young man who had a most unwelcome habit of intruding in their lives, for his prompt action during an incident which had fed the gossips of Singapore for several delightful sessions. The whole colony had enjoyed the news that the wild young Beresford boy had performed a drunken stunt at the Oxenford party, which had led to his plunging into the sea just short of the paddle-wheels, from where he had been dramatically rescued by the unstable godson of the colony's most revered judge. Despite the plain facts, details of the affair had been outrageously exaggerated, until the whole island now firmly believed Alex had been snatched from certain death amid the paddle blades by a war-hero who had dived unflinchingly into danger, while the remainder of the guests had watched paralysed by fear. Beside themselves with anger over their son's behaviour at a party which he had been forbidden to attend with Thea dressed as a Chinese, the Beresfords had nevertheless felt obliged to make a public gesture toward Martin Linwood and the Weyfords in order to satisfy social demands. To say it went against the grain for them would be a gross understatement of the way they felt about that whole sorry evening.

Martin had personal reasons for not wishing to visit that family, apart from the fact that he had repeatedly explained that there was no necessity for the gesture. Sir Hartle dreaded the evening, because Lady Weyford had only been constrained to attend after a bitter exchange and was making no secret of the fact. Fay Christie had been similarly compelled to accompany her indulgent aunt and uncle to what she felt would be a dull affair in the presence of Thea, whom she heartily disliked. She was still smarting over the sensation the girl had made at the party in her Chinese dress.

Austin was in a blacker mood than anyone had suffered. His son's escapade, coming after the quarrel over Thea's dress earlier that evening, had been the final straw to break his forbearance. Alex had created the proof of family wildness he had struggled all his life to banish. He had spent the following two nights at his club, not trusting himself to be in the same house as the son who had let him down so totally. Margery was wretched and miserable over the chasm which had opened in family ranks, over the hold Thea apparently had on her son, and over the decline in Lydia's behaviour since that girl had been welcomed into the household. She blamed Austin for being too lenient with Alex, and blamed herself for ever agreeing to her brother's request to mother a girl who was no real relative. Everything else, she blamed on Anna du Lessier's liberated daughter.

Alex, himself, was sick to death of the whole affair. It needed no strictures from others to tell him he had made a fool of himself that evening, yet he could tell no one why he had done it. Although he had known in his heart Thea would respond as she had to his plea to travel to England with him, the blow had not been lessened when she had done so. She was under his skin in a way which had no cure, yet she seemed unaware of the pressure she was putting on him from all directions. He was afraid to leave her behind when he put half the world between them, for he would surely lose her, yet his relationship with his parents was now so strained he knew the best thing to do was announce his decision and go. All he lacked was the chance to do so. With his father shunning the house, he had no hope of announcing anything. Small wonder he dressed and went downstairs, after watching the day die slowly behind the fan palms, dreading the coming few hours.

In the sitting room his parents were silent and tense, making little effort to drink the pale sherry Ling had poured for them. Lydia, in a gown of pink slipper-satin, looked radiant and excited. Alex frowned. Was his sister really heading for trouble where Martin Linwood was concerned? She would have to be stopped, if so, but what was the best way of going about it? Any hint to his parents would be disastrous for her. It was not something he felt able to broach with his sister, so the alternative was to warn Linwood. His frown deepened. That man was caught up in so many aspects of his life, it seemed, yet something told him Martin was no happier about the curious bond than he. Was there even some secret link between him and Thea? They had certainly been lost in each other on the steamer.

Alex had seen nothing of Thea since the affair he wished he could be allowed to forget. For three days, she had been locked in her room working on her book. He hoped it meant that she had decided to sail with him and was completing as much of it as possible before leaving the East, but when he had scrambled over the roof to her room at night, however, those doors had also been locked against him. Denied the opportunity to mend the breach he felt had opened between them, and uncertain where he now stood, he determined to clarify the situation tonight. Then he would tell his family that he was relieving them of the embarrassment of his presence in the colony. His departure would constitute the final sensation performed by Justin Beresford's grandson. Perhaps he could then simply live his life without his every action being viewed through a social microscope.

Thea was apparently waiting until the last minute to join the family which held her responsible for their present woes. Alex prayed that she would not choose to be too much of an individualist this evening. It promised to be difficult enough without adding an outrageous dress certain to shock and offend those who had no understanding of her personality, as he had. When she did put in an appearance, however, it coincided with the arrival of the hero-designate. The pair entered the sitting room side by side, but any suspicion Alex had of their relationship was instantly dispelled by the optical exchange between Martin and Lydia that fairly sizzled across the room. If this man was the reason for Thea's determination to remain in Singapore, he was plainly unaware of the fact. No one could fail to interpret the message flashed to Lydia. It was a disturbing one. Martin Linwood was clearly greatly affected by Alex's young sister, and in a manner that made him less than happy. Was Damien Lang right in suggesting that he was a damned sight deeper than anyone guessed? Alex was further disturbed when his father came forward to recite a stilted speech of thanks for the prompt action on the steamer. Their guest feigned unawareness of the hand offered him as he, just as stiltedly, disclaimed any credit for the rescue of a man who had not required help. There was a curiously hostile attitude in the supposed hero which, in view of the fact that the evening was being held in his honour, deepened Alex's conviction that the next few hours would be unmitigated purgatory.

"Take that scowl off your face, darling," said Thea, as her hand slipped through the crook of his arm. "You should be tickled pink that Martin is so honestly relieving you of the public obligation to owe him your life."

He turned to look down at her. "The courage was his, nevertheless."

"Nonsense!" She smiled in a manner that told him nothing had changed between them. "He was tighter than you were, and equally reckless. That insufferable creature Lang, and his cronies, had clearly given him some kind of potion designed to render him paralytic. It's the kind of stupidity that would amuse idiots like them. Poor Martin was hardly aware of where he was, when I came upon him trying to climb over the side in the belief that he was going ashore. I was in the midst of talking some sense back into him when you created your diversion. Once you slipped, Martin jumped in before I could stop him." Her head wagged admonishingly. "You men really are impossible. A woman would never indulge in such pranks simply to express her personality."

The evening had suddenly begun to glow. "A man would never dress in Chinese costume to attend a party, just to create a sensation."

She laughed. "All right, I deserved that . . . and I do so love you when you're roused."

"I've been roused for the past three days," he told her pointedly. "It hasn't helped, you know, to be shut out so completely."

"I'm sorry, Alex. I didn't mean to be such a bitch to you. I was so inspired, I just had to keep going until it was all down on paper."

"All through the nights, as well?"

She made a face. "The locked verandah doors were for our own good. I was in the perfect mood to be seduced, so I barred us from temptation."

"Thea! If I'd known that, I'd have kicked down the doors."

"Exactly!"

"Are you still in the mood?" he asked eagerly.

"Yes, darling . . . but it really wouldn't help you, in the long run," she told him apologetically, "or me. If we become lovers, you'll never go to England without me. I couldn't be responsible for holding your back now you have the bit between your teeth, so I'd go with you. No, listen," she urged, at his dawning delight, "if I go back to England with you, I'll never finish the book. It means so much to me that I'd let it stand between our happiness. I don't want that, Alex. When we give ourselves to each other, I want my surrender to be total."

Feeling like a starving man who has been offered a meal only to have it snatched away, he asked yet again, "Why is this book so damned important?"

The amber of her eyes clouded momentarily. "It'll give me back my . . . my soul."

He was uncomprehending. "Your *soul?*"

"There's only one other person in the world who would understand that. I don't expect you to, and it would be useless to try and explain." Her fingers linked through his as she squeezed his hand. "I was beastly to you at the party. My only excuse is that I was in a rebellious mood after your family's bigoted objection to my Chinese dress, so I hit out at you when you also began to criticise my actions. I know they were what prompted your stunt on the paddle guard, and I'm truly repentant. But, please, Alex, follow your star. Just as soon as the book is finished, I promise I'll follow you and give you anything you want, with or without a gold ring."

Thrilled, born again at such reviving words, he murmured huskily,

"You choose bloody inconvenient times to make such promises."

Her smile was a mere shadow of its usual brilliance. "Perhaps that's why I make them."

"You drive me nearly crazy sometimes," he told her then. "You're doing it now, and the evening has barely begun."

"Oh dear, I'm trying my best to be well behaved, for your sake, darling. I put on a frock that is so infernally dull, you showed more interest in Martin than me when we came into the room, but I can't promise to keep up such goodness all the evening. The feline Fay will feel one up on me over the dress, so I fear I might have to deflate her some other way."

His smile broke through at that. "You have my full permission to do whatever you like with Fay . . . and thanks for the dress. You might consider it infernally dull, but the body inside it is the only thing that'll get me through this terrible evening."

It certainly promised to go from bad to worse. The Weyfords arrived extremely late, and it needed little imagination to guess that they had quarrelled *en route*. Sir Hartle was over-effusive, his wife was icy as her well-bred stare assessed the contents of a house she had never before deigned to grace. In consequence, Margery grew over-effusive, and Austin became icy. Fay, clad in jade-green lace, mewed insincerely in reply to every remark made to her, and smiled at Thea in her unexceptional beige dress as if she were a sacrificial mouse. Martin was mostly silent, his jaw so rigid it hardly moved whenever he was obliged to speak. However, it was not until they all sat down to a dinner on which Margery had lavished so much thought and effort, that the fur really began to fly.

After staring for some time at the huge sapphire on Thea's finger as if she suspected it must be glass, Lady Weyford suddenly looked up at her to ask, "Why do you have your mother's name, Miss du Lessier? I have heard it hinted that your father was related to the composer, Tosti."

Thea's lovely eyes gazed back at the stern-faced woman in utter innocence, and Alex adored her when she said, "Yes, but on the disreputable side of the family, unfortunately. Father was a bastard, you know. Mother was heartbroken when she found out, but it was too late. They were married by then."

Lady Weyford appeared unable to rise to that, so Fay stepped into the breach. "Hardly a pleasant thing to discover about the man one has just married."

Thea turned to her. "Exactly. It meant she wouldn't get her hands on any of the Tosti money—a dreadful disappointment. She was obliged to start writing risqué books in order to keep body and soul together.

When I was born, she decided that I would derive greater benefit from being a du Lessier than a Tosti." She dipped her spoon into the clear soup before adding, "I no longer wish to be connected with her shocking reputation, so I intend to change my name before long."

"To Tosti?" enquired Sir Hartle.

Thea sipped her soup delicately, then smiled at him. "Oh no. I have in mind something much more respectable and English."

Alex began to tingle with awareness. He knew she was finding it impossible to contain her rebellion against this kind of polite play-acting, and was baiting them all. All the same, he could not help relishing the fact that she was speaking of their shared secret. It was soon obvious that her words were telling Fay something entirely different, however.

Seated next to him she said quietly, under cover of the removal of soup plates, "They make an attractive pair, don't you think?"

He could not mistake her meaning, and she was right. His mother had deliberately placed Thea beside Martin at the table, and there was a certain aura about them which was indisputable.

"It must be quite a problem for her," Fay added.

"Problem?"

The girl smiled her cat-like pleasure at his confusion. "To decide between you and him. At the moment, Uncle has full control over Martin's money, but a girl like Thea could soon change that." At his frown, she asked in feigned surprise, "Don't tell me you have never considered that. Why else would she waste her time on a man like him?"

"Thea is probably quite as well off as any of us," he put in caustically. "Don't tell me you have never considered *that*."

"Everyone can always use more. You see, there's very little to choose between you, so far as she is concerned. You and Martin are the same age, and both pretty unstable, but she'd have to fight your entire family to get you. Martin is there on a plate, just so long as she can take his muddled mind off your little sister. He has been looking at her the whole evening as if she would make a better meal than the one being served to him at this table. You really should do something about that, Alex."

The comment touched too many raw spots, and sounded far too plausible. He hit out. "You really should do something about Damien Lang, my dear Fay. That fellow has a doubtful reputation where girls are concerned, and he mixes with a very rum crowd. You'll soon find yourself the subject of some very unpleasant gossip."

Her pointed face sharpened. "Isn't that a case of the pot calling the kettle black?"

"Maybe, but I know I'm a pot. You seem to think you're the cream jug."

175

"Alexander, Sir Hartle has twice asked you a question," admonished his mother, flushed and flustered over an evening that was fast falling apart.

"Sorry, sir," he apologised swiftly. "Fay was just telling me a most amusing story."

Lady Weyford smiled indulgently. "My sister Cynthia is renowned for her charm and wit. She has passed those qualities on to Fay."

"Is Cynthia Christie Fay's mother, Lady Weyford?" asked Thea with genuine interest. "I met her a number of times at the home of Countess Levinsky, and liked her very much. She invited me to one of her house parties, but I was unable to go because of my work on the suffragette committee."

The elderly aristocrat could not decide whether to show interest or disapproval, so merely said, "Oh?" in a neutral tone.

"The Countess left Russia during the revolution, I understand. She's a marvellous woman with immense courage, and a brain to equal that of any man. So different from most of the Czarist blue-bloods, who were interbred perverts bent on robbing the people of their right to freedom. Civil war was the only answer," Thea declared as she tackled her fish.

Into the startled silence caused by such a statement by a young woman at a dinner table, Martin said quietly, "Socialist nonsense! War is never the answer, Thea, especially when it is led by men who don't care how many are killed so long as their personal dreams are realised."

She turned to him, alive with interest. "Is this the historian, the warrior, or the politician's son speaking?"

"All three . . . with a dash of the human being thrown in," he retorted smartly. "You really do talk out of the top of your hat sometimes, girl. Not too long ago, you were lecturing me on the foolishness of abandoning my studies to go and fight for what I believe in. Why should it be wrong for me to want freedom for my people, yet right for Russians?"

Thea laughed gaily, and held up her hands. "I surrender, sir. You have demolished my defences with one blow. All the same, we must get together for a longer discussion on the subject. I have other theories which I wager you'll not flatten so easily."

Margery suddenly looked happier, and said gloatingly, "How very pleasant it is to discover that my niece is so well acquainted with your sister, Lady Weyford."

"How very pleasant it is that we were enabled to make the discovery because of Martin's commendable rescue of your son, Mrs Beresford," she responded haughtily. "But for that, we might never have gathered around your table."

Fay studied the fillet of sole Ling had placed before her, and said languidly, "Poor Martin had little choice. Hero of Arras, with shell shock to support the claim, what a fool he'd have looked if someone else had dived in first."

"I didn't notice anyone making the remotest sign of doing so," Thea put in smoothly.

"What fools the other men would have looked if Martin hadn't dived in," said Lydia with sudden and surprising fervour. "They would probably all have stayed where they were and watched Alex drown."

Margery looked at her daughter in astonishment, so Thea put in quickly, "Alex wouldn't have drowned. You should know that, Lydia. Although he was doubtless grateful to know someone else was at hand while the boat was being lowered, Alex didn't really need Martin's rescue attempt. He's a brilliant swimmer."

"Ah, that may be true of a bright daytime dip in the sea at the Swimming Club, Miss du Lessier," Sir Hartle began sternly, not caring for his godson's bravery being dismissed. "It was dark, and the steamer was some distance from the shore in the main shipping channels. One man bobbing about in the darkness would never have been seen by merchantmen plying the Straits. Dear me, yes, there could have been a very nasty accident. Very nasty indeed!"

Whilst being served with vegetables by the gentle, courteous Ling, Thea looked across at Sir Hartle with a dazzling smile.

"I in no way intended to suggest that Martin's plunge into the sea was not extremely heroic, and I really did see no one else on deck preparing to do anything about the situation when Alex fell so unexpectedly. It was undoubtedly your godson's quick reactions which saved the day."

Sir Hartle positively puffed up with satisfaction, until Thea's next words arrested the process.

"I'm sure you have already decided that such heroism deserves positive recognition, and have now removed your objections to Martin's wish to buy a car, Sir Hartle. He derived such pleasure and benefit from discussing history with the Sing brothers, I thought it a great pity that he should be denied further visits to those men who share his intellectual interests. It was when I asked if I might accompany him there again that he confessed your attitude. I immediately offered to lend him the money for an indefinite period. His old-fashioned notions wouldn't let him borrow money from a girl—quite absurd, in my opinion—so I was thinking of getting a car for my own use, which he could borrow whenever he wished." Flashing a glance at a stony-faced Martin, she then said, "I hope he's not so stubborn that he will regard *that* offer as unacceptable, also."

Thrown into a state of mixed anger and protest so soon after the self-satisfaction of a moment before, the judge glowered at her from beneath his brows.

"I should think very little of any man who took money from a young woman, Miss du Lessier. Martin acted exactly as I would expect, and there will be no question of his 'borrowing' your motor-car, if you should decide to purchase one. The matter was one between my godson and myself, in the irksome rôle as trustee of his finances. I am astonished that he should have discussed this with you. Yes, indeed, most astonished."

Eating her lamb cutlet with obvious relish, Thea paused to say with a hint of apology, "He never would have done, I'm sure, except that he was suffering from the effects of intoxication deliberately induced by the group of acceptable youngsters led by Damien Lang, who had invited themselves to the party that evening. He was so tight, he hardly knew what he was saying, poor man. He was treated with far more courtesy and respect by the Sing brothers, you know."

Feeling that Thea had them all on strings like puppets that evening, Alex waited to see what would happen next. His parents were now as statue-like as they had been on first sight of this girl. Lydia was flushed, and gazing at Martin the way she had once gazed at a bird with a broken wing which had crashed on to the verandah. Martin was looking almost murderously at the sparkling girl beside him. Lady Weyford's eyes were closed in social pain, and Sir Hartle seemed lost without a jury to direct on the charge to levy. Beside Alex, Fay whispered with acid delight, "That's cooked her goose. She'll never get Martin now."

At that moment, the silence was broken by a flurry at the doorway. Alex turned to see Ling being pushed aside by a tall figure in evening clothes, who walked in without ceremony and took in the scene slowly. His bow tie was dangling, his trousers were unpressed, his tail coat sprouted patches of green mould, and his opera hat was partly concertinaed. He stood with a lop-sided smile on his face as he studied them all with inebriated interest.

"Good God, a wake!" he announced. "Who's expired?" Catching sight of the Weyfords, he bowed. "Sir Humphrey and his good lady. Who, on setting eyes upon you, madam, would doubt that you were good?"

Moving unsteadily towards Martin and Thea, he bowed again.

"A whey-faced youth and his love, it seems. I envy you, sir. Ah, and my upright brother with *his* good lady." He tut-tutted rather wetly, then said, "You'll stay like that if the wind changes suddenly. Not nice, that face, you know. Not nice, at all."

Alex watched in utter delight as the visitor trod carefully around the table to peer closely at Fay, and say, "A pretty little kitten who has been at the cream jug, no doubt."

Jumping to his feet, Alex offered his hand with affectionate eagerness. "Welcome back, Your Grace. How's the Duchess?"

"Ha, ha, ha," came the boisterous response from his uncle, as they shook hands with matching energy. "Never forget, do you, boy. Her Grace is as chipper as ever. Having tea with the Sultan today, you know. S'why she couldn't accompany me." Swinging to challenge the silent group, he cried, "Is this splendid boy the only one with a warm welcome for the Duke of Beresford after an absence of so long? Judging by your expressions I left it too damned long before paying a visit. You've all bored yourselves to death with your own inconsequence."

He thought that such a good joke he laughed loudly, and spun round to face Alex again.

"Must tell Her Grace that one," he chortled. "She'll be tickled to death."

The arrival of Marmaduke Beresford gave the *coup de grâce* to a social occasion at which everyone save Thea had been labouring under severe strain. On one person in that room, the eccentric planter had a disastrous effect. His unsteady gait, his overloud voice, and the taunts to those whom he approached all reminded Martin too vividly of those months spent in a hospital full of men doing much the same thing. Desperate to escape the walls surrounding him, he rose to his feet with the other diners and left the fracas to stumble out on to the verandah he knew so well. It was humid and still, heavy with heat and the unmistakable smell of the tropics. It was hotter out there than it had been in the room cooled by overhead fans, but there was darkness lit by no more than a sickle moon and the wide freedom of the sky to disperse that sensation of claustrophobia. He moved to one of the great stone columns flanking the top of the steps to the garden. Taking hold of it, he gazed at that luminous sickle and fought memories of a hospital ward containing the lost and terrified survivors of war.

"Is everything all right now?" asked a gentle voice behind him.

It represented sanity and all that was clean, sweet and tender. He let go the pillar and turned slowly to face the girl in a pink shimmery gown. The appealing beauty of her was greater than ever, yet his only thought in that moment was the one which had been in his mind from the first sight of her that evening. Lydia Beresford was dominated by a man with warped passions. He longed to protect her from him.

"Yes, everything's all right now," he assured her. "I needed some air, and believed no one would miss me."

"I did."

"You're very kind."

"Is that the only way you think of me, Martin?"

"You're many more things, all equally unforgettable." He reached out to take her hand in a light clasp. "Lydia, those other times . . . well, it's been so long since I was with a lovely girl. I'm not normally as brutal as that. Can you forgive me?"

"Yes, yes, *of course*," she breathed. "If we could meet more often I'm sure it would help. You'd grow used to being with me. All the time you go out of your way to avoid me, we'll never become friends."

Stroking the back of her hand with his thumb and thinking of George's words, he nodded. "Yes, it was very foolish of me. When we see each other at the Cricket Club or the races, or at some social function, I'll come over and speak to you from now on."

She drew nearer. "Couldn't we meet alone?"

"I doubt it," he responded, thinking of how well she was chaperoned. "I suppose if I invited Thea and your brother as well, you could come to tea at my place sometimes."

"Would you come here, if I invited you?"

"If your parents consented . . . and on condition that I'm not expected to play tennis."

"It wouldn't be a party, just me," she told him with what he knew to be a false hope. "We could talk and get to know each other better. It won't be for absolute ages, unfortunately. When Uncle Duke is in Singapore, no one is invited to the house, in case he walks in. Look what happened just now."

"I suppose your parents have a point, although the evening was hardly a roaring success before he came, was it?"

"That was Thea's fault."

"Not entirely, although I could have wrung her neck on more than one occasion."

Her upturned face studied his searchingly. "Every other man in Singapore seems to find her fascinating. Why don't you?"

Because his self-control had been shaken by Marmaduke's arrival, he caught himself being honest with her. "There's no peace in Thea. In her own way, she's as uncertain and lost as I am. Instead of admitting her own weakness, she tries to compensate for it by bullying other people over theirs. I don't think she realises the dangers attached to that."

"Does she bully you, Martin? I won't let her."

He took her other hand to kiss them both gently. "Sweet defender! Don't worry. I have her measure, and she knows it." Changing a potent subject swiftly, he went on, "Tell me about your uncle. All I've heard about him from others is that he's eccentric, with behaviour to match. I should find much in common with him."

"Don't, Martin," she cried in soft distress. "You shouldn't say things like that."

"Others do," he pointed out, then relented quickly as he remembered that he was not with a girl like Thea. "All right, I'm sorry."

"Uncle Duke really is the limit," she began. "He never gives us any warning of his arrival, and takes delight in refusing to tell Daddy when he plans to go back. The one consolation is that he always stays at Raffles, and not here. They keep a room for him, and put a sign on the door calling him the Duke of Beresford. Raffles is that kind of place."

He smiled. "No doubt the other guests are delighted to extend the joke by treating him accordingly. It's all harmless enough, I should have thought, so why does your father dislike him so much?"

She sighed. "He doesn't really dislike him—no one could—but Daddy can never forgive him for something which happened long before I was born. I only know the story Alex told me."

"Am I allowed to hear it?"

She smiled up at him. "Of course. Everyone out here knows, so it's not a close secret. I expect you have family skeletons, too."

His entire family were skeletons. He made no reply to that as she tugged him by his hands to sit on the top step beside her. Leaning back against the stone balustrade so that he could study her in what little light there was, it struck him that all he now longed to do was to draw her against him while he circled her protectively with his arms. Had his confession to George damped down the fire, or had Austin Beresford's obscene vice caused this change in his feelings?

"Uncle Duke was sent to England to be educated, while Daddy went straight into the business with Grandfather," Lydia began. "Being the older brother meant that Daddy was expected to learn about shipping instead of Latin and Greek. Neither he nor Grandfather knew about it when Uncle Duke was sent down from Oxford and began to live a rackety existence with a group of wild young men addicted to horse racing, who spent their days at racetracks all over the country. Uncle and one of his friends made so much money, they bought a racehorse between them and set out to make even more."

Martin realised that she was just repeating what her brother had told her, for the choice of words and expressions was surely not hers.

"A year later they had a long run of bad luck, and were desperate to recoup their losses on the last race of the season," she continued. "Their horse beat the two favourites by several furlongs. It made the other owners suspicious, and they demanded an enquiry. It proved that the

181

other two horses had been drugged. Strong evidence pointed to Uncle Duke and his partner, but no charge could be brought against them. However, enough doubt was cast on their honesty to get them expelled from the Jockey Club, and blackballed from many others. Finally, they were both declared bankrupt." She looked up at him sadly. "This all happened shortly before Grandfather was disgraced, and shot himself. Daddy never forgave Uncle Duke. He brought him out to Singapore and installed him up at the plantation, with orders to stay there for the rest of his days."

Martin thought that over in relation to what he now knew of Austin. "Your uncle must have been only in his early twenties then. Rather severe punishment, wasn't it?"

"Do you think so?" she asked in astonishment. "Poor Daddy had to pick up the pieces of the company all on his own *and* try to live down the disgrace of two scandals in the family at much the same time. I think he has been marvellous. I only wish Alex would see him in the same light."

"Oh, I think he very definitely does. It constitutes his greatest problem."

"I don't understand. What problem?"

He squeezed her hand. "Tell me more about your uncle."

"Well, every so often, Uncle Duke turns up in Singapore when we all least expect it."

"Does he come on business?"

"Sometimes, but more often it's because he says he felt an urge to see civilisation. He's quite out of touch with it, and still thinks this is the Edwardian heyday. Although I quite like him, I do wish he wouldn't come. It always puts Daddy in a dreadful mood, and Mummy gets very irritable. It has been bad enough lately with Alex being obstinate, and Thea prancing around speaking her mind. Now, it'll be a hundred times worse at home."

Restraining himself admirably, he merely said, "Poor little thing."

Turning immediately, she urged, "That's why it would be so wonderful if I could see you a lot. I'd be able to bear everything else then."

Recognising danger, and hearing the sound of car doors which told him the Weyfords were leaving, he stood up and pulled her up with him. "The others are going, Lydia, and so should I. Will it be all right if I use the garden gate?" He gave a swift smile. "I seem to make a habit of it, don't I? Will you give your parents my thanks? They seem pretty well occupied by your uncle's unexpected appearance."

Disappointment was all over her. "*Must* you go?"

"I think it would be wiser," he told her with his new gentleness. "The party is very much over."

Refusing to release his hands, she asked, "When will I see you?"

"I'll send an invitation to tea . . . soon," he promised, not sure he could be this good for much longer. Freeing himself, he backed down the steps. "I can find my own way out."

Following him step for step, she asked desperately, "Are you quite sure you're all right now?"

On level ground he looked up at her and smiled. "Yes . . . and thanks for being so understanding and sweet."

It was all she needed. Two steps, and her arms went up around his neck as she kissed him inexpertly in the region of his mouth. "Goodnight, *dear* Martin," she whispered.

Telling himself he was only following George's advice to kiss and cuddle her, Martin demonstrated what an embrace should really be like. She surrendered so completely, he demonstrated further. It delighted them both, she for the obvious reasons, and Martin because he was retaining control of the situation, this time. Although strong desire was only just beneath the surface ready to surge through, the compulsion to protect her from the bestial realities of life pursued by her father was stronger. In consequence, his kisses were tender, his mouth against her temple murmured soft endearments, his hands in her pale hair were cherishing. All the same, only the sound of Margery's voice stridently calling the girl's name forced him to release her.

"You'd better go in," he told her softly. "There'll be the devil to pay if your mother comes out here and finds us together."

She looked as ethereally lovely as any young girl who suddenly finds her dreams have become reality, as she said, "Promise that I'll see you soon."

"I promise."

Halfway up the steps, she turned. "You *can* behave yourself with a girl, you see. You mustn't think you're different from other people, Martin . . . just a great deal nicer."

She ran indoors leaving him to make his way through the garden to the side gate beyond the pergola where he had first set eyes on her, wondering what his friend would make of the situation now. Lydia was starting to fall in love with him; a sweet girl he could never have and make happy. Kissing and cuddling had not solved the problem, but enlarged it. He was still a danger to her. The ability to feel sexual response was a curse, he decided. He had been better off without it. Even so, peacefulness pervaded his soul and mind so that the room which had witnessed his despair and loneliness seemed almost welcoming when he returned to it. As he lay beneath the mosquito net watching palm fronds create moving filigree patterns against the moon through

183

his open window, his thoughts were of poetry and music which were synonymous with the silver and black beauty of this night. For once, moonlight brought no visions of barbed wire standing black against it, no sounds of wounded men screaming for humanity.

That night, Alex succumbed to an attack of his recurring malaria; that which had deprived him of the chance to fight in the Singapore mutiny in 1915. It prevented his supposed return to Manila on the date arranged, and delayed the announcement of his impending departure for England. With the problem hanging over him, he found convalescence irksome. Restless for action rather than constant mental revision of the possible outcome, the wisdom of leaving Thea in Singapore when he sailed, and the best way to go about seeking employment in England, he got back on his feet several days too soon and made his way along the corridor to Thea's room, bursting to discuss it all with her. Her door was locked again, and a tray containing the remnants of her lunch was outside it on the floor. He sighed with frustration. That novel again! Very well, he would go ahead without further discussion. She claimed the book would give her back her soul; his new future would give him back those years during which he had yearned for freedom.

Dressing in the usual crisp linen suit, he left the house and drove himself to the office with the idea of making a start on tying up loose ends and packing personal items. No one would think it curious, for he would do the same if going to Manila rather than England. Once in his office hung with gold-framed paintings of vessels of the family line, the full implications of his break with *Berondel* hit him. He had been regarded by everyone as heir to the company since Charles died. There was no doubt his departure would be viewed as ingratitude by some, and as many other things by the rest. Probably no other person in the colony save Thea, and a few of his closest friends, would believe he had every right to walk away from an unwanted inheritance, and wish him well. It would not worry him, because he would leave public censure behind when he sailed. The censure of his family, however, was something he dreaded. Despite Thea's brave words on his rights as an individual, and although he agreed that his parents had used what she called "emotional blackmail" to keep him at home, twenty-four years of life could not be put aside without a certain amount of pain. Knowing they would do nothing to make the break easy for him, he decided nothing would be gained by delaying the announcement any longer. Might as well tell his father now, here in the office, and have that part over before having to face his mother's tears and accusations.

Tense, but determined, Alex abandoned the task of clearing drawers to make his way along the hushed corridors to his father's office. The quietness of it typified *Berondel*, he mused. Nothing was happening; no rush of activity disturbed the plodding serenity of a shipping line run by old men. All he had achieved in Manila had been a waste of time. If he did not go there to run the sub-office with determined insight and enthusiasm, the project would be allowed to die. If he wanted justification for what he was about to tell his father, it was here in the tranquillity of a company just ticking over.

Austin Beresford had left early, his secretary told Alex. After tiffin at his club, he had complained of a severe headache and returned home. Frustrated and annoyed, Alex realised they must have passed each other. His father had probably downed too many stengahs at the club after a heavy meal, and was now paying the price. He always drank more when Marmaduke was in Singapore. That, combined with suppressed anger, played havoc in any constitution suffering tropical temperatures. It was not the best time to tell a man his son was making his bid for a future on the other side of the world.

Returning to his own office, Alex continued clearing his possessions from a desk which had witnessed so many hours of bored rebellion. He should have gone long ago, he told himself. Only Thea's support and love had broken that inbred sense of obligation to a yoke his brother had left on his shoulders. If she would only sail with him, his joy would be total.

He was preparing to leave an hour later, when a knock on the door leading from the outer office heralded a visitor. Alex smiled with pleasure and went forward to greet him.

"Uncle Duke, what brings you here?"

"My feet, old sport," came the laughing reply. "Can't abide motors, and it don't seem right to let another chap pull me along in a rickshaw when I've got legs, same as him. As for the horse—ah, that's a different matter altogether—but no one uses them here now except to play games. Great pity. Something very impressive about a man on a horse, but he looks bally stupid being pulled along in something resembling an infant's perambulator. Takes away his dignity, you know."

Alex laughed as he went straight to the decanters on the sidetable. Marmaduke had a great partiality for port, at any time of the day.

"There you are." He handed his uncle the glass, then perched on the corner of his desk as Marmaduke settled in the chair and sipped appreciatively, before looking up with a twinkle in his dark-blue eyes.

"You should have been my son, young Alex. I've never understood how you could have sprung from the loins of my muffin-faced brother." He sipped again, then smacked his lips noisily before saying, "Your

185

brother was muffin-faced, too, you know. I'm sorry the poor little chap died, but he'd never have amounted to much, in my opinion. The girl was pretty—like little Lydia—but girls . . . well, they can't do much really, can they?" After a longer sip at the port, he leaned back in the chair to give Alex a rueful glance. "Is Austin in a pucker?"

"I'm afraid so. You couldn't have chosen a worse time to arrive unannounced."

"If I had announced it, you'd all have gone out," he complained.

Alex grinned. "Mother was entertaining high-flown guests, and you were well under the influence, you know."

Marmaduke hunched his shoulders and gave a grunt of resignation. "Yes . . . well, it gets damned *lonely* up there. You have no idea, old sport. The monsoons started early, and the sound of that bloody rain thundering down night and day gets under a man's skin. There's no one to talk to, and the gramophone is useless." He grinned impishly. "Fact is, I threw something at the bally thing one night. Don't work at all now."

"What about Tiyah?" asked Alex of the Malayan woman who lived with his uncle.

Marmaduke's face crumpled. "She's been a good girl to me all these years but, you know, I can't get away from the fact that she's not one of us, at times. It's not like having an English wife, lad. Take my advice and find yourself a nice English girl to marry, before it's too late. You're fortunate. There are so many out here to choose from. The war took most of our young men except those, like you, who stayed in the colonies. Lucky dogs, you can take the pick of the girls."

Not liking the subject under discussion, Alex said then, "Did you come to see me about anything in particular?"

"Apart from having a glass of your excellent port? Yes, yes, of course," he declared. "Problem, old sport. Those ships of yours aren't nearly big enough. Clunes is talking of using *Nimrod* instead of *Berondel*, in future. We had a larger than usual consignment on the last run, which meant that some of his stuff had to be left on the jetty all night during a monsoon. Wasn't too pleased, I can tell you."

Alex rose from his perch on the desk, and thrust his hands into his pockets angrily. "Clunes is one of our oldest and most loyal clients. Are you certain he mentioned going to *Nimrod*?"

"Certain."

"My God, some idea of loyalty, after just one unfortunate incident!"

"Don't shout at me, boy, I wasn't there."

"Sorry, Uncle. It's just damned annoying to hear this sort of thing. I've been pressing for bigger ships on that run ever since the start of the year, but Father won't hear of it. Since the war, trade is building up fast. If we don't expand, we shall be ousted by rivals like *Nimrod* who are far more enterprising. We've had a recent example of it with *Rochford-Kendal*. One can't afford the old approach, these days, but dashed if I can make him see it."

Marmaduke made a face. "If you can't, boy, no one will. Still, you'll be taking over soon, when Austin relinquishes the reins."

"He'll die in harness rather than allow me to run *Berondel*," Alex told him bitterly. "He has no intention of handing over anything."

"Start up your own line, in competition, then. By the by, is there any more of that port?"

Alex thought over the idea which had just been flung at him, as he poured port. It was one that had never occurred to him. Was it an alternative solution to his problem? It would certainly allow him to stay in Singapore with Thea, but it would really be no solution to those daunting twilights. Besides, the pioneering world of aviation beckoned too strongly now he had allowed himself to cherish it. In a swift rush of decisiveness, he asked his uncle to excuse him while he wrote a note. Sitting at his desk he penned a request for a single first-class cabin on the first available sailing for England. Taking the envelope into the outer office to be despatched by hand of a messenger, he returned to his uncle. There, he picked his topee from the hat stand, and invited Marmaduke to take tea at the Beresford house.

"There are no guests, and Mother will be reasonable, I promise," he said persuasively. "I can't vouch for Father, but I really want you to meet my girlfriend—sober, this time."

"Tipsy last time, was she?"

Alex poked him in the chest. "No, you old rogue, you were."

Marmaduke's face lengthened into a suitable expression of remorse. "Oh dear, how naughty of me."

Alex laughed. "I wouldn't have minded except that you matched her up with some other fellow, and not me."

"Very remiss," agreed Marmaduke solemnly, "but what was she doing with him? Must have been doing something for me to think . . . not her brother, is he? Could've made a mistake there easily enough."

Opening the door to usher his uncle out, Alex said, "Actually, you can come and meet him. I'm calling in at his place with a message." They walked together to the lift. "When we reach home, I'll help you to persuade Father to invest in some new modern vessels."

"Not me, boy," Marmaduke said, setting his panama hat at a rakish angle. "Never had the slightest influence on my brother, even before he cut me out of the company. Wasn't even given any shares in the line, you know. I'm simply the rather grey sheep who runs the plantation; an estate manager who has the family name."

Alex adroitly changed a subject inclined to make his uncle maudlin by saying, "There's only one Duke of Beresford, however."

"True, true. Rum joke, that," he chuckled. "They still believe it up there, you know. I receive regular invitations to the Sultan's little shindigs."

Martin was reading a book on ancient Chinese art when the family car drew up at the front steps. He put down the book and walked along his own verandah, to greet them and invite them in.

"Do you mind sitting out here? Lang often fills the sitting room with his cronies, and they are usually more than I can take at the end of a working day."

"We won't be staying long," Alex told him. "I've called in about your invitation to tea on Thursday. Thea is too involved in her novel, and I'm rather busy, too. Lydia couldn't come on her own, naturally. I'm sorry." He thought it dealt with the matter very reasonably, and it was one way he could intervene in whatever was developing between this man and his sister.

Showing little reaction, Martin simply said, "Another time, perhaps."

"Yes, perhaps. As we had to pass your place on our way home, my uncle decided he would like to come in and meet you."

"How do you do, sir," said Martin, as if he had never come across his eccentric guest before. "Would you care for a drink?"

"Port would be very acceptable," Marmaduke said promptly. Then he caught sight of the scar on Martin's neck, and pointed to it. "My word, someone take a poke at you, lad?"

As he walked inside for the bottle and glasses, Martin called over his shoulder, "Something like that."

Alex found that he could not let the other man dismiss so lightly something which brought guilty memories of that tennis party.

"It's a war wound, Uncle Duke. He's something of a hero. Won an MC at Arras," he said.

"Well I never. How splendid! I won a medal once, you know. I'm a crack shot, except when I've been imbibing unwisely. Ever do that, lad?"

"Get drunk?" queried Martin, returning with the port. "I'll say. I once got so tight I walked across a pontoon . . ." He broke off momentarily as his dark gaze flicked to Alex. Then he decided to finish what he had begun. "I walked across a pontoon bridge near the front line without realising there were bullets whistling past my ears."

Marmaduke took the glass of port and sipped, before saying reflectively, "I see tigers when I'm in my cups. Damn beastly striped creatures all over the place. Never know which of 'em is real and which isn't."

"My godfather says they still roam freely in the wilder areas up-country." He indicated the bottles. "What'll you have, Alex?"

"Nothing, thanks. Tea with the family is imminent."

"They're killers, you know," pronounced Marmaduke.

Martin looked startled. "Who?"

"Tigers. Damn beastly striped creatures. I hate 'em." He stared at Martin. "Aren't you going to join me, old sport?"

Their host shook his head, and he explained to Alex, "It's my night for dinner with the Weyfords. That's an exercise which demands a clear head."

A smile broke through before Alex could stop it. "It shouldn't be too bad tonight. They'll be holding a full post-mortem on their evening with us. It should give you a bit of a rest."

Martin smiled back, and Alex suddenly realised how rarely he had seen him do it. It banished the strained look and gave him a shy kind of charm. He looked at his watch, saying, "I think I've time for a G and T, after all. I can always say I was held up at the office."

"A man's perennial excuse," commented Martin indicating chairs to his guests with a wave of the hand. Pouring the gin and tonic, he handed it to Alex, then perched on the verandah rail facing them.

"Stupid man, my brother, young sir," Marmaduke said suddenly. "Been trying to run the whole thing by himself ever since the old fellow retired, with the help of a bullet. Forty odd years!" He held up his glass for a refill. "I ask you, lad, is that reasonable?"

"In this climate, I'd say it would take a lot out of any man."

"Could have had my assistance all this time," the older man informed him sadly. "Wouldn't hear of it. Hard man, Austin. Inflexible. Has to have things his way, so he keeps complete control." He looked up at Martin from beneath bushy eyebrows. "Married a very silly woman. Broody hen, that's Margery. Wrong to neglect husband for children. I've a Malay woman. Been with me for thirty years. *Marvellous*. Keeps the place very comfortable. Gentle, loyal, very good when I go down with the old fever. Ever had a Malay woman, old sport?"

Martin shook his head solemnly. "Never."

"Married, are you?"

"I haven't had the chance to think about it."

"Of course. Went off to the war. Defending some girl, I suppose."

"No. I was only seventeen and a half—a schoolboy, really."

"Defending your mother, then."

189

"She had died several years earlier."

"Must have been a sister," Marmaduke decided, sticking to his theme. "Girls are always sending us off to do things. Weep and wail about it, they do, but they never go themselves, you notice. Your sister did the same, I'll wager."

"I had just one brother."

"Had?"

"He was killed at Ypres."

"There you are! Some girl behind it, mark my words."

Martin shook his head. "He was even younger than I was."

The ageing planter's face creased up disapprovingly. "Your father should never have allowed it. Both sons off to the war over some girl! Not right, that. I'd speak to him about it, lad."

"He died last year," came the low answer.

The glass of port stilled in the air. "What, him as well? Oh dear, oh dear, oh dear! You poor lad. All alone in the world, and people taking pokes at you like that."

While his uncle rambled on, Alex stared out across the gardens of the bungalow toward the tropical skyline. It was that haunting time of day again. Three hours before the spectacular nightfall. Ten thousand twilights stretching before him, then ten thousand more. He would count them in triumph from now on. He intended to live, *really* live, before he died.

When he turned back to the pair on the verandah, Martin was asking, "Were you ever married, sir?"

"Not legally. Didn't want it when I was younger. What bright spark does? Afterwards, no girl would come up there. Don't like it, you know. Too lonely. Those who do, turn broody. Or go mad. Ever seen a woman run amok with a carving knife? Terrible sight. The tigers don't help, of course. Damn beastly striped creatures. I hate 'em. Killed every servant in the place, and the planter."

"Good lord, a man-eater!" exclaimed Martin.

"No, the woman with the carving knife," came the sad reply. "Dreadful to-do. Locked her in the madhouse. Well, what else could they do? Defence tried to blame the natives, but she was found with the knife still in her hand. Respectable white woman! Not too long ago they'd have hanged everyone in the nearby village instead, just to be on the safe side." He slapped his hand on the arm of the chair, making Martin jump. "Got it! Come up for a visit. Time young Alex came to inspect the factory and godowns, talk to the agent and the clients. Having some trouble with 'em, you know. Thinking of going to *Nimrod*. It won't do. He'll bring you with him. Might even see a tiger," he added by way of inducement. "You look due for a holiday, young sir. Very washed out, if you pardon my saying. Been walking over too many tight bridges with a pontoon."

It was then Alex realised how many glasses of port his uncle had drunk, and his heart sank. He should never have asked him home to tea. Small hope of a calm atmosphere into which to throw his own bombshell!

"It's getting late, Uncle," he said vigorously. "We must go."

The shaggy head turned to regard him. "I'd much rather stay here talking to this poor lad. Hasn't anyone in the world, you know. Very sad, that. Liable to turn broody . . . or go mad. They do. Seen it often."

"It's past four, and you know how Mother hates delaying tea," he said firmly, taking Marmaduke's arm.

Turning to Martin, the old eccentric said apologetically, "Pity, but I suppose I must pay my respects to my muffin-faced brother." Leaning confidentially toward Martin, he confided, "Upset him the other evening, you know. Don't take much to do that—people are forever doing it—but I get the blame every time. Had a lot of fusty people to dinner, they did, and didn't care for my arrival. Wish I'd stayed up there. The tigers get too much for me, however, and I have to come down to civilisation. Thing is, don't have horses any more. Damned motors, or those perambulator things. Won't have another man pulling me when I've got feet of my own!" He gripped Martin's shoulder. "You really are a splendid fellow. I look forward to seeing you up at the plantation." Peering closely at the scar again, he whistled through his teeth. "My word, whoever did that made a marvellous job of it."

Alex waved a farewell to Martin, then led his uncle to the steps. He continued his theme in typical fashion. "Bring him up with you when you come, Alex. Bit pasty, poor fellow. Not surprising. All alone in the world, and drinks very poor quality port. Not half as good as yours. I'll show him some tigers. Seems keen on them, for some reason. I don't like 'em. Damn beastly striped creatures! Well, come on, let's face your father. How he came to have a son as splendid as you, I can't think. Should have been mine. Often thought so."

It hardly seemed worth climbing into the car just to be driven several hundred yards down the road, but Alex was preoccupied with thoughts of how best to reveal plans he knew would cause an uproar this evening. They would trot out the same reasons and pressures they had used before, but this time no one, not even Austin Beresford, could prevent him from leaving. Yet he did. On reaching the house, they found an ambulance at the entrance, and the women of the household being comforted by Thea. Austin had suffered a severe stroke fifteen minutes before.

191

Chapter 11

Those first weeks following Austin's stroke took all Alex could give by way of stamina, patience and business flair. By day, he worked hard to reassure clients known to be investigating the possibility of transferring their business to another line, and went all out to maintain the reputation for stability in *Berondel* despite the collapse of the line's controller. By night, he pored over contracts, cost lists, and a fresh plan for the Manila sub-office under the management of a youngster from the list of applicants he was interviewing. During that period he glimpsed life as it could have been, if his father had ever allowed him true partnership. The feeling of holding an entire company in the palm of his hand was heady after the restrictions he had suffered, yet it in no way compensated for his bright new future. So, whilst he put all he had into seeing the company through a difficult period, his troubled eyes followed the departure of homebound liners, and his restless spirit ached for true freedom.

One morning after a particularly frustrating board meeting, a visitor was announced. Alex was greatly surprised and not a little wary when Randal Forster walked in, smiling that easy assurance and greeting him like an old friend. There had been no time to make enquiries about the man amongst his business acquaintances, for the drastic change in Alex's own plans had occupied all his thoughts since returning from Manila. It was something of a puzzle to find Forster there in Singapore, and he voiced the fact.

"I thought Manila was to be the venue for your activities. Don't tell me you were unsuccessful in finding suitable premises there, despite your numerous connections."

Forster made himself comfortable in one of the heavy leather chairs. "Still weighing up the pros and cons, old chap. Thought I'd see how the land lies in this little corner of the jolly old empire. A shade more civilised than Manila, wouldn't you agree?"

"Property is just as difficult to acquire, unfortunately. If you've come for advice on that subject, there's little I can do to help you, I'm afraid."

Forster leaned back, very relaxed. "Have you a cigarette, Beresford?"

Alex pushed the carved box across the desk toward him, the sensation of wariness increasing every minute. They both helped themselves to a cigarette, then Alex lit them both before tackling the man again.

"What is all this about, Forster? I'm up to my eyes in paperwork whilst my father's in hospital so, unless there's some way I can help you, I'm afraid I can't spare the time for a chat on your problems in finding premises for your distribution centre."

"Actually, we can help each other, old boy."

"Oh?"

"Are you still after lucrative contracts in Manila?"

Taken unawares, Alex hesitated.

"Ricky Reynolds told me last night you have ships returning from there with half-empty holds. That smacks of very bad organisation. Your old man can't be that short-sighted, yet continue to prosper."

Alex caught himself firing up in defence of his father. "Ricky Reynolds says a damned sight too much, if you ask me. The major exporters could fill the holds of our relatively small vessels regularly, but Father won't break faith with long-standing and valued clients even though their goods don't always constitute a full cargo. I support him in that. However," he went on carefully, "we are interested in one-off contracts, or any which would supplement what we already carry." He frowned through the cloud of smoke at the big man facing him. "There are any number of lines operating from there. Why the interest in *Berondel?*"

The visitor brushed ash from the leg of his immaculate cream tropical suit. "I don't hold grudges, old boy. I told you I could put some business your way. I have a client in Manila who would just suit you. Any time you have cargo space, he'll fill it for you."

Alex was immediately wary. "Fill it with what?"

Thick fair brows rose in injured surprise. "My dear fellow, the usual commodities, of course. Spices, cloth, dyes, wood." He drew slowly on the cigarette, watching Alex through half-closed eyes. "There'll also be occasional consignments *en route* from Canton. This client brings Chinese goods out in a couple of junks he owns, but they're not up to making the full journey down to Singapore." Adjusting the knot of what looked to be the tie of a famous public school, he smiled with faint derision. "Your agent can inspect all the cases before loading, naturally. I have heard of the celebrated Beresford caution."

Although his offer appeared to be what *Berondel* badly needed, Alex had no intention of seeming too eager. "Righto, I'll discuss it with my father and let you know."

Forster stubbed out the cigarette in the ashtray beside his chair, and Alex noticed that the knuckles of his right hand were badly bruised. Did he do business with the help of his fists when charm failed? he wondered.

"Ricky Reynolds warned me that it was really old man Beresford who ran *Berondel*. I can't keep this offer open long enough for your father to make a full recovery and get back at the helm. If you really want this contract, surely we could sort it out between us. We're both men of intelligence and ability, aren't we?"

Alex was not taken in by that piece of flattery. "Too much so to take this all on spec. I'd need to see some sample manifests before considering this any further."

"Only what I'd expect of a sound businessman." Forster reached into his pockets for some folded papers, which he tossed on to the desk before standing up. "Look them over. If you're interested, send me a chit by the end of the week." He gave the lazy smile again, adding, "I could arrange to have the cases marked with the stamp of one of your existing clients. Then no one would be any the wiser." He gave a broad wink, "Including the old man."

Alex had to ask, "What part do you play in this, Forster?"

The man turned in the doorway. "I'm the lad who distributes the stuff when it arrives here. Good contacts. You'll find me in the business register. Chin-chin!"

Alex glanced at the manifests as soon as his visitor had gone. They were for substantial quantities of goods transported by a Japanese line which had recently given up the Singapore route. Nothing wrong there. Then he looked up Forster in the business register. A very impressive Hong Kong address. Although something about the man still made him feel slightly uneasy, friendship with Ricky Reynolds was surely enough to recommend him. The proposal would suit *Berondel* perfectly. After thinking it over for the rest of the day, he decided to direct the bright young Scotsman he had now engaged as the manager in Manila to go ahead with the deal. The opportunity would be lost if he waited for his father to recover sufficiently to discuss the future.

The subject of the future dogged his waking thoughts and disturbed his sleep. The doctors had been pessimistic. There was no chance of Austin making a full recovery. The paralysis of the right side of his body might lessen its grip slightly, but he would remain disabled; a permanent invalid in danger of suffering further strokes unless he took life at a slow pace. Alex could not begin to guess how his father would face up to that life sentence. His mother had shown surprising strength after the initial shock, but Lydia was deeply affected by the suddenness of an attack which had taken away the man who ruled her life and left him a twisted frame in a hospital bed. Alex worried about his sister. Would her sensitive personality suffer in a household dominated by a sick man, and would their mother now cling even more to the girl who had little hope of breaking free?"

His own hopes of breaking free had suffered a severe setback, which was only remotely bearable because it meant he was still with the girl he so passionately loved. Thea had him in a spin, never knowing whether it was easier on those days she locked herself away, or when she emerged to swamp him with affection and dazzle him with the promise she still withheld. Perhaps she was right in saying that if they became lovers he would never leave without her. He had suggested instant marriage, but she had declared that would only worsen the situation he was having to face with his family. One thing she stubbornly maintained was that her novel must be finished before she would consider any deep tie with him. When he had bitterly pointed out that she had given freely to some other man what she was withholding from him, her strangely sad reply had been that he had the answer in that very statement. The mystery of her former lover added to his tormented love for her. It occurred to him that she might have no idea what she was doing to him but, when he had very forcibly told her, she had been stricken with remorse and her means of comforting him had only worsened his condition. He had kept quiet on the subject since then, and the fact that she could find such fulfilment with the writing of her book at a time when he was worried, overworked and frustrated, only served to emphasise the lack of fulfilment he found in running a shipping line and increased his longing to escape from it. Yet, how could he now?

On an afternoon when he felt jaded, dispirited and claustrophobic in his father's dignified office, he turned his back on it all and had himself driven to the Cricket Club, where he knew the members of the First Eleven would be at practice in the nets. He had not attended for several weeks, so the prospect of physical exercise, and male companionship of the vigorous youthful variety was very attractive. Waving to those already in the nets, he entered the pavilion to change into cream flannels and shirt, then took pads, gloves and bat from his locker to join the convivial sporting group in the area to the rear of the building. They were all pleased to see him but, dedicated as they were to the sport, exchanged no more than greetings and the expressed hope that he would be available for the coming match against their arch rivals from the military garrison.

His decision had been a wise one. The open air, the company of young people after the ancient members of *Berondel* staff, the pleasure of a sport at which he excelled, and the chance to relieve stress and frustration by swinging a bat very forcibly at a ball to hear the unmistakable crack as he sent it away in dashing style, all took his mind from the problems besetting him. For an hour or more, Alex was no more than a virile young man enjoying a pastime of carefree youth. The breeze ruffled his hair and put billows in his shirt as he abandoned the bat to take his turn at bowling, and he derived almost sensual pleasure in stretching his body and limbs in an effort bordering on punishment. The sun beat down on his head and burnt into his bare arms as he worked the aggression out of himself with physical force.

Only when the light began to fade, did they begin to collect their gear and make their weary way to the pavilion for a shower and sundowners, talking about their chances in the annual marathon against the Army. Only as they trooped into the changing room did several then ask Alex about his father's progress and quiz him on various rumours concerning *Berondel*. His replies, as he stripped off and walked under the shower, were somewhat brusque. Reality was returning faster than he liked.

Feeling refreshed, and dressed in clean underwear beneath his suit, Alex then strolled into the large fan-cooled lounge with its verandah open to the green view of the field and beyond. The room with its scattered furniture smelling of cigars, haircream and linseed oil, and its framed photographs of past and present teams alongside the glass-fronted cabinet containing silver trophies, was a room of so many memories. He recalled his first match with the club, at the age of sixteen, when he had scored a thrilling fifty then been knocked out cold whilst fielding when a ball had come at him out of the sun's dazzle. So many afternoons of sporting pleasure with men he had known all his short life; so many laughing congratulations followed by horseplay in the showers. At such times he had felt his own man.

"Your usual G and T, Mr Beresford?" asked the white-coated steward, as Alex stood lost in sunny recollection.

He turned to the Malay with a smile. "Yes, Husain. How is your young daughter now?"

"She is well, still remaining with her aunt in Malacca. We are so grateful to the gentlemen of the Club for the money to send her there."

"It was worth it to put the smile back on your face," Alex told him with a laugh. "We'd grown used to it."

A voice hailed him, and he turned to see one of his more regular friends in a chair beneath one of the circling fans. He crossed to him and sat down. "What are you doing here, Giles? Don't tell me the First Eleven has decided to give you a second chance after chucking you out for getting too many ducks."

"Cheeky blighter!" growled the other man, who prided himself on his athletic prowess. "I came to see you, as it happens. Wondered if you might be here today as the big match is looming near. Everyone seems to think the cause'll be lost if you aren't in the team. Can't think why."

Avoiding an answer to that, Alex offered Giles another drink. Signalling the order to Husain before he came across with the gin and tonic, Alex then leaned back to study his friend.

"What did you want to see me about?"

"To ask what's behind your trip to England. Came as no end of a surprise, as you'd made no mention of it."

Alex was dumbfounded. How could Giles possibly know of his plans. "My trip to England?" he hedged.

"Had to postpone it because of your pater's illness, I suppose, but you kept it bally quiet, didn't you? Wilfred would've been a bit shirty. Missed the match if you'd gone, wouldn't you?" He took his drink from the tray brought at that moment by Husain, took a gulp of it, then repeated, "What's behind it, old chap? Single cabin, and all that, so can't have meant to elope with the delectable du Lessier."

Still shaken, Alex asked, "How the hell did you know about the single cabin etcetera?"

Giles's eyebrows rose. "How does anyone in Singapore know anything? Grapevine, naturally. Gordon Craythorne has a chum in the offices of P & O. He was understandably curious when your name cropped up on a passenger list, so he asked Gordon what was afoot. Gordon asked me. I was as much in the dark as they were."

"Oh God," he exclaimed in great consternation. "How many others know about the cabin?"

Giles grinned. "By tomorrow morning, almost everyone. You should know that well enough. Come on, out with it! What's going on?"

He was furious, with Giles for spoiling his oasis of calm pleasure, and with himself for not realising that his note, sent to reserve a cabin before he had broken the news to his father, would notify the entire colony of his intentions.

"All the time I remain on this damned island my life won't be my own," he said savagely. "If word of this reaches the directors of *Berondel*, the fat will really be in the fire."

"Of course it'll reach them. They're most closely concerned in the affair, I suspect. Alex, what the hell is going on?"

There was no alternative but to confide his plan to Giles Fancot, who had been his friend for some years. With the twilight performing its spectacular colour change outside, turning the cricket field pink and gold, he spoke of his eventual realisation that he could not condemn himself to the future mapped out for him by destiny and Austin Beresford.

197

"I've never wanted it, Giles."

"I thought it was because the pater held you on such a tight rein."

"I was fooled into that belief myself, but going down to Manila brought the truth out into the open. Even with some measure of responsibility, I derived no more than an assurance that I could do something else far better. Father sacrificed his life to *Berondel*, and I've grown up feeling it to be my duty to vindicate that sacrifice. Then Thea arrived. I'm in love with her, you know. Very seriously. She made me see that a second life sacrificed in no way compensated for the first. I suppose she also made me see how I've allowed myself to be manipulated." He appealed to his friend. "At what point does a strong sense of filial obligation turn into personal weakness? I'm not certain which has governed my actions since 1914, but all at once I could stand this life no longer. I booked passage—foolishly, I now realise—and headed home to tell my father. I found him in an ambulance and my mother and sister in floods of tears. Bang went my hopes for the future!"

Giles studied him for a moment or two. "I don't see why."

"For God's sake, man! He's had a stroke."

"Very few were surprised at the news, you know, Alex. Your pater held himself on such a tight rein in his determination to attract no censure whatsoever of his behaviour, it was inevitable that something would have to give under the burden. It could have happened at any time—a week after you sailed; a day, even. Perhaps it was fortunate that it was *before* you left, or you'd have blamed yourself for it. This way, you can't feel guilty, and he has had you on hand to steer *Berondel* through the initial panic. From what I've heard, you've done it damned well. But, old chap, nothing has basically changed, has it?"

Alex got to his feet, disturbed by his friend's words. "Of course it has damned well changed!"

"In what way?" was the calm challenge. "Have you now discovered a taste for shipping after virtually running the company for a while?"

"No . . . but I can't walk out on him now. I can't desert the family."

Giles stood up to put a hand on his shoulder. "If this had happened whilst you were on the high seas, your family would have coped without you."

"I wasn't on the high seas, I was here!" he cried.

"They were very fortunate. You've held the company together magnificently and stood by your mater and Lydia through their early dilemma. Isn't that enough?"

"They wouldn't consider it to be," he murmured bitterly.

"Forgive me, Alex, but whatever you do for them will never be considered enough. Everyone in Singapore knows that."

He looked at Giles in astonishment. "They do?"

"My dear fellow, it's certainly not personal weakness which has governed your actions since 1914, but exceptional unselfishness. Not too many men would have stood up to the strain of family demands as you have, trying to compensate your parents for the children they lost by putting aside your own wishes. Small wonder you broke out now and then. The longer you delay your departure, the smaller your chances of ever going."

"I can't tell a sick man I'm abandoning him," he said slowly, shaken by his friend's surprising words.

"You'll have to, Alex. Now this story is circulating the colony, it's only a matter of time before the *Berondel* directors hear it. I think you'll discover that Singapore will make the decision you appear to find so difficult."

The directors of *Berondel* were told immediately, in the strictest confidence, that Alex would be resigning and sailing for England as soon as his father was well enough to be consulted on the future of the line. Alex suggested that they form an interim committee to consider alternatives. The elderly gentlemen were deeply shocked by the news, regarding his decision to take to the skies as an even more dastardly deed than abandoning his family. For a shipping man to consider learning to fly was no less than criminal, in their opinion.

Relief at public knowledge of the fact, at last, was augmented by Thea's approval of what he had done, although they were both so busy during the next few days they saw little of each other. Alex was lucky in that his mother and Lydia spent so much time at the hospital, they shunned social engagements. He hoped against hope that they would not hear of the booked passage to England before he had a chance to tell his father. He determined to have company affairs in a flourishing state when he did. The new manager was now in Manila and proving his worth. The contract with Randal Forster's clients had been ratified, and consignments of goods were already filling holds that had once been half empty. Two old clients had taken their business elsewhere, but Forster had introduced several new ones with lucrative prospects. All in all, there was every reason for satisfaction.

Six weeks after being taken ill, Austin was sent home. Alex was busy in his father's office that same afternoon when the secretary entered holding a sheet of paper in his hand. The man's jaundiced face was a picture of uncertainty.

"What is it, Beamish?" Alex asked absently.

"These instructions have just arrived, Mr Beresford. I'm not at all sure what to do about them."

"Instructions?" queried Alex. "On what?"

"Instructions from Mr Beresford senior, sir, to arrange for the files, books and all business communications to be transferred to the house immediately. In addition, he instructs me to attend for business there, instead of here in the offices."

Alex stared at the man wondering if the old employee had lost his wits. "What are you talking about, man? How can you have instructions from my father?"

"Your syce delivered them a moment ago, sir. Direct from Mr Beresford senior, he said."

Getting to his feet as a curious brand of rage began somewhere in his breast, Alex took the sheet from the secretary's hand. On it he read evidence of something he could not credit; something so utterly humiliating it turned him cold. Hardly knowing what he was doing, he stumbled from the room with a muttered command to ignore the letter, and ordered the car to be brought round. During the drive home, the coldness reversed into the burning fury of a man finally pushed beyond his tolerance.

Reaching the house, he ran up the stairs and along the corridor to the suite which had been converted to cope with an invalid. His heart was pounding as he burst in without knocking, but he soon halted. In a hospital bed his father had looked a travesty of the man he had once been; in a long chair filled with pillows and flanked by bottles of barley water and medicines, he looked incredibly pathetic. His face, twisted by palsy, was dry and yellowish; the moustache was grey with a few remaining dyed tufts to betray the vanity. His useless arm lay on a pillow, the leg had been carefully placed beside the normal one. He looked far older than his sixty-four years; a man broken in body as well as spirit.

Twenty-four years of filial regard and loyalty formed a lump in Alex's throat as he gazed speechlessly at his father. He had seen disappointment, incomprehension and occasional pride in those pale eyes, but never hatred. It was there now, and it made him hesitate too long before speaking.

"I had not anticipated the honour of your return from the office in order to welcome me back," Austin said with difficulty. "You should have waited for the normal close of business for the day. Now you are here, I'll have a report on what has been happening during my absence, ready for my resumption in the morning."

Alex found his voice. "You can't mean that! You can't really mean to retain your monopoly and attempt to run *Berondel* from an invalid-chair."

"What choice do I have? My son is going to England to learn how to fly. Why haven't you already left? You are six years behind in your bid to become a hero."

Deeply shocked and distressed Alex cried, "Who told you that news? I made the announcement in the very strictest confidence, so that they would all have an accurate picture of the future situation and be able to consider the alternatives. No one should have spoken to you of it."

"They naturally assumed that your father would have been the first to be told of your treachery."

"You were too ill to discuss the future . . . and it's not *treachery*."

"When his son plots behind his back to leave a sinking ship, what else can a man call it?"

Alex moved nearer the chair. His father still exuded the mixture of smells found in hospitals, and it intensified the sense of guilt the accusation had instilled in him.

"I made the decision to leave some time ago, soon after my return from Manila. On the evening I had intended to tell you and explain the reasons for my decision, I returned home to find you had collapsed. There was never any intention of leaving a sinking ship. How can you suggest I would do such a thing?"

"Can you deny that you intend to do just that?"

"Of course," he protested hotly. "I have worked very hard to weather this storm. *Berondel* is in perfectly calm seas, I promise you. The situation has stabilised, and trade has even increased. The past six weeks have been spent holding the company together and organising a governing committee which will have you as its nominal head. Edwardes and Leigh fill the two major posts. Their election was unanimous, and we all feel they'll do a splendid job"

Saliva was dribbling from the corner of his father's mouth, but he was unaware of it. His agitation was betrayed by the clenching and unclenching of his hand as he continued to glare at Alex.

"Oh, do you? Then let me tell you that you have been wasting your time. I may be a twisted wreck now, but there is nothing whatsoever wrong with my brain. A Beresford began this company, and a Beresford will be at the helm as it goes down. It will go down honourably and nobly, despite your treachery, and no one will ever have cause to say Austin Beresford did not repay his father's debt to the world."

This was said in a voice Alex hardly recognised, and took a great deal of painful effort. It muted his aggression as he sat in a chair beside the stricken man, intending to reason with him.

"Father, the world doesn't expect you to almost kill yourself in the process. No one owes it that much," he said with feeling. "You can't possibly carry on. The doctors have ordered you to lead a much more restful life. From now on, there'll be time to enjoy things like your butterfly collection which is still waiting to be labelled and catalogued, and there's that set of books on old merchantmen the club members gave you in appreciation of the sterling work you put in, which you've been too busy to read. There'll be other benefits. You'll have more time to spend with Mother—she'll like that—and it may be possible for you all to take a holiday, later on." The expression in his father's eyes made him hurry on to say, "Being at home all the time doesn't mean you'll lose contact with everyone. There's no reason why you can't retain your place on some committees if they'll agree to hold the meetings here. There's that history of shipping you always intended to write," he added with fresh inspiration, "and . . . well . . . there are any number of ways you'll be able to occupy your time."

As he ran out of ideas and fell silent, Austin glared at him with cold weariness. "I was the same age as you are now when my father put a pistol to his temple. I took over *Berondel* lock, stock and barrel along with all its debts. I lost my friends, my pleasure in life and my self-estem on that day your grandfather was denounced as a villain. I had no sooner changed his name to mine on the plate glass of the office door when Marmaduke was branded a rogue and came running to me to bail him out of trouble. It took me ten years to gain acceptance from other businessmen in Singapore; another five to earn their grudging respect. I married a very worthy, unimaginative woman who promised to do her duties well enough to help my professional aspirations, but not attempt to interfere in them. We had four children as a result of marital duty rather than pleasure. Eight years ago two of them died in the same month. Half our family gone in four weeks! All those years of rearing them wasted. All our hopes for them dashed!"

He tried to move his head, found it to be impossible, and had to remain staring at his son while saliva from his slack lower lip ran over on to his chin. "Your mother refused to have me in her bed after they died. I discovered that I didn't much mind, and sought my pleasure elsewhere. I have been discreet, and we have kept up appearances all these years for our own reasons, and for the sake of our two remaining children. We shall not rejoice at having more time together. We have nothing in common, and have said all we ever wanted to say to each other years ago. I can't recall the last time I really looked at her. That's what it always comes to in the end; two unhappy people tied together because it would be too inconvenient to sever the bonds.

"As for our two surviving children; the girl is a pretty but ineffectual creature who will marry a dedicated colonial, bear him children, then turn into a pathetically coquettish copy of her mother. Then, of course, there is our son, our one surviving son. He is going to turn his back on us when we need him most . . . but only because some dark-eyed, acid-tongued female says he should. He's never had the courage to make the decision himself."

The voice grew curiously stronger and, to Alex's horror, tears gathered to roll down the wasted cheeks. "That is what my life has all been for; what I have sacrificed everything to achieve. You think I'm finished. Well, I'm not, damn you. You've witnessed the loss of my manhood and strength, but you won't take away *Berondel* and give it to some committee unless it's over my dead body. Go off and learn to fly. I swear you'll be in your coffin before I'm in mine. Go! Get out of my house . . . and take that mistress of yours with you! You'll not spend another night here, you traitor!"

Thea was shopping. The fuss surrounding Austin's return from hospital had made the house so frantic with sound and bustle, it had been impossible to concentrate on her work. Reluctant to be present when the medical entourage arrived, she had deemed it wise to let the dust settle before entering the scene. In view of Alex's coming departure, she decided to move out when he did, anyway. He had coped so superbly with the emergency, she sincerely hoped Austin would now appreciate that his son really did have those qualities he had consistently refused to recognise, even though they were to be used for a vastly different career than the one which had been planned for him. Thea was also sincere in her hope that Austin's affliction would enable him to see the world and those around him in a more human light. He had sacrificed his life to a misguided obligation. He surely now deserved to enrich his remaining days with time to appreciate the warmth and beauty around him. That stroke might have been a blessing, in a curious way.

Lydia appeared to be the biggest loser from the drama. Daily visits to the hospital with her mother, more to satisfy society than through their concern for the invalid, Thea suspected, had effectively put an end to the girl's social life. It had dashed her hopes of encounters with Martin. Feeling sorry for Lydia, the object of whose powerful infatuation lived no more than a few hundred yards away, Thea had invited them both to tea with him. He had been hardly less delighted with the arrangement than Margery, who saw the chance to throw together her unwelcome guest and any man other than her own son. She had accordingly found other occupations for Lydia that day, so that she should not spoil a twosome. Thea had sent an apology and explanation to Martin, then worked on her book, instead. Fate would have to take over the reverse match-making, she decided, for the affair stood no chance of success.

As she wandered amongst carpets, curios and chopsticks this afternoon, it occurred to her that it might have been better to move to the hotel immediately. Although Margery had been grateful for her support in the initial stages of the drama, the relationship had cooled again. With an invalid in the house, which gave a guest the perfect excuse to leave, Margery would no longer risk social censure for not housing her extremely distant relative. A hotel would be more conducive to writing, particularly when Alex was about to break his news.

It was while she was pondering this, and gazing at a jewelled fingernail shield which might look exciting on her own hand, that she was accosted by Fay Christie.

"Gracious, the budding authoress in a dusty old curio shop!" she exclaimed in her sharp tones. "I had no idea that you engaged in anything so mundane."

Thea looked coolly at the girl in sherbet-yellow muslin. "I also eat, wash behind my ears, and yawn when I'm bored. Even genius is human, Fay. How about you?"

The other girl could afford to ignore that. She had a juicier bone to gnaw on. "What's this about Alex going to England . . . *alone?*"

"Exciting, isn't it?" she responded. "Have you any idea of the date he plans to sail? I'm sure he'd like to know."

Fay's bright eyes regarded her suspiciously. "Don't tell me you've thrown him over and mean to try your luck with Martin."

"No, I won't tell you that, Fay. Instead, I'll ask your opinion on this fingernail shield I'm tempted to buy. The last empress wore them, you know. Martin told me that she not only lopped off heads, she also scratched out eyes when she had a fit of pique."

The barb went home. Fay's suspicion turned into open malice as she said, "You won't get his money. Uncle intends to keep a tight hold on it, especially if he feels his idiot godson is at the mercy of a gold-digger."

Thea was angry. "Martin is no idiot. He's saner than a great many people on this island. You didn't hear him talking to the Sing brothers."

"Who has been talking to the Sing brothers?" asked a masculine voice behind her.

Thea turned to see a big blond man with the slightly dissipated handsomeness of many colonials. She had seen him on various occasions, mostly in the company of Damien Lang, but they had never been introduced. For once, she stood on ceremony.

"Unless you have the most deplorable manners, I must assume that you are well enough acquainted with Fay to feel free to join our personal conversation."

He stood fully six feet four inches, so used his advantage to look down at her with an insolent smile. "Quite correct, Miss du Lessier. Fay and I have the pleasure of long acquaintance. I have been intending to negotiate an introduction to you, but these things tend to be shelved until chance brings it about." He offered his hand. "I'm Randal Forster."

"I know," Thea told him, declining to shake hands. "I'm afraid chance has chosen the most inconvenient time to bring your shelved intention to fruition, because I have to get straight back to work."

"On the great novel?" asked Fay with a sneer. "She's writing a book, Randy. All about the mysterious Orient."

"I heard. Emulating your mother," he queried, studying Thea with intense interest, "or attempting to eclipse her?"

The remark halted Thea in her tracks, and inspired curiosity for this man. Surely it had been no more than a guess . . . yet, what a perceptive one. He was deeper than she imagined.

"You've read my mother's work?" she asked.

"From cover to cover. It shouldn't be difficult to topple her and mount the throne yourself."

He had captured her attention. She forgot Fay and the dark cluttered interior of the curio shop as she took up his challenge with a sense of intrigue.

"You're assuming a great deal, Mr Forster. Are you always so forthright?"

"Aren't you?" he countered smoothly. Putting a hand beneath her elbow, he began to guide her through the mingling tourists seeking souvenirs, toward the door. "I heard, the way one does in this part of the world, that you were nabbed by the estimable Linwood whilst attempting to gain local colour for your work in the Chinese quarter." With another of his faintly insolent smiles, he went on, "I am nowhere near as upright and law abiding, so I can promise you a sight of the most astonishing and colourful cult ceremony of the East." He raised his hand, and a waiting car edged several yards forward to stop beside them. "It's no more than a short drive."

Captivated by someone vastly different from the topee-wearers she normally encountered, and curious about the promised ethnic treat, she allowed him to hand her into the expensive vehicle, and settled in the corner of the broad seat. Fay followed her in, looking none too pleased. Looking pointedly at the luxurious interior and fittings, Thea smiled at the girl.

"I see what you meant about gold-diggers, my dear."

Randal Forster settled on the folding seat facing them, and the car purred along the broad avenues of mercantile Singapore heading toward the sector housing temples and close-packed dwellings wrapped by the aroma of curry and other spices. Fay was huffily silent during the journey. Thea also chose to sit quietly, watching the passing scene whilst acutely aware that she was being scrutinised by the powerful enigmatic man opposite her. He inspired a chilled excitement in her. For once, she felt she had no control over the situation, or over a man. It made her wary, yet the experience was novel enough to intrigue her and she was happy to let it continue for a while.

The uniformed syce took the vehicle slowly through narrowing streets where mangy dogs and dark-skinned children wandered in matched resignation, using the gutters as a communal lavatory and watching the long sleek car with dark fathomless eyes. Then, Thea grew aware of the sound of distant noise and excitement of the kind created by the Asian residents of the colony during one of their exotic celebrations. Remembering how she had been cautioned by both Martin and George on intruding upon such personal occasions, she looked at her companion.

"Are you quite certain that we shall be welcome here?"

His mouth twitched. "I was told that was something which never deterred Thea du Lessier."

"You appear to have been told a great deal about someone whose acquaintance you shelved until chance took a hand."

"Piqued?"

The curious sense of excitement stirred again. He read her thoughts far too well. "I've been told nothing at all about you, Mr Forster. Can you really be that dull a person?"

"I'm certain you'll discover the answer to that for yourself before the afternoon's over."

Fay intervened in their verbal fencing. "It's getting most disgustingly smelly, Randy. How long is this going to take?"

"You're perfectly at liberty to give it a miss," he told her equably. "I'll instruct Mahmoud to drive you home, then return for us later."

"No need for that," she said with sharp irritation. "It's simply that your friends almost always live in the more unsavoury areas of the island."

"Unsavoury to you, but not to them. You're a hopeless snob, Fay. Live, and let live."

Thea had turned back to study the street scene. It was hardly more than a track running into jungle, yet it was thronged with people in vivid festive clothes, bedecked with flowers, who were in a state of high expectation. Fay was basically right. There was an overwhelming aura of crowding humanity which, mixed with that of the surrounding fetid undergrowth, was almost more than Thea could take. The sun had clouded over to leave the afternoon particularly humid. Thea's lime silk dress, with diamond points at the hem and a huge pompom at the hip, was sticking to her skin. It was difficult to breathe in the stifling atmosphere, and she was starting to regret the rare meekness that had allowed her to be swept off by the large man facing her, who must be sweltering in his immaculate cream suit. He gave no outward sign of discomfort, however, and his air of calm was curiously disturbing in the face of universal bustle.

The car halted, and he leaned toward her. "We must go on foot from here."

"Not too far, I hope," put in Fay testily. "My shoes aren't designed for hiking."

"How about yours, Thea?" he asked, adopting her first name too easily for her liking.

"They're like Fay's, but they'll doubtless stand up to whatever you have in mind."

"Attagirl! Game for anything, as I was told."

His choice of words annoyed her. "Not quite anything. You'll know soon enough when I'm not, I promise you."

"Should prove interesting," he murmured, climbing from the car and standing ready to assist his passengers.

He led the way along the track which headed further into the jungle some five hundred yards ahead. It was lined by so many people, Thea wondered where they all lived. The car had passed through small clusters of dwellings, but none big enough to call a village. She could only guess they had gathered from all over the island to witness something which must be very momentous. Only Randal Forster's influence could make this possible, she knew, for no one seemed worried by their presence. Like George McGregor, he must have many friends among the non-European races of Singapore.

The track was not totally blocked, and the distant sound of trumpets, gongs and drums told her they were almost at their destination. Randal turned to them, cautioning them to stay close behind him as he made his way to the front lest they be swept away by the shifting mass.

"I can't vouch for your safety, if that happens," he said.

Fay immediately closed behind him, leaving Thea to bring up the rear as their escort shouldered his way through. Despite her supposed reputation for "gameness", Thea hardly enjoyed the next few minutes. Fighting her way through an eager surge of people in a temperature of a hundred degrees was bad enough. Doing it dressed in a close-fitting silk dress and elegant lime-green kid shoes, made the experience definitely harrowing. Perspiration drenched her face and body, her head began to swim, and her legs threatened to fold up. She now realised the penalty of so many hours spent indoors beneath a cooling fan over the past few weeks, eating spasmodically and without appetite. The humid airless atmosphere clogged her nostrils with the sickly scent of the flower garlands, body oils and another smell she could not identify. What she was about to see had better be worth all her discomfort, she told herself ruefully.

They broke through to a clearing at the foot of an endless flight of steps disappearing between trees. In the far distance, a temple could now be seen on a rise. From this, there was a slow procession wending its way toward them, at the head of which was a sight which drew Thea's horrified attention. Men stripped to the waist and wearing only a cloth wrapped around their loins, had been clamped into heavy metal cages comprising inward-pointing knives which pierced their skin on chest and back in a hundred or more places. They looked to be in a state of agony which included paroxysms as they offered up prayers in monotonous chanting voices. Behind these victims of torture slowly plodded others with skewers more than twelve inches long plunged through the fleshy part of the throat, or through the upper lip. Still more were covered with huge dangling weights fastened to the chest and back by short pins inserted through the skin. With every step, the agony of the dragging weights sent grimaces across their sweat-sheened faces. A few men in the procession walked on sandals fashioned from upturned nails, in addition to the other tortures, and some bore crowns of metal thorns which penetrated their heads in a myriad places.

The scene began to swim before Thea's eyes as nausea swept over her. She now saw the most terrible sight of all. Borne aloft by others was an old, emaciated man on a throne of knives, which sank into his buttocks and back as he sat gazing into some far haven of purgatory.

"Religious martyrs scourging themselves, or celebrating their excessive piety," breathed a voice in her ear.

She turned swiftly to see amusement in the man's clear blue eyes.

"They're all in a trance induced by religious fervour. After volunteering for this incredible form of torture, they walk from here to their main temple enduring the scourging qualities of severe torment. When they reach it, the knives are withdrawn, the *kavadis* removed, the sandals unstrapped. They are then covered with a mysterious ash-like substance, and not a drop of blood gushes from the wounds. Incredible!"

Staring at him as if in a trance herself, Thea said, "I find it terrible. Almost obscene."

"Not in the least! Scourging of this nature is an essential religious ritual for these people. It's extremely hallowed and reverent." His face hardened momentarily. "You disappoint me. I was certain it would amuse you."

"Amuse me?" she echoed in disbelief. "Who could find it amusing?"

"My dear girl, don't be so naïve! There are those who find immense gratification from watching a public flogging, or from more discreet and inventive humiliations of the body, but this is by far the most colourful and bizarre, don't you think?"

Turning from him, Thea found Fay gazing at the procession, lost to all else. There was no suggestion of revulsion on her pointed face. It wore the same brand of marvelling awe which touched the expressions of all those around them. Swallowing hard, Thea forced herself to watch once more, but the sight of this anguish passing before her eyes, plus the deafening sound of the alien music created such turmoil within her, the vision swam, dimmed, then faded into darkness as she felt herself falling.

Her eyes flickered open to see the interior of a room painted bright blue. The unmistakable smell of Singapore hung in the air; that unique mixture of spices, oils, rotting vegetation, rain-refreshed blossoms, and joss sticks. She knew her surroundings were alien and felt a faint unease. The bed she lay on was a native *charpoy*. There was no pillow beneath her head, and only a thin, brightly-coloured covering over her body. Beneath it, she was practically naked. Since arriving in Singapore, she had abandoned the restriction of a bodice, so wore no more than panties under her dresses. Who had removed her lime-green frock and shoes?

Angling her head in order to see the rest of the room, it came as a shock to find someone watching her. Randal Forster had on a loose cotton gown and thonged sandals. There was no one else in the room. Instantly aggressive, Thea clutched the inadequate cover against her as she struggled to sit up. Her movements were disturbingly sluggish. Memory returned. She had fainted from the oppressive heat, and the garish cruelty of what she had witnessed.

With her head still swimming, she demanded, "Where is this place, and where is Fay?"

Randal smiled as he stood and crossed to her. "You passed out and missed the most exciting part of the affair. I had greater faith in your stamina."

"Where is Fay?" she repeated, conscious that he could see her bare back from where he stood.

"I sent her home. Mahmoud is coming back for us later this evening."

"He can come back for you later this evening, Mr Forster, but I'm leaving now. Where is my dress?"

Plainly enjoying her situation, he gazed down at her unperturbed. "My friend Haji is outside cleaning it for you. This is her house, by the way. So fortunate that it was nearby when you suddenly dropped to the ground. Mahmoud carried you here, and Haji felt you should be given a mild sedative to counter the shock. You've been asleep for two hours."

By now unsure of whether she was more afraid than angry, Thea hid both emotions behind her usual façade of sophistication. "As I now feel perfectly refreshed, I'll relieve you of any further responsibility. Ask your friend for my dress, whatever stage in cleaning it she has reached."

He sat on a cane chair beside the bed and ran a lingering glance over her bare shoulders. "Aren't you being just a trifle melodramatic? I heard you're a liberated woman whose byword is utter frankness."

Still clutching the cover against her breasts, she told him icily, "I don't know where you've heard all these supposed facts about me, but they've plainly been given to you by people I've never met. Now, listen carefully, because these are real facts. One, I find your attitude extremely offensive. Two, contrary to your belief, I have no intention of remaining here a minute longer. Frankness *is* my byword, Mr Forster. It leads me to suggest you stick to alley-cats like Fay Christie. She's more your style."

He began to laugh softly, and his eyes brightened in appreciation. His continued composure alarmed her more than aggression would. It suggested that he knew he had the upper hand, as well he might. She would stand no chance if he forced himself on her, but he appeared to enjoy the cat with mouse game. Thea noted the position of the door, and the distance between it and the *charpoy*. He would catch her easily if she made a dash for it. It was an incredible situation to be in. The woman Haji was just outside that door. Thea could hear water running and the soft slap of sandals on a stone floor. Through the large open window, she could see another house beneath the shade of the trees where several women moved back and forth. The ripple of childish laughter, the barking of dogs, and the soft continuous clucking of fowl gave all the signs of normality, yet she was a virtual prisoner of this man no more than yards from it.

"Seeking a means of escape?" he asked in chillingly gentle tones. "My dear Thea, you don't understand the situation in the least. Using force on women is not in my line. For one thing, they are usually more than willing and, for another, there's no pleasure to be derived from using my strength on unequal opposition. I prefer to subdue other men. Much more satisfying! Go, if you wish."

Taken aback, she studied his relaxed expression. "You're right, I don't understand the situation. What is this all about?"

"It's about a chance meeting in a curio shop, and an offer to show you some local colour to include in your great novel," he replied with the urbanity that hid his thoughts and feelings. "You were the one who fainted, if you recall."

"So?"

"So I brought you here to recover, and very gallantly persuaded our hostess to clean your dress which was greatly soiled from your fall. What happens now is up to you, so discard that ridiculous maidenly martyrdom. It so happens that I like women who are well used, which is why I've waited this long to make a move. I knew it was inevitable, so was in no hurry. If you choose to walk out, so be it. You'll get around to it eventually."

The inference of his words was clear and deeply insulting. She began to tremble with the echo of humiliation from the past.

"My God, you really have been speaking to the wrong people about me," she told him in a low voice.

He shook his blond head. "Everyone knows Anna du Lessier is a whore, and so is her daughter. She excuses it on the grounds of 'artistic inspiration'. Your excuse is 'emancipation', but it amounts to the same thing. You're both tarts, albeit high-class ones."

An old pain began to burn in her breast. An adolescent ghost on her knees, cried *What have I done?* as she clutched the hem of her lover's jacket.

"No," she whispered painfully. "You're wrong. You're wrong."

The insolence of his smile added to her sense of vulnerability. "I think not. I knew Dominic Grant during my schooldays, before he was devoured by your mama as an aspiring poet. I met him again during those early days of fame, and he spoke with immense gratitude of your uninhibited inspiration. When I heard he'd moved on to du Lessier senior, I was surprised he could consider abandoning such a rich torrent of undiluted passion. Later, after spending an entire weekend with your mother, I understood his move to more mature experiences. She really is the most erotic and stimulating creature—far more talent in the boudoir than she has with her pen. I'm intrigued to discover how you measure up, both as an author and as a whore."

Feeling as though she were being torn apart, she scrambled from the bed clutching the cover to her body, even though she felt utterly exposed and degraded.

"You expect me to stay here with you simply to persuade you to keep quiet?" she asked in an unsteady voice.

"Much too melodramatic again, my dear," he admonished, wagging his head. "I could have spread that story long ago had I known you cared so deeply about hushing it up. I really can't imagine why. I always felt it added to your extrovert personality." As she stood uncertainly before him, he stretched lazily to put his hands up behind his head. "Don't tell me you mean to have Mad Alex, forsaking all others! You haven't confessed your past to him? Dear, dear, that does put you in something of a quandary, doesn't it?"

Shaking from head to foot now and feeling totally helpless, she asked, "What are you going to do about it?"

"Nothing. No, nothing at all," he assured her in tones of genuine sincerity. "It'll be our little secret." That supercilious smile broke through again. "It does rather create a special bond between us, though, don't you agree? One with exciting future possibilities."

Drawing in her breath, she asked, "What secret do you share with Fay?"

"Ah, little Fay came to me willingly," he confessed. "Recognition of another alley-cat, perhaps. Yes, I like that simile, Thea. It has a deliciously low ring to it," he finished with a soft laugh.

Near to breaking now, Thea began to inch her way toward the door, although she sensed he would make no attempt to stop her. He had degraded her as much with words as if he had forced himself on her.

"You have certainly given me local colour for my book," she said, in an attempt to retire with dignity. "You're the perfect example of the human flotsam to be found in the East."

Two steps further on, the length of cotton was dragged from her hands leaving her naked save for the brief panties. Randal Forster's foot was firmly planted on the free end which had dragged the floor. He looked her over from head to foot as she momentarily froze beneath his scrutiny.

"It's the least reward I deserve after the trouble I took to amuse you today, wouldn't you agree?" he murmured.

Martin was driving home in his new car. It was the very latest model available to him, sprayed an impressive green. It had turned George a matching shade with envy. The afternoon was excessively hot and airless, so he was glad of the retractable hood which allowed the small disturbance of air caused by his progress to provide a little relief. Thanks to Thea's intervention, Sir Hartle had given his consent to the purchase of this vehicle, which gave Martin a modicum of pleasure in the life he hated. He had written a short note of thanks to Thea but, after sending it, felt his words might have sounded less than gracious. He had intended thanking her in person when she brought Lydia to tea, but the visit had been cancelled making the note obligatory.

Rumours were flying concerning Alex's astonishing plan to return to England very suddenly. No one was quite sure why, but the favourite guess was that he was being sent by his family to negotiate a partnership for *Berondel* with one of Margery's many nephews, also in trade. Many felt it was also the Beresfords' latest attempt to free their son from du Lessier's clutches. Martin listened to the gossip with an open mind. Any news concerning the shipping family was of interest to him. Austin's illness had put paid to the chance of meetings with Lydia and, although thoughts of her continued to torment him, he felt it was probably just as well. Where they might have headed was anyone's guess, but no direction could have led to mutual happiness. He was finding individual happiness elusive, as it was.

He was passing through an area still littered with the crushed flowers and other debris left by those who had been watching the procession this afternoon. Although he had seen holy men and occasional martyrs undergoing the fervent ordeal, he had not been present at the temple today. It was no place for Europeans. Yet, even as he formed the thought, he saw a white girl come from a side street in a manner that suggested she was also in a trance. He trod the brake pedal automatically. The girl was all alone in an area normally avoided by her own people. Switching off the engine in deep concern, he was climbing from the car when he realised that he knew her. Angry and incredulous, he strode across to where she stood gazing into space.

"*Thea!* What the hell have you been doing?" he demanded. "I've warned you before about unwarranted intrusion in these areas. Haven't you *any* intelligence?" Then, growing aware of her wet dress and filthy shoes, he raged on. "Look at the state you're in! I'll wager you have no inkling of how lucky you are to have escaped so lightly. You little fool! Do you really want an even more scandalous reputation than the one you have already?"

Her face was white; her eyes shocked. She stared at him while a building emotion rose to overwhelm her, so that she cried in a wild shaky voice, *"Don't you shout at me, you brute!"*

It halted his tirade. To his consternation, he then noticed that she was dangerously near to tears. This girl who always acted as if she had the world on a string.

"Are you all right?" he asked, in vastly different manner.

For some moments she struggled for control of herself, then whispered helplessly as the tears finally won, "Oh, Martin. *Martin!*"

The sight of her misery moved him to draw her close in comforting fashion. "It's all right," he said, in almost parental fashion. "Come on, my car's over there. I'll take you home."

She clung to him, her tears running into his starched jacket to turn the material limp as he led her across the road. All manner of suppositions ran through his startled brain all the while, but he knew better than to question her yet. Her distress continued as she remained within his encircling arm, clutching him as if he were a lifeline, while they sat in the front seats of his car. Totally mystified, and not a little shaken by this evidence of her breakdown, he let her cry herself to a standstill. The residents of the area passed in complete unconcern. The behaviour of English colonials was eccentric, at the best of times, so nothing they did surprised them.

Thea grew quiet, then slowly drew away from him. She made no attempt to speak, however. Martin hardly knew how best to break the strained silence. Eventually, he said, "Your mascara has run. You have a striped face."

"Have I?" she asked, her voice husky from weeping. "Will you wipe it clean for me?"

Taking out his handkerchief, he began the task. Halfway through it he asked, "What happened to you this afternoon?"

Refusing to meet his eyes, she murmured, "Nothing."

"Don't lie to me," he instructed gently, still rubbing at her streaked face. "I am in the right department to take action, if you've been harmed in any way."

She shook her head, causing him difficulty with his task. He gave her the handkerchief. "Here, finish it yourself. There's just one stripe left under your chin." Watching her spit on the grubby cloth before scrubbing at her skin, he probed further. "Were you up at the temple?"

"Yes."

"How many times . . ." he began, then broke off. He had no wish to upset her again. "Will you tell me what happened?"

"I passed out," she informed him with relative composure, as she handed back the now filthy handkerchief. "A woman kindly took me to her house until I recovered." Her large amber eyes were still shocked as they gazed at him. "I couldn't stand the sight of that self-inflicted torture. You see, I'm not as heartless as you think."

"I've never thought you heartless. You're an inveterate meddler, that's all." He put the handkerchief back in his pocket. "You also never listen to advice."

She tried to smile, but it was a wobbly one. "I will from now on."

"I don't believe that any more than you do," he told her quietly. "Have you any notion of the risks you ran up there all alone? If you don't care about your own safety, think of Alex. How do you think he'd feel if any harm came to you?"

"I'm sorry, Martin."

He sighed with faint exasperation. "I wonder!" Looking at the state of her dress, he asked, "Would you like to go to a hotel to clean up before going back? Or you could do it at my place, if you prefer."

"There's no need for that, thanks."

He switched on the engine. "Are you all right now?"

She nodded. "What a nuisance I am."

"You can say that again," he told her emphatically. "It's a good thing I was passing right now." Still deeply concerned over her surprising lack of control, he drove in silence for several hundred yards, then said, "I suppose I shouldn't berate you, since you're riding in the beautiful new car your meddling obtained for me. What do you think of her?"

"Very splendid. May I borrow it occasionally?"

"Certainly not! It's bright and shiny-new now, and that's the way I plan to keep it."

Normally, she would have put out the tip of her tongue, or riposted with a clever remark. Today, she said nothing. He was seeing a totally different side of this girl, which he had always suspected, but what had forced her to reveal it remained a mystery. He decided to attempt to find out.

"I have two theories about you, Thea. The first is that you've grown up in the shadow of your mother's notoriety and feel the compulsion to match up to her. Your clothes and behaviour are about right, but the urge won't be satisfied until you also become a sensational author."

"What's the second theory?" she asked, in subdued manner.

Taking his glance from the road to study her reaction, he said, "It's by far the simpler. Someone has hurt you so deeply, you can only hit back through prose." He studied the road again. "I can't wait to read the novel and discover the answer."

"You might have to wait a long time," she murmured, her faraway expression giving nothing away.

He tried again. "Singapore says Alex is planning a trip to England. Is there a business merger afoot?"

She shook her head. "He's leaving *Berondel*. After learning to fly, he plans to join an aircraft company. That's privileged information, by the way. The rest of Singapore will find out soon enough."

The news took him by surprise yet, on reflection, he realised it was the perfect life for a man who craved constant excitement.

"I wish him the best of luck," he said.

"Really? I thought you were both daggers drawn."

"Good heavens, no! I envy him, to a certain extent, however."

"And he envies you. What fools you are!" she declared, in a near normal manner. "You're both such marvellous individuals. Why not concentrate on following your own stars, instead of wallowing in this stupid resentful admiration of each other?"

"Alex is now planning to follow his," he pointed out, trying to get back to his original theme. "Where does that leave you?"

"When are you going to follow yours, and abandon this wasted existence Sir Hartle has forced on you?"

Two could play the game of refusing to answer awkward questions, he decided, as he turned the car into the broad avenue leading past his own bungalow to the Beresford house.

"I visited the Sings again last Saturday." Squeezing the rubber horn to warn a Chinese who was taking his pig for a walk right ahead of them, he continued, "There's no doubt one slips back in time during that ride in the sedan-chair. On reaching the top of the hill, it's quite clear that the Emperor is presently regarding the young Queen Victoria as a minion ruling a tiny island floating somewhere in the vast seas surrounding the world of China." He looked at her to impress her with his next words. "A century dispensed with during a ride up a hill. The curious thing is, I don't miss it all the time I'm up there."

"You would when you came down," she pointed out quietly. "There'd be nothing here but jungle, hostile natives and tigers."

Negotiating a bend, he said, "That sounds like a description of the Beresford rubber plantation. Marmaduke seems obsessed by tigers. He invited me to accompany Alex when he next goes. Lost the opportunity now he's going to England, haven't I?"

"Marmaduke probably wouldn't remember inviting you, anyway," she suggested, as they turned into the driveway and drew up at the door.

Martin got out and walked round to open the door for her. Before he did, however, he looked at her closely. "I know you are incurably independent, Thea, but if you were molested this afternoon, it's your duty to tell me. I'll treat it as strictly confidential, and do all in my power to avenge it."

She gave him a strange, sad glance. "I think you would, my dear. You're a knight at heart, aren't you?"

"Good God, no. But you're a rebel."

"Is that so very wrong?"

"Not in itself, but it's a stony path you've chosen to tread."

Putting her hand over his as it rested on the car, she said, "I simply trod on one of the stones this afternoon. Please leave it at that."

After no more than a moment's hesitation, he nodded. "Fair enough . . . but take care of yourself."

"I promise," she said, allowing him to help her alight. "Thanks for your handkerchief, and the shoulder to cry on."

"Think nothing of it. It's a long time since it was used for such a gentle purpose. Goodbye, Thea."

He drove away still absorbed by the mystery she was withholding, and also wondering how Alex could risk booking only a single cabin for his trip to England.

Chapter 12

Entering the house, Thea walked straight into the heart of a storm. The sound of raised voices drew her to the sitting room, where she found a family divided. Lydia was on a chair near the window. She had plainly been crying. Margery stood beside the elegant grandfather clock, staring at Alex, who gripped the back of the central settee, his face pale and set. Thea knew instantly that he must have announced his intended departure. Although she felt he had been unwise to do so on the very day Austin returned from hospital, her heart went out to him as she guessed the number of daggers they must all have plunged into his loyal breast.

Her own distress put aside, she moved across to him swiftly. The man who looked at her was almost a stranger, lost somewhere in the pain reflected in his eyes. Her hand gripped his as she realised, probably for the first time, what it had cost him to free himself. His attempts to spell out for her the concept of family loyalty and obligation—something she had never known—had left her impatient with him. Now she saw too clearly the demands such things made on a man. In her present low state, momentary guilt touched her. Had she driven him to this? Had she imposed too severe a choice—herself or his family? Yet, surely this was a choice between himself and them. He was entitled to his own life, with or without her by his side. Six years ago, he had selflessly bowed to their demands on his allegiance. Now, they owed him his new dawn after so many daunting twilights.

"You are responsible for this," cried Margery in the voice of wrath. "In a matter of months, you have driven my husband to a state that has rendered him helpless for life. You have shocked and distressed my daughter to the extent of robbing her of her vitality. Now you have exercised your destructive powers over my only remaining son, turning him into a slave prepared to do anything you say. You have destroyed a close loving family, and robbed me of the little I have left to live for." Fighting for control, Margery demanded, "Are you proud of what you've done? Anna du Lessier has a daughter in her own mould, that's very clear."

Coming on an afternoon of such painfully degrading treatment from a man who said the same, Margery's words hurt very deeply.

"No, oh no! My mother destroys for selfish reasons. I could never do that," she offered in self-defence. "Although I possibly added a further pinprick to Austin's rigid life, it must have been obvious to everyone in Singapore that his collapse was inevitable. No man can surely live and work in this deadly climate, year after year, measuring his every word and action in order to present a model of total perfection. In the few months I have been here, I never once saw him less than immaculately dressed, never heard him laugh or cheer, never saw his tight control slip by the slightest degree. Margery, he has been driving himself like that since he was the age Alex is now. The wonder is that he's survived this long without breaking down."

Although she had spoken in gentle, almost compassionate tones, Margery saw only further emnity in her words. "How dare you speak to me in that manner? How dare you criticise a man who has devoted his blameless life to the family you have irrevocably split?"

"Austin devoted his life to his *ideal* of a family. He forgot that its members were individuals who did not necessarily share that ideal."

"My son did, until you dazzled him with prizes beyond his reach."

"They were only out of his reach because you made them so," Thea cried emotionally. "If you really loved Alex, as you're so fond of vowing, you'd be giving him your blessing right now. Real love means being willing to let go."

"Then practise what you preach, you wicked girl!" cried the demented woman.

"I'm not holding him, Margery," Thea responded then. "My love for him has urged him to cross the world, leaving me here."

"Daddy's ordered him out," put in Lydia, in a broken voice. "He's told poor Alex to leave the house immediately and never come back."

Stricken, Thea turned to Alex. "He couldn't be so cruel, after the way you've tormented yourself over making the decision."

"You've been thrown out, too," added Lydia. "Whatever will people say?"

"To hell with what people will say," cried Thea, the stress of what she had suffered that afternoon finally making her lose control. "That's been the trouble with this family all along. You've been so obsessed with ensuring that people say the right things, you've forgotten how to be human. You, Lydia, have been so repressed, you now feel guilty over perfectly normal emotions. Your brother has been named 'Mad Alex' simply because he has indulged in the usual high-spirited capers all young men enjoy. You're both delightful young people who have never been given a chance to live."

"Stop it!" commanded Margery hysterically. "Stop it, at once! Haven't you done enough to hurt me without resorting to such cruelty?

"All right, everyone," said a quiet, weary Alex. "I think enough blame has been laid at various doors." Turning to Thea, he added, "I allowed you your right to reply, darling, but now the important thing is to decide on the best way out of this mess."

"There is no question of you being denied your own home, Alexander, but I will not have that creature here," cried Margery. "*I will not!*"

"Be quiet, Mother," he responded with great firmness. "You are far too overwrought to decide anything, at present. It's Thea and me who have been told to go, so we must do so in a way which will hurt you and Lydia the least. As she said, people are going to talk. I can't see how that can be avoided completely."

"Your father didn't know what he was saying," his mother pleaded. "Give me time to talk him round. Of course you must stay here. He's confined to his room and need not be aware of the fact."

"No, Mother. What he will never forgive is the humiliation of being told of my plans by old Brimmicombe. I understand that and have enough remorse to do as he wishes. I'll not remain here behind his back, but I have to think of the best place to go when we leave."

Thea stared at him with unwelcome suspicion crystallising fast. "Alex, you are still going to England, aren't you?"

"Yes, yes . . . I've no choice now. I wasn't expecting this, however. I imagined there'd be a period of adjustment before I sailed."

"What was that about Austin being told your plans by Brimmicombe?"

He still looked dazed and deeply hurt as he explained. "I advised the board of my resignation in strictest confidence. The members observed it with everyone save Father, whom they assumed had been the first to be told. It must have been a terrible blow to him, Thea. He now sees me as a rat deserting a sinking ship, and I can't blame him. It's how everyone will see it."

Thea knew it was presently how Alex himself saw it. Knowing how vulnerable he was to accusations of disloyalty, her heart went out to him as she imagined what must have passed between sick father and guilt-ridden son.

"Darling, listen. Contact all the shipping lines and get on any vessel leaving Singapore in the direction of England," she advised.

He sighed. "That really would be like the rat leaving. I . . . this is so unexpected a development. I hadn't ever considered the possibility of his . . . his refusal to have me in the house." His throat worked convulsively as he struggled for words. "Thea, you must see that I can't just walk out on a situation like this. He's an extremely sick man, yet he

220

intends to continue working from home as if nothing has happened. It'll kill him.''

She took his hands in hers. "It'll kill him if he ever stops. Alex, this must make you see that your decision is the right one. If you had given up your ambition in order to stay here after his stroke, you would still only ever be as good as the office boy. He has no intention of giving up control until he gives up breathing. We'll move out to a hotel. Wah and Ah Toy can send our things across when they've packed them.''

He shook his head. "We can't do that. It'll cause too much talk.''

"Oh, not you as well!'' she cried impatiently. "They'll make a scandal from this whatever you do. Why worry?''

"I'm not worried for my own sake, I'm simply trying to minimise the problem for Mother and Lydia.''

"I've never known them try to minimise anything for you.''

"Leave the boy alone, Dorothea,'' snapped Margery. "You have caused all his unhappiness, as it is. Pack your clothes and go!''

Alex rounded on her. "When Thea leaves, I shall leave with her, but I have no intention of going until I'm satisfied that everything possible has been done to spare you and Lydia distress. So please spare me distress by ceasing your attacks on the girl I love. They don't help the situation, in the least, and are totally unjustified.'' He added with great weariness, "Father has precipitated this situation and, in his absence, I am the man of the house. Please leave me to make the necessary decisions.''

Thea watched him with growing concern. He seemed disorientated, as if the rug of his life had been snatched from beneath his feet. She had drastically underestimated what this would do to him after weeks of concentrated work to keep the family line afloat. Austin's reaction had dealt him a near-mortal blow. He needed time to come to terms with it; time to hide away and lick his wounds, like a hurt animal before returning to the fight. With that simile came a solution, as she recalled Martin's words concerning an invitation to see tigers.

"Uncle Marmaduke!'' she exclaimed eagerly. "We'll go to the plantation for a while. No one'll think that's unusual. It'll give you a chance to think, and Margery will have time to talk Austin round. What do you think, Alex?''

Passing a weary hand over his brow, he considered her idea. "Well, I do go up fairly regularly. He's been in Singapore recently, so no one would be surprised if I took you with me.''

"They'd think he issued the invitation whilst here.''

"Yes, they probably would,'' he agreed, apparently accepting the plan. "Lydia had better come, too. Not only will it seem more natural for her to make the trip with us, it'll halt any speculation on the fact that we've left the house together with such suddenness. She ought to get away for a while, anyway. Father's illness has upset her, and so has this bombshell."

"Lydia will most certainly not go to Serantinggi," ruled Margery. "I need her here with me."

"It's the best arrangement, Mother," Alex said firmly. "Since Father collapsed, she's had no life at all apart from visits to the hospital. When we go, she'll be faced with nothing but sickness and stress in this household. A trip to Serantinggi will do her the world of good."

It will also do Martin good, thought Thea out of the blue. *It might help those two to see so much of each other, they won't even be speaking by the time the trip ends*. It did not occur to her that she was starting to meddle, once more.

Martin had been at the Beresford plantation at Serantinggi no more than a few hours before he knew that was where he would like to spend the rest of his days. The large white-painted sprawling bungalow was reached by an earth track running from the coast ten miles away, where a jetty and godowns supplied *Berondel* ships with latex. That track gave the visitor his first insight into the jungle and hills terrain of the Malay States, and provided an emerald cloister deceptively suggesting that it was leaving the world behind and running to Nirvana.

The giant lush undergrowth housed a teeming variety of birds, magnificent butterflies and chattering monkeys that leapt from tree to tree; the brilliant green foliage was broken every now and then by bright flame-of-the-forest, rioting purple bougainvillaea, pale hibiscus, and the wonderfully-scented white frangipani. This was the outer edge of the jungle; the beautiful face. The other face was in that area where the sun never penetrated. There, the slimy, ugly or dangerous creatures roamed. The swamps housed snakes, leeches, and crocodiles; the depths concealed elephants, buffalo and tigers. There, the plants and trees were swollen and grotesquely twisted, tangled with creepers that almost strangled the weaker plants. Man wisely remained on the jungle fringe, unless driven into the savage interior by strong motivation.

The rubber plantation lay in an area of cleared jungle. From the bungalow built on a slight rise, there were magnificent views of Serantinggi Valley and the verdant surrounding hills which were soft on the eye and infinitely alluring to a man searching for tranquillity. The isolated wooden bungalow with its shabby old-fashioned comfort, the warm familiar smell of its stables, the heavy perfumes of blossoms and fruits, the neat rows of rubber trees stretching in every direction, and the distant sound of music from the huts of the Indian tappers all charmed Martin from the moment he arrived to an eccentric and hearty greeting from his host.

He supposed some men might have been upset by the willingness with which his department had granted him leave of absence at virtually a moment's notice, but he had never been under the illusion that he was a valued member of staff, and he wanted this trip too much. He wanted it, in spite of the conditions under which it had been offered. Thea had arrived at his bungalow whilst he had been taking a refreshing bath after dropping her at the Beresford house, and he had dressed swiftly in a robe, feeling certain only dramatic circumstances could have brought her there.

At first, he had been inclined to agree with her view that what people were liable to say about Austin's renunciation of his son really did not matter. Then he thought of what his own attitude would have been if scandal had touched his lost family. Of course he would have done his utmost to protect them. It had been uncomfortable enough during his father's campaign to halt publication of Anna du Lessier's novel, when newspapers had been full of misquoted exchanges between them and details of the Linwood family had been available for public reading. The memory of his feelings on reading about those dear to him, now led him to sympathise with Alex Beresford's bid to minimise the distress of his mother and sister before he left.

His opinion of Austin, already extremely low, now reached rock bottom. His opinion of Thea was more difficult to define. Knowing full well her principal motive in arranging for his inclusion on this trip, only her forceful personality could have persuaded Alex to accept him as one of an intimate foursome on an isolated plantation during a time of emotional stress. How had she done it? Should he have agreed to accept? Only the forthcoming days were likely to provide the answer to that, and Martin was too eager for the chance to go up-country to worry about the outcome. He would face that when the time came.

On the overnight voyage in a *Berondel* ship, the other three had retired to their cabins early, leaving him to sit contentedly on the deck to watch the dark coastline slipping past by the light of a full tropical moon. Morning had brought arrival at the jetty, and the delight of discovery during the ten-mile drive to the bungalow. Marmaduke was boisterously pleased to see them, and prattled endless entertaining nonsense throughout dinner, until his guests were almost asleep in their chairs. He then conducted them to their rooms—the two men very correctly on one side of the bungalow and the two girls on the other. The Malay woman who lived with Marmaduke did not put in an appearance, so Martin deduced that she would remain out of sight throughout their visit. It was a pity. He would like to have met her.

Even had the girls occupied the adjacent rooms, Lydia would have been unmolested, for Martin fell asleep almost immediately and had to be gently shaken awake by a Malay boy in starched white jacket and colourful sarong, who brought him morning tea and several fresh figs on a silver tray.

The dawn bore an atmosphere of fresh beginnings, as if the burden of the past had been removed at some time during his sleep. Pulling free the mosquito net, he slipped his feet into mules and walked naked to the window, where the boy had thrown back the shutters. The view was magical. Mist hung through the valley as the growing warmth of the day encountered the moist depths of the jungle, and the sun was still no more than an apricot glow behind the hills. In that hushed stillness, the tappers were setting out to collect the milky latex which had dripped into the cups wired to the trunks. Their swaying figures could just be seen in the infant light, and Martin watched them out of sight as he drank his tea feeling unbelievably contented.

The shower consisted of a stone-floored cubicle, where an overhead tank was filled with water from buckets brought by a *kebun*. To receive the deluge, Martin was instructed to pull the rope at the side of the tank. This opened a perforated section which sent sporadic gushes of tepid water over him, so long as he stood on the cross marked on the floor. Its antiquated delight was one more aspect of Serantinggi that made him feel right in such a place. Having been warned that the only way of getting around up-country was on a horse or elephant, he dressed in the expensive breeches Sir Hartle had insisted he bring from England, which he had not yet worn, and tucked into them a long-sleeved white silk shirt. As the group was an informal one, he considered a jacket unnecessary so knotted a cravat loosely around his throat to substitute for a tie. It hid the scar perfectly.

When he followed the verandah around the side of the building he discovered the headboy, Marek, standing patiently beside a table covered with immaculate linen set for four with cutlery polished to a dazzling shine. Seated at the table was Alex, in breeches that looked impressively well used and a shirt with a Cricket Club tie. His face was set, and with his unruly curls slicked down after a shower he looked suddenly older and a deal more sober.

"Good morning. Sleep well?" he asked, nodding to Marek, who pulled out a chair for Martin.

"Marvellously." Looking around with continuing pleasure in the misty apricot vista, he added, "This is my idea of paradise."

"Is it? Uncle Duke would never agree."

"How about you?" Martin probed, as Marek poured coffee from a silver pot before setting before him a slice of pineapple chilled and frosted with sugar, which rested in a silver coupe lined with a paste of ground nuts mixed with the juice of the fruit.

Alex shook his head. "Not my idea of paradise either. You should experience it during the monsoons. Men can go crazy out here."

"Men can go crazy anywhere," he replied quietly.

At that point, the girls appeared from their side of the bungalow, Lydia in a white cotton blouse and neat breeches that gave her a schoolgirlish air, Thea wearing an almond-green costume which would not have disgraced a Turkish sultan.

"Don't look so horrified, darling," she told Alex, as both men got to their feet. "These are the only clothes I have in which I could conceivably ride a horse and, since I've never done it before, I don't expect to remain on it for long." She kissed him full on the mouth before sinking into the cane chair Marek held for her. Then she glanced up at Martin. "You look astonishingly fit this morning."

"I feel it," he replied, thinking how one girl's vividness emphasised the other's pallor and lack of vitality. "Good morning, Lydia."

"Good morning," she replied, sitting on his right and waving the pineapple away as the boy offered it.

"Where's Marmaduke?" asked Thea starting on her fruit.

"He breakfasts in his room. Porridge and a boiled egg; the same every bally morning," Alex told her. "Marek is in his element with guests to pamper. We'll be treated like royalty, believe me."

"Sounds heavenly," Thea declared. "After that middle-ages contraption the little Malay girl told me is misnamed 'a shower' I feared the worst. Royal treatment from Marek will compensate nicely." She sipped her coffee, looking at Martin over the rim of the cup. "Have you one of those unbelievable arrangements in your room?"

"Fun, aren't they?" he commented, looking appreciatively from the dish of scrambled eggs to the one of kedgeree Marek offered, wondering if he could have some of each. Deciding on the kedgeree and taking a man-sized helping, he continued without thinking. "We had even more ingenious contraptions in France. You'd never credit the lengths we went to just to douse ourselves—fully-clothed, of course."

"Fully-clothed," echoed Lydia faintly. "Why?"

"To get rid of the . . ." He pulled himself up just in time. Alex was frowning at him. Lice and other assorted bodily torments were not a suitable subject for breakfast at a rubber plantation, or for three young

225

people who had no comprehension of trench life. He tried another subject. "Where do you propose we should go this morning?"

"I thought we'd make a brief tour of the plantation," Alex replied. "We'll keep close to the bungalow in case the girls want to turn back. Lydia's fairly competent on a horse, but tires quickly; Thea's a total novice." He signalled Marek to bring more coffee, asking casually, "Have you had much experience in the saddle?"

Martin nodded, making eager inroads into the kedgeree. "I did a bit of steeplechasing in my youth, and hacked around the estate, of course. It wasn't until the regiment went to France that I learned what real riding was. Cavalry horses are strong-willed beasts difficult to control under fire."

The other man stared at him as colour crept into his face. "You were in a cavalry regiment?"

He nodded. "Hussars."

"You have never told us," came the accusation from the star rider of the polo team and Turf Club.

"I don't recall any of you ever asking me," Martin returned in level tones.

Silence fell between them then, and it continued until Marek offered Lydia the cooked dishes, only to be waved away again. Martin looked at the girl in concern.

"Aren't you going to eat at all, this morning?"

"I'm not hungry."

"You must be! You left most of last night's excellent dinner."

She shook her head. "I couldn't manage a thing."

"Nonsense, you must have something inside you if we are going to ride around the plantation."

"Leave her alone," Alex interceded wearily. "She knows what she wants."

Martin studied him for a moment or two, then put down his knife and fork deciding that the only hope of enjoying this sojourn was to clear the air right then.

"Look," he began, "I know it wasn't your idea that I should come here, but perhaps we could get a few things straight. When Thea came round with the invitation, she explained the reason for this trip. I have every sympathy and understanding for your situation and, if there's anything I can do to help, I'll be glad to support you. It was with that notion in mind, apart from my eagerness to take up your uncle's offer to show me around, which made me agree to come. A foursome is always more enjoyable than three, and I am looking forward to Lydia's company while you two thrash out your problems."

When Alex made no immediate response, he continued doggedly, "It does seem to me, however, that it would be a great deal easier for us all if we relaxed and enjoyed what this place has to offer us. He turned to Lydia. "Starving yourself into a decline will solve nothing, besides putting additional worry on your brother. He needs all the love and support he can get from you, right now. Instead, he's confronted by a wraith who can't even conjure up a smile first thing in the morning."

Flushing, she looked down at her empty plate. "I'm sorry. It's just that everything has been so beastly lately."

"All the more reason why you should do your utmost to put an end to the beastliness," he insisted gently, to the top of her head. "Now stop being foolish, and let Marek give you some egg with toast." So saying, he glanced round to signal the Malay, and caught sight of Thea's expression. "Why that smirk, Miss du Lessier?"

"I was merely thinking that the air at Serantinggi appears to have brought out the meddling trend in you, too," she told him pointedly.

He smiled. "I didn't mean to sound officious. It's just that I find this place so marvellous, I was hoping we could behave like four young people on a holiday, and enjoy ourselves."

Taking out his cigarettes and offering one to Martin, Alex said, "You can't have much of a holiday in a place like this. There's very little to do except drink and go riding. Any planter will tell you that."

"Planters don't necessarily have two attractive girls to entertain," Martin pointed out, leaning toward the lighted match Alex held out. He settled back and exhaled smoke slowly. "We can't expect them to spend their time as planters do. Come on! If Lydia is prepared to eat a breakfast she doesn't want in order to cheer you up, you owe her a few happy memories before you leave for England."

"How about providing a few for me, darling," put in Thea persuasively. "Let's forget about the problems in Singapore for a while."

With lingering reservations Alex said, "I appear to be outnumbered three to one, so let's get *this* straight, Martin. I'll provide the drinking and riding, but you'll have to conjure up all the additional entertainment. It was your bally idea."

Chapter 13

During the first three days at Serantinggi Alex still felt the effects of shock. Being ordered from the house was a move he had never foreseen, had never remotely considered. Anger, recriminations, reminders of his obligations, all these he had expected. Not a total and irrevocable severance. The vision of an embittered crippled man with saliva running down his chin had haunted him during the journey to the plantation, and continued to haunt him. He knew his shining new future had been robbed of its flavour of freedom. It was no longer his own decision to go to England; his father had made it inevitable. Even in this, Austin had assumed total control.

Hours of concentrated thought on the situation had produced just one clear conclusion. If Thea remained adamant about staying on in Singapore, she would be obliged to take a room in a hotel where she would be prey to all the raffish, unscrupulous men in and around the colony once he sailed. If she were his wife, his name would protect her until the novel was finished . . . or until she missed him so badly she was driven to join him. He had placed his proposal before her during the overnight voyage to Serantinggi, asking her to consider it while they were at the plantation and give her answer before their return to Singapore.

He had agreed to invite Martin whilst still reeling from shock, having some vague notion of four being better than three whilst trying to make important decisions with Thea. From the first day at the plantation, however a remarkable change had occurred in the man who had always inspired a mixture of admiration and resentment. The hesitant, reserved manner had vanished beneath a confidence bordering on command.

Three days spent continuously in his company had shown Martin to be a different man from the one Alex had known in Singapore. A skilled horseman, an intelligent questioner on all aspects of rubber production, and a surprisingly inventive house guest, he had somehow drawn them all close in companionship at a time of stress. Finding himself liking the man more than he had thought possible, Alex considered Damien Lang's suggestion that they were all being duped by a man playing the part of a fool. If he ever had been, he certainly was not now. By the fourth day, he had won Alex over completely. The two girls had been captivated from the first evening, when Martin had produced a book of ghost stories from Marmaduke's neglected library and read them aloud with such drama they had declared themselves too scared to go to bed. The subsequent appearance at their windows of a sheet draped over a chair, to resemble a spook, whilst obviously human wails rent the air, had brought forth a hail of pillows, cushions and other soft weapons from the shrieking female occupants.

Alex had been too preoccupied by his overwhelming problems to participate then, but by this fourth evening he had recovered sufficiently to respond with genuine pleasure to the news that Martin had finally succeeded in mending Marmaduke's gramophone, with which he had been tinkering for some while. Accordingly, all four young people, plus their host, dressed for dinner as if the meal were to be eaten in a smart hotel, placing Marek in his seventh heaven with such a grand occasion in the offing. At precisely seven p.m. the two young men in correct evening suits marched around the bungalow to present themselves as escorts to their chosen partners. The girls emerged from their rooms almost simultaneously, and there could hardly have been a more striking contrast. With her golden-fair hair dressed high for the occasion, and wearing a demure gown of pink georgette, Lydia gave the appearance of a girl embarking on the first engagement of her coming-out season. When Martin presented her with a corsage of hibiscus he had picked and given to Marek to keep on ice, she was thrilled. Thea's dark vividness was highlighted by a clinging gown of violet shot-silk, with a long swathe of ivory satin hanging from each shoulder to form a hip-length loop at her back. Around her head she had wound a band of ivory material and fastened it with an antique brooch of amethysts and pearls. Alex gave her a lingering kiss instead of a corsage, murmuring, "You look ravishing."

The couples walked arm in arm to where Marmaduke awaited them in the sitting room. The older man was highly delighted with the histrionic flavour of the evening, so rose to the occasion with such glee the youngsters flattered him by calling him *Your Grace*. Conversation at dinner was very lively, and if decorum slipped a little after the first course of glazed prawns, no one was there to frown on them. The dining room filled with dark, heavy Victorian furniture was lit by oil lamps from the same era and cooled by punkahs operated by the motor-driven generator outside. Martin was charmed by the sensation of being in a past age, and said so to his host.

"Your ancestral home is extremely impressive, Your Grace."

"Owned by the family since Cromwell, young sir," Marmaduke stated, with equal solemnity.

"It was that Cromwell fellow who installed the showerbaths, I suspect," put in Thea dryly.

"Tut, tut, madam, not nice to say such things at the dinner table," admonished Marmaduke, before breaking into a chuckle. "Must tell the Duchess that one. Tell you what. Take you to meet the Sultan while you're here."

"How splendid! I'd adore being introduced to a real sultan."

"Going to put one in the book?" queried Martin teasingly.

"No."

"Why, not, Thea? You can't get much more Eastern than that," Alex pointed out.

"I have too many characters already. I'm thinking of taking some out."

"Good lord, can you do that when you're halfway through it?" asked Martin.

"What makes you think I'm halfway through?" The response was tense and wary.

"You've been working on it every afternoon since we came here."

"I haven't done much. It's not easy to write lying down, and all that riding each morning makes it too painful to sit for long."

Martin smiled wickedly at her. "To be a genius, it's necessary to suffer. You'll create a greater masterpiece if you sit to write it."

"Oh, very amusing," was her acid comment. "Just because you were once in the jolly old Hussars, you think everyone should be a born rider."

"No, I don't, but I think you'd get on better if you borrowed some breeches. That Turkish potentate's outfit makes the poor beast believe it must be an elephant, so it moves accordingly."

Putting out the tip of her tongue at him, her eyes sparkled as she said, "I'll wager you're not such an expert at the two-step. You'll regret that ungallant remark when the orchestra hired by the Duke plays for dancing after dinner."

"The hero of every ballroom I used to be," put in Marmaduke reflectively, as the consommé was served by the elated houseboy. "Very neat feet, you know. Twinkled over the polished boards—positively twinkled. There was not a hostess in London who refused me a card for a ball, and the young ladies practised their steps for days just in case I wished to write my name in their dance-cards. Couldn't keep up with me, half of 'em," he ran on in typical style. "*Twinkled* over the floor."

Thea smiled at him. "I suggest that the arrangements are changed, in that case. You must partner the ladies while Martin operates the gramophone."

"He'll have to," put in Alex with a grin. "He's the only one who knows how to work the bally thing since he mended it."

230

"It takes brains and considerable skill," Martin pointed out immediately.

Lydia, who had said little yet, put down her spoon to say, "If Uncle Duke is going to twinkle over the floor with Thea all evening, I'm not going to dance with my *brother*. You operate the gramophone, Alex."

"It takes brains *and* considerable skill," repeated Martin, with a straight face.

"Dear me! Had no notion the contraption was so complicated," marvelled Marmaduke. "Threw something at it during a monsoon, you know. Wish I hadn't. Given you all this trouble to put it right. How did you learn to do that, young sir?"

"In the army," he replied. "Good thing you didn't throw the records instead. I'm not too hot at mending them."

"Quite so," the older man agreed, nodding his head. "Can't read music myself, either. Nothing to be ashamed of."

The soup was followed by chickens stuffed with nuts and spices, served on a bed of rice and surrounded by sweet potatoes. When it came to the desserts, Marek had allowed the occasion to go to his head by encouraging the cookboy to produce three. They were each so magnificent to the eye, it seemed a crime to disturb them. They did, of course. Fruits, and a selection of cheeses finished an excellent meal created from the contents of the vast store cooled by huge blocks of ice made each day by the cookboy's assistant.

When they returned to the sitting room, Alex and Martin moved the furniture so that it lined the walls, while Marek took up the numerous rugs to leave the floor free for dancing. Marmaduke was indulging in his second port since dinner, having had several before the meal, so Alex murmured to Thea that she should encourage his uncle to "open the ball" without delay. Nodding, she went across to the sidetable bearing the decanters, and took his arm to lead him away from it to the centre of the room.

"We haven't dance-cards, Your Grace, but there is a lovely young lady over here who has been practising her steps very determinedly and will be devastated if you don't twinkle over the floor with her."

He looked at her with great sadness. "Oh, my dear, you know I haven't done it for many years. Many years. Muffin-faced brother sent me here. Very unforgiving." His face, ravaged by too many glasses of port and an unrelenting climate, drooped into a doleful expression. "Only a slightly *grey* sheep, you know. Not black, at all."

"Still the hero of the ballroom, I'm sure," she put in quickly, at a gesture from Alex. "Allow me to present the Honourable Lydia Beresford, Your Grace. The orchestra is about to strike up."

Martin had wound the gramophone and selected a record. It was a waltz from the Boer War era, and the recording sounded as old. With Thea in his arms, Alex called across, "Brains and considerable skill . . . to produce *that*?"

Martin looked affronted. "I have never claimed responsibility for what is on these round things. The gramophone is a triumph of repair work, but don't hold me responsible for the music."

To the amazement of all four, Marmaduke did twinkle across the floor . . . almost. Extremely light and elegant on his feet there was plain evidence of his youthful skill, which only age and an excess of port presently marred. Lydia did very well under his guidance, despite the fact that she spent most of the dance gazing at Martin, betraying her wish to be in his arms rather than those of her uncle. Her wish was soon granted when Alex volunteered to keep an eye on the precious machine for the next dance. Thea twinkled with Marmaduke to the rhythm of a rather scratchy two-step, while Martin proved her right as he partnered Lydia no more than adequately.

"You going to marry that young fellow?" her host asked Thea loudly, as he executed such a complicated manoeuvre she had difficulty in copying it.

Avoiding an answer, she merely said, "He's asked me if I will."

"Lonely, you know, since his father died."

"His father recovered from the stroke. Surely they told you," she said indignantly.

"Never said a word to me," he insisted. "Still, I'm glad, for the lad's sake. Not right for a man to be on his own. He refused to admit it to me, of course, but his sister was behind it all."

"Lydia?" she said, baffled by his conversation.

"That her name? Same as my little niece there. Very pleasant young fellow. Taken a fancy to him. Clever—very clever. Mended that gramophone, d'you see? Two things against him, though. Likes tigers, for some reason, and serves very poor port."

Understanding him, at last, she shook her head. "I'm not going to marry him."

Her partner halted in mid-twirl, looking deeply worried. "Oh dear, oh dear, oh dear! Was it mention of the tigers, or the port? Shouldn't have said anything. Disregard it completely. Give the fellow a fair chance. No tigers in Singapore now, and you can pass him a tip about the port."

"It's your nephew Alex who has asked me to marry him," she explained patiently.

"Gracious, him too! Difficult decision for you. Mustn't try to influence you, naturally, but he's a splendid boy. Muffin-faced father, mind you. Should have been my son, instead. I never had a son, you know," he went on regretfully. "Second thing I'd have liked."

"What was the first?" she prompted, hoping to lead him from the subject of marriage proposals.

"Partnership of *Berondel*," he replied immediately. "Wasn't even given any shares in the company. Packed off here to live and die. Hard man, Austin. Unforgiving. If you do choose that nephew of mine, take him away somewhere. Family almost smothers him, and he's such a splendid fellow."

The record ended, and Martin came to a halt saying apologetically to Lydia, "That can't have been very thrilling for you. I can't boast of ever having actually twinkled over the floor, but I seem to have lost what little skill I did have."

Remaining as close as if he still held her, she gazed up at him. "You were *marvellous*. You mustn't continue to believe that you're not as good as other people, Martin. You're much, much better. I told you that once before."

He smiled. "That was in a different context. Even your generous nature can't blind you to the fact that I'm a deplorable performer at the art of ballroom dancing." Even so, as he walked beside her to the chairs lining the walls, he recalled the Military Ball at which he had not dared to dance for fear of making a total fool of himself. What progress he had made since then owed itself mostly to the past four days. This place offered all he longed for; his *real* new start in the East. This was what he wanted to do with his future. He would buy a rubber plantation. There, he would gain the peace he sought and could not find in Singapore.

These days at Serantinggi had been magical. Cantering through sun-dappled paths in company with a man who was entertaining, warmly friendly, and eccentric enough to make Martin feel the sanest man on earth, he had seen every aspect of the plantation from cutting the trees and fixing cups to catch the liquid rubber, right through to the factory where the latex was processed and baled for transportation to the *Berondel* jetties. He had spoken with the tappers—mostly Indians —and visited their lines to meet their wives, and laughing brown children already possessed of the handsome features of their race. He had studied Marmaduke's books on the production of rubber and the care of trees, and had spent long periods with the Eurasian manager and overseers discussing labour and production problems, returning to the bungalow for tiffin or sundowners feeling happy, pleasantly tired, and full of a new confidence. He felt a different man: he *was* a different man. The doctors had been right in their promise of eventual recovery. Since his arrival in this paradise his hands had been perfectly steady, he had not once lost control of his temper, and his feelings for Lydia had been blessedly normal. Small wonder he was possessed by a happiness he had not known for a long time—so long, he now almost ached with it.

Marmaduke retired early. The four younger people made no attempt to detain him. Twinkling across the floor had made him maudlin with reminiscences of his youth and unwilling exile at Serantinggi. He bade them an elaborately affectionate goodnight before heading off along the verandah, port decanter in his hand, telling them to enjoy themselves but to exercise discretion. It was easier on their own. Delightful though he was, the self-styled "Duke of Beresford" had made the numbers uneven and put restrictions on their conversation. They found it was possible to dance without someone manning the gramophone, although there was an occasional laughing scramble to wind the machine when the music began to slow and drop several octaves. It was great fun, and they were bound together in a state of friendship and understanding only possible now because all outside influences had been removed. They drank enough to make them reckless and relaxed without being actually inebriated, so that between dances they sprawled unselfconsciously in the chairs to talk about everything under the sun, including the kind of stimulating teasing indulged in by those who find each other attractive.

After a while, the night beckoned. They carried the gramophone on to the verandah, which was lit by one of the huge moons only seen in the tropics, seeking the closer harmony nocturnal enchantment could provide. Amongst the records they had found a batch of more modern ones, mostly wartime favourites. These were now placed on the turntable, and the dancing grew slower, more intimate, as the sentimental tunes brought to the surface the desire for more demonstrative expressions of their harmony.

Thea enjoyed the closeness with which Alex held her while they danced. His body was youthful and strong against hers, offering the promise of excitement and comfort with its nearness. That evening she had a curious desire for the latter, yet had no idea why. Perhaps it was due to hearing the old wartime tunes, which threatened to awaken the ghost of a kneeling girl clinging to the hem of a khaki jacket and crying desperately, *"What have I done?"*

His mouth bent to her ear to whisper, "How about giving me your answer now—tonight?"

Coming from the humiliating memory of her meeting with Randal Forster, she looked at him. "Alex, you gave me until the end of this trip to make my decision."

234

Drawing her even closer as they circled dreamily, he said, "This is how it would be all the time. What more would you want?"

The answer to that evaded her. Sliding her hand up his back to caress the curls at the nape of his neck, she murmured, "You've recovered from the shock a little now, haven't you? The first painful step has been taken, darling. Don't start to introduce complications. All you now have to do is concoct a story which will spare your family as much gossip as possible, then book your cabin."

He kissed her temple. "I'd rather book a double cabin."

"Oh, Alex, I have to . . ."

"I know," he interrupted savagely against her hair. "Why is this damned book so important?"

The ghost of a kneeling girl stirred in its shroud once more. "You'll know, when I've written it. Hold me close, Alex—very close."

When the music stopped they continued to sway together, loath to break apart. The record began again, after noisy winding of the machine by Martin, and the words of "Let the Great Big World Keep Turning" touched them all once more. Words telling of need, of love, and of surviving anything through the strength of that love. With that simple evocative melody, the throbbing of the cicadas, and the pulsing of the distant generator filling her ears, Thea made no attempt to prevent Alex from guiding her along the verandah and around the corner. On that side of the bungalow where she slept, the moonlight was partially blocked by the wide overhang of the roof and by a tree planted to give shade. In that seclusion they kissed with growing passion, both swept by mutual attraction that had been denied true fulfilment for so long.

The inexplicable wish for comfort now manifested itself as involuntary desire for something her body had long ago frequently gloried in. As Alex slid the dress from her shoulders, and his warm mouth began to travel over her skin toward her breasts, she ached deep within for that touch which would set in motion the joyous agony of release. Instinctively, her hands unbuttoned his jacket and sought warm flesh by tugging the shirt free from his waist.

Her touch on his skin put the torch to his passion, and he said huskily, "We'd better go inside your room before I undress you completely."

The faint voice of sanity spoke to her then. Longing to do as he suggested, she moaned a soft warning. "We can't go there yet. The others will come looking for us."

"Not if they've any sense," he argued, forcing her to back in the

235

direction of her door. "Thea, I can't stand this much longer. For God's sake, let's get in there."

"No, Alex, we *have* to wait until they go to bed," she insisted, struggling to keep her head while he lost his.

When her back was against the wall, he pressed his whole body to hers as he said, "I want you like hell and I want you *now*. Now, Thea. I've gone too far to stop."

She knew it, but forced herself away and began tugging her dress back in place. "Thank God, I haven't," she told him in a voice that shook. "We daren't leave those two alone."

"What?" he demanded, a man highly excited and unable to reason sanely.

"Alex, please don't look at me that way," she begged, already in the cold throes of denial. "A few hours, and you can have all you want of me, I swear."

He was deaf to all but his basic need, however. Turning swiftly, he clattered down the three wooden steps into the garden, then stood breathing heavily as he fought for control.

"Damn you, Thea," he said eventually, over his shoulder.

"I've deliberately thrown them together on this trip," she replied quietly from the verandah above him. "It's my responsibility to protect Lydia from the possible consequences."

Round the corner of the bungalow, on the main verandah, the record had ended. Martin released Lydia and walked to the gramophone, where the needle was clicking back and forth over the grooves at the centre of the disc. He lifted the arm and returned it to its rest, saying, over his shoulder, "You can choose between 'After the Ball' and 'Beautiful Dreamer'. We've played all the rest."

"Let's not bother with music," said Lydia from behind him.

He turned to her with a smile. "Is my dancing that bad?"

She was very close, and very aware that they were presently alone. He wondered how he would handle what was surely coming. At that stage, he was reasonably calm.

"You look awfully nice when you smile," she told him softly.

"So do you."

"You look altogether different, Martin. Breeches suit you, and you're wonderful in the saddle. So much time out in the sun has made you as brown as a planter, and you seem so much younger when you laugh instead of being angry all the time."

"Hey, I should be the one paying compliments," he told her in teasing manner, trying to keep things on a light level.

"You like it here, don't you?"

He perched on the arm of a cane chair, nodding. "Very much. The rubber business is fascinating, and this valley is so beautiful. Above all, it's so utterly peaceful," he added, on a sigh. "I shan't want to go back to Singapore and that confounded job of mine."

Moving forward to stand between his spread legs, she took his hand in hers. "Don't worry about it. I shall be in Singapore, too. With Daddy now tied to the house, and Alex off to England, it'll be easier for us to meet than it was before. I can wait until Mummy is with one of her committees, or resting in her room, then slip out through the garden gate to your bungalow."

He shook her hands from side to side with gentle chiding. "No, my dear, that's quite out of the question. We can only meet in circumstances which would in no way compromise you."

"I wouldn't care about that," she declared fervently. "Since Daddy collapsed, I've missed you dreadfully. Every day seemed like a whole week, and knowing you were so near yet so far away made it worse." Her colour rose slightly. "I actually came to see you once, but that hateful Lang person was on the front verandah and saw me. I had to pretend I was simply passing."

"There you are; the very point I'm trying to make," he said emphatically. "That man could have spread a highly-coloured story about you around Singapore within twenty-four hours, and that would have been the end of any hope of meetings between us. Lydia, promise me you'll never be so foolish again."

She looked down at their linked hands. "I wanted to see you so very badly."

Moved by her ingenuous confession, he tilted her face up to his very gently. "I also wanted to see you. You've no idea how badly."

The kiss was tender, born of his present contentment and confidence in his future. It was more the kind of kiss she could expect from young men who observed the rules of under-age courtship. Yet, when he attempted to lift his head, her arms locked around his neck to force his mouth harder against her own, while her body began to press so insistently against him he was in danger of falling backward into the chair.

An angry voice shattered the moment. "What the hell is going on here?"

Lydia tore herself away from his tightening hold, and looked across at her brother with guilt at being caught in the act. As Martin got to his feet, one sight of Alex's expression told him what must have happened between the other pair. It would account for the man's unreasonable anger, he guessed, and he tempered his reply accordingly.

"Much the same thing that has been going on between you two, I imagine. It's that kind of evening, isn't it?"

They confronted each other in silence, until awareness of their mutual need for action eased the tension enough for Alex to say, "Oh, for God's sake, let's have another drink!"

In contrast with the aggression of the frustrated men, the girls were quiet and lost in thought as they drank. No one wished to continue the dancing, yet they were reluctant to part. Sitting restlessly in chairs which faced out to the throbbing night, there was a sense of waiting for the unknown. Suddenly, Martin got to his feet and went into the bungalow, reappearing with a bowl of nuts. Then, he carefully placed six ice-cubes on the verandah rail, six inches apart. Returning to his chair he put the bowl of nuts on to the floor, saying, "Whoever knocks all six cubes into the garden with the least number of nuts will win a stupendous prize. Any cheating will be mercilessly punished, and any contestant who is so bally hopeless the cubes melt before they're sent flying will be drummed out of the Cube-whacking Club, and forced to pick up all the nuts at the end of the contest. Who cares to have a crack at it first?"

They all revived as nuts flew fast and furious over the verandah and into the garden beyond. Cheers and boos accompanied each person's performance, cheating was rife, and the ice had to be replaced frequently as the humid atmosphere melted it fast. After a great deal of hilarity, during which the men discarded their jackets, Alex was declared undoubted overall winner.

"So where's this stupendous prize you promised?" he asked Martin, lying back in his chair to squint up at him.

"Ah . . . yes." He looked swiftly around for inspiration. Then, taking up the ice-bucket, he said, "Mr Beresford, you have earned this stupendous prize with your stupendous skill at cube-whacking." So saying, he tipped the ice-cubes over Alex's head, adding solemnly, "Well done, sir."

Alex yelled as the icy deluge touched his heated body, and the two girls shrieked with delight at such clowning. Wisely, Martin armed himself with a small rattan table until he was satisfied that reprisals were not threatening. All the same, Alex was eager to satisfy his frustration with more active horseplay than the mere throwing of nuts. With his white shirt plastered to his body, he tugged off his bow tie and climbed on to the verandah rail, inviting them to lay bets on his ability to walk the narrow rounded bar without falling.

"I'm not wasting my money on you," Martin told him rudely. "Any fool could do it."

Alex grinned and jumped down. "We have a volunteer, ladies. Come on, up with him!"

Grumbling and protesting, Martin was obliged to perform the deed he had derided. Alex then went one better by doing it with the ice-bucket balanced on his head. Then the challenge was on as each man thought of greater and greater handicaps, until Martin was pronounced the outright champion after traversing the eighteen-foot length on his hands. It was touch and go as he swayed upside down several times, bringing gasps from Lydia and Thea watching with baited breath. Alex could not better the feat, Martin quickly declined any prize which might be offered, and a break for refreshments was called.

While they were enjoying lime juice and soda brought by a grinning Marek, Alex looked across at Martin. "What now?"

He thought for a moment. "An officers' mess favourite was horse racing. The bigger men used to take the light ones on their backs over a set course. Absolutely exhausting, but tremendous fun!"

"Couldn't we take turn about being horse and jockey, as we're much the same size?"

"We could, but there'd be no race with only one horse."

"No, there wouldn't."

They looked at each other in growing conspiracy. Then Alex said, "Of course, we could both be horses, if we only had two riders."

"Yes, we could," agreed Martin solemnly.

"In that case . . ." reasoned Alex, with a smile.

Slowly and simultaneously they turned their heads towards the girls, putting down their drinks as they did so. Thea read their intention, and shook her head vigorously.

"Oh no, I'm doing no more riding today!"

"Which do you fancy?" Alex asked of Martin, rolling up his sleeves.

"The one in pink. She has a better seat on a horse."

Lydia was wide-eyed with curiosity for what was afoot, and turned to Thea. "What do they mean?"

"They imagine that we'll agree to ride pick-a-back while they have some nonsensical race, but they're both wrong."

"Are we?" demanded Martin, rolling his sleeves back also. "Let's find out."

In a flash, the girls were up from their chairs, driven by the subtle sexual thrill of flight and pursuit. There followed a wild, crazy chase along the verandahs and through the bungalow, with the men blocking the way with chairs, or cutting off the girls' retreat by leaping over the furniture. Thea and Lydia ran with their skirts clutched high, shouting with laughter and filled with the joy of freedom to express their youth as they twisted away from capture time and again. When the men decided that it was time they were caught, the chase was over swiftly. The danger then was how to avert the natural conclusion to familiar mating activity, and the actual race was the only alternative. Marching the girls outside again, Alex and Martin agreed on a course and told their female jockeys to mount.

As Thea climbed on to Alex's back, she glanced across at Lydia and wondered fleetingly what Margery would make of this radiant laughing girl, with her dress pulled past her knees, clinging to Martin as she participated in the most natural of all youthful pleasures. There was no sign of anguished infatuation or self-sacrificial compassion in her delight at light-hearted flirtatious fun. How would she cope on her return to Singapore, when the bars closed around her again?

The noise they made must have awoken the entire plantation as Alex and Martin galloped around the verandah encircling the bungalow, deciding that the winner would be declared on the results of three races. Honours were even when they started the third and, after circuiting the building neck and neck, the two men clattered down the steps into the garden and headed into the night with their shrieking jockeys. The race finally ended when the two steeds sank exhausted to the earth. This was not England, however, and the ground was neither comfortable nor safe for long. Worn out, but unanimously happy, the two entwined couples walked slowly back to the rooms occupied by the girls. There, they said goodnight. Kisses were not exchanged; they had gone beyond that. Thea merely gave Alex an optical message he read very well, as she opened her door and went in. Lydia looked up at Martin with shining eyes.

"This is the most marvellous night of my life."

He shook his head. "There'll be others twice as marvellous . . . but perhaps not quite like this one."

The men walked round to their own rooms in comfortable silence. On reaching Martin's door they both stopped, knowing the night was not quite over for them. Martin took out his cigarette case and offered it to Alex as they turned to look out at the night, which was alive with noisy nocturnal creatures.

After smoking in relaxed manner for several moments, Martin asked quietly, "Won't you miss all this?"

"I suppose so—it's the only life I've ever known—but not in any regretful way, I'm certain."

"Why weren't you sent to England for your education? It's the usual practice in climates such as this, isn't it?"

He nodded. "My father was so shattered by Uncle Duke's sacking from Oxford and the subsequent scandal of the racehorse, which came almost immediately after Grandfather's suicide, he refused to let any one of us out of his direct control. All four of us had a private tutor. After Charles and Eleanor died, Lydia was taught by a crusty Scotswoman who had been governess to children of a Russian count, and had escaped during the civil war. I received tuition from a local professor for several years, but Father thought it was more important for me to learn the business than Latin." Giving a faint smile, he added, "He was probably right in that. I haven't so far needed knowledge of the language of the Caesars."

Martin nodded. "I don't think it's a necessary qualification for a pilot, so you'll be all right there. Most of those I knew during the war were men very much like you."

"In what way?" he asked with quickening interest.

"Sociable, aggressive, reckless . . . and very young. They all had a quality that somehow marked them as different from we earthbound troops. The ground staff at various airfields all said that fliers were two men in one. In the air they were giants; once they landed they seemed lost and without motivation. Rather like you were when we first met."

Memories of that unforgettable tennis party had to be smothered, so Alex asked, "Didn't flying ever appeal to you?"

"Not half," came the hearty response. "It appealed to every man who'd had enough of mud and gas attacks. We all volunteered for the RFC at some time during those four years. I was cock-a-hoop when they accepted my application, but I was chucked off the course and sent back to the Front."

"Why, in heaven's name?"

"Every time I left the ground I was so bloody airsick I almost passed out. They decided I was more use to them on a horse."

Alex was curiously saddened by the admission. This man he admired and envied, this honoured hero, had revealed that he was the victim of a most unheroic weakness. Because of it, the new friendship forged at Serantinggi allowed him to ask what pride had forbidden before.

"What was it like?"

"Airsickness?"

"War."

The other man drew in smoke slowly before exhaling just as slowly. "Do you want the truth, or the glorified version?"

"The truth."

"It's a state of existence which obliterates all the world and its inhabitants save those within a radius of twenty miles. You live in holes in the ground like rabbits knowing, as rabbits do, that the minute you pop up someone will try to kill you. You make friends of men you loathe because they're the only ones left; you see the ones you love being blown into little pieces or burst apart by a hail of bullets. In winter, your body and senses ache with the endless cold, and you're afraid to close your eyes in case the lids freeze and you'll be unable to open them again. In autumn and spring, you wallow in liquid mud, you eat it, you drink it and you sleep in it. Your clothes never dry; you catch trench fever and bronchitis; your stomach is clawed by dysentery. In summer, you sweat all the time and there's never enough to drink. You go down with trench fever and heatstroke. The lice on your body and in your hair breed, multiplying in their millions. You can no longer remember what a flower looks like . . . or your mother's face.

"All civilised behaviour is abandoned. Men vomit or urinate in the mud at your feet. They pretend they're ill and in pain so that they won't have to go when the whistle blows; they snatch a gas mask from a wounded man because they have lost their own and don't want to die the most revolting death of all. They lie and they cheat. They abuse each other sexually. They rape virgins in villages they pass."

He drew on the cigarette again until the tip was glowing red in the darkness, then exhaled on a sigh. "They also risk death to save others. They sob over the death of a stray dog picked up only two days before. They write letters full of lies to forgotten families, saying that everything's fine. They joke while death stares at them from a distant wood, they sing when they're so weary they hardly know how to put one foot before the other, and they give their last cigarettes to the homeless in villages they pass. They go time and again when some schoolboy subaltern blows his whistle. The godless pray, the proud weep, the mean and shifty shine like gold as they wriggle on their stomachs into no-man's-land to bring in total strangers." Dropping the stub to the floor, he crushed out the glow with his shoe, as he added, "Oh yes . . . and they kill the enemy."

It was some time before Alex could speak, then all he could say was, "Thanks." For some deeply rooted reason he held out his hand. "Goodnight."

Martin shook hands with him. "Goodnight."

After stripping off and taking a shower, Alex lay on his bed lost in a labyrinth of thoughts. Thea waited in vain for him to go to her.

Chapter 14

On the following morning they all took the plantation launch up the brown silky river to a local beauty spot. Marek had produced a picnic lunch worthy of the occasion, which the boatman loaded in the stern before assisting his passengers into the small canopied craft. The four young revellers of the night before were dreamy, leaving Marmaduke to talk without interruption throughout the voyage through Serantinggi Valley. The slow-moving water, hiding crocodiles and other dangerous creatures, was thick with tangled weed and bizarre flowering plants, in parts. The banks were lined with the dark-green trees which stretched as far as the distant hills rising against a morning sky of silvery blue. Beneath the canopy it was shady: watching isolation slide past had an almost mesmeric quality.

Martin sat with his arm along the side of the boat behind Lydia, and she gradually inched along the cushioned seat until she rested against his shoulder. Alex thought he had never seen his sister look so startlingly lovely as she did this morning. Youthful vitality shone in her eyes, her expression and her smile whenever she glanced up at the man beside her. That the pair were totally in accord was obvious. Not so himself and Thea. She had greeted him speculatively at breakfast, and had been unusually quiet since then. There had been no chance to speak with her alone, and he was still thoughtful about the surprises of the previous evening. New light had been thrown on old ideas. Time was needed to consider and reach conclusions.

They tied up to a rickety jetty, then scrambled ashore to walk the short distance to a spectacular waterfall with a series of smaller cascades over rocks worn smooth by erosion. They were all eager to arrive. If conditions were right, it was possible for visitors to have an enjoyable time travelling down this lengthy waterslide on light bamboo rafts. The thunder of water could be heard when they were still some yards away, and the coolness created by the falls touched the humid air as they approached.

"Long time since I indulged in this delight," announced Marmaduke over his shoulder. "When I first came up here, parties of young rips and their bubbly ladies used to have the most marvellous fun. Deserted now. Sad, very sad. All down in Singapore, d'you see? Planters' wives don't *bubble* any more. Grown weary; grown old. Understandable. Lonely up here, you know. Very lonely."

The waterfall was certainly spectacular. They stood before the great foaming plunge of water which seemed to come from the sky, as they gazed up at its source near the tops of tall surrounding trees. The spray created by the falls was deliciously cool against their skins, and the crystal water gliding swiftly over a downhill series of flat rocks promised the fun they sought. They disappeared to segregated areas, the men to strip and don shorts, the girls to change into loose cotton frocks which had to substitute for swimming costumes. Then, they scampered out to take up the rafts and climb to the large dark pool at the foot of the main falls, which fed the minor cascades.

Marmaduke descended first, clutching the sides of his raft as he raced downward on the surface of the swiftly-gliding water. It was plain that some skill in guiding the bamboo rafts was necessary, and Alex exchanged grins with Martin as the girls expressed their doubts about the fun element of something looking decidedly risky.

"If the Duke of Beresford can expose his elevated person to it, we lesser mortals should not hesitate to follow," Martin reasoned.

"You insult our manhood," protested Alex. "It's child's play."

The girls allowed themselves to be persuaded and down they went, Thea clinging to Alex, and Lydia clutching Martin as they careered madly toward the flat stretch of water at the base of the falls. Once there, they all declared it to be the most exhilarating pastime they had ever known, and climbed up to repeat it again and again. The isolated clearing rang with laughter, shrieks and frenzied splashing as they raced down the aqua-chute one after the other until, finally, they linked up to form a snake of five for a truly spectacular last descent before the picnic. Alex led. With the other four behind him clutching each other around the waist, he pushed off into the current, shouting, "Tally-ho!" at the top of his voice. It was at that precise moment that he sensed the feeling of confidence which told him he was free and his own man, at last.

They ate patties and cold meat, with a macedoine of chilled vegetables and crisp buttered rolls, all enhanced by a light white wine which had been standing in the water while they frolicked. Then there was a fruit fool, a large lemon cake and a basket of cheeses to follow. With appetites sharpened by physical activity and the sheer stimulation of happiness in such surroundings, they worked their way through everything as they perched on rocks above the water in their dry clothes, dabbling their toes in the tiny clear eddies at the very edge of the torrent as they chattered and ate unrestrainedly.

After the meal, a decision was made to explore a ruined temple Marmaduke said was nearby and well worth seeing. The boatman carried the picnic basket back to the launch, collected his parang, then rejoined them to lead the way through jungle known to hide giant

244

deadly snakes and other venomous scourges of mankind. Thea declined the adventure, and Lydia only went because Martin was keen to see the Malay relic. When Alex volunteered to stay and safeguard Thea, it seemed perfectly reasonable for him to do so. Yet he knew the moment for truth had come. He had watched her throughout the water games, when her wet dress had clung to her and her face had been at its most expressive. He had watched her during the picnic, when her extrovert personality had been given full rein, and his love for her had deepened even further. Although he had given her until the end of this trip to make her decision, he meant to demand it now.

The others set off and were soon out of sight. As it was out of the question to stretch out on the ground for a cat-nap, Thea declared her intention of returning to the boat where cushions would provide some comfort. Picking up her towel and the damp dress, she turned to leave.

Alex stopped her quickly. "Now we're alone, I want to talk to you."

"What about?" she asked, as if there was no vital issue between them.

"Our future together."

"Why now?"

"Because it's now that I want your answer."

"To what?"

"My proposal of marriage."

Taken by surprise, she studied him assessingly for some moments, the only sound being the thunder of the cataract as it threw off the spray which was turning her hair into a jewel-dotted cap.

"What happened last night, Alex?"

"You know what happened."

"*After* I went to my room."

He cast around for the right words. "I think I somehow came of age. Everything seems clear cut, at last."

"Darling, I'm so glad," she said quietly, but with genuine warmth. "It means no one can influence you now."

"Except you. Winning through won't make any sense unless you're with me. My future happiness lies in your hands."

"No, Alex," she told him with a firm shake of her head. "If that's true, you still haven't come of age."

His anger was born of a sense of fear that she was about to reject him. "My God, I sometimes wonder if you know what love really is. No one is a complete person. We all need someone . . . save you, apparently. It makes me wonder if this former lover of yours ever existed. Is he merely an invention to give added mystique to Anna du Lessier's daughter, to make foolish men like me jealous? If he did exist, I pity the poor devil."

The change in her was astounding. The amber of her eyes darkened with a semblance of pain, and she looked as shocked as if he had struck her. Pushing past him, she began to run along the path toward the river—a slim figure dappled by light and shade thrown by the lofty trees. He went after her, distressed by her reaction, until he overtook her and held her steady before him.

"Darling, I'm sorry. I'm sorry," he panted.

She shook free of his hold, saying in a tone he had never heard from her before, "Don't pity *him*. He died. I was the one left to suffer the aftermath. Oh yes, Alex, I know what love really is. It's anguish, humiliation and loss of pride. I'll not suffer that again, ever!"

His distress deepened as he saw a girl she had kept hidden from him until now. Beneath her pose of sophistication, her elaborate pretence of sexual assurance, her façade of modern resilience, she was frighteningly alone and vulnerable.

Taking her in a close hold, he said urgently, "True love isn't like that, Thea. I'll make you so happy; I'll give you everything in my power to give. We'll go to England and begin an exciting life together. There'll be no time to think of the past, because we'll be too busy basking in our new dawn. Darling, I love you. I love you so much, I'll make you drunk on it, too."

He kissed her then, feeling the same sense of triumph and confidence he had known when racing down the rapids this morning. Soon, she began to respond with matching desperation, and he knew that he had his answer. Picking her up in his arms, he carried her the short distance to the launch. On board, he kicked the cushions to the floor and sank on to them with Thea still in his arms. He had wanted her for so long, possession was unbelievably thrilling in its mutual abandonment. He had been with Chinese and Eurasian girls now and again, but she was the first conquest of love he had known and even the evidence of her experience with another man barely dimmed the quality of his passion. When they were both spent, they pulled on their clothes in case the others returned unexpectedly, then sat close together in the gently-rocking boat while Alex smoked and outlined his plans.

"When we return to Singapore, I'll arrange for a swift marriage. It might be expedient anyway, darling," he added, kissing her temple lightly. "I wasn't prepared for love in a launch, so I might well have to make an honest woman of you for the sake of our child." He drew on his cigarette, then exhaled before saying, "It'll also serve the purpose of providing the gossips with an acceptable explanation for our removal to hotel rooms, and give them so much about us to chew over they'll leave Mother and Lydia in relative peace. As soon as we're married, we'll sail for England. Funds will be rather short for the first year, but after that we'll be more than comfortable on my inheritance and what I earn as a pilot."

They sat together with only the lapping of the water against the boat and the far-off muted roar of cascading water to break the silence. Then she said, "I'll marry you as soon as you like, darling, but I can't sail with you." At his quick movement of protest, she added, "Please wait until you hear what I have to say. My reasoning is very sensible."

He tightened his hold around her, saying, "After what we have just done, it's impossible for me to be sensible."

She tipped her face up for his lengthy kiss, then smiled her contentment. "They call you 'Mad Alex' in Singapore. Now I know why."

He chased her mouth with his own again. "You are the only girl who knows, Thea."

"The *only* one?"

He shrugged. "I've done the rounds, like every other man, but it was never like this before. You've knocked me for six, and I'm likely to remain in that state for the next sixty years."

"Alex, behave," she warned, catching his hands to hold them still. "I have things to say, and the others might come back before I have finished. You'll need a spell in England sorting everything out, and you'll do that best alone. Darling, listen," she said insistently, "you have to find a place to live and someone willing to employ you. I was in England recently, and know that there are large numbers of former RFC pilots seeking jobs with aircraft companies. They are already trained fliers. You may not find it easy, and have to settle for less, at first. A bride would be an additional responsibility until you sort out your future—our future."

He could not help seeing the sense in her words, but passion still echoed inside him to make the idea of separation unbearable.

"A bride would provide consolation after disappointments; encouragement to try again and again. I might be tempted to find both elsewhere if I'm on my own."

Touching his mouth with her fingers, she said, "Don't try that on, Alex, because I could do the same. There are plenty of men in Singapore who would be only too happy to console a lonely wife."

"That's why I daren't leave you here."

"When I become Mrs Beresford, I'll never betray that loyalty, you should know that, Alex." Smiling her love, she added, "My reasoning makes sense, doesn't it? Be honest."

He nodded reluctantly. "Damn you, yes, but I'll miss you like hell."

"It won't be for long," she said consolingly. "I know you'll succeed, because you now have the right determination, and the book is more than half finished."

He grew still, letting go her hand. "I see. The real reason for remaining here is that damned novel, isn't it?"

Drawing away so that she faced him across the boat, she said, "I've just given you my body; I've promised to take your name. I have undertaken to join you in England for a wonderful future together. Isn't it your turn to give something?"

He gave a long sigh, knowing he must surrender. "All right. I just don't understand why it's so important, that's all."

Looking out across the gliding brown river, she said reflectively, "I don't quite understand why myself, lately, but it is. Even more so than before."

The news of the impending swift marriage was greeted with enthusiasm from all, so the fun and contentment was even more enjoyable as it continued into the middle of their second week. The evenings would be spent dancing to records they now knew by heart, or they would contrive further innocently flirtatious games. Often, the four would sit quietly after Marmaduke had retired, and talk of what they would like to do with their lives. Their strengthened understanding of each other allowed Alex to comment frankly on Martin's dream of buying a plantation like Serantinggi.

"You don't seriously mean to live up here and grow as eccentric as Uncle Duke, surely?"

It also allowed him to reply, "I have the advantage of being eccentric from the start. Lady Weyford assured me that all loose screws make a fortune from rubber, so you see before you a future multi-millionaire."

Lydia was always upset by such comments from him, but the other pair treated them lightly and responded in the same vein. Even so, during a moment spent alone with him at the breakfast table awaiting the others one morning, Thea taxed him on the subject.

"You're not serious about running a plantation, are you?"

"Perfectly."

"It's a form of running away."

He stirred his coffee. "Isn't that what you did?"

"I'm not sure what you mean."

"Yes, you are, Thea. Whether your novel is intended to make you as notorious as your mother, or whether you're hitting out through prose at someone who hurt you, as I once suggested, you had no real need to cross the world in order to write it. The East, itself, doesn't fascinate you, I've seen that. It's the people here who've got under your skin, instead. I'm pretty certain you ran away from someone or something when you sailed here, and I suspect it still isn't far enough. Are you going to marry Alex because you love him, or because becoming Mrs Beresford will provide metaphorical distance from your *bête noire*?"

"Mind your own business," she told him smartly.

He smiled. "Coming from an inveterate meddler in that of everyone else, that's rich!"

Unabashed, she urged, "You'd be a mental wreck within six months on a plantation. Go home, where you rightly belong."

All he said was, "Typical behaviour of brides-to-be. Can't resist trying to make others climb on to pink fluffy clouds, too."

She dropped the subject as Lydia joined them, and the day's activities prevented further discussion on Martin's plans. They once more took the launch up-river, this time to visit the Sultan. It was something of a disappointment that it could not have been for one of the grand occasions demanding the full splendour and regalia which Malay rulers produced to impress royal or diplomatic guests. During the voyage, Marmaduke described, in great detail, the trains of decorated elephants bearing elaborate curtained howdahs in which honoured guests travelled to shoot tigers, or to witness grand spectacles of Malay dancing and martial arts during religious festivals. He told of the levees, at which the lesser chieftains and court dignitaries were obliged to demonstrate their loyalty by approaching the throne overhung by a huge ceremonial umbrella, sitting cross-legged and dragging themselves forward with their hands on the ground before them. The Malay sultans were reverenced by their subjects, who regarded them as divine, yet they all had most human personalities when not on official show and made a determined effort to maintain good relations with the British.

However, it was an additional personal fondness for "The Duke of Beresford" which governed the relationship between planter and ruler, so he was delighted to welcome the four young people Marmaduke brought with him. He greeted his guests wearing a European suit, and offered them tea with little cakes more in keeping with an English country vicarage. They recognised the honour he was according them by providing what he would see as their favourite fare, but would have preferred to try traditional Malay refreshment. Similarly, their host spoke of English matters such as cricket, on the rules of which he proved to be an authority, and his favourite European dance, which was the schottische. This confession led Marmaduke to relate the story of his own ability to twinkle across a ballroom floor, and the two older men delved into reminiscences leaving the others to listen with growing boredom. The visit improved a little when they began a tour of the palace, its grounds, and the elephant houses but, out of hearing of Marmaduke because he had kindly arranged it, they all declared the experience to have proved decidedly flat. Martin went so far as to suggest that Thea in her Turkish potentate's outfit far outrivalled the Sultan in magnificence, for which remark he received from her a gesture with her tongue no sultan would dream of making.

Nothing particular was planned for the next morning. The two young men went riding straight after breakfast, before the day grew too hot, returning at ten o'clock to find Lydia lazing in a chair waiting for them. Thea was in her room working on her book, she told them, and asked not to be disturbed. Marek brought tea to set on a small table beside Lydia, and it was while they were all refreshing themselves that Marmaduke appeared from the direction of the factory, and stumped up the wooden steps to join them, full of obvious excitement.

"Well, I never! Well, I never! Doesn't happen often," he exclaimed loudly, punching Martin's shoulder gently. "Couldn't have come at a better time, eh? Taken a fancy to them, I know. Can't think why. I hate 'em. All the same, there's one about, and we'll get him. We'll get him." He headed for the door. "Calls for a glass of port, eh? Perhaps even two."

"What are we going to get?" Martin asked curiously.

"A tiger, young sir," Marmaduke called over his shoulder as he entered the bungalow. "Old Stripes himself! Soldier, weren't you? Handy with a gun. Must be. You've been accorded the honour of bagging your first kill."

He returned with a generous measure of port to regale his guests with details of the hunt that afternoon, his excitement mounting minute by minute. The conversation around Martin faded to a background noise as he sat looking at the green vista which had given him so much pleasure. Somewhere out there rested a hunter who was soon to become the hunted. Out there in the dim interior of a kingdom ruled by creatures of the jungle, lay a beast of great grace and beauty, who must be regarded as an enemy. Out there, peace would soon be shattered by gunfire, the green growth would turn red with blood; beauty would be destroyed by death. He caught himself willing the animal to make its escape, to run into the hills before the sun began its downward way; willing this creature of sharp instincts to sense the danger and go while it was still free.

The tiger had not attacked humans, but it had taken a buffalo and some goats from a nearby village. That, plus sightings of it in Serantinggi Valley, had so frightened the local people the tappers were refusing to work at the farther end of the plantation. Marmaduke was the most respected man in the area, his supposed dukedom making him second only to the Sultan, so it was his responsibility to hunt the animal and remove the threat from those who looked to him for help. Yet there was a personal vendetta against tigers in the breast of the planter, which gave his preparations for the hunt a "yoiks and tally-ho" flavour that amused the natives but left them uncomprehending of its inference. In Martin, it aroused growing revulsion.

The sequence of kills had pinpointed the tiger's position as being in dense jungle, halfway along Serantinggi Valley and near to a large village. It was arranged that a horseshoe of beaters would drive the creature into relatively open terrain near the plantation boundary, where guns would be stationed along the west bank of the river. The marksmen would be Marmaduke, his Eurasian manager, Alex and Martin, to whom Marmaduke enthusiastically promised the very best chance to bag the kill.

During the remainder of the morning there was a tenseness in two of the young people, which Marmaduke appeared not to notice. Martin had grown broody and withdrawn, a state even Lydia's presence did nothing to ease. The girl herself was pale as she followed Martin's every movement with an anxious gaze. Alex enthused with his uncle over the excitement of the coming hunt, and spent much time examining the rifles before choosing one. When Thea emerged from her room she seemed unusually listless, greeting the news of the hunt with no more than a plea for the men to take great care in the face of danger.

Tension mounted after tiffin. The guns were cleaned before the men went off to change into breeches, and jackets with special pouches to hold the ammunition. The horses were then brought round. The plan was to meet up with the headmen of nearby villages, who had been organising the teams of beaters. They expected to take the tiger just before dusk but, as a precaution against the faint chance of the beast slipping through the trap and heading into the plantation itself, the girls were ordered to remain indoors. Fires were to be lit as daylight died, and a cordon of plantation employees would stand guard from behind them with flaming brands to ward off the animal.

Martin mounted silently, heedless of the enthusiastic chatter of the other men around him. A strange inner transition had taken place. The khaki breeches and jacket he wore had become a warrior's uniform; the horse was now a cavalry charger. A rifle butt pressing against his knee as he rode was a well-known sensation, and the ammunition belt hung with familiar weight around his waist. That stomach-churning mixture of fear, loathing and self-disgust over what he was setting out to do brought the usual struggle against the need to vomit. Fighting it, as he always had, he rode on knowing that he was a prisoner of the inevitable, unable to choose his actions or speak his true thoughts; a prisoner of the drive to kill or be killed. Those surrounding him laughed and joked. It was the way many of his comrades covered their fear. In the early days, he had been like them, but too many had died leaving their ghastly screams ringing in his head to drive out the ability to feign light-heartedness.

The muddy cratered landscapes of France gradually turned green, lush and innocent again as he progressed. He shook his head to dispel lingering confusion, remembering that he was in that peaceful valley which had made him so happy and confident. The only sounds in his ears now were those of steady hoofbeats, men's fearless voices, and the exotic chatter of jungle creatures warning each other of their approach. The pain in his stomach subsided as his muscles relaxed. This was not war, merely a hunting jaunt similar to those enjoyed in the sleepy countryside of England. Fox, partridge, stag . . . or tiger; what difference did it make to the thrill of stalking and outwitting a wily creature?

The reed huts of a small village clustered in a clearing ahead. The open space they encircled was filled with dark-skinned men wrapped by sober garments. Some carried machetes, others were armed with knives and heavy sticks. In the doorways of many of the huts stood dark-eyed handsome women, watching with their children this event which produced some sensation in their calm routine now threatened by the tiger. Marmaduke was greeted with enormous respect by the several headmen, making Martin witness to another side of the eccentric planter who exchanged correct civilities with his Malay neighbours then took command of the gathering, as was expected of him. When in the element he totally understood, it was possible to glimpse the man Marmaduke Beresford might have been if scandal had not led to his banishment from society.

After watching the exchange for several minutes, Alex looked across at Martin with a smile. "Would you like a translation?"

He shook his head. "Not necessary. Plans of campaign follow much the same pattern everywhere, and sign language is very easy to read."

"Done much shooting in England?"

"Not half as much as I did in France."

A shadow crossed the other's good-looking face as he subconsciously straightened in his saddle. "You must be such an expert shot, there's no need for me to emphasise the need for swiftness and total accuracy. A wounded beast is highly dangerous, besides proving almost impossible to follow through dense jungle. There'll be no more than a few seconds during which to aim and fire."

Martin said through a tightening throat, "That's all I'll need."

"Good. Uncle Duke, Rajeed and I will all be ready in case you can't get a good fix on him from where you're positioned. We'll all be in visual contact. At the first sign from you, one of us will take him."

"Righto," he murmured, as the Malays bent to take up the drums to sling over their shoulders.

With the scheme now perfectly understood by beaters and guns alike, everyone set off. Scouts had come in no more than thirty minutes before to confirm sightings of tiger spoor in the vicinity, heading toward a village on the banks of the river. The residents had vacated it speedily, and the beast was to be driven toward an adjacent small clearing giving excellent cover for the marksmen. For a while, the riders followed in the rear of the silent beaters, then Marmaduke indicated that they should take a narrow path through the thickening trees, diverting from the Malays who would push through more difficult undergrowth.

They rode single file, Marmaduke in the lead and the Eurasian bringing up the rear. It was a silent procession, each man occupied with the chilling thrill of knowing that soft-footed danger moved somewhere in the jungle closing around them. Martin found it difficult to believe that vast numbers of men were making their way through the emerald walls to the west of them, taking up their positions for the horseshoe drive down to the river. Apart from their own progress, the only sounds were raucous alarm calls from the branches overhead, sent by invisible furred or feathered watchers who resented the intrusion by man into their territory. They pursued a narrow track cut by the local people, who used it to move from village to village. It was lengthy and tortured. Heat closed in on them as dusk approached, and Martin began to wander once more in the realms of unreality. The oppressiveness took on a sinister aspect; the growing chorus of jungle calls added to the suggestion of hostility. Then, breaking into the sultry aspect of the dying day, came the sudden thudding of distant drums providing a pulsebeat beneath a chorus of human cries designed to send the tiger seeking a peace he could not know would prove to be final.

The track led up to the river, where Marmaduke halted. Dropping from his saddle he swiftly surveyed the surrounding trees for the best vantage points. By now almost obsessive in his command he selected places for them all as they dismounted, drew their rifles from the saddle-clips, and affirmed the plan of campaign. Martin was allocated the position which offered the finest view of the clearing into which the beast was intended to be driven. The other three concealed themselves amongst the foliage to form a horseshoe of guns. The boy who had ridden with them then took the horses off to a safe area to await the kill.

Watching silently concealed for the unsuspecting foe was no new sensation to Martin. The accelerated heartbeat, the tensing of nerves and muscles, the ache behind eyes searching constantly for the first sign of movement all suggested the continuation of all he had known for four interminable years. As he stood behind the screen of dark fleshy growth, he could just see Alex away to his right, and Marmaduke to his left. They were both in visual contact with Rajeed, who was most likely to sight the tiger first if it came from the direction they anticipated. Its approach would be signalled to Martin, then the three would stand by ready to finish off the beast in the unlikely case of Martin being unable to make an instant kill. There was no doubt whatever in his own mind that he could fell with one single bullet any living thing within his range. Failure to do so could cost him his own life. He had never yet failed.

Dusk was arriving swiftly through that close vegetation. Now was the time an enemy chose to creep stealthily from behind trees to surprise the unwary. The thudding of drums and the chilling wail of human voices began to draw significantly nearer. It was similar to the bombardment usual before an advance, when artillery attempted to drive men from their trenches in terror so that the hopeful new occupants would find no more than corpses to share the mud-filled ditches with them. Before long, the tattoo thundered in Martin's head to tell him the unseen beaters were closing in all around him. The eerie cries were now augmented by the crashing of undergrowth that had to be slashed with machetes to be penetrable. Beads of perspiration now stood all over his face. His hands were clammy as they gripped the rifle; his clothes stuck wetly to his skin. Alex was little more than a pale shape in the distance, yet Martin saw the movement of his arm which signalled success. The striped hunter had been outwitted, outnumbered and driven to its certain end.

Martin's whole body tensed until it was rigid. He gave a return signal to the concealed Alex, then to Marmaduke practically indiscernible to his left. With great care he raised the rifle to his shoulder, and narrowed his eyes to focus on the clearing. Twilight was cacophonous with the sounds of the tiger's death-song. The beaters were no more than a hundred yards away, elated by the primitive aspect of killing a foe. Martin swiftly wiped his eyes with his wrist to clear his vision, then stared at the open space intently, reflexes poised for the first sign of movement.

The quarry came silently, an exquisitely graceful combination of rippling stripes, and great yellow eyes filled with the wisdom of jungle lore from aeons past. The tiger stood squarely in the sights of Martin's rifle, sensing danger yet confused by the deafening noise all around him. As the beast hesitated, its head swung to look right at Martin concealed within the cover of its own natural habitat. Glorious amber eyes met his own as Martin curled his finger around the trigger. Nothing happened, and the beast started forward again to flee from the beaters.

There was an aura of drama about the afternoon which made the girls restless after the men had departed. Lydia spent much of the time clutching one or other of the verandah posts, and gazing out over the valley where anything could be happening. Thea sat lost in thought. She could make no progress on the book, even had she been in the mood to do so. An abundance of characters appeared to be confusing the plot. In addition, the plot itself was twisting and turning so frequently, her view of the eventual outcome had now become ridiculously clouded. On this particular afternoon, her view of most things seemed clouded, she realised. Why was she so full of apprehension? Why did she find it so impossible to concentrate on the task she was determined to fulfil? The answers to those questions were as clouded as everything else, and for a reason she did not comprehend. Alex had been an exciting and passionate lover during these last few tropical nights. Her future was assured; it promised variety and excitement. Why, then, was her mind so full of questions and theories which made no sense?

Tea was served, but both girls ignored the sandwiches and cake. They said little to each other, conscious that both the twilight and what it would bring were inevitable, and beyond their control.

As the heavy afternoon closed toward the hour when the call of a far-off oriole sounded like a poignant farewell, the brilliant blue of the sky paled to grey and the nearest hills grew deep emerald as the sun ceased to gild their slopes. Then, into the hush of approaching night came a distant sound which set the girls on their feet, running to look out over the lush valley. The steady thud of drums, the clamour of gongs beaten at random, and a chorus of human shrieks designed to set animals running in wild fright had begun somewhere in the dense jungle. It sounded sinister, spine-chilling in its significance and highly evocative of danger. At the far end of the plantation where rubber trees gave way to untamed growth, the Indian overseers put torches to the perimeter fires, then stood ready with cymbals and gongs in case the flames were not enough to deter the hunted cat. The sight of those burning piles put the finishing touch to Thea's sensation of unease. There was some emotion deep within her as she watched and waited, which was as basic as that ancient jungle spread before her.

Lydia was gripping the rail along which Martin and Alex had balanced so light-heartedly last week. Her knuckles were white with the strength of her grip as she stared and wondered what was being played out unseen down there.

"They will be safe hiding in the trees, won't they?" she asked, in a small voice.

"Of course," Thea assured her. "Your uncle knows the procedure well, and would hardly expose them to danger."

"No . . . I suppose not."

They said little more, yet derived comfort from each other's presence as the minutes passed and the noise swelled to reach the surrounding hills, which threw back an eerie echo to add to the clamour. Soon, the entire valley seemed to be filled with phantom hunters, and there was no way of telling which way they were driving the tiger. Thea watched the flames and smoke rising against the edge of the jungle as the answer to those questions within her suddenly hung on the brink of recognition. It continued to hang there while each minute dragged past, and the sun finally vanished behind the hills to leave a luminous violet dusk which would last no more than fifteen minutes. Then, just as she felt her pulse thudding in time with the drums, and her nerves jangling to the din of the gongs, the twilight was split by a fusillade of sharp cracking shots. She jumped to her feet to stand beside the other girl and stare into the near-darkness surrounding them.

"Does that mean . . . ?" asked Lydia, with her hand to her mouth.

"I hope to God it does," she replied tautly. "I couldn't have stood much more of that din."

Next minute, Lydia burst into tears, turning her face against the pillar in her distress as her shoulders started to shake.

"Poor thing! What chance did it have? It must have been terrified out there, not knowing which way to turn. Why do men have to be so cruel?"

"It wasn't all that cruel, Lydia," Thea told her, putting a hand on the girl's arm. "They're all expert shots. The first bullet would have killed the tiger. Your uncle said it had to be destroyed because it's been taking animals which provide food for the local people. It could have attacked children next."

Lydia turned to lean back against the pillar, still weeping. "It's a tiger's instinct to kill for food. We do the same, but no one comes after us with guns to shoot us down."

"That's different."

"How?"

"Man is the superior animal . . . for the present, at any rate. Try not to feel so upset. They had to protect the Malay villagers, and us. The creature could have come up here to the bungalow."

"Not with all those fires burning," she retorted, brushing the tears away with the back of her hand. "Imagine being pursued through the night by that terrible wailing and beating, then finding your only path blocked by flames. The tears formed again. "It's so *unfair*! A hundred or more beaters and four marksmen, all against one tiger. It's such a beautiful creature."

She tried to reason with the distraught girl. "They only did what they felt was their duty."

"Did they? Is that what you really believe? Uncle Duke enjoys every revolting minute of it. He lives for tiger shoots. They break the monotony of this life he hates. The Eurasian manager has the usual native indifference to animals, and Alex could scarcely contain his excitement over something he hoped and prayed would be dangerous. As for Martin . . ."

"Martin didn't want to take part," Thea interrupted, with sudden insight. "He would have given anything not to have been obliged to go."

"But he did," pointed out Lydia, as she tried to conquer her tears.

"He had little choice. Your uncle made it seem as if the whole thing had been especially arranged for Martin's benefit, telling him the 'honour' of killing the beast would be his. In the face of that, what man would . . ." She broke off, suddenly aware of the cessation of all noise from the valley. The contrast was as startling as the sudden descent of night, which now blotted everything from view save the row of flaming beacons. That silence was now as nerve-racking as the earlier din had been, and somehow even more ominous with its suggestion of everyone having been killed by that volley of shots.

More than two hours passed before the men returned. The girls had gone inside to dress for dinner, then returned to wait in the sitting room, anxious and edgy. When they finally heard the horses being led away to the stables, and then the heavy tread of boots on the verandah, they leaned forward expectantly, their gaze on the door. Only two men came into the room. They both wore sweat-darkened shirts, and breeches stained by foliage. Marmaduke had flushed cheeks and an unsteady gait, which suggested that some celebratory port had been taken in his saddle-bag and consumed on the spot. Alex seemed strangely reluctant to face them, appearing neither triumphant nor filled with a quiet sense of achievement.

"Where's Martin?" asked Lydia almost hysterically, jumping to her feet.

"Gone to his room," was her brother's brief reply.

"Oh dear, oh dear, oh dear, what a frightful thing to happen," muttered Marmaduke, heading for the sidetable. "Felt sorry for the boy. Looked pasty. Needed a holiday, I thought." He poured port generously into a glass, drank some, then turned back to the girls. "Wish I'd never asked him here. Told him so. Had to. Can't have that, d'you see. Really can't have that. Never known such a thing to happen before." Waving the glass warningly at Alex, he said, "Shouldn't associate with people like him, my boy. Do you no good at all. Oh dear, oh dear, oh dear, what a treacherous ungrateful fellow. Had to tell him to leave. Nothing for it. Really can't have that."

Thea turned to Alex in alarm. "Whatever is he talking about?"

He perched on the back of a sofa, saying with obvious reluctance, "I'm afraid Martin damn near ruined everything. He had the beast right in his sights, and was too petrified to fire. It's true. I saw him quite clearly from my position nearby. He was shaking with fright. It took three of us to finish the creature off, because no one had the chance of a fatal shot. It was touch and go whether we got the beast before it slunk off into the jungle. A wounded tiger would have been highly dangerous." He gave a heavy sigh. "It was a rotten business all round, and I'm thankful it's over."

Marmaduke swayed across to Lydia, taking something from his pocket. "Brought this back for you, my dear. Fox's brush . . . or some such thing."

He held out a long thin striped article with reddish-brown matter encrusted on one end of it. Lydia stared at it in mounting horror, then rushed from the room with her hand over her mouth.

"S'matter with the little thing?" exclaimed Marmaduke in drunken surprise. "Cut off the tail especially to bring for her. Damn beastly striped creatures. I hate 'em."

The smoke from Martin's cigarette kept the mosquitoes at bay as he stood by the open window of his room, looking at the crimson embers of the perimeter fires. He had been drinking steadily and still had the shakes. The bungalow had fallen silent, although it was not yet ten p.m. Marmaduke had been roistering very noisily since his return, and it was likely that the girls had eaten dinner in their rooms. The eccentric planter was not fit company for them tonight, and he had now probably sought the Malay woman who knew and understood him in every mood.

Martin drank deeply again, appreciating how peaceful, how wonderfully peaceful it was. Yet his head still rang with the echo of the hideous din of the afternoon, and still he mourned the loss of a living creature. He could clearly recall that great gold and black combination of power and grace, on huge paws that could step so delicately the beast had appeared to glide practically unseen through the striping of dark and pale treetrunks. He had felt his heart leap with admiration and excitement as the huge head had tilted to look right at the barrel of his rifle, offering the full impact of dilated golden eyes, neat ears, a mouth almost primly closed, and a vividly striped face full of sad dignity. No power on earth would have forced him to pull the trigger, in that moment.

The tiger had been moving away when the other guns had fired from awkward angles, the staccato cracks inducing the familiar shakes and the dizziness which made him want to vomit. They had literally destroyed the splendid animal. The carcase had been torn and bloody; the dignity of that magnificent head had been replaced by the frozen agony of its open jaws. One sight of it had driven Martin to retch, and moan his distress. They had all thought him a poor specimen, a coward in the face of danger. He had seen condemnation even in Alex's face. Yet he had known all along that he would never fire the rifle they had given him; known it from the moment Marmaduke had mentioned hunting a living creature and killing it.

As he stood drinking brandy and chain-smoking, he stared at the distant ring of dying fires and recalled an incident which had haunted him several years ago. His squadron had ridden through a sweltering afternoon to a village held by New Zealanders in dire need of reinforcements in the face of an expected attack. There had been time only to feed the horses, not themselves, before manning the rough gabions facing a dense wood. The Huns had come at dusk, driven into the trap by a pincer movement. On the point of firing, Martin had realised that he was looking at the face of a youth so beautiful he hesitated to destroy him. In that suspended moment, the boy's first shot had killed Martin's leading subaltern, not much older than the German lad. Seconds later, Martin had felled his adolescent enemy. The boy's body had lain, blue eyes staring sightlessly at him until orders had been given to retreat and re-form.

The vision of that boy with sky blue eyes, petal mouth, and flaxen hair as soft and shiny as a girl's had filled Martin's thoughts to the extent of obsession. In the hospital, a year later, he had confessed his guilty love for this unknown lad, suspecting it to be responsible for his lack of sexual response. The neurologist had laughed, saying that most men at some time in their lives, felt fantasy desire for a pretty boy, and that there was no significance in it. Yet Martin had remembered that German boy's face with the greatest clarity as he had waited and watched for the tiger. He had been under orders to kill that boy: nobody in the world could have forced him to put an end to another creature of such heartaching beauty this afternoon.

At that point in his thoughts he heard movement and spun round, glass still in his hand. She stood no more than a few feet away in an ankle-length wrapper of pale cambric, her eyes as blue as those of the lost German, her mouth as petal-soft, her hair as golden-shiny as his had been before the mud had caked and stiffened it. Then, as she moved toward him, he saw the sparkle of tears on her cheeks.

"What are you doing here?" he demanded harshly, glaring his anger at her intrusion into his past hell.

She moved nearer and it was plain that she was in genuine distress. "I don't care what the others say about you," she cried thickly. "I'm *glad* you didn't shoot the tiger, Martin. *Glad* you didn't kill such a beautiful animal."

"I had no intention of shooting it."

"You hadn't?" she marvelled on a sob. "You really hadn't?"

"I shall never fire a gun again."

"Oh, *Martin!*" She flung herself against him, pressing her body close in search of comfort as she wept. "Uncle Duke brought back the tail all covered in blood. He's . . . he's nailed it on the wall like a trophy. I can't bear to go into that room now. It's *beastly!*"

Instant, uncontrollable need raced through Martin as his hands closed over her body, warm and vital through the thin material. She was peace and unspoilt beauty; gentleness and innocence. He could only lose his past through her. Forcing her head back, he began to kiss her with almost savage desperation, sighing his anguish against the childlike lips crushed beneath his own. Her tears flowed warmly over his own cheeks, and he was suddenly weeping the whole world's misery, bearing it alone.

The bed was simply a few steps away. He took them with her clasped in his arms. The flaxen hair spread out around her head as she fell beneath him, moaning his name in matching anguish. Frantic for the beauty and solace she offered, he tore the cambric from her shoulders to assault her breasts and their rising nipples with his hands and mouth. Almost instantly, she began to pant and sigh with a self-induced orgasm of passion, which swamped him with the familiar agony of an unstoppable tide. He dragged her trailing garment higher. Her bare thighs, rounded golden and biddable, parted at his first touch on the most vulnerable area. Then, they snapped together again as a voice suddenly cried a terrible warning across that lamplit room.

"Lydia, no! For God's sake, no!"

A nightmare of shouting and screaming began as Martin felt himself being dragged from the girl with hands which dug deep into his shoulders. He fell away to see another girl, with tragedy flaring in her eyes, pulling at the clothes of his symbol of peace as she lay, almost hysterical with the shock of too many simultaneous passions. Thea seemed

260

half-demented herself as she slapped the other girl's face, before pulling her to her feet and holding her close in comfort to ride out her spasms.

Overcome by the familiar nervous symptoms, Martin rolled on to his face as the whole procession of bizarre events that day rioted through his shattered senses. Then a new voice broke into the sounds of female distress; a voice betraying emotion of a different kind.

"Just what the hell is going on in here?"

"Alex, thank God you've come! We were both so worried about Martin, we came to talk to him about what happened this afternoon. He'd been drinking heavily, and resented our intrusion, I'm afraid. What he said to us was rather too much for Lydia. She's dreadfully upset over the shooting, and by that damned tail your uncle offered her. Martin's behaviour was the last straw. I suggest we give her a stiff drink and try to calm her before she breaks down completely."

They went, leaving Martin with thoughts of what he had almost done. His limbs now felt leaden; his mind was full of fears. Fantasies, images, floated somewhere out of reach in that room which throbbed with the sound of cicadas. Tigers mingled with boy soldiers; boys with girls. His body ached from the shock of sexual drive so brutally interrupted which, now it had turned cold, was channelled into untamed aggression. Dragging himself to his feet, he stumbled to the table bearing the bottle he had told Marek to bring to his room earlier that evening. Ignoring the glass, he put the neck of it to his lips, tilted back his head, and drank lengthily until the fiery brandy ran down his chin on to his bare chest.

The room was spinning when he straightened up, and there was a dark-haired girl in the room with him. Her face was ashen, stiff with shock.

"I'm sorry," she whispered, so faintly he only just heard. "I'm so desperately sorry. Please try to understand why I had to do it." Fighting for composure, she went on, "I couldn't let it happen . . . for both your sakes. It would have destroyed you."

His aggression exploded. Hurling the bottle at the wall just above her right shoulder, he cried in utter despair, "This is the result of your bloody scheme to throw us together, your damnable constant meddling! Are you proud of yourself? *Are you?*" he repeated, on an agonised roar.

She appeared to sway, then catch at a chair to steady herself. "No, Martin, no. Forgive me. I was wrong; quite wrong. It's this damned place. The jungle is too elemental. No wonder planters go out of their minds. Let's go back to civilisation, for God's sake, before we all go mad!"

Chapter 15

Martin left the Weyfords' house in a fury. Coming from the interior cooled by fans, the humid airless night seemed to stifle him. The mixed odours of rotting vegetation, human refuse and food being fried in the servants' quarters at the rear added to the sensation. He slammed the car door with unnecessary force and drove down to the main gate. Turning into the street he narrowly missed two squatting figures using the monsoon gully as a latrine, and a rickshaw-boy who hawked as he ran. The mosquitoes descended to whine around Martin's head, and torment him by puncturing any area of his flesh not covered by clothing. As he dabbed savagely at his perspiring face and neck with his handkerchief, two pi-dogs raced across his path in a frenzied, bloody fight to the death, causing him to brake so hard he stalled the engine.

He sat at the side of the road in the car he had been so grudgingly allowed to buy, while his anger raged. This was not the uncontrollable whiplash variety caused by the effects of war, it was the result of rank injustice. He hated Singapore with its extremes of poverty and wealth, its mixture of cultures, its double standards. He would never grow used to colonial life, or begin to understand it. His job was monotonous and totally unfulfilling, the city oppressed him with its heat, squalor and smells. Those with whom he had to mix were narrow in outlook and a decade behind the times. Here, he was a prisoner of society, branded as unstable by those whose eccentricities often exceeded any of his own. On a plantation up-country he would be free, a man in command of his own life and destiny. Yet Sir Hartle controlled the means of achieving this, and therefore controlled his whole life. Surely any man would rail against such restriction?

After a while, he started the car again and continued his journey to the bungalow shared with a man he disliked. There was no ending in sight, no hope for future happiness to which he could cling whilst enduring this present misery. He drove past the Beresford house, and fury surged once more. After what had happened at Serantinggi, it was vital that he should get away. Both Thea and George had been proved wrong. Lydia was not safe from him. If it had been Alex, not Thea, who had first walked in on the scene, if Thea had not lied so convincingly when he had, there would now be hell to pay. Martin dared not consider the outcome of being accused of the rape of an over-protected virgin of barely eighteen. Her life would have been ruined; he would have been in serious trouble indeed for the offence. The colonists would have felt totally vindicated, and would have put their madman in a strait-jacket whilst he awaited trial.

He had arrived back from Serantinggi only that morning, so had had no opportunity to confront George with the disastrous failure of his advice to kiss and cuddle Lydia whenever he felt like doing so. All the same, he felt that his only friend on the island must be asked to help him now. Barred from buying a plantation, he would try to find employment as a manager or overseer. At Serantinggi he had studied the business quite fully, and felt confident that he could learn the ropes very quickly. George had many friends, both in Singapore and up-country, who might advise on likely openings or on the best way to advertise his availability to work in those isolated areas. Failing that, Martin resolved to visit the Sing brothers at the first opportunity. They would surely be in a position to help him escape an experiment in resettlement which had gone wrong.

Looking back on that tennis party, Martin realised that it had never really stood a chance from then on. Between them, the Beresfords had picked him up, swung him round and round, then allowed him to fly through ten days of pure contentment only to land with a thud which had knocked the last breath from him. At this precise moment, he felt totally defeated. Yet there had been ten days which had proved that it was possible for him to build a new fulfilling life, given the right conditions. That thought was the only factor keeping him going after his godfather's unequivocal refusal to release the sum of money needed to achieve it.

"I have never heard anything so foolish, my boy," Sir Hartle had said, almost laughing at the prospect. "Even sane men go mad up there all alone. It would be the finish of you, Martin, believe me. Just because you've spent a few days with an amiable eccentric, you imagine the life of a planter is one long holiday. It can certainly be very beautiful up there—didn't I tell you so myself? But it can also be soul-destroying. No, no, my dear fellow," he had concluded, putting a hand on Martin's shoulder to console him, "you're coming along quite nicely here. Not made quite as much progress as I had hoped, perhaps, but Sir Frederick reports that he is satisfied with your work for the department, and now you have the car you were determined upon, you should make every effort to get out and about more, mix with other youngsters like yourself."

"There aren't any other youngsters like me in Singapore," he had pointed out heatedly.

"Now, now, mustn't take that attitude. Mustn't start feeling sorry for yourself," the ageing judge had admonished sternly. "You must forget the past, pull yourself together, and make up your mind that you *will* succeed in this wonderful chance for a fresh start."

He drove to the bungalow, and climbed wearily from the car that he had looked upon as his symbol of freedom. There was no such state, he now realised. Although Damien Lang's side of the building was in darkness, indicating that he was out, Martin still decided to let himself into his own rooms via the side verandah. He did not want Wah fussing around him. Bed, and a few stiff brandies was all he had in mind. The room was hot and airless, so he switched on the overhead fan before taking off his jacket and flinging it into a chair. Pulling the bow tie undone as he crossed the room, he then poured a drink to keep him going until he could climb beneath the mosquito net with the bottle. While he was enjoying the fiery liquor he heard a car arriving, followed by the noisy slamming of doors. His heart sank. Lang was back with a crowd of his cronies. Impulse drove him to switch off his light to give the impression that he was not there. Solitude was what he needed tonight, not colonial high jinks.

His door suddenly crashed open, and his light was switched on again. Lang stood inside the room with a sneering smile on his face.

"Knew you were in, Linwood, because your car was outside."

Thinking the man was aggressively intoxicated, Martin spoke carefully. "I'm feeling rather knocked up after the overnight journey from Serantinggi. Sorry, Lang, but I'm planning to get to bed right now."

"Change your plan," he responded harshly. "I have something to say to you."

"Can't it wait until morning?" he asked with a touch of impatience.

Another figure pushed into the room, and Martin recognised Randal Forster from the night they had all gate-crashed the paddle steamer party.

"No, it won't wait, Linwood," he said with violent emphasis. "I've come here tonight especially to see you."

Martin then sensed that there was something wrong, and the feeling strengthened when the other members of that night's group crowded into his room in what appeared to be a curiously ugly mood.

"What's this all about?" he asked sharply, in no shape for collective inebriation.

"My God, you're cool," exploded Forster. "You're surely not intending to deny that you arranged the closure of Ammul's little love-palace while you were away up-country."

"What?" he queried, trying to make sense of what was going on. "Oh, you mean that place we all went to. If my department has finally tracked it down and closed it, I think it's a jolly good thing, but I certainly had nothing to do with it. Whatever gave you the idea that I had?"

"It was doing very well before I took you there," Forster replied in grating tones. "I made it very plain that you were given the privilege of an introduction because we wanted a friend in the right place."

"You had your wish. I've said nothing to anyone. I gave you my word on that, didn't I?"

Forster looked at him disparagingly. "The word of a man like you is worthless. The very day after you went up-country, the place was swooped on and closed. Too much of a coincidence, Linwood. Far too much of a coincidence."

"You rat!" cried Lang with venom.

The group began to close in on Martin. As he looked at all their faces in turn, the first suspicion that they were there to mete out some kind of punishment occurred to him. Hiding his apprehension, he stood his ground with outward coolness.

"It was only a matter of time before the place was discovered and closed during one of my department's systematic purges. It was probably some dissatisfied client, some well-known figure who feared being seen there who gave Sir Frederick the tip to close it before scandal could ruin him." As they closed in tighter, he began to back, saying, "Look, aren't you all getting a little too hot under the collar over the affair? There are dozens of other whorehouses in the colony."

At that, Lang stepped around the table to confront him, and it was plain that he was possessed by more than mere anger.

"It was through me that Forster took you there that night, so I'm held responsible for what you've done. You knew he had a nice little deal going on with Ammul. He made no secret of the fact, and told you that you'd be given special treatment as a friend of his. If any hint of Forster's involvement gets out, or any suspicion . . ."

"I have no notion of how involved Forster is with anything," Martin said quickly, "and I've already sworn the closure had nothing to do with me. From the way you're all behaving, it seems you must have very strong reasons for not wanting Ammul to be caught. If you've been indulging in sins other than fornication with children, that's none of my concern, and I'd be glad if you'd all leave."

Before he was truly aware of imminent danger, they clustered around him to trap him in a corner of that stifling room.

"Yes, we have strong reasons for not wanting Ammul caught," snapped Forster. "We also have strong personal reasons for deciding to teach you a lesson you'll never forget. It's time you understood something, Linwood. We have accepted rules of behaviour, certain understandings between ourselves. Out here, we have to live cheek by jowl with the natives, and they with us. We have to give and take, solicit trust in each other. We are colonisers, who take the rough with the smooth. We spend our lives out here in this damned awful climate, go down with malaria, snakebite, and fever of the brain. If we go out without a topee we're smitten by heatstroke. Most of the food we eat comes from tins; most of that which doesn't, gives us dysentery. All day long we are surrounded by beautiful brown women, but we're not supposed to live with them. So we go to England to find a wife, then bring her back here to discover that she hates the climate, hates the natives, hates the insects, and hates sharing her husband's bed. We become so desperate, we have to go to brothels to avoid raping our own wives."

When Forster paused for breath, Lang continued. "That's how we live out here, Linwood. We might not be like the stout upright fellows who fought with you for King and country, but we do have a code of honour. We don't like those who rat on us. We don't like being asked to befriend a chap who is supposed to be some kind of hero, then find he's no more than a righteous prig. We don't like outsiders who use influential relatives to get them a post some poor devil has sweated for years out here to deserve. Most of all, we don't like slimy bastards who crawl to the authorities at the first opportunity. In case all that isn't clear enough to you, we're here to make certain you'll understand it in the future. You'll think twice about playing the shell-shocked fool again."

Martin was seized by four of the men and forced back into the corner. He had suspected some kind of punishment, but would never have anticipated what then happened. Between words of vitriolic abuse, Forster struck him again and again on mouth and eyes, sending his head cracking back against the wall and forcing grunts of pain from his split lips. It seemed to go on endlessly, while Martin tried to understand what was happening, what could have unleashed such ferocious reprisal. Soon, one eye was closed over, blood ran from the corner of his mouth, and he was no longer capable of reasoning. Every moment, he expected the man's fist or boot in his stomach to signify the end of the attack. There was something far worse to come, however.

As he gasped in air to counteract the waves of pain flowing through his head, he felt himself being dragged from the corner across the room to one of the big leather armchairs. He had no chance to struggle before he was forced over and downward, so that he was bent over the back of it. He was held in that position by wrists and ankles while first Forster, then Lang lashed his back and legs with a leather belt until, crying out in his agony, he believed his flesh must be pulp. At that point, they hauled him up so roughly he screamed even louder. Supporting his drooping body beneath the armpits, they forced the neck of the brandy bottle into his swollen mouth. He had to swallow or choke, and he continued to swallow until his head rang with the clamour of a thousand bells. He believed they must now be slowly tearing him apart, limb by limb. There was a great heat within him; his flesh was burning like the fires at the tiger hunt. That beautiful striped creature was tearing the skin from his body with red-hot claws. Blood was filling his throat to choke him. The night had grown as black as pitch when the world began to recede. He swallowed liquid fire once more. There was oblivion.

Thea had spent the night alone in a hotel room. They had returned from Serantinggi to be greeted with the news that Austin had been readmitted to hospital on the verge of collapse due to his attempts to continue running *Berondel* from his home. Enforced convalescence was his only hope of avoiding another stroke, doctors had told Margery. With Lydia still in a highly emotional state, and his mother in need of his support, Alex had had no alternative but to stay at home with them. Margery refused to have Thea in the house, however, and had greeted the news of the forthcoming marriage with silence and a blank expression.

In truth, Thea was glad to be back in civilisation again, even if it took a form she did not entirely understand. Serantinggi had unsettled her. During the first few days of that visit personalities had changed, relationships had altered, some in dramatic fashion and others in more subtle ways. Attitudes and beliefs, long held during years in close communion with others, took on a different bias when isolated in a place of elemental nature free of social poses and prejudices. Away from parental repression, Lydia had become a relaxed radiant girl enjoying a normal adolescent infatuation with an older man who represented all the excitement her life had so far lacked. Freed from the sensation of being an experimental curiosity viewed through a microscope, Martin had revealed something of the boy he had been and the man he could become. Alex had come to terms with himself, and gained strength. Although he would never admit it, Thea knew the change had been wrought by his curious new rapport with the man who had induced strong responses from their first meeting. Whatever had been exchanged between them on the night Alex had failed to come to her room, it had turned his envy, resentment, reluctant admiration—call it one or all of those—into an understanding beyond casual friendship. Then, a creature as wild and ancient as the jungle had been hunted and killed. The idyll had died with it. Better by far to have remained beneath the umbrella of social posturing than to have glimpsed truth only to have it snatched away again.

All Thea could now remember of the trip was the clamour of the unseen beaters in that dense green valley, and the shock of rifle fire which had brought an ominous silence. The image of a blood-encrusted tail as Marmaduke had spoken of his disgust for a man who had not revelled in the slaughter, as he had, would not go from her memory however hard she tried. Nor would the recollection of walking softly to Martin's room in the sure belief that he was in need of help, only to discover an insane passion near to consummation. Looking back on it, she did not know how she had had the courage to intervene at such a stage. The memory haunted her, the pair of entwined bodies constantly changing identity so that they were first Lydia and Martin, then became Dominic Grant and Anna du Lessier. Her mother and former lover had completed the act as she had watched in silent anguish. It had proved impossible to watch it happen a second time.

Lydia was now suffering from shock, but to a lesser degree than the loss of her virginity would have induced. Martin had reverted to the bitter, disturbed person Thea had first encountered in a garden chequered by clouds over the moon. If he had been allowed to possess that young girl, if she had become pregnant as a result, surely the consequences for him would have been far more damaging? Had it been wrong to stop the ultimate union? Had it been wrong to contrive Martin's inclusion in the Serantinggi trip? Had it been a mistake to come to the East in a bid to escape, only be involved in a situation as tangled and emotional as the one from which she had fled?

As she ate an early breakfast in the fan-cooled restaurant the day lay empty before her. Work on her novel was out of the question in her present state of mind. Alex had more than enough to occupy him before joining her for dinner tonight. As it was Sunday, the shops would be closed, and the colonials would be asking for guidance in their various churches. Thea had no god. Guidance, therefore, had to be the result of instinct or intellect. It was the former which led her to leave the breakfast table, collect a shady hat, and seek one of the rickshaws waiting at the hotel entrance. Giving the address of Martin's bungalow, she sat back telling herself she would either be greeted with the succinct advice to leave immediately, or with a flow of invective he would consider she well deserved. Perhaps it was from a masochistic desire to be thus punished that she was going to him, she reasoned. If she truly was to blame for what had happened, the affair must be properly concluded, one way or the other. She could not leave it as it was at present.

The bungalow stood silent beneath the morning sun, as if the residents were still sleeping. Thea was surprised. Although it was already nine a.m., there was nothing to suggest any sign of life. The verandahs were deserted; the wooden shutters still bolted over the windows. There was no sound from within, no mattresses airing on the sills, no smell of breakfast being cooked. The whole place appeared deserted.

Feeling mystified, Thea told the rickshaw-boy to wait then went up the stone steps fronting the building, and on to the terrace. It had been swept that morning, and still smelled damp from the water thrown over it by a *kebun*. Someone must be at home or the servants would never bother with such chores. She banged the dragon-shaped knocker several times, then listened for the sound of movements from within which would suggest that the residents were astir. There were none, yet the door was opened almost immediately by the houseboy wearing the usual soft black shoes which made no noise.

"I've come to see Mr Linwood, Wah," she explained. "Is he at home?"

His reaction was almost one of fright as he stepped back to allow her entry, then led the way across the spartan sitting room dimmed by closed shutters. The fans had not been switched on, so it was oppressively stuffy. A door on Martin's side of the bungalow stood open, and Thea could see that it was a bedroom. She grew even more mystified as Wah led her in silence toward it. What was wrong? she wondered. Could the events at Scrantinggi have affected Martin more than she guessed, and brought a return of his nervousness? With curiosity deepening into concern she walked into the room made shadowy by shutters closed over the windows, but was drastically unprepared for what she found. The place was a shambles, as if the owner had run amok.

Martin was sprawling face down across the width of the bed, arms stretched out above his head, ominously still. His white shirt was tattered and stained with blood, which had darkened and congealed. There were similar marks on the legs of his evening trousers. The tips of his fingers were tightly curled, as if clutching the counterpane for support, and the backs of his hands were purple with bruising. So was the left side of his face, just visible as he lay against a blood-soaked patch on the snowy bedspread. There was an overwhelming smell of brandy filling the room.

Thea stared at him appalled. She had had no idea that shell shock could produce violence of this order. How could any doctor have allowed a man as ill as this out of his hospital? She approached the bed on legs that had turned rubbery. Martin lay so still he could be dead. With her heart pounding, she bent over him. The smell of brandy was even stronger, but he was still breathing.

"Thank God," she breathed, forgetting that she worshipped none. "Oh, thank God!"

"Missy tell what do," said a voice beside her, and she turned to find Wah looking as shocked as she felt.

"What happened?" she demanded, fear making her tone aggressive. "What has been going on here?"

The Chinese was very upset, but managed to say that he had only just discovered his master. He was afraid, he said, and was glad that someone had come to instruct him on what should be done. Trying to collect her thoughts, Thea stood looking down at the bed feeling unbearable disappointment. Martin plainly was the mental misfit everyone but herself had seen. Her disappointment was swiftly replaced by sadness so great, his image shimmered before her eyes. She thought of the studies sacrificed for war, the sharpness of a brain which could be normal for long periods at a time, the complex personality no one had bothered to try to draw out, the love he had for a young girl out of his reach. She thought of the laughing man astride a horse at Serantinggi, the inventive, impudent participant in games of an innocent, flirtatious nature, the vital individuality of someone who had recently found peace and sanity in a green jungle plantation: a man who had seen so much of death he could not bring himself to shoot a beautiful animal, even if he earned the contempt of others. His image shimmered even more. What a waste! What a tragic, senseless waste of a young life!

Wah touched her arm insistently. "Missy tell what do."

Turning to him, she tried to pull herself together. "First bring a bowl of very warm water and some small towels. While you're fetching the water, I'll write a note for you to give to the waiting rickshaw-boy. Tell him to deliver it to Dr McGregor, at top speed. After that, make a large quantity of black coffee to sober your master up."

The little houseboy went off swiftly. Thea sat at a table to write a brief emergency summons to George, telling herself as she did so not to give in to weakness. Life had to be faced. There were hundreds—even thousands—like Martin Linwood, and probably just as many who were far worse. Wah returned with the bowl and towels, then went off again with the note.

Feeling more resolute, Thea began to sponge those areas of Martin's back where his shirt was stuck to his skin by congealed blood. By the time it was possible for her to ease the material completely away, the water in the bowl was crimson. She then pulled the shirt free of his trousers and folded it back as far as his armpits. A chill of horror crept over her as she looked at a series of scarlet weals, where the skin had been split to expose raw flesh now starting to ooze fresh blood. Around each stripe there was severe bruising.

Thea began to feel sick. Such injuries could never have been self-inflicted, no matter how inebriated or unbalanced a man might be. It was physically impossible for Martin to have lashed his own back with the strength and ferocity required to produce such a state. The obscene truth then became obvious. He had been systematically flogged.

Turning away from the sight, she clung to the bedpost for a while, fighting rising nausea while her brain teemed with questions, accusations and vows of vengeance. Wah returned with a large pot of coffee and cups on a tray. His fearfulness redoubled at the evidence of such violence, but Thea seized his arm as he hastily put down the tray and made to leave.

"Help me to turn him round on the bed," she ordered in raw tones. "Then you must fetch fresh water to wash away the blood."

They gripped the comatose Martin beneath the armpits, heaving him upward and around ninety degrees. Then they swung his legs up so that he was lying flat on the bed. Their efforts brought an agonised cry from him, which was all the more disturbing because it came from a mouth that was split and swollen in a face darkly contused and smeared with blood. One of his eyes was puffy and completely closed; the other flickered feebly as his cries continued. The little Chinese had had enough of something his oriental mind saw as the work of devils, and he vanished in the direction of the kitchen saying that he would fetch water.

Feeling tears dangerously near again, Thea fought them back. What Martin needed was help, not feminine weakness. Reaching gently beneath his prone body, she began to unbutton his trousers, then his underpants. When Wah returned, she told him to put the bowl on the bedside table, then help her to strip his master as she sponged the torn clothing free of his body. As the task progressed, she grew more and more appalled at his injuries. Fury bubbled inside her, just below the surface of her control. Who could have thrashed a man until his back was practically broken? Who could have lashed his buttocks and thighs so that they grew bloody and raw? It was the first time that she had seen the results of man's inhumanity to his own kind at first hand. The war casualties she had seen in England had all been neatly bandaged before being presented to the public. This evidence of brutality shocked her to the core.

By the time Martin was naked and every trace of blood had been cleansed from him, Thea found she was trembling. At that moment she heard George's voice outside, and hurried to meet him, thankful to have someone with her to administer the medical aid she was not able to give. One look at her face must have been enough to tell George he had not come on a simple errand, for he went into the bedroom with her immediately without pausing for an explanation. The sight horrified even a man used to sickness and violence.

"However, in God's name, did this happen?" he demanded, going swiftly to the bed and taking up Martin's wrist to feel his pulse.

"Who knows?" Thea responded. "Wah said he thought both men were away for the whole weekend. He hasn't seen Damien Lang since yesterday morning, and he didn't hear Martin's return so has no idea when that was. It's not surprising, really. His quarters are well to the rear of the bungalow. Only when he spotted the car outside did he suppose Martin to be in and sleeping late. He claims to have heard nothing during the night, so was very scared when he decided to come in here to ask if his master wanted breakfast."

George nodded abstractedly. "What are you doing here, may I ask?"

Thea had never known him in professional guise, so bridled at his tone. "Visiting. What else do you suppose I was doing?"

He glanced up at her shrewdly. "Been a bit of a shock, eh? Go outside and ask Wah to make you some tea—strong and sweet. I'll take over now." He smiled reassuringly. "You've done marvels with him, my girl. Why not become a nurse instead of a novelist?"

She shook her head. "I hated every minute, and was almost sick halfway through it. I'd make a very poor nurse . . . but I couldn't let him lie there and do nothing to help."

George dropped Martin's wrist, and approached her to turn her away from the bed. "Not quite the self-centred, self-possessed creature you pretend to be, are you? Go on, sit out on the verandah and have some tea. I'll call you when you can come back in."

"But I . . ."

"Do as I say, Thea. I don't want two patients on my hands."

She went out, still trembling. The garden was hushed and peaceful, making the scene she had just left seem even more shocking. Perspiration beaded her face, and her dress was sticking to her body as she stepped blindly from the verandah into the garden. There, she wandered along a path edged by trees bearing long hands of the small, sweet monkey bananas. Somewhere nearby a golden oriole sang its rich melodious call to another, and cockatoos squawked raucously as they savaged the branches amidst which they sat. These creatures thrived in the humid heat of this colony: Thea wilted in it.

The East was a contrast of beauty and cruelty, she decided. Life was uneasy; the people a law unto themselves. They were easily inflamed to mixed passions and they protected what they had with ferocity resulting from suspicion of each other. Yet, incredibly beautiful flowers flourished amongst tangled creepers, birds displayed unbelievable colour and song from a perch above a pile of human refuse, and the native people produced articles of exquisite design and form in the midst of squalor. A man of sensitivity and courage could be thrashed almost to a pulp without anyone hearing or knowing of it, and for no apparent reason. How could she hope to write about the East when she found it impossible to accept or understand? All at once, she longed for home, longed to run and tell Alex to whisk her on to an ocean liner there and then. A feeling akin to fear invaded her as she recognised an overwhelming desire to run away. From what? How could she tell when the impulse had only just touched her?

Halting at the far end of the garden, she leaned back against a tree, pushing up her damp hair from her equally damp forehead, and told herself it was the heat making her ache for gentle green pastures and soft balmy English days. It was never cool in Singapore; it was either hot and dry, or hot and rainy. The climate sapped one's strength and dulled one's wits. That was why she had been unable to think positively back there in Martin's bedroom; why she could not analyse her impulses now. This heat made the simplest task seem an enormous effort, and movements soon grew sluggish. Yet the colonists ruggedly and determinedly played tennis, danced, indulged in cricket matches, dinner parties and grand military reviews, defying the climate to prevent them from being European. They succumbed to fevers, dysentery and heatstrokes, but stoically pretended that such evils were a normal part of their lives. They refused to go outside without a topee in the belief that it would act as some kind of talisman whilst they continued to live as they would in their homeland. In Thea's opinion, they would all cope far better if they dressed like the native people, ceased their never-ending sporting activities, and drank less alcohol. It would be asking too much of them, of course. They had to dupe themselves into believing they were still in the land of their birth, or end like Marmaduke Beresford and his ilk.

Sharp pain made her look down, then move smartly away from the tree, brushing her legs with her hands. A column of vicious red ants winding its way up the trunk had made a detour to embark on a feast from her flesh. Perspiration broke anew on her brow. That was another pestilence of this island. Ants, and more ants. If one was not troubled by ants, it was by cockroaches, giant spiders, snakes, praying mantis,

273

centipedes or hornets, to say nothing of the bats which swooped from the sky the minute darkness fell, to catch the myriad moths and mosquitoes in that swift change from twilight to night. Add the smells, the monsoon rains which fell in solid sheets to make green mould sprout on shoes and clothing, water which had to be boiled before drinking, fruit that turned bad within a day if not eaten, and the red itching rash known as prickly heat. The sum total produced a place where unknown and unseen attackers could invade a man's home and lash him until he was near to death.

She wandered on, her thoughts deeply troubled until, in a tangle of greenery, she found evidence of the other face of this island. Hanging from a leafy arch was a spectacular pendulous flower. It was exotic, beautiful and green in colour. The jade-flower, rare and much prized for its decorative shape and colour, was growing there in a neglected garden ignored by occupants and passers-by alike. With a swift surge of delight Thea reached up and plucked it, letting the heavy bloom lie against her palm as she held the short stem between thumb and finger. Here was the exotic, fabulous East—here in one single blossom.

When George called to her she went back with the flower, as if its beauty would somehow counterbalance what had occurred in that room. Martin was now lying face downward in a bed made up with fresh sheets and pillowcases. The vivid marks on his back looked even more grotesque against the spotless linen, and were sheened with sweat. The strong smell of brandy had been dispersed; the shutters were now folded back and the overhead fan was circling to freshen the atmosphere laden with the clean scent of antiseptic. Wah had cleared away the coffee tray and all Martin's clothes.

George was sweating profusely, his shirt crumpled and wet. "It wasn't quite what I thought," he told her quietly. "He wasn't so much drunk; more in a state of shock, I'd say. The brandy appears to have been mostly poured over him, judging by the condition of his clothes. He was probably fairly sober when he was attacked, but his assailants tried to force him to drink against his will. That makes the business more serious, and infinitely more bizarre."

"Who would do this to him?" she cried. "It's absolutely brutal!"

George shook his head. "There are a great many people in our world capable of such an act. They do flog offenders to death whilst lashed over a frame in some Malay States, you know, but this is quite mystifying. What could Martin possibly have done to invoke this manner of revenge, and from whom?"

Pushing back her damp hair once more, she sighed. "The police will have to discover the answer to that. They're certain to mount a major investigation into an attack of such ferocity on a colonial servant who deals with ethnic affairs."

"He won't hear of it."

"Who won't hear of it?" she asked, uncomprehending.

"Martin. He refuses to let me report this to the authorities . . ."

"*What?*"

"He's quite adamant, Thea."

"Adamant!" she cried emotionally. "How can a man in his state be adamant about anything? Of course it has to be reported. Whoever did this must be a maniac, who should be locked away."

"I told him all that, but nothing will persuade him."

"Then you'll have to act without his consent."

"I can't do that," George said quietly. "As you pointed out just now, there'd be a massive inquiry into this if we called in officialdom. An English civil servant subjected to flogging by a typically Eastern method in his own home, for no apparent reason! They'd rake up every fact possible concerning Martin, in case it proved relevant. That would include his periods spent in a mental hospital. I can understand his reluctance."

"Oh, can you," she raged. "What *I* understand is my reluctance to let this ever happen again . . . to Martin, or to anyone else. The whole of Singapore has already decided that he is a half-witted dolt from a lunatic asylum, because they know about his time spent in a hospital for men shattered by war. That is something they try to ignore, because it makes them feel uncomfortable. However, what has recently occurred here is something they *can't* ignore. Never mind that they have treated Martin abominably themselves, they can't have the jolly old natives thrashing one of *us*, and getting away with it. They'll move heaven and earth to find a culprit somewhere, you know damn well they will."

George looked back at her steadily. "Calm down. You'll help no one, least of all Martin, by growing hysterical."

"I am never hysterical," she snapped, shaken by such an accusation. "What I am, at this moment, is immensely angry, and much of that anger is directed against you, George. I thought you were a friend of his, yet you are apparently quite prepared to shrug your shoulders, murmur 'c'est la vie' and merely dab iodine on his hideous wounds. Some friend!"

"I can't go against his express wishes," he stated firmly.

"I can," she flung at him. "Being a woman, I am unaffected by your ridiculous masculine code of 'old boy' loyalty."

"Fine, fine," George retorted, watching her shrewdly. "You want to be emancipated and equal, but all too soon fall back on female traits

275

when it suits you. All hell will break loose if this business is made public. Martin knows that. I know it. However, if that's what you truly want, go ahead and report it. I *am* his friend—probably the only one he has out here—and I'm not prepared to betray him when he asks for my silence. I have always suspected that you two were rather more than friends, but if you take matters into your own hands now, he'll never forgive you."

She looked at him hard and long. "Neither will you, I take it."

"No."

Turning away, she went to the open window, filled with anger, a sense of impotence, and another emotion which defied identification. What should she do? Normal human compassion cried out against doing nothing to avenge such cruelty, yet she knew George was right in saying Martin would never forgive her if she defied him and set the colony alight with this affair. Fresh waves of heat washed over her, renewing the urge to leave this deceptive tropical paradise with its disturbing contrasts. Realising that she still held the jade-flower in her hand, she looked down at its exotic green beauty and her eyes filled with tears.

George came up behind her and turned her by the shoulders to face him. "Come on, girl, summon up that famous self-possession," he instructed gently. "It's not like you to go to pieces like this."

She shook her head slowly. "No, it isn't, is it? It's just that there's something so . . . so . . . ."

"*Eastern* about this?" he suggested with continuing gentleness. "More atmosphere for your book."

"To hell with the book! George, did he say anything about what happened, give any clue as to why?"

"Not really. Only something about breaking the rules."

"Breaking the rules? Whatever does that mean?"

"Who knows?"

"Is that all he said about the affair?"

"I'm afraid so, but you might coax some more out of him." He gave an encouraging smile. "Go on, have a try."

"Is he conscious?" she asked in surprise.

"Probably not enough to have followed our conversation, but you'll get through to him if you go right up to the bed and speak into his ear."

She drew up a chair, sat on it and leaned close to Martin's broken face to speak his name. After a moment or two, his least injured eye opened slowly to squint at her. The smile she summoned refused to come. Instead, she felt close to weeping again.

"Did you know you had a rare plant growing at the end of your

276

garden?" It was all she could think of to say, and he just looked back at her helplessly. "I picked it to bring in for you," she went on, holding it up for him to see. "It probably won't last longer than today, but it's so lovely even a single sight of it is worth having, don't you think?"

As he lay in silent study of the green bloom, she asked softly, "Why won't you let George report this?"

The question prompted a mumbled response as his gaze left the flower to fasten on her face. "I'll . . . be all right."

"No, you won't. It's not safe to leave you here alone. Martin, are you misguidedly trying to protect whoever did this?"

He made no answer, and she grew quickly angry with him. "If the pain isn't enough to tell you that serious damage has been done to your back and legs, I'll enlighten you. Without George on hand to deal promptly with your injuries, I would have called an ambulance. You would now be in hospital being closely questioned by the relevant authorities. They wouldn't accept your stubborn attitude, I can assure you, so why should your friends?"

"Go away, Thea," he told her with great difficulty.

"If I do, it will be to the nearest police station."

"No." His voice was stronger in protest. "Don't . . . meddle!"

Defeated, she looked down at the flower in her palm. It was already starting to wilt. "There's no compulsion for you to be a hero any longer, you know. This isn't war," she said, meeting his damaged eye once more. It had closed, and he appeared to have drifted from consciousness.

George helped her up from the chair. "Nothing to worry about. I gave him morphia." Leading her from the bedroom to the sitting room, where Wah had placed a fresh tray, he added, "Have a cup of tea, as I instructed. It'll do you good."

While she drank the tea, he outlined his plan. "Martin will need watching. I daren't move him to my place in anything less than an ambulance, and I'll not get hold of one without an official rigmarole. So I'll move in here for a while. As far as the department is concerned I'll be on duty, which is perfectly true. I'm rarely in the office, in any case, so no one will miss me. Can you hang on here while I go to fetch my things?"

"Of course," she murmured. "George, what is this going to do to him?"

"Mentally or physically?" he asked, stirring his tea vigorously.

"Will the cuts heal?"

He nodded. "Should do. That kind of open wound is more vulnerable to germs in the tropics, and soon becomes infected. That's why it's essential for me to be on hand during the early stages. He'll have to exercise to prevent the muscles from seizing up, but I guess he'll bear the scars forever. With luck, he'll recover physically all right."

"And mentally?" she asked tentatively.

"I can't answer that. It's not my field of medicine. The only evidence we have to go on is that he seems in perfect command of his senses at the moment." Leaning back in his chair, he mopped at his neck with his handkerchief. "Tell me something, my dear. Do you know of any association with Malays or Indians which Martin had? The injuries suggest that he was tied or held down over a piece of furniture whilst the lashing took place, which is a form of punishment unlikely to be used by Chinese, in my limited opinion. It's quite commonplace in parts of Africa, I've been told, but I think we can rule out the possibility of Africans being responsible. There are so very few here. Martin works very closely with me in the department, so I'd be aware of any event which could conceivably evoke such reprisal. The only instance recently was the department's closure of a particularly disgusting brothel, and I have definite knowledge that Martin had no hand in that. The information came to us in a letter penned undoubtedly by one of our own countrymen, because the phraseology was the crisp businesslike kind used by native Britons. It arrived several days after you'd gone off to Serantinggi, so could not have been posted in Singapore by Martin. I should guess the sender is more likely to be a former patron of the so-called 'love-palace', who has recently discontinued his patronage either through fear of discovery or because his own advanced years denied him the ability to use the services on offer. He has covered his tracks by ensuring that the place was closed. The owner is unable to avenge himself on anyone, because he's tucked behind bars."

He poured himself more tea, sipped it gratefully, then frowned at Thea. "Martin could only have fallen foul of some group or family over something outside his work. Did he mix socially with Indians or Malays?"

"Not so far as I know. He visited the Sing brothers, of course, but they're Chinese."

"And totally incapable of this attack. They thought too highly of him, in any case. No one else?"

"Martin avoided people whenever he could," she pointed out.

"Then the only possible explanation is that the attackers punished the wrong man. Maybe Lang was the intended victim. I could easily believe that snake capable of deserving a flogging."

Thea felt herself turning cold at the thought of Martin receiving what Lang deserved. "That's terrible!"

"More terrible than accepting that Martin really has done something deserving of such vicious reprisal?"

"Oh, I don't know what to think," she cried. "The whole affair is too beastly to take in. You didn't see what I saw when I walked in here this morning. All that blood! He was clutching that bedspread as if trying to hold on to life itself."

George got to his feet, and stood looking down at her. "You're not half as brittle as you pretend to be, Miss du Lessier, and you have never fooled me for a moment."

Glaring up at him, she demanded, "What is that supposed to mean?"

He smiled, and touched her hair with a light caress. "Work it out while I go off for my things."

Thea stayed at the bungalow even when George returned, departing reluctantly only when time demanded that she meet Alex for dinner, as arranged. During the rickshaw ride to her hotel, she witnessed one of the spectacular twilights her lover found so taunting. This one would bring him nothing but joy, she reflected, because she intended to tell him that she would sail with him to England as soon as he wished.

Chapter 16

In two days it would be Christmas Eve. The balls, dinner parties and sporting events had followed one after the other since Alex had returned from Serantinggi almost a month ago. For once, he had participated in very few of them, and had only agreed to play in today's polo match because he felt in need of strenuous physical exercise after so long without it. As he slaked his thirst with the other players beneath a marquee during the interval, he watched the spectators strolling around the field to catch up on the latest news or scandal. The Beresford family had given them a great deal to talk about recently, and there was more to come shortly.

Austin had suffered a second stroke four days after they had all returned to Singapore from the plantation, which had once again delayed Alex's plans to sail for England. His father was now an extremely sick man, severely paralysed and unable to communicate either by written or spoken word. Alex had visited his bedside at the hospital only once since the second attack. It had proved a distressing experience for them both. Austin had been powerless to forbid his son's entry or to tell him to leave, so hostility had been expressed in his eyes as he had lain immobile, a victim of his own impossibly high standards. Alex had determinedly embarked on what he had felt obliged to say, but soon realised that every word he spoke and every minute he remained there multiplied the helpless man's anguish. Smitten by a mixture of sadness and guilt, he had left the sterile room knowing that he would never see his father again. There was enough filial devotion still within him to create deep regret at parting from a parent in such manner, but his strength of purpose was now great enough to allow him to accept the fact and pursue his responsibilities.

In view of Austin's unfitness to control *Berondel*, Alex had been granted temporary legal powers to act for his father. As it was now impossible to receive any instructions from Austin, the members of the board instead studied the terms of the older man's will before reaching a unanimous conclusion. The document, drawn up only a few weeks before, excluded Alex from any monies or business connected with the shipping line. In short, Austin had virtually disowned his son. However, since the terms of the will would only apply after death, Alex's position in the family company was still valid, allowing him to draw a salary as usual. Denying his heir, Austin had specified that his daughter

Lydia should inherit *Berondel* as a "sleeping" chairman, while the company was managed on her behalf by the present directors, their sons or appointees.

For the past weeks Alex had been engrossed in legal complexities whilst deputising for his father in all outstanding contracts, agreements or long-term plans. Mercantile panic had set in once more when it became known that Austin was a dying man and his son was leaving the business. *Berondel* lost a few nervous clients, but most of the long-standing ones were reassured by the knowledge that the present directors, cast in Austin's cautious mould, would be in control of their business. Alex spent a great deal of time explaining and outlining the future arrangements to Lydia, and to his mother who would be as financially secure as before. There was also much to sort out regarding the house and domestic finances, all of which had been handled by Austin. In every aspect of his life, he had maintained total control, which now left Margery bewildered over payment of household bills, and expenditure such as servants' wages, the maintenance of several cars, and subscriptions for membership of those clubs she had always felt free to use. If Alex felt an obligation to remain at the head of his family placed in this situation, it was soon dispersed by his mother's implacable attitude toward Thea and his marriage. In the past, he had been torn by the desire for freedom pulling against a sense of duty. He was torn no longer.

Thea had suddenly and surprisingly surrendered, agreeing to sail with him when he was free to go. That being so, and in view of his father's second stroke with all it had entailed, she had suggested delaying the actual wedding until they were on the high seas. With her family in England, and his certain to shun the ceremony, there seemed little point in marrying in Singapore. Thea had expressed a desire to pledge her vows at sea, and he had agreed. He was really so embroiled in tying up every loose end before he left, there was no time in which to arrange a wedding, anyway. The urgency no longer applied, because her hotel room provided the privacy for frequent lovemaking. Alex was deeply and wonderfully happy. Possessing this unusual girl was even more fulfilling than he had imagined it might be. She was generous, imaginative and stimulating; she set him afire with the confidence that he would reach those distant goals he sought. Her novel appeared to have been discarded, and her eagerness to sail for the homeland she had left six months ago was patent. Passages were booked on a liner leaving Singapore three days after Chinese New Year began, by which time he felt he should be able to have family and business affairs running smoothly.

With all Alex presently had to occupy his mind there had been little time to think of Martin Linwood, yet strange unease over the man touched him whenever he happened to witness one of those ten thousand twilights he had dreaded. That last day at the plantation had shown Martin to be every bit as unstable as everyone had claimed. It had been a sharp disappointment after the early days up-country, and Alex felt very sorry for an inescapable truth even Lydia could surely no longer ignore. She had been sobered by it, and by their father's irreversible illness which was bringing such drastic changes to her life pattern. Alex's imminent departure from it had been accepted by her, for she did not once join in their mother's pleas to him not to abandon them so heartlessly. In redoubling his resolution against emotional constraint, Alex also set out to sever his ties with the island which had been his home for so long, and with those inhabiting it, including the man who had first incited his revolt against the future he did not want.

He was thinking of Martin as he mounted for the next chukka, however. The polo pony he was riding was a spirited animal requiring skilled handling, and into his mind came Martin's words concerning cavalry horses which were difficult to control under fire. As he rode out on to the field of sporting battle, that old sensation touched him momentarily. After what Martin had told him of war, did he really envy him the experience? No, in all honesty, he no longer did. Yet, despite the other man's humiliation over the tiger hunt, Alex still experienced that faint sense of not quite measuring up to him. It was totally absurd. Even Thea had abandoned all mention of him. Why, then, was the man still under his skin? Thank God Martin Linwood would be left behind on this island, once they sailed.

Introspection was forgotten during the energetic game he always played with skill and enjoyment, and he helped his team to victory with two splendid goals. They rode from the field to the applause of the crowd, and Alex swung from the saddle to hand his pony to the syce before heading toward the pavilion and a refreshing shower. His progress was delayed several times by enthusiastic friends eager to chat and discover the latest version of his plans to leave all this behind and learn to fly. Some of them thought him quite crazy: his close friends wished him luck, others gushed and kept their thoughts to themselves.

Freeing himself, at last, Alex walked on only to find his path blocked by a big blond man, and a girl whose sharp eyes took in with undisguised admiration, every detail of his boots, well-cut breeches, silk shirt and polo helmet.

"Ah, Beresford, I've been wanting a word with you," Randal Forster said. "Tried your office several times, but was told you were ensconced with your decrepit directors."

"Quite probably," Alex said, stopping beside the man and nodding to his companion. "How are you, Fay? I didn't realise you two were so well acquainted."

Lady Weyford's niece smiled. "Polo is such a *virile* game, isn't it? I love watching all those rippling muscles and daredevil charges on horses."

Ignoring that, he addressed Forster. "If the matter is urgent, I'll shower and change then meet you in the refreshment tent."

Forster shook his head. "No need to primp up, old sport. I just want to hear from the proverbial horse's mouth whether or not all I hear about *Berondel* is true."

Alex took off the protective helmet to allow the sun to dry his thick curls, dampened by exertion. "What have you heard?" he asked shortly, never having particularly liked this man.

"The latest hum is that your baby sister is now the governing force behind the company, not you."

"Really?" he commented noncommittally.

"I hope that doesn't mean any change in our little arrangement."

"We both signed a five-year contract, if you remember," Alex pointed out, then added disparagingly, "You gave me the impression that you were a shrewd businessman when we first met, Forster. Don't tell me that you're one of those who panic at the first item of tittle-tattle they hear. One needs business acumen and confidence in one's own judgement in this game, you know."

The other man plainly disliked having the tables turned on him, and snapped out, "Lack of both is behind your impending departure to England, I hear. Daddy had more faith in little Lydia than he had in you, it seems. Rippling muscles are all very well when it comes to impressing silly creatures like Fay, but they're no substitute for intelligence."

Alex smiled. "That must explain why Fay is hanging on your arm." Turning away, he said mockingly, "Chin-chin, old sport."

Next minute, his arm was seized as he was dragged around to face the arrogantly handsome features of a man flushed with an astonishing display of vindictiveness. "You think yourself highly amusing, I take it. Have a care, Beresford. Against the business interests I control, *Berondel* is insignificant. If I chose to, I could swallow baby sister whole and no one would miss her."

Jerking free, Alex found himself firing up in defence of his own. "That's just about your style, I should imagine. Try swallowing someone as large and obnoxious as yourself. I'd be interested in the outcome of that, Forster, because it would take brains as well as those rippling muscles you flex a damned sight too quickly, to digest equal competition. I doubt you could do it." Turning to Fay, he told her, "I've never liked you much, but you deserve better than this as a boyfriend. If you take my advice, you'll sever contact right away . . . before he swallows *you* whole."

Sidestepping, Alex walked on toward the pavilion, disturbed by the incident. There was no question of the man harming Lydia, because the business would be controlled by a board of shrewd directors, but the latent unpleasantness in Randal Forster still made him uneasy. It was as well that the only contract with him was in the hands of their own agent in Manila, and the merchandise handled by a client who had been exporting through them for years. All the same, it might be as well to alert the members of the board and recommend that they think twice before extending their business with Forster. As he entered the pavilion, he told himself ruefully that the elderly group of men would never deal with anyone of that ilk. They had been drilled in caution and respectability under his father's rule, and would continue that way. The single contract between *Berondel* and Forster had been negotiated under his own initiative. He had checked it thoroughly, at the time, and found it perfectly satisfactory.

All the same, Forster's inexplicable swift violence continued to bother him until he left the clubhouse and almost bumped into Fay, standing alone just outside the building.

"Taken my advice and given your rough friend his marching orders?" he asked pointedly.

Fay studied him from head to foot, a tight expression on her feline face. "You have undoubted physical appeal, Alex, but it's no more than boyish charm. I'd advise you to grow up before taking on a man like Randy."

He gave a cynical laugh. "Still think he's marvellous? Well, there's no accounting for taste. Do Sir Hartle and Lady Weyford know you're in his company so much?"

"For someone who's lived his whole life in Singapore, that's an extremely naïve question. You know tittle-tattle relates every move we all make . . . except, apparently, details of what goes on in the native areas." Her smile curved her mouth. "Wouldn't the sharp tongues be interested in the liaisons formed within the walls of some of the out of the way hovels there, Alex dear?"

Hardly following the trend of her remarks, he moved off, saying, "Watch your step with Forster, Fay. You're liable to get hurt."

"So are you," came her voice after him. "Ask your lady love what she does during sultry Hindu afternoons."

It halted him. Turning back to her, he demanded, "What are you getting at, Fay?"

Her smiled broadened, but there was a touch of real malice in it as she said, "In all fairness to her, we know she has never pretended to be anything other than what the polite world calls 'a woman of experience', but you're wearing rose-coloured glasses if you imagine her adventures have ended now you're on the scene. For a while, I imagined her unrestrained tastes led her to fancy poor, dotty Martin, but it seems she finds erotic satisfaction in secret rendezvous at forbidden venues flavoured with the scent of ghee and curry. Watch your step with her, sweetie, unless you have no objection to sharing her favours with the natives."

Shaken, angry and greatly disturbed by the girl's words, he would not rise to the bait visibly. "Fay, you have always been an acid-tongued creature, but have a care when you embark on serious accusations of that nature. Yes, I have lived all my life in Singapore, so I know that tittle-tattle is vastly different from slander. You're liable to end up in court. Ask your learned uncle, and he'll tell you the same."

Not in the least perturbed, Fay shook her head. "Slander, my dear Alex, is when lies are spread about someone of good character. In this case, I'm speaking the truth about a girl who deserves all that is said about her."

At that point, Forster emerged from the clubhouse, and Fay fell in silently beside him without a backward glance. The pair walked off leaving Alex feeling as if he had run into a wall. Fay was a vindictive, sly creature, yet she would never have broached such a subject without some foundation for her words. Sick with doubts, and anxious to thrash the subject out with Thea in order to get to the bottom of it, he tackled her the minute they met in her hotel room that evening.

"Everyone knows the girl is a complete bitch," he said, after telling Thea some of Fay's hints, "yet she can't be allowed to go around spreading lies of that nature. I won't have it, darling. Gossip is one thing; hints of that type of liaison between you and . . . and . . . well, the colony will take an entirely different view of that."

Looking pale, as she had for some days, Thea surprised him with her lack of response over his revelation. Normally, she would have flamed with anger, or have laughingly accused him of being as stuffily colonial as those he was afraid of offending. Tonight, she appeared desperately evasive as she said, "Who knows what Fay means by anything she says? You know she loves to put the cat amongst the pigeons—the cat being

Fay herself. Alex, she was simply hitting back at you for what you said to her about that brute Forster."

He frowned. "Do you know Forster? When did you come across him?"

Still appearing evasive, she said, "I've heard enough about the man to know she's in excellent company."

"But why would she mention *Hindu* afternoons?" he persisted. "She's not a fool. Thea. It's such an outlandish piece of misinformation to think up on the spur of the moment, she would surely know I'd never take it seriously."

"But you are, aren't you?" she charged, getting to her feet to walk away from the bed where they had been sitting together after their initial embrace.

He sighed. "Only inasmuch as it arouses in me the obligation to silence her. Darling, tell me there's some simple explanation for her malice; some connection with Hindu people or areas that she has exaggerated to use as a foundation for such ridiculous lies. Have you been taken to visit Indians or to see their temples by George McGregor, in his mistaken attempt to help you with your book? No matter how long ago it was, have you ever had the slightest contact with Hindus?"

"George took me to visit the Sing brothers, that's all. Even then, Martin was with us."

Worried and unhappy after all the recent upheavals in his life, he looked at her with regret. "She also hinted that you had designs in that direction, poor devil. Thank God no one in Singapore knows what happened up at the plantation."

Taking him unawares, she came to stand before him, plainly close to tears. "Take me away, Alex. I don't think I can stand much more of this island and the people on it. Take me away from here and make me forget about everything but the years ahead of us, and the happiness we're going to share."

In deep concern, he drew her into his arms. "Darling, I didn't mean to upset you over Fay, but I love you so much the urge to defend you is very strong."

She kissed him with strange fierceness. "Let her say whatever she wishes. It can only hurt us if we let it. Make love to me, Alex. Please make love to me, and drive away old ghosts."

It was such an easy command to obey, and thoughts of Fay soon fled as he found matching oblivion from old ghosts in her willing arms.

Martin lay prone on a charpoy. With his chin propped in his hands, reading was an uncomfortable pastime. Small wonder the human

286

animal usually chose to recline facing the sky! After thirty minutes, he abandoned the novel and lay flat watching a small colourless lizard emerge from behind a picture. He followed its progress toward a fat mosquito digesting the dose of blood it had just sucked from his neck, and wished the lizard luck. Then he fell to thinking about the book he had been reading. Although only halfway through it, he was finding the prose disturbing and already knew the ending. The characters did not live happily ever after. Did anyone, he wondered, and if they did would they grow complacent, boring and self-centred? Did suffering truly make a person stronger and more multi-faceted? Who could ever answer that?

Admittedly, his own recent suffering had made him strong in the determination for revenge. It would have been pointless reporting the facts to the authorities. They had known that, and been confident of his silence. The word of a man generally accepted as being so unstable he could not manage his own financial affairs, would never be believed against that of five solid, upright colonials, so they must be made to pay for what they had done to him by more subtle means. Having experienced public school and officers' mess practices of "teaching a lesson" to those who broke the rules or tried to be too individual in a conformist group, Martin would have accepted token punishment from Forster and his friends for something they really believed he had done. They had gone far beyond the bounds, however, and had half killed him in a session of such dedicated savagery, he had no doubt there was much more behind it than the mere closure of their favourite brothel. On his return to the office three days ago, Martin had set in motion an investigation into the affairs of the sadistic importer; a move the man had clearly not foreseen whilst wielding that leather belt.

After four weeks, Martin could now walk reasonably well, although sitting for long periods was still an ordeal because his skin pulled painfully over the healing wounds. The bruising on his face had paled, and the punishment to his eyes no longer hampered his vision. His message to the department that he had fallen down the steps of his bungalow in the darkness and damaged one eye, had been accepted without question. His general unpopularity had ensured that no one came to visit him with grapes and solicitude, to discover the true extent of his injuries. Fortunately, Sir Hartle had gone up-country to sit on the bench during a complex trial, so there had been no awkward probings from that direction, either.

George had proved to be a friend indeed. Martin was exceedingly grateful for his medical care, and for his discretion. He had also been glad of his company during those first terrible days. After George had returned to his own house, Martin had continued to live in the bungalow with Lang, taking all his meals in his own half of the place. Moving out would suggest that their brutality had intimidated him. By remaining in close proximity to one of the men who had so viciously lashed him, and saying nothing about the affair, Martin hoped to make them all uneasy and strengthen Lang's suspicion that he was "so bally deep he had them all fooled". In any case, his tenure would end as soon as he was fit enough to implement his plan to seek work on a plantation.

Although doubting the advisability of such a move, George had agreed to contact a number of friends living in the various Malay States, who might help with the project. It was through George that Martin had heard of Austin's second stroke and subsequent critical condition. He guessed it must be delaying the marriage between Alex and Thea, which his friends confirmed had not yet taken place. He had seen nothing of the pair since Serantinggi, although Thea had somehow featured in the events of that awful night—or the morning after, to be more exact. He could only vaguely remember her presence beside the bed with a curious green flower in her hand. George had elaborated.

"That girl arrived here first thing in the morning. Don't ask me why; she informed me quite sharply that she was merely visiting. I ask you, paying a visit all alone at the crack of dawn! Anyway, she exercised amazing command of the situation. By the time I got here, you had been stripped naked and tenderly washed by someone who claims to have no place for sentiment in her life." He had grinned then. "Our Miss du Lessier thinks herself so damned clever, yet she can't see what's perfectly obvious to me. You're just as bad."

"What's that supposed to mean?" Martin had demanded.

"Work it out," had been the brief advice.

Martin had, and found the conclusion ridiculous. His friendship for Thea had been deeply damaged. The knowledge that she had taken off his clothes to see the results of that flogging, made him burn with an echo of the searing fire which had consumed his pride after she had walked in on him and Lydia. For her to have witnessed his sexual frenzy, then physically dragged him from his partner whilst in that state, was totally humiliating. For four weeks he had hoped never to see her again, yet he had now discovered reason for a modicum of understanding which slightly negated his own sense of humiliation.

Where Lydia was concerned, the case was vastly different. He had had no previous experience with over-protected virgins, who believed seduction to be complete when self-induced excitement brought the hitherto unknown erotic spasm. Over the past few weeks, he had received notes from the girl suffering the agony of desire denied.

Luckily for him, she had been low with fever since arriving back from Serantinggi, and this had prevented her from begging him to visit the house. His own physical state would have prevented it, and Lydia was so mad to see him again, he had no doubt she would have thrown caution to the winds and come to his bungalow. Thank God, she had been unable to, and subsequently had no knowledge of the flogging he had received. One girl knowing of it was bad enough. For Lydia to know would complete his degradation.

He had not replied to her letters, because he knew any sign from him would be viewed as a return of the love she claimed to feel for him now. The passionate letters filled him with the kind of longings which told him, with depressing certainty, that his only hope of peace lay in isolation at a plantation like Serantinggi. He wished George would speed up his contact with planter friends, so that he could leave Singapore at the first opportunity. If he had to break Lydia's heart, he wanted to do it before having to meet her again. Unwilling to read the distressing consequences of his assault on her that night, he nevertheless scanned each letter through. The fierceness of her desire for him both dismayed and astonished him. Beneath her innocent, pure exterior, there lay a girl seething with emotions she found impossible to contain. Knowing he had been responsible for bringing them to the surface, only increased his sense of guilt over that uncontrolled attempt to ease his own pain in her. The guilt kept him awake at nights, and plagued him during the long daylight hours.

Having put aside his book on this afternoon two days before Christmas, he became prey to thoughts of Lydia again. There had been severe storms all through the night, which had disturbed what little sleep he could get whilst lying face downward on a hot, damp bed. The day was even more humid than usual as the sun beat down on the saturated earth and, unwilling to read more of the novel, he decided to take a shower. It would cool him temporarily and give him something to do. In the midst of easing himself from the charpoy, however, Wah entered to announce a visitor.

"Lady fliend come see you. I show her in; you come velandah?"

His heart sank. An impassioned confrontation with Lydia would be hard to handle. How could he possibly end the affair without hurting her too deeply? Would she accept an end to it? Oh God, was it too late to pretend he was out?

"I show her in?" prompted Wah.

"No," he said sharply, looking at the bed and imagining all manner of things. "No, Wah, I'll see her on the verandah. Bring some tea, please, and make it snappy, will you?"

He was presently dressed in just a short cotton robe, so he pulled on linen trousers and a silk shirt. It was a slow, painful business during which he ran through ideas on how he could best deal with the coming equally slow, painful business. Splashing his face with water, he then ran a comb through his thick straight hair before pushing open the shuttered doors leading to the verandah, praying Lydia would accept what he must say to her.

The girl turned as he appeared. Her vivid looks were enhanced by a tomato-red silk dress with a tracery of black leaves running diagonally from the right shoulder to the flounced hem. The expression in her amber eyes was unreadable in the shade cast by the verandah, and all manner of strong emotions ran through him as he faced this girl who had intruded so dramatically in his life.

"I thought the events at Serantinggi would have put an end to any social contact between us," he said forcefully, "so to what do I owe your determination to continue it?"

"It's the season of goodwill, and all that nonsense," she returned in semi-bitter tones. "Hard to remember the fact in this steam bath atmosphere, but the jolly old colonials are instructing their cookboys to prepare plum puddings, and are tucking holly sprigs into their topees with total abandon." Pausing a moment as she looked him over, she then asked, "How are you now?"

"Fine." The word was short and sharp, echoing his resentment at the fact that she was the only person apart from George who knew about the vicious beating he had taken that night.

"You look far from it."

"And you hardly present the picture of wedded bliss. I take it you are now Mrs Beresford."

"In all but name."

Curiously shaken by that frank admission, he said, "Well, lucky Alex . . . or is he?"

Her eyes darkened. "If all we're going to do is fight, I'll leave."

"If you told me why you came, we could discuss that instead of all this polite questioning on each other's health and wellbeing," he said crisply.

"Are you able to sit down?"

"Of course." As she sank into one of the chairs, he sat in a matching one facing her, glad of the cushions at his back. "So what can I do for you, Thea?"

"Are you ready yet to tell me what happened that night?"

Angry again at her insistent probing into a humiliating episode, he snapped, "Certainly not. In any case, George told me you were on the spot before he was, so you probably have more details than I on the subject."

"I can describe how you looked when I arrived, if that would interest you," she told him quietly. "I thought you were dead."

"I'm sorry you had such a shock," he said, with a touch of regret.

"I would have grieved for you, Martin."

Helpless in the face of her irrepressibly candid personality, his anger melted away. "Thanks for what you did. George commends you highly, you know. I meant to write, but I didn't know where you were staying or who you were now."

"Why won't you tell anyone who did it?"

Wah arrived beside him with tea on a tray, and a cakestand bearing the usual dainties he served when ladies visited either of his masters. It provided a diversion, so Martin deftly avoided answering Thea's question by asking one of her.

"Why has the wedding been delayed?"

She poured tea for him. "Dear me, you have been cut off from the gossips!"

"You do still intend to marry him?"

She nodded. "On the voyage to England."

"You're sailing with him? What about the definitive novel of the exotic East?"

Avoiding his gaze, she sipped her tea. "I've seen all I want of it. Martin, do you know a man called Randal Forster?" she continued with disconcerting swiftness, watching him intently.

Caught off guard, he bent forward to add extra sugar to his cup, hoping to hide his expression from her. "I've heard of him, of course. Why, is he a friend of yours?"

She seemed to be equally taken by surprise by his question, and he sensed an adopted airiness of tone when she said, "Gracious, no. It's just that he appears to be one of those ubiquitous creatures who inhabit the Far East. I simply wondered if your department had had any dealings with him."

"No."

With something suspiciously like relief, she changed the subject again. "George said he's trying to get you a job on a plantation. We both agreed it's a terrible mistake, on your part. Sir Hartle told me a little about the Linwood estate, you know. It has rolling farmland, a trout hatchery on the river running through it, a section of forest providing timber, and a vineyard. The house is apparently set in spectacular countryside, where the air is very bracing due to its proximity to the coast. You'd find peace, open spaces and the chance to be master of your own life, Martin. Why not give up this ridiculous idea, and go home?"

Her words brought back vivid pictures of his home, as it used to be. For a moment or two, he was lost in memories of that estate; Giles and he eagerly running across to the hatchery to watch the young trout emerge, cantering through the forest with the smell of newly-sawn timber in their nostrils, lolling on their stomachs at the side of the village green to watch the cricket on drowsy summer days. There was his mother, beautiful, elegant, soft-voiced, entertaining friends to tea on the sloping lawns, or coming to his room to kiss him goodnight, dressed for evening in a gown of vivid shade which rustled as she bent over him with a loving smile; his father, riding with the hunt, reckless and alive with wellbeing, strolling through the vineyard in deep discussion with his manager and reaching up to pick a sample grape.

Recalling where he was, he shook his head. "I can't go back there."

"Why not?" she asked with unusual gentleness.

"Home no longer exists."

"Of course it exists. You'll have to go back one day."

"They've all gone," he told her harshly. "The place is empty."

"Then fill it again—with a wife and children. You're the only one left who can do it."

"It's not that simple."

"I didn't say it was," she retorted warmly. "Nothing is ever that simple, but people go on trying. You've given up."

He was angry again. "You really are impossible! You go amongst us preaching doctrines you don't begin to understand, in the belief that you're guiding those who have lost their way. May I suggest that you concentrate instead on sorting out your own life because, God knows, you need to."

"What's behind that impassioned statement?" she demanded calmly.

"I've had time on my hands recently, so I've filled much of it with reading. This morning, I picked up a newly published novel in a bookshop. It was written by someone called Anna du Lessier, and its title is *Domino*." Although he had known she would react to his words, the strength of that reaction took him by surprise, to cause him to hesitate. However, he had to continue now he had embarked on the subject. "Thea, the character named Dorothy is you, isn't she?"

She rose and turned toward the garden, so that he could no longer see her distressed expression. Easing himself from his chair, he stepped up behind her knowing he had been right about her flight from a past hurt.

They were now on equal terms, because he had just stripped her naked with his perception.

"Human cruelty doesn't necessarily leave visible wounds," he said quietly. "You've hidden yours remarkably well. Only because I've been close to such things for so long, did I see what everyone else missed . . . even Alex, I suspect." When she remained silent, he asked, "Who was the man your mother calls Domino?"

He had little expectation of an answer yet, after a further pause, she said, "Dominic Grant."

"The war poet?" he queried, in surprise.

She nodded.

"Grant was your lover?"

She nodded again.

After thinking over that unexpected information, he took the subject further. "I deduced that the character Anna du Lessier calls Amber, is really the author herself. That novel is no work of fiction, is it? In truth, your mother took Grant from you."

"No." The denial was little more than a whisper. "She merely provided for the demands of his talent when it outgrew my tiresome adolescent bondage."

Gazing down on her glossy dark hair for a while, deep in thought, he reached a conclusion. "You seek vengeance for this book, not for his betrayal of your devotion? I see. Your grand novel is intended to show hers for the rubbish it is. Oh, Thea, can't you see that you'll only topple her from her tawdry throne if you produce something as sensationally cruel and erotic as *Domino*? Whatever you may have written so far, I'll wager it doesn't fit that description."

Still gazing out over the garden, she confessed in thick tones, "He plainly told her every single detail, and she simply wrote it down verbatim. My humiliation is there for everyone to read."

Having read it himself, he was filled with the urge to comfort her. Drawing her back against his chest, he said, "Very few people will recognise it. It's possible to learn to handle one's humiliations, in time. I speak from experience, my dear."

She turned quickly to face him, her expression wild and stormy. "Martin, I'm sorry about what you consider as my meddling in your life, which doesn't seem to have been totally successful. You're such a worthwhile person, a damned sight saner than some who point the finger at you, so I can't stand by while you allow them to drive you into becoming one of the outcasts of the East, like that man Piers Massingham."

Thrown by her sudden switch back to their earlier conversation, he

293

stepped back from her with a frown. "No one's driving me to do anything."

"Of course they are! I am, at least, trying to exercise revenge for my humiliation. You've just taken a terrible beating, yet won't do a thing to punish those responsible for it. Do you intend to let them get away with half killing you, and creep away up-country to a soul-destroying future without making any effort to fight back?"

"If you want to put it that way, yes," he said bluntly. "I had four years of fighting back, and learned that it might hurt the other fellow but in no way removes one's own wounds. I know the jungle had an adverse effect on you, but when a soul has already been destroyed such a place offers salvation. I'm now better able to recognise your motives, Thea, but please don't concern yourself about my future." Summoning up a faint smile, he added, "I shall have to cope without your misguided championship once you sail off into the sunset with young Alex."

A hint of puzzling desolation touched her mobile features for a brief moment, before she challenged him yet again. "What are you going to do about Lydia?"

It was indicative of the present mood of rapport between them that he was able to confide in her. "The only thing I can do, with the least amount of brutality possible. I hope to God that once I go off up-country, she'll gradually learn to forget me."

"As you'll learn to forget her?" At the sight of his expression, she asked swiftly, "You're not really in love with her, are you?"

Although he shook his head, it was not a denial. "What I feel for Lydia can't be listed under such an obscure heading. I imagine you're 'in love' with Alex, and he with you, yet I'll wager you both have vastly different emotions centred on that happy state." Running a hand through his thick hair to lift it from the dampness of his brow, he searched for the right words. "Lydia represents all the things I'd forgotten. She's peace and tranquillity; innocence, trust and breathless wonder. The first time I set eyes on her, it was as if those four years of war had never happened. She made me human again." He sighed with memory. "I met her at a time of great unhappiness with this new environment chosen for me by Sir Hartle. After twelve months in hospital with others who felt as I did, it was inexpressibly lonely here, especially as I was made very aware of the resentment of those around me. Then, one curious afternoon, a girl walked forward from the midst of a group of hostile staring youngsters; a pretty slender creature with a blue ribbon in her hair. In that moment, I knew she was all I had ever wanted." His throat tightened, as he added, "For a while at Serantinggi, I fooled myself into believing . . . but I have to face the truth. Going away is the only answer for us both." He looked at her with frankness to match her own. "I may learn to live without seeing Lydia, but I'll never forget her."

"You won't have to forget me, Martin," said a soft young voice from the garden below.

Thea spun round, and he stepped forward quickly as Lydia came up the steps toward them, her face glowing. Dismay vied with a leap of inner excitement as he took in the fresh, clean beauty of the girl dressed in green and white spotted voile with a large shady hat. There was that same quality about her now as there had been at that tennis party, and it was just as potent. She was all he had ever wanted.

"How long have you been in the garden?" demanded Thea apprehensively.

"Long enough to hear Martin tell you he could do without your advice," the other girl told her hotly. "You're supposed to be marrying Alex soon, so what are you doing here, Thea?"

"Saying goodbye, it seems."

Regaining his senses, Martin said swiftly, "You can't go yet."

Her dark glance met his. "Don't hurt her any more than you can help. I did what I could to prevent this, yet I ignored the voice of reason when ruled by a similar passion so it was unlikely that she would heed it."

He could not believe she intended to walk away after all her attempts to protect Lydia from the harm he could bring her. "Thea, for God's sake, take her with you," he begged, the long disturbing session with one girl leaving him unequal to the prospect of a harrowing emotional scene with another, who looked set to demolish his every resolution. "There could be hell to pay, if you don't."

On the steps, she looked back at him over her shoulder. "Hell would solve your problem nicely, wouldn't it? Shotgun wedding, marital bliss on a rubber plantation. Gradual mental decline, and let the great big world keep turning well out of your sight."

"That isn't the way I want it!" he cried.

"It's never the way any of us want it . . . save Lydia. I saw the way you looked at her just now, and she's been burning to make the ultimate sacrifice for your sake. You shouldn't be such a damned wounded hero, my dear."

"*Thea!*" he urged desperately, "you can't walk out now."

On the pathway, she turned. "I'm finally taking your advice to cease meddling in your life. You can hardly make a worse mess of it than I have. Goodbye, Martin."

He watched her vanish around the curve of the driveway, then found himself being firmly turned around to face the girl who was all Thea was not. As she smiled up at him, he sensed a new strength of purpose in the face which had haunted him for so long with its promise of peace.

"When you didn't answer my letters, I was heartbroken. Now I realise it was because you're afraid to be with me. You've grown angry again, Martin."

"Not with you," he murmured, trying to marshal his thoughts of what he must say to her.

"With Thea?"

He shook his head. "With myself."

"Because of what happened at Serantinggi? There's no reason to be angry over that." Her colour rose becomingly. "I had no idea love could be so wonderful."

"That wasn't love, it was . . ." He broke off, disturbed by the hunger in her gaze. "Lydia, if your brother had walked in on us, I would have been rushed into an asylum to await trail and permanent incarceration. You would probably have spent the rest of your days in a convent. Only because Thea lied so promptly and convincingly to Alex did we escape the consequences so easily." He took a deep breath. "When a man loves someone, he doesn't expose her to such risks. I can't be trusted not to do that. Is it any wonder I'm angry?"

Before he knew it, her arms were up around his neck and she was kissing him full on the mouth. He broke contact, trying to keep the situation under control.

"You shouldn't be here alone with me like this," he ruled.

"Thea was."

"Her reputation can stand association with a man like me."

Her hand went up to the scar at his throat. It was no more than a gentle touch, yet it set him alight. "I heard you tell her I made you forget all the bad things that had happened to you," she said softly. "I want to go on making you forget. I want to make you happy, darling, so stop trying to send me away."

"But I can never make you happy," he said with desperation, as he put distance between them by retreating behind the cane chairs. "I was in a mental hospital for a year, and I'm still considered unfit to handle my affairs. You know Sir Hartle can prevent me from spending one penny of my own money, if he chooses to. No parents in their right mind would allow me to court their daughter."

"But if I told them . . ."

"Please listen, Lydia," he interjected firmly. "Apart from those considerations, I'm really no fit companion for a sweet girl like you. I find it almost impossible to socialise. When I do, I drop things and embarrass everyone including myself. When I'm depressed I drink myself insensible. I can grow violent without any warning. You've had ample evidence of that. I also sometimes . . ."

His catalogue of vices was halted as she stepped forward to stand in one of the chairs, and smother his words with her mouth. Then she drew back slightly to regard him with misty eyes.

"I shan't listen to any more, because you're simply being foolish. I know you dropped a glass at the tennis party, and upset Mummy and Daddy because you scattered the sandwiches, but that was because the others had been so beastly to you. *Anyone* would have been nervous. Alex also drinks too much when he's depressed. So do most of his friends. Men can't seem to help that. As for being violent with me, we both know why you were."

"Lydia, you . . ."

"Shhh!" she admonished gently, putting her fingers against his lips. "You're not like that with Thea, are you . . . or with any other girl? Answer truthfully, Martin."

Having been prepared for tears and emotional pleas not to cast her aside, he was totally disarmed by this approach.

"Of course I'm not."

A radiant smile broke through. "There you are then, silly! I've told you before to stop imagining you're different from other people."

"It's not imagination," he insisted heavily. "You've never witnessed one of my really bad attacks."

"That's because you don't have them when I'm there," she declared, pulling his head down to kiss him with fervour.

No longer able to resist her, he drew her slender body closer and the embrace grew heady as it went on and on. When he slackened his hold on her, his careful defences had collapsed.

"Oh, Martin," she whispered unsteadily, "you made me yours at Serantinggi, so you can't ever send me away. I'll live with you on a plantation, if that's what you really want."

Knowing it was exactly what he wanted, he nevertheless shook his head. "It's an impossible dream. I'd never get your people to agree to that proposition."

Her eyes clouded in pain. "What are we to do, then? I can't bear it without you, and you'd be unhappy again."

Gazing down at her troubled upturned face, a faint surge of hope touched him. This girl offered the peace and happiness he thought could never be his. After all, he had been a different man at Serantinggi; confident, relaxed, full of optimism. Only that damned tiger hunt had spoiled it. Up there in a tranquil valley with brown smiling people, the past with its burden of fear and loss would recede until it vanished to trouble his mind no longer. With Lydia to give him a reason for his future, the world would revolve to present its joyous side to him once more. He had experienced the dark side for too long.

"Daddy's too ill to object," she pointed out urgently, "and Alex is going to England soon. There's only Mummy to overcome. If we show her we're determined to be together, she'd have to agree."

Tightening his hold around her again, he allowed himself to say, "If we could meet frequently, under the usual circumstances, maybe everyone would come to realise how normal I can be."

"I'd help you, darling," she cried eagerly. "I wouldn't let anyone upset you, or make you angry. Thea's leaving soon, so she won't be able to interfere any more. Oh, I do love you so much, and want to make you as happy as you were at Serantinggi. Say you'll let me."

Total surrender came, as he smiled his love at her. "I'll let you do anything you like, so long as it makes you happy too."

Wah appeared at that moment to take away the tea tray. He looked in astonishment at Lydia standing on a chair with her arms around Martin, having ushered Thea in only a short time earlier.

"Other lady flend go?" he asked, perplexed.

"Yes, Wah," Martin told him, helping Lydia down from the seat of the chair. "She won't be coming here any more."

The servant wagged his head regretfully. "Velly solly no come back. Wah likee. She velly good missy. Bad she no come back."

"I shall be coming, Wah," Lydia told him sharply. "I shall be coming here a lot."

The Chinese began stacking cups and plates. "Other missy velly good. Master sick, she makee better. Bad she no come back."

Lydia looked at Martin curiously. "What does he mean?"

He touched her hair, caring only that she would be coming to visit him often. "When we're constantly seen together, all the tongues in Singapore will start wagging. You won't mind too much, will you?"

She laughed softly. "Mummy will. She'll have to let you marry me in order to silence them. Oh darling, make it soon."

There on his verandah, in full view of anyone who might be passing, he drew her close and buried his face in her fragrant hair. If they were about to set the colony alight, it no longer mattered what they did. The future shone with brightness. Thea was wrong. All they would bring each other was joy and fulfilment.

Chapter 17

Alex held the obligatory farewell party three days before they were due to sail. The event coincided with the four-day festivities for Chinese New Year, traditionally heralded in at midnight by a deafening and continuous explosion of firecrackers. Europeans were without their Chinese servants for the period, and few managed to sleep through the din. In consequence, all Alex's invitations had been gratefully accepted, and the large private salons of the hotel were full on an evening of such high humidity, even those used to the climate found it distressing.

The fans were circling as fast as possible, and all doors to the terraces were open despite the risk of plagues of flying ants and beetles at that time of the year, which could swarm in attracted by the lights, then smother food, drown in revellers' glasses, or drop unceremoniously down the bodices of ladies' gowns. Despite the fans, the atmosphere was soon thick with the smell of cigar smoke and perspiration, as men in wilting starched shirts and evening clothes assembled, mopping their wet faces whilst downing gin slings or stengahs which made them sweat even more. The women, carefully smothered with lavender water or eau-de-Cologne, also dabbed at their faces with lace handkerchiefs and worried about dark patches appearing on the pale materials of their dresses.

Nothing would have kept them away that night, however. They all wanted to be present at a party to celebrate the departure of the young shipper who had been disinherited by his vindictive father, and a liberated girl responsible for her lover's downfall. It was an occasion sure to be remembered for years to come. As if that were not enough to tempt them there, there was the additional spice of wondering how little Lydia, who had supplanted her brother at *Berondel*, would behave with the unstable ex-officer Martin Linwood. Their astonishing courtship was rocking the colony, now eagerly awaiting the scandalous denouement which would surely come.

Alex greeted his guests with an air of gaiety, yet a curious sense of depression began to creep over him as time passed and the atmosphere grew more and more suffocating. He had lived in Singapore all his life. His only home had been that large square house with its tennis courts and airy verandahs. His twenty-four years had been concerned with colonial affairs; his business and social activities had run concomitantly with those of the Eastern races. He was used to the sight of garish temples and the noise of many religious festivals. Everywhere he looked there were people in bright ethnic clothes, vivid profusions of exotic blossoms, colourful screeching birds, brown-sailed junks on the waterways, and hooded rickshaws on the roadways. He felt at home in clubs with circling overhead fans, lowered blinds to keep out the white-hot sun, soft-footed native bearers. He was known wherever he went, and was invariably welcomed. His working days had been spent in cool dim rooms within the dignified white colonnaded building flying the *Berondel* flag: evenings had found him in the homes of wealthy friends, or in the familiar surroundings of hotels. He had been the golden boy of polo and cricket teams, the frequent winner of steeplechase and amateur jockey stakes, a skilled high diver, a wild young man. All that was about to end: an era was almost over.

Freedom stood waiting, yet the golden moment of which he had dreamed so often seemed tarnished. He hid it, even from Thea, but deep inside was the unhealed wound of estrangement from the family which had provided the background against which he had lived out those twenty-four years. Whatever their differences, however much he might have felt their possessive hold on him, the dramatic severance of that bond still troubled him. This evening, this farewell party which heralded his new exciting future, was spoiled by the absence of his parents, and by the knowledge that many of the guests had come in the hope of some further Beresford sensation to entertain them. He presently felt as he had done on that paddle guard, when he had looked up to meet Martin's gaze and realised the gesture had been foolish and full of bravado. Perhaps he had planned this party knowing that it was a similar gesture, yet it had seemed inconceivable to leave without saying goodbye to all who had played a part in the era which was ending.

As his future wife, Thea was acting hostess, as she always would from now on. Yet, ridiculously, he missed his mother's fussing over the arrangements, her last-minute panic over the dress she had chosen to wear, and her plump familiar face creasing into smiles as she welcomed the guests. There was no Austin to shake men's hands, exchange business news, share a social warmth. Parents, however one viewed them, were an integral part of one's life, he realised. How could such a bond end this way? His freedom was sorrow-tinged, and less desirable because of it. Halfway through the evening and he wished the party was over; wished he was already on that liner steaming out of Singapore harbour. All the time he could see the palms outlined against the swift glorious twilight, he continued to hope for some sign of forgiveness from his father. Yet he knew there could be none; could be none from a man who was a silent prisoner within a crippled body.

Lydia had surprised him. She appeared to be coping with the new situation remarkably well, her confidence almost certainly being due to the fact that she was spending so much time with Martin. Alex, along with the whole of Singapore, knew they were meeting at every possible opportunity. Austin, isolated in his sick-room, was totally ignorant of the relationship, and it survived only because their mother was too afraid of the possible consequences to tell him. Margery herself no longer appeared to have control over her daughter. How the affair would end Alex dared not think, but the kaleidoscope was turning too quickly, these days. Patterns formed and changed, while he looked helplessly on. In three days he would be gone. Those left behind on this island would have to work out their own salvations, as he had.

As if reading his thoughts, Martin chose that moment to make his way through the throng to where Alex stood temporarily alone. They had not come face to face since Serantinggi. Alex had been too busy, even if the outcome of the tiger hunt had not intruded into their curious relationship to mar what had been allowed to blossom up there near the jungle.

"God, it's humid," Martin said, arriving beside him. "I almost envy you the prospect of England in March. I think this is the hottest and wettest I've been since coming here."

"Twelve months ago, wasn't it?" he asked

"Less than that. Chinese New Year was over long before my ship docked last year."

"The date varies, you know, according to the Chinese calendar."

The other man offered him a cigarette, saying, "I'm in the department dealing with ethnic affairs. I've done my homework on local festivals." He snapped the tortoiseshell case shut. "I think we British should have a few more. Any excuse will do, it seems, and we might all let our hair down a little more."

Alex drew on his cigarette. "Still find us too stiff and conventional, do you?"

"Us?" came the gentle probe. "Three more days, and that won't apply to you any longer. Do you have regrets?"

"Good lord, no," he exclaimed, too heartily. "It's what I always intended to do when the right moment came."

"With, or without, Thea?"

Alex let that pass. "We plan to marry on the voyage."

"So she told me."

"You've seen her recently?" he asked in surprise.

"Just once. She came to say goodbye."

"I see."

"I'm sorry about your father's second stroke. It must have put a great deal of pressure on you whilst trying to wind up your own affairs," Martin said, then, "I was tempted to get in touch with you several times, then thought better of it. I wasn't sure how things stood between us after that business with the tiger."

Alex hesitated over his reply. Then, knowing they were unlikely ever to meet again after tonight, said, "I never have been sure how things stood between us. For almost a year, you've been constantly in and out of my life, yet a normal kind of friendship has always somehow eluded us."

Martin's dark-brown eyes studied him shrewdly. "Perhaps neither of us is a normal kind of man. Although we're both searching, it's for completely opposite things. Deep inside, I've always envied you, Alex."

He was astonished. "Envied me?"

"Why the surprise? When we first met, you were a young man of my own age who had been untouched by war. Your family was still complete. You had a large comfortable home, plenty of friends and associates, a stable future in a colony you knew and easily accepted, and your wild behaviour was the kind which results from restless youth. Sometimes, I believe I would have given anything to change places with you. It began on the day of the tennis party. I walked into your garden and saw carefree young girls and men laughing and flirting together. My brother and I used to do that kind of thing before the war and, when I came upon that scene suddenly, I felt as if I were outside a wonderful multi-coloured bubble, unable to burst it and join you."

Whatever had happened between them since that first meeting, the memory of it still made Alex uncomfortable. To cover the feeling, he said with feigned nonchalance, "You're welcome to it. I've discovered that it's liable to burst of its own accord."

Martin nodded, stepping sideways to avoid a surge of over-enthusiastic young men heading for the buffet. "It always does, sooner or later. That's when you have to find something more tensile. Flying will suit you far better than shipping; the element of danger will answer your needs. I remember your telling me how lacklustre you found your professional life, that day you introduced me to the Swimming Club. I grew so interested in all you were saying, I forgot my fear of making a fool of myself in your presence."

Another wave of depression hit Alex at the memory of swimming and diving beneath the tropical sun off palm-fringed shores. Would it be as enjoyable in the ice-green waters of the Atlantic buffeted by strong winds?

Something of his feelings must have been betrayed in his expression, because Martin said then, "It's never easy to adjust to a totally different life and environment. It takes time—sometimes a very long time—but one day you realise you've completely forgotten how it used to be. My problem has been in trying to get back to the original, after growing so used to war."

Alex suddenly recalled the night this man had answered his eager question on what it had been like, and rapport was instantly between them again.

"Are you still keen to go up-country?" he asked. "The environment seemed to suit you . . . and tigers only become a menace very occasionally."

A great cheer went up somewhere in the salon, where a few of Alex's wilder friends were indulging their high spirits. Martin smiled, saying, "We had some fun up at Serantinggi, didn't we? Remember the waterfall?"

How could he forget: the afternoon Thea finally became his. "It wouldn't be like that if you became a planter, you know. There's usually very little company, and the rainy season can drive a man crazy."

"No, Alex, it might make him a drunkard or deeply eccentric, but I've seen men who are crazy. They could never run a plantation."

"So you're going ahead with your plans?"

"A modified version, yes."

"Where does my sister fit into them?" he demanded, knowing the subject must be broached. "Since Christmas, she's defied Mother with astonishing determination in order to go around with you." Dodging a large monocled man bent on following a waiter bearing a tray of drinks, he continued. "I know I'll be relinquishing my obligations to Lydia soon, but the relationship between you two at the plantation appears to have grown a great deal more serious over the past few weeks. The whole of Singapore is talking about you, and what they're saying is not altogether welcome."

"Is it ever?"

"Look, once I leave here I'll have no influence on what she does, but you're six years older than she and a whole generation wiser. If you're genuinely fond of her, I must warn you that talk soon turns into damaging gossip, then into downright scandal. Is that what you want?"

Martin looked back at him steadily for a moment or two. "What I want is to make her my wife. I know I'll probably have to wait until she comes of age, and the waiting will seem endless, but I'll be established up-country by then and have a place ready for her. I have no need to study your present expression to know you disapprove . . . but it's what *she* wants, Alex. You, of all people, should appreciate that. We love each other. She provides the perfect stabilising effect I need, and I give her the experience of life she so desperately wants. I'll take very great care of her, I swear, and protect her with my life, if necessary." He took a glass from a tray proffered by a persistent waiter, but made no attempt to drink from it. "I grew up feeling responsible for my young brother, as you have Lydia. I watched over him during childhood sprees and protected him from bullies at school. I was proud of the job I had done. Then someone blew him into so many pieces he has only a token resting place. That was when I realised that each of us has a destiny which takes no account of the efforts of others during its unfolding. Your destiny dictates that you now leave here for whatever lies in store elsewhere. Go to it, without doubts or feelings of misplaced obligation. May it prove glorious for you."

Alex hesitated, then shook the hand Martin offered. "Thanks. I hope all goes well for you, too."

Thea was deliberately living up to the reputation she had acquired. With only three days to remain in a colony which had turned her whole life topsy-turvy, she was determined to leave with as big a bang as the traditional firecrackers. With her full-length gown of scarlet silk heavily beaded with jet, which fitted like a skin and left her back bare to the base of her spine, she sported a hair ornament which looked uncannily like a pair of jet horns, and black satin shoes decorated to resemble cloven hooves. Even Alex had been shocked, but she had swept from her hotel room saying that even if she wore virginal white this was what people would see, so why not give them what they wanted?

The only absentees were Sir Hartle and Lady Weyford, in company with a few others of that ilk, who plainly felt their presence would have constituted disloyalty to Austin and Margery Beresford, those staunch supporters of British colonial life. Fay Christie was there, however, in the midst of a large group containing Damien Lang. The girl appeared in fine fettle when Thea met up with her on leaving the ladies' lounge to make her way back to the main salons.

"So you really are going to marry Mad Alex, despite the absence of an engagement ring!" marvelled Fay, her eyes bright with malice as she walked beside Thea in a dress of orange crêpe which clashed with the scarlet silk.

"It's the marriage service which binds people together, not flashy rings," Thea told her. "They're a relic of pagan rituals."

Fay's sharply pretty face hardened. "I know all too well how you dislike strange rituals, although I still haven't decided whether or not that faint was genuine."

For once, Thea was not able to counter the girl's acid comment. Memory of that day with Randal Forster still filled her with a curious sense of degradation. So far as she knew, he had not spoken of it to anyone. Yet it was that expectation of hearing barbed comments on the subject from those she met, which constituted the kind of baiting the man plainly enjoyed. Just when she felt safe from him was when he was likely to act. Martin knew of her heedless passion with Dominic Grant, yet had not condemned her as a whore. Because of his own suffering, he had understood. However, Thea wished more than anything to keep the truth from Alex. He knew she had had a lover, and accepted the fact. She could not add to his present problems and stress by allowing him to discover the erotic details of that conquest by a poet.

Fay took advantage of her silence to add more venom. "Did your beloved ask you about Hindu festivals, by any chance? If he didn't, perhaps I should suggest again that he should. Or, if he did, and you wriggled out of it, perhaps I should tell any one of these people here tonight. The news would reach Alex like wildfire. What do you think I should do, Thea?" she finished, as they re-entered the salon.

Thea stopped and faced Fay with great seriousness. "You are a bitch, and will probably remain one into old age, but you're a girl running no end of a risk with that man, Fay. I suspect that he's totally evil, and I'd hate to see you fall victim to his particular brand of it. If it's not too late, break off your relationship with him. He might seem very exciting, but it could end in tragedy. If you're not prepared to listen to sound advice from someone with no reason to wish you well, perhaps I should tell any one person here tonight what he revealed about you that day. That news would reach your aunt like wildfire. Don't play with it. It burns."

With that, Thea walked away with every intention of joining Alex. He was deep in conversation with an ageing churchman, so she halted uncertainly. Then she spotted Martin, and it served to revive the advice she had just given to Fay. The notion of Forster inflicting the injuries to Martin's back and legs was almost unthinkable, yet he had spoken of those who derived pleasure from watching public floggings. He had also mentioned other, more private, humiliations of the body. However, Martin had denied knowing the man. In any case, she could not imagine how they could have tangled on an issue great enough to invoke such inhumanity as revenge. Even if her suspicions were correct, why would Martin remain silent and let the man go scot-free?

She made her way across to where he stood by an open french window. He was watching Lydia as she sympathised with two elderly matrons who wanted the cool relief of a fan directly overhead, yet who were worried about the damage it caused to their coiffures. A slight smile played around his mouth as he watched, and Thea experienced a surge of fierce protective anger. He was a basically gentle person. It seemed inconceivable that he could have done anything to warrant that savage beating, or that he could allow the perpetrators of it to go unpunished. Yet he had successfully persuaded George to say nothing, and she must also abide by his request for silence.

He straightened up as she neared, and pulled out a chair for her. "Hallo, have a seat."

She declined it with a shake of her head. "I'd prefer an April shower, if you happen to have one handy."

"Would I had," he quoted poetically. "I might even share it with you. I'm not sure I can stand this Turkish bath atmosphere much longer."

"I'm glad you came this evening," she confessed. "I wasn't certain that you would. I know Alex hasn't been in touch since Serantinggi—he has been exceedingly busy—but it meant a lot to him that you should be here to say goodbye."

"Did it? How about you?" he asked, dark eyes searching her face.

"We said goodbye three weeks ago, didn't we?"

"So this is hallo, again, is it?"

Unusually, she could think of no smart answer, and spoke her thoughts instead. "It's too late for that."

"Yes, it's too late, Thea," he agreed quietly.

Pulling herself together, she embarked on something only slightly less provocative. "It's not too late for you to abandon the plan to bury yourself on a rubber plantation, when you know full well the right decision is to return to Larkswood and your true destiny."

"Mmm, *destiny* appears to be a significant word tonight," he mused. "Farewells tend to breed introspection and a flood of impetuous emotion."

"I hope it's not the latter which is behind your courtship of Lydia, which has Singapore hopping with excitement." Seeing his expression, she said more gently, "Whatever's behind it, she's very obviously making you happy, Martin. You look even younger than you did during those early days at Serantinggi, and full of confidence."

"I am. Lydia's putting back into my life all those qualities I last knew before 1914, and making me see the war years in the right perspective." He smiled. "Alex will be equally good for you, you know. He loves you very deeply, and will give you back all that Dominic Grant took so brutally. No, don't look at me that way. You've known my private pain

306

too, don't forget. Maybe that provides us with our strongest grounds for compatibility. We both owe our hopes for the future to the Beresford family."

They were facing each other in the open doorway when the night outside was suddenly rent by a shattering, stuttering outburst of deafening explosions that seemed to be all around them, above and below. The darkness was pierced by showers of sparks, flashes of flame, and small rivulets of fire that ran along the ground momentarily then petered out as if they had never existed. The silence was broken by an instantaneous incredible volume of bangs, thuds and chattering cracks of explosive sound which hurt the eardrums and suggested violence and insurrection on a massive scale.

Thea jumped nervously, covering her ears against the din as she cried sharply, "Oh God, the firecrackers have begun. It must be midnight. Alex warned that it would sound like all hell let loose."

The man beside her no longer knew she was there. His thin face had taken on a frighteningly grim expression, which turned him into a stranger. The dark-brown eyes were searching restlessly for distant danger and registering such fearfulness, Thea's heart chilled. As she stared in shock, he began speaking jerkily; broken savage sentences that accompanied his slow advance into the room, while he gazed at some distant sight that lay years ago beyond a hotel salon.

"*Keep going whatever happens . . . close up, or you'll lose each other . . . hold your fire! . . . where are you? . . . over here, over here . . . look out, you bloody fool! . . . close up! . . . thirty yards to go.*"

While the deafening celebrations to mark the start of Chinese New Year continued outside, the assembled company within fell gradually silent to stare in horrified fascination at the involuntary reactions of a man who had no idea they were there. His slow progress across the room was made in half crouching position, an imaginary revolver held in his shaking left hand. Still muttering orders in a voice grown husky, he staggered against small tables, collided with stunned onlookers and tripped over expensive rugs scattered over the polished wood floor as he approached his supposed enemy.

Another table was knocked aside to collapse with more smashed glasses, and he turned to scream at the space left by it, "*Leave him, he's already dead!*" Looking around wildly for a few moments, he whispered in chilling manner, "*They're all dead. Christ Almighty, they're all dead!*"

Feeling sick, almost melting with compassion, Thea could only watch with the rest as he suddenly dropped to his knees with a cry of pure terror, throwing up his arms to cover his head as he cowered from something he imagined was coming through the air at him. Doubled up in the throes of a paroxysm of shaking, he began muttering incomprehensibly as he knelt reliving some terrible nightmare which had again become reality.

The rest of the room was in total silence as dinner-jacketed men, and women in elegant old-fashioned evening gowns stood in the sweltering atmosphere, staring at the wreck of the party and the jibbering figure in their midst. No one moved; no one spoke. It was as if horror had put them all in a trance while the joyous firecrackers that sounded so exactly like a thousand machine-guns continued all over Singapore, as they would for the next three or four days.

Finally, it grew too terrible for Thea to bear. Her limbs unfroze to allow her to walk across the kicked-up rugs, and across the scattered mess of canapés and broken glass littering the floor. Reaching Martin, she sank down to take hold of one of the arms protecting his head, but it was clamped so tightly in position she could not move it.

"Martin," she ventured gently, then more insistently, "*Martin*, it's all right. They've gone."

She had no idea of the right thing to say. Her words sounded like reassurance to a frightened child, and a frightened man was much the same, she supposed. As she knelt beside him offering love and understanding, she forgot the room and all those filling it, forgot the heat, and that alien island celebrating the start of a new year of mixed fortunes. All she recognised was that elusive key to understanding which showed her own imposture of the past few years for what it was.

Gradually, the man on the floor beside her stopped shaking. Gradually, the iron-hard arms relaxed and slid from their position across his head. Gradually, he uncurled to reveal that he was aware again. His staring brown eyes now focused on her face; his sweat-sheened features relaxed their savage lines. A frown creased his brow as he attempted to understand time and place. However, returning sanity betrayed the inescapable truth. His glance took in the party wreckage strewn about him, the rugs kicked aside, the circle of horror-stricken upright citizens staring at him. When Thea saw humiliation start to darken his eyes further, she put a hand on his shoulder to steady him, but his gaze had fixed on a distant corner of the room. The quality of his expression made her turn to look over her shoulder.

Lydia Beresford, white-faced and trembling, stood with eyes dilated and one hand clenched into a fist against her mouth, as if to prevent a scream as she stared back at Martin with a mixture of fear, disgust and revulsion. Her entire posture suggested imminent flight from something she could neither accept nor face. All eyes in that room now became fixed on that optical exchange between man and girl, which left their emotions publicly exposed. The fact that a multitude of people witnessed it, made Lydia's rejection all the more cruel.

Thea turned cold, despite the heat, as she watched a girl destroy a man with just one look. Then, before she was aware of it, Martin struggled to his feet and stumbled out through the open french windows. One last look she gave at the outraged perspiring faces before she ran out after him. Looking swiftly in both directions, she spotted him at the far end of the terrace, slumped against one of the stone pillars. Her determination waned as she drew near; her steps slowed. In the moonlight, his motionless figure appeared to be in a world of his own. Dare she intrude?

Hesitantly, she spoke his name. Then, thinking her soft call had probably been drowned by the din all around them, she circled the pillar to face him. Any further words were swallowed by her sigh of deep distress. As he gazed unseeing over the night sky brilliant with the cascading lights of revelry, Martin was crying. This silent, helpless weeping was like none she had ever seen before. His pain instantly became hers, his despair found an echo within her. Sophistication fell away as she put a hand over his as it gripped the stone.

"*Don't*," she begged softly. "Please don't let this destroy all you've built with such courage. Go back in there and calmly apologise for the damage. It's no worse than youngsters often cause through high jinks at these kind of affairs." Moving closer to slide an arm around him, she urged him further. "Please, Martin, listen to me. You *must* go back in there; you must look their world in the eye and tell it to go to hell. I'll come with you. We'll do it together."

He began to move away from her down the steps, and she called out desperately, "If you run from it now, you'll run for the rest of your life."

Whether or not he heard, she could not tell, but his stumbling progress continued through the garden, his steps growing faster and faster until he was running. No more than a moment passed before she set off after him.

He sat for several hours silently staring at the white walls of his bedroom, where tiny pale lizards moved about in the darkness. It had been easy enough for Thea to walk into the bungalow, via the verandah, when she had reached it only a few minutes after he. Since then, she had been sitting in one of the chairs unsure whether or not he was aware of her presence, finding a strange kind of peace in that shadowy room despite the pandemonium outside. Satisfied that she was on hand if he should need her, she was content to wait for the inevitable reaction to set in. What form it would take, and whether she would be competent to handle it she was unsure, but he would not be alone.

Although she had switched on the overhead fan to full speed, it was stifling in that room. Some time ago she had discarded her dress, stockings and cloven-hoof shoes, and sat now in only a short cotton robe Wah had put out ready for his master. Martin still wore his thick white dinner jacket, dark trousers, shirt and bow tie of the evening, oblivious to the heat. Sooner or later, normal feelings were bound to overtake him.

Her thoughts drifted from the events of that evening. The past filled her mind with memories and pictures of faces she had not seen for some years. It was now easy to realise how lack of normal loving relationships had caused her to erect barriers around herself, until even she could not reach the girl so securely within them. Then, she had encountered a beautiful, selfish, doomed poet who had demolished the barriers with one glance, one stanza of tragic verse. Eventually, he had spurned her adoration and reverence, turning instead to vile destructive coupling with a woman who had then exposed the truth publicly. Thea had believed herself recovered, until it had happened only an hour or so ago between two other people and revived her own pain.

Martin began to stir, tugging the bow tie with sluggish movements. Thea remained where she was, saying nothing, as he forced himself to his feet and dragged the tailored jacket off to drop it on to the floor. Like a man in a daze he stripped off the rest of his clothes, then went toward the bed to pour himself a drink from the carafe set on the small table by the houseboy. She heard ice clink against the glass as he poured—a cool familiar sound amidst those of oriental festive celebrations out in the street. Pulling the mosquito net free, Martin sank face downward on the bed, one arm hanging loosely to the floor.

After a while, Thea stood and went across intending to lift the arm and place it on the bed, before tucking the net in. Faint light filtered in to illuminate the stripes across his back, as he lay in the same manner in which she had found him that Sunday morning. She knew then that she could not leave him alone tonight. Slipping beneath the net, she settled on the bed beside him filled with a curious sense of peace.

How terribly lonely she had been all these years! To compensate, a sense of bravado had led her to tell the world she did not need it. She had hung on the fringes of political movements, emancipationists, and the Bohemian set. The attempt to substitute something—anything—for the affection she had never had, had been a failure all along. What a moment for such a revelation, and under what desperate circumstances! Her hand moved restlessly on the sheet and came into contact with

310

Martin's. Their fingers lay alongside each other's for a while, then gently curled until they were interlocked. Thea's sense of contentment grew as that involuntary contact remained unbroken. She lay watching the *chichaks* at play on the far wall, while thoughts which had once been too painful to contemplate drifted in and out of her head. None of them seemed important now.

It was a considerable time later when Martin's fingers began to curl tighter and tighter around hers until his grip grew almost painful. Coming from half slumber, she rolled on to her side toward him, putting her other hand on his back by way of comfort. She felt the scars, like scaly ridges, and her fingers feathered over them from side to side as if attempting to remove them and all they stood for. At her caressing touch his body began to tremble. Then he gave a long shuddering sigh and turned to reach for her. He was wonderfully gentle as his hands slid the robe from her shoulders, leaving her as naked as he. She could see his dark, desperate eyes by the faint light within that room, yet there was nothing desperate or brutish in the way he sought relief from her body; no evidence of the rough passion she had witnessed between him and Lydia.

Yet, somewhere along the way, fiery desire raced unexpectedly through her, so that her own responses grew wild and urgent. Her hands began to explore and arouse until what had begun as a tentative exchange between a seeker of comfort and the comforter, became a mutual release of something they had both denied for too long. Physical possession by Dominic had been brutally selfish. By Alex, it was joyous and shaded by his love and gratitude. When Martin gathered her beneath him for the culmination of their unlooked-for passion, possession by him encompassed every sensation of delight, honour and surrender. They finally lay spent in each other's arms, listening to the deafening firecrackers outside knowing nothing could touch them for the remainder of that night.

When Thea walked into her hotel room at ten that morning, Alex immediately knew that he had lost her. The party had broken up shortly after the scene that had shocked any sense of fun or enjoyment from the guests. By the time Alex had arranged for his distraught sister to be escorted home, and seen the departure of shaken or disgusted friends, he had realised that Thea would not be coming back to the hotel. Unable to bring himself to go to Martin's bungalow in case he found them there together, he had gone instead to her room where they had made love together so joyously. He had walked restlessly about the place, touching her perfumes, a hairbrush, pots of cream; running his hands over the material of her clothes scattered about the room, holding them to his cheek caressingly, as if by doing so, he would banish the vision of her kneeling protectively beside the only person she had observed in that wrecked room. By dawn, he could no longer hide from the heartbreaking truth.

When she finally returned, it was there in her eyes and in the softness of her expression, despite her air of sadness. The scarlet silk dress was crushed, looking tawdry in the bright light of morning. Her face appeared surprisingly youthful without the cosmetics she loved to use.

It was as if she emerged from reverie when she caught sight of him and halted just inside the door. "Oh, Alex, my dear!" she breathed, in distress.

He got to his feet stiffly after his long vigil, feeling unkempt in last night's evening wear. All the speeches he had rehearsed for hours seemed melodramatic now she was there facing him. All he could manage to say was, "Is he safe to be left now?"

Closing the door behind her, she nodded wearily. "Just very tired. He said, he's always like that afterward."

"After what?" he asked painfully.

She levelled a look at him. "After a neurotic attack. One of us should have thought to warn him about the firecrackers."

"He can't go through life expecting to be warned of anything that might set him off. The tiger hunt was bad enough; now this. He should be in hospital."

"Don't, Alex! That kind of remark isn't worthy of you."

"What kind of remark is?" he countered bitterly. "As the man you have promised to marry, am I allowed to ask what you were doing with him all night?"

She walked to a chair near him, and sank into it wearily. "Yes, of course. You have every right to ask that."

"So what's the answer, Thea?"

"The answer? An answer gives you nothing but plain facts. There's so much more to any situation. A question of feelings, in addition to actions. I'm not sure you'd understand."

"I'm damn sure I would," he retorted. "I'll ask you again more specifically. Did he become your lover?"

"Yes, he did."

He turned away to strike at the bedpost with the flat of his hand. "My God, you always swore there was nothing between you save a desire to help Lydia."

"I'm desperately sorry," she offered in broken tones.

He swung round. "*Sorry!* When you rushed off to console him, didn't it once occur to you that you were making me as pitiful a figure as he?"

"I thought of nothing save the urgency of trying to save a man from possible self-destruction. Not one other person in that room made a move to help him . . . even you, Alex."

"All right," he conceded, "I'll accept that you were motivated by compassion. However, the treatment for such cases doesn't require the nurse to take off her clothes and roll about the bed with her patient." He fought to speak through his thickening throat. "If you had to break me apart, why did you have to do it in public . . . and why, of all the men in Singapore, did it have to be him?"

After a significant silence, she said, "It's not the fact that I've allowed a third man to become my lover which has upset you, is it, but the fact that he was Martin? You have never been able to come to terms with him. Alex, tell me this. Would you like to now be sitting in solitary state wondering how on earth you're going to carry on living amongst those who were at the party? Would you be happier having your future totally governed by a trustee and a set of doctors, your days clouded by the fear that some day one of those attacks might start and never end? Would you like to be regarded with derision and mistrust? Would you? Would you truly like to be Martin Linwood?"

He looked back at her with crushing pain in the region of his heart. "If it meant winning your everlasting love, then I would."

It proved too much for her. She rose and came into his arms, crying helplessly against his shoulder. He held her comfortingly, although he knew the tears were not entirely for him. When she grew calmer, he drew her over to the bed where they had made love so uninhibitedly. How could such happiness be lost?

Sitting beside her, he asked heavily, "What happens now, Thea?"

"I don't know," she confessed, gazing at him with tear-drenched eyes. "I still love you; I think I always will, my dear. After Serantinggi, I discovered that I also loved Martin. In a vastly different way, however." She sighed. "It is possible for a woman to be dedicated to two men at the same time. History's full of examples."

He stared at the silk picture hanging on the pale washed wall of that hotel room, finding it difficult to accept such a complex theory. Part of him urged a total break with her; told him to walk away in justification for what she had done to him. Yet his love for her was still strong. He tried to persuade himself that she had merely been carried away by the drama last night; that her nature had compelled her to champion the underdog. Pity was close to love. Could she be mistaking one for the other where Martin was concerned? Yet he could not ignore

313

the undeniable bond which had been between the pair from their first meeting, could not forget the way she had looked up at Martin after running in from the rain on the night of the Military Ball.

He sat for some minutes, as confused as she. Then, looking across at her through eyes bleary from lack of sleep, he said brusquely, "He must have said something to you when you left this morning. Surely it wasn't just 'Thanks, and goodbye', was it?"

"Actually, he was very worried about you."

That touched him on the raw. He left the bed in a violent movement, turning on her in anger. "That's bloody rich! He violates my future wife, then worries about how I'll take it!"

Rising also, to go to him, she said, "There was no question of violation. I told you I wasn't sure you'd understand."

"Oh, I understand, all right," he raged. "He became your lover last night. How he did it is immaterial."

"No, it makes *all* the difference," she argued urgently. "It began as a kind of comfort. He wasn't aware of where it might lead."

He shook her hand from his arm. "Are you trying to tell me that he didn't know damned well which woman he had under him?"

"Oh no, he certainly knew it was me," she affirmed quietly. "I believe I was the only person he could bear to have beside him, at such a time. My hand was there in the darkness, and he held on to it like a lifeline. Thought didn't go beyond that to the extent of considering relationships. He needed help, and I was there."

His stomach was churning and his palms were wet. The strain of that nocturnal vigil in her room was taking its toll now. "You begin to sound like Lydia. Another little fool worshipping the hero."

"He's no hero, Alex, just a man who has lost his way."

"So have I. *So have I*," he cried from the heart. "Put me back on the path, if it's at all possible. You've just told me how he feels about me this morning, and I don't need his concern. How does he feel about *you* now that passion has flown? Tell me that!"

Looking exhausted and unhappy, she had to confess that she did not know. Then, with typical honesty, she looked him in the eye to add, "As a matter of fact, he did say 'Thanks, and goodbye'. Not in so many words, but that was the basic message."

"*The bastard!*"

"What else could he say?" she demanded, in his defence. "He can't think straight yet. He's grappling with the fact that something he thought he had conquered still rules him, the future he had all mapped out has probably collapsed, and the girl who adored him now regards him as some kind of disgusting monster."

314

"Isn't he?" he cried involuntarily, then realised what he had done when he saw the pain of her disbelief that he could say such a thing.

"If you truly believe that, why have you envied him from the moment you first met?" She walked to the door and held it open for him. "Goodbye, Alex."

He left his love in that room despite all that had been said between them, and prepared for his voyage to England in a daze of misery. He did not sail on the *Princess Maria*, however. On the day before his planned departure, he was told by the authorities that he could not leave the colony. He was amongst those wanted for questioning in a case being brought against the exporter, Randal Forster, for serious criminal activities in which *Berondel* was one of the companies implicated. The inquiry had been set in motion two months before by Martin Linwood.

Chapter 18

Austin Beresford had a third and fatal seizure before news could reach him of the scandal implicating the company he had dedicated his life to freeing from such taint. The residents of Singapore nevertheless agreed that Alex's dealings with Randal Forster, negotiated without his father's approval, must have killed the dedicated shipper. Their version was a more titillating one to go down in the annals of colonial history, and there was much more to come as *Berondel* was not the only shipping line connected with the biggest scandal the island had known for some years. Martin's instigation of discreet inquiries into the exporter's affairs had stirred up a hornets' nest. Many small businessmen of indeterminate nationality were leaving Singapore covertly on junks and sampans, one step ahead of the authorities. Those like Alex Beresford, who would not run, waited numbly as revelation after revelation showed them how they had been duped and used by a man who had taken advantage of all the East offered the born rogue.

Martin was not immediately aware of the consequences of his actions. After the events of the farewell party, Sir Hartle, the Civil Service, and the outraged residents had insisted that he spend a period in hospital, ostensibly to rest and recover, but mainly to put him out of harm's way while they decided what to do with him. George McGregor fought the intention to instal the patient in a solitary room where he could be watched through a window in the door, and won for his friend a place in a small ward occupied by men from up-country when recovering from various tropical fevers. Isolation would have increased Martin's introspection at a time when it might have proved fatal. George visited him frequently, encouraging him to talk freely about what had happened and offering reassurance. Their mutual trust and liking made it possible for George to relate news Martin was sure to find upsetting, then help him to come to terms with it.

Austin Beresford's funeral had been attended by the entire business population of Singapore as a mark of respect for a man who had worshipped the gods of integrity and honesty. It was no consolation to his corpse that he was honoured in death as he never had been in life, or that he was now regarded as a very fine man who had been betrayed by his ne'er-do-well son. Lydia, on the verge of nervous collapse, was sailing for England with her mother. She had assigned to Alex the legal power to act on her behalf in respect of *Berondel* and he, hardened by tragedy and confident of exoneration from complicity in a case growing daily more unpalatable, took on the task gladly. The Beresford house was to be sold and the contents shipped to England for use by the widow and her daughter.

George broke all this to Martin gradually, and he accepted it with inscrutable calmness. Deep inside, however, he shouldered responsibility for it all. His first instinct that any association with Lydia would prove dangerous had been right. He had shocked and distressed her beyond forgiveness; had harmed her reputation and made her ill. As for Alex, there was not a lot more Martin could have done to ruin his life and happiness. The investigation of Randal Forster had apparently been responsible for Austin's death, and involved *Berondel* in a scandal which had not yet reached its sordid denouement. In addition, he had seduced Thea on the eve of her marriage.

Martin could hardly remember how it had happened, only that it had. She had been there in the depths of that black night, and he had turned to her wanting the comfort only a woman could give. It was not until some time later that he realised Thea had broken his sexual abstinence in the most natural way; that he had taken her as tenderly as any normal man would. He did not bother to analyse why, thinking simply that she had saved him from possible destruction that night. In doing so, she had betrayed a man who did not deserve to be broken in the cruellest way.

A month later, George insisted to the hospital authorities that there were no longer grounds for keeping Martin there, and he drove his friend back to the bungalow promising to return that evening. Martin felt no joy at leaving the small ward which had provided a retreat for the past four weeks. The set of familiar rooms seemed no more agreeable than the hospital, and held too many memories he wished to forget. Wah was delighted to see him back, however, and the warmth of the welcome on that round friendly face touched Martin in ridiculous fashion.

There was no welcome from Sir Hartle when he arrived at the bungalow about an hour later. Martin stood to greet him warily, his godfather's disinclination to visit him in the hospital hardly improving the situation between them now.

"Hallo, sir. How did you know I was back?"

Sir Hartle nodded brusquely by way of greeting, and ignored the question. "Came to see how you are, and to sort out a few things. Thought it was time."

"Would you like a drink, or is it too early for you?" Martin asked.

"Eh? No, no," was the irritable reply as he settled himself into a chair. "I wouldn't advise you to have one, either, boy."

Martin had had no intention of drinking, but the manner in which the advice was given made him pour himself a stiff brandy and toss back half in one defiant gulp.

"After four weeks of enforced abstinence, I think I deserve one, don't you, sir? Have you been away up-country again?" he asked pointedly as he sat facing his godfather. Then, noticing that his hand holding the glass was shaking, he put it on the table beside him.

"Up-country?" queried Sir Hartle, missing the sarcasm of the question. "Heavens, no! Been up to my neck in this damned affair you've stirred up."

Martin frowned. "How are you involved in it?"

Bushy eyebrows rose. "How am I . . . you have the gall to ask?"

"I've been locked away, out of touch with what's been happening."

"Yes, a damned sight too late, unfortunately."

Martin challenged him uneasily. "What do you mean by that, sir?"

"Dammit, boy, you know all too well what I mean," came the response accompanied by a fist thumped on the arm of the chair. "You've let me down all along the line! Have you any idea what I had to do to secure you a post out here, where promotion is slow and greatly coveted? Do you know how many people I had to bribe, how many favours I had to perform, how many assurances I had to give to gain you entry to clubs, societies, and the houses of all who wield power in this colony? It was my name, my influence, my wealth that persuaded people to accept you." His protuberant eyes glared a challenge. "How have you repaid me? I gave you every chance, offered every assistance toward making a new start. I told you on a great many occasions that it was simply a case of pulling yourself together. Did you work on it? Not a bit. Instead, you tangled with that poor little Beresford girl, at a time when her father was unable to protect her, and have now ruined her reputation," he accused, waving an angry hand in the air. "You ignored my warnings about drink, and apparently became so inebriated one night you fell down the steps here and were off-duty for a ridiculously long time. Yes, I heard about that, even though it happened when I was on a case in Kuala Lumpur!"

Looking at Martin from beneath lowered brows, he continued. "You have made no attempt to be sociable with your fellows, preferring the company of men such as the Sing brothers, and George McGregor—a loose screw, if ever there was one. This aloofness has made you unpopular in the Department, and your association with the Beresford girl has become the talk of the colony. Poor young Fay has suffered immeasurably because of her vague connection with you." He paused, panting with the extent of his anger for a moment or two. Then he

318

wagged his head vigorously. "I do not consider that pulling yourself together, sir, and I tell you that I have never been more disappointed in my life. If it were not for the fact that you are Frere Linwood's son, and I gave your father my word that I would look after you, I would be strongly inclined to let you go to the devil."

Passing a distracted hand over his brow, he sighed gustily. "Nevertheless, I shall honour my word. I shall honour it, despite all this. You are still a very sick man, Martin. I had hoped it would be possible for you to live a normal life. I wasn't present at young Beresford's farewell party, but I have been given numerous vivid accounts of what happened there, aside from Fay's description of something that has never before been witnessed in Singapore. I cannot allow it ever to happen again. Indeed, the residents *demand* that it does not."

Martin tucked his hands into his pockets as the shaking grew worse. He had no idea what he had done that night; he never knew how he acted during severe attacks. All he remembered of the affair was one minute standing with Thea at the open french doors of the hotel, then finding himself kneeling on the floor in the middle of a wrecked room, with a hundred pairs of disgusted eyes watching him and the girl he loved in a state of shock. However, he had seen other victims of shell shock when in the grips of fear so strong it overcame reality, and his imagination filled in the scene for him. His bravado vanished.

"I'm sorry, sir," he said quietly.

"Yes, I expect you are . . . but it really doesn't help the situation, does it?" Sir Hartle pointed out in softer, but equally firm, tones. "You can never be sure when it might happen again, and it really is not . . . not . . . *fitting* to subject people to that kind of frightening behaviour, is it?"

"I . . . no, I suppose not."

"You really should be with those who understand and know how to deal with such outbursts."

Martin rose, his stomach muscles tensing. "What are you suggesting, sir?"

"Now, now, there's no need to get excited, my boy," said the elderly judge, heaving himself from his own chair with a great deal of effort. "There is great justification for the decision."

"What decision?"

"To . . . er . . . well, to fill your post in the Civil Service with someone more . . . hmm . . . suitable."

Martin had never enjoyed the work, had often longed to leave it for something more active in peaceful surroundings, but he nevertheless felt that unqualified dismissal was extremely unjust.

319

"I always did my job in a completely satisfactory manner, and no one could honestly say otherwise," he said defensively. "As my health problems have never affected what I did for the Department, I don't see how they can find someone more suitable than a man who is already first class."

For the first time during the interview Sir Hartle appeared slightly uncomfortable and evasive. "Yes . . . well, it's not just your health, you see. It's this other business."

"What other business?"

"Oh, come, come! It's useless to pretend you are not very well aware of why they can't keep you on," his godfather said testily. "It has already killed poor Beresford, and God knows how many more will go under before the thing is finished."

"Are you referring to the investigation into Forster's enterprises?" Martin asked, reaching for the brandy again because he suddenly needed it. "It was in the interest of my Department. For a start, he was putting honest native traders out of business by under-cutting their prices with goods brought in illegally. We are supposed to protect ethnic relations; ensure peace and stability on the island. You're surely not saying, sir, that my Department *resents* my action against Forster?"

Sir Hartle's complexion reddened, and he cleared his throat noisily. "You have been with us for a year, Martin, and still haven't the first idea of how we go on out here, of our values and rules, have you?"

Martin's back began to tingle as he recalled much the same being said to him on another occasion. "I thought the laws of this administration were the same as we have in England, since it is run by the British. Crime shouldn't go unpunished. Forster is a criminal of the nastiest kind. He makes capital from poverty, and from the simplicity of some native minds."

"That's as may be," came the impatient answer, "but there are Forsters in every city in the East. One can never stamp them out. As soon as one is removed, another moves in to take his place."

"So they should be left to prosper?" he demanded.

"Better the devil you know," blustered Sir Hartle, avoiding his eyes. "So long as they don't overstep the mark we . . . well, we let sleeping dogs lie," he finished on another maxim. "You now see why. Once officialdom is forced to intervene, it stirs up all manner of unpleasant business involving more and more innocent people. The minute your report was officially filed, they had no option but to follow it up. You put Sir Frederick in an impossible position, Martin." He took a pace or two about the room in agitation. "He is scarcely speaking to me now . . . nor, I might add, are quite a few others who feel that you are my responsibility. What, in heaven's name, made you do it?"

Martin was incredulous. "Made me do it? It was part of my job."

"Of course it was not! You should have had enough sense to leave well alone."

"Are you suggesting that the Department, in which you secured me a post at great personal conniving, exists only to fill in forms and field a team in the cricket competition?" he asked furiously.

"That remark is offensive, sir," snapped Sir Hartle. "You have overstepped your responsibilities, broken all the codes of our society. Running this colony is no easy task, I'll have you know. With so many races, creeds and temperaments with which to deal, it's the devil's own job to maintain harmony. You have been a soldier and should know that to command one has to be respected. Your damned inquiry has exposed some high-ranking men to censure, if not to charges of complicity in criminal activities. The backbone of our society has been weakened —by one of our number, of all things! A traitor, sir, that is how you are now regarded."

Martin's back was tingling more and more as the exchange continued. "Is that worse, or on a par with being regarded as 'a rat, a righteous prig and a slimy bastard'?" he asked through tight lips.

"Eh?" queried the older man, unaware of the significance of Martin's words.

"You've been a soldier, too, sir. You should know that respect in command has to be earned, not maintained by covering up one's faults."

"I don't know what you mean," snapped Sir Hartle.

"My health and background history has nothing whatever to do with this, has it? It is simply because I have unwittingly proved that several puffed-up men are little better than some of those they are appointed to govern. If the investigation had revealed *all* the villains to be men of native origin, I'd have been the hero of the Civil Service. Let me tell you, sir, that four years of living in holes dug in the ground showed me that a man is only as good as his inborn character. There's more than one way to be a traitor to one's countrymen. I venture to suggest that respect would be easier earned by showing that everyone on this island is subject to its laws, rather than letting sleeping dogs lie, especially when they are dogs like Randal Forster."

He tossed back the rest of the brandy, then gave his godfather a tight smile. "I'll tender my resignation. That will save you the reflected ignominy of my dishonourable dismissal from the service. As for the suggestion you couldn't quite bring yourself to make, namely that I should enter an institution permanently, that really isn't the only way out of your promise to my father. Release enough of my funds to install me on

321

a plantation up-country, and I'll be off your hands for good. As a planter, it will be quite permissible for me to be as mad as I wish. After all, when Marmaduke Beresford creates chaos at a party, everyone smiles indulgently and regards it as jolly good entertainment. It's only when some half-demented outsider does it that colonial dignity is outraged, and everyone demands his blood." He picked up the brandy decanter and filled his glass to the brim defiantly. "Cheers, sir . . . and goodbye."

After Sir Hartle left, red-faced and badly shaken by behaviour that did not suggest pulling oneself together, Martin embarked on a bout of drinking. He soon abandoned it as futile. There was some truth in what his godfather had said. He very much regretted that an innocent man like Alex Beresford would be tainted by the charge of shady dealing, because he did not believe the person he knew would have approved shipping stolen goods, drugs and weapons for the growing revolutionary Chinese based in Singapore. Apart from his personal integrity, Alex had too much respect for his father's insistence on honest trading to have risked breaking Austin's spirit so blatantly. Martin was sad to have been the cause of bringing *Berondel* into a criminal investigation. If he had had any inkling that Alex was dealing with a man like Forster he might have thought twice about filing the report, or at least have warned the man to pull out before he did. Then, full of disgust, he realised that he was regretting the very thing he had just condemned so forcefully to his godfather.

He sat for a long time thinking of many things, and trying to put his future into some kind of perspective. The glory of it had faded, somehow. Impossible dream it might have been, but a life with Lydia up there with lush jungle, lazy waterways, brown smiling people, vivid birds, and a beautiful peaceful valley had been worth dreaming of, for a while. Yet, even after several hours of concentrated thought, a new dream had not evolved to take its place.

Quite when the other resolution occurred to him he was not sure, because his mind had been confused for some time, but he had no sooner heard Damien Lang return from his office than he picked up his leather belt and crossed the communal sitting room to enter the man's bedroom without knocking.

Lang looked around quickly, his face darkening when he saw Martin. "What are you doing back here?"

"I escaped from my padded cell," he responded with a smile. "I missed your charming company too much."

Lang put down the jacket he had just taken off, trying to look unconcerned. "You are boringly unfunny, Linwood, and I don't care for halfwits. Now clear out of my room!"

"Not just yet," he said, crossing the coloured rugs until he was face to face with his good-looking neighbour. "I've come to teach *you* a lesson, this time. You see, I don't like rats either—especially those who implicate friends of mine in corrupt activities by pretending they are above board. Do you know what we stout upright fellows who fought for King and country used to do to rats that ran around our trenches, feeding on the corpses of our unfortunate friends? We used to swipe them with our Sam Brownes until they were unrecognisable."

Smiling grimly at the fear and uncertainty playing across the other man's face, he added, "I haven't four others to hold you over a chair while I do it, so you can either stand there like a man and accept your punishment, or run away squeaking in fright. Which is it to be?"

Lang backed against the wall, upsetting a small table holding a cigarette box, ashtray and several glasses which smashed on the floor. Staring at the belt in Martin's hand, he panted, "You're mad . . . *mad*."

"That's right," he agreed equably. "You'd better run, in that case. The only snag is that I locked the door as I came in, which limits your possible destinations."

With that, he swung the belt viciously. It cut across the man's cheek to draw blood, which caused him to let out a muffled scream as he darted across the room to the door. Martin followed, lashing at the back covered in no more than a thin shirt.

"Sorry, old bean, forgot to tell you the key's in my pocket," he taunted harshly.

Lang turned from his fruitless rattling of the latch. His face had grown putty-coloured against the vivid stripe which spoiled his looks. "You ought to be locked up, Linwood."

"I was, but I broke down the door. We lunatics have superhuman strength, you know, and that's what you'll need if you hope to get away from this."

Another lash from the belt sent Lang headlong for the window. He was frantically trying to clamber on to the windowsill when Martin's blow caught him across the knee, setting him shrieking with the pain of it.

"Don't try that," warned Martin. "I get very angry when thwarted. *Don't*, I said."

From then on it was a case of frenzied flight and dedicated pursuit. The belt made a sickening sound on Lang's flesh with each blow, until Martin suddenly realised that the uncontrollable urge to kill, which overcame men in battle, was starting to rule him. The business ended quickly then. His victim was sweating with fear and pain, and so demoralised, it was easy to seize him, march him into the bathroom, and unceremoniously drop him into the tub of tepid water prepared by Wah, who had vanished to his own quarters. Martin left the man sobbing and terrified to return to his own room. There, he threw down the belt and sank into a chair, head in hands, while tremors shook his entire body.

"Dear God, let me get away from this place before I really do go mad," he prayed.

The inquiry into Randal Forster's activities revealed the usual pattern of blackmail, corruption, and disregard for the law in the shipping of stolen goods, drugs and arms. In order to move his merchandise without the knowledge of those lines he used, he had bribed men in official posts—some very high indeed. Heads had to roll, and the European population laid the blame squarely on the shoulders of someone they felt should never have been allowed into the colony and their homes. There were ways of dealing with cases such as this, other than forcing a full official investigation, and it was the last straw that the man responsible should be one of their own number.

Martin was dismissed before he could offer his resignation—an eye for an eye style of punishment—and his membership of clubs and societies was immediately cancelled. Sir Hartle Weyford continued to receive very cool treatment, and those in power demanded to know what he proposed doing about his unwelcome godson. In such cases, the culprit was normally sent packing with all speed, but the old judge retained enough of his standing in Singapore to earn him the courtesy of being allowed to deal with Martin himself.

The colony had yet to sustain its worst shock, however. One of Forster's slow junks from Canton was searched when it eventually docked, and crates within its hold were found to contain kidnapped Chinese boys between the ages of seven and twelve, destined to be sold for homosexual purposes in Singapore's brothels. The children had been caged throughout the voyage, and fed through the bars.

Scapegoats would no longer suffice. Church and welfare bodies raised a terrible hue and cry, and this movement of protest was seized and used by Chinese revolutionary groups who took any opportunity to enhance their bitter campaign against foreign intervention and the corruption of the East, despite the fact that they were the customers for the arms shipped by Forster. As the affair mushroomed, the vice rings in Singapore were split, setting any number of men to nocturnal flight when the investigation drew too close. Amongst these were the Sing brothers, who vanished from their hilltop paradise for an unknown destination taking their priceless possessions with them. The colony then became ripe for outbreaks of violence of the kind being perpetrated in China and the British Crown colony of Hong Kong. The obvious targets for reprisal were those responsible for the greatest cause of dissatisfaction. Alex had been living in limbo since Chinese New Year. First, he had lost Thea, then his father had died. Next, his mother and Lydia had sailed for the motherland they hardly knew, unable to face a fresh scandal over *Berondel*. The evidence showing that the one transaction he had made with Forster, unknown to his father or the board, had branded the company as one of a number involved in the illegal shipping deals, had dealt Alex one of the worst blows of his short life. Knowing that most people believed the news had killed his father, was the cruellest blow of all to a man who had fought such painful inner battles over filial loyalty.

For hour after hour, he had endured concentrated questioning during the heat-ridden days, until his thoughts had grown confused and his body ached. The *Berondel* files, books and records had been seized, and the penalty of Austin's rigid personal rule of the company was never more dearly paid by Alex than whilst trying to explain details of past contracts he had never been allowed to handle. He had had no alternative but to admit sole responsibility for the instigation of the Manila office, and for agreeing to carry Forster's cargoes through that port. He fought long and hard, however, to prove that *Berondel* had no knowledge of the actual contents of several shipments the company had carried. The young manager Alex had installed in Manila had been one of the men bribed by Forster. He had also vanished into the labyrinth of the East, taking with him all available funds from the sub-office.

After long deliberation, *Berondel* was crossed from the list of companies to be charged with criminal complicity, although Alex would be required to give evidence in the case against Forster. It had been his original intention to remain in Singapore for the purpose, but the discovery of child slavery on a large scale would start a major scourge of the East and delay the trial drastically.

Alex booked passage for England yet again. By doing so, he knew he was forcing himself to make a very difficult decision. He had not seen Thea since that terrible morning following the party. In truth, he had been too stunned and worried by developments coming so soon after each other to find time to analyse his feelings for a girl who claimed she loved two men equally, albeit in different ways. He also could not analyse his feelings for the man who had been responsible for destroying the fabric of his life over the past twelve months. Did he despise or pity him? Did he hate Martin for the scandal involving *Berondel*, or admire his courage in exposing something destined to rock the East for months to come? It had never been easy to define their relationship, yet Alex knew he would never forget Martin Linwood.

He also knew Thea had been unable to forgive his one heedless remark condemning Martin, so did he really want a girl whose heart and mind were equally occupied with another man? Each time he asked himself that question, the answer was yes. His love for her was still as deep; his need still as strong. As the date of his departure drew nearer and nearer, he was haunted by uncertainty. During his long deliberations, it was easy to believe that Thea would forget Martin once they sailed to England and became husband and wife, but not so easy to ignore the implication of her failure to contact him during this long period of family and business disasters. Was she telling him that she no longer cared for him, or was she simply waiting for a sign from him that he forgave her for that one night with Martin?

The problem occupied his thoughts once more as he returned to the house two days before his planned departure. The syce drove in leisurely manner dodging cars, trams, bullock carts, rickshaws, bicycles and an occasional smoke-emitting motorcycle ridden by a daring young European in goggles and the obligatory topee. The late afternoon heat hung in the crowded streets filled with the smells and dirt common amid the hotch-potch of buildings which formed the mercantile core of the city. The scene went unnoticed by Alex as he wondered if he really could simply shrug his shoulders, murmur *c'est la vie*, and make no effort to see Thea before he left. Once that liner pulled away from the shore, there would be no turning back. Would he be repeating 1914 in reverse; himself on the deck desperately yearning to be on the jetty? There were only two days in which to act. What should he do?

Being obliged to pass Martin's bungalow each day to reach home had not made things easier, for he had been unable to resist the urge to look for Thea there. He did so now, but the only sign of life was provided by the servants who clustered excitedly at the gates of the place. It was an odd circumstance for the entire staff to be neglecting their duties. Alex had heard that Damien Lang had moved in with a friend since Martin's release from hospital, making it clear to the colony that he had no wish to share quarters with a madman. Alex now wondered if Martin had run amok again and been taken off, leaving the staff to their own devices.

It was at that moment that he grew aware of several ominous things simultaneously. Distant shouting suggested a large number of agitated people, smoke was billowing across the road ahead, and there was an unmistakable smell of burning. The infant bubble of apprehension burst into outright fear, as he realised that the smoke rising in thick black clouds came from behind the row of fan palms bordering his own garden. He immediately guessed what was happening, and was incredulous. Several high-ranking men who were implicated up to the hilt in the Forster scandal had been attacked by stone-throwing mobs; more had been besieged in their homes by politically roused Chinese carrying all manner of weapons including flaming brands. All those connected with the case had been warned, but Alex had been so very slightly involved he had not dreamed reprisal would be taken against him. He could scarcely believe it now.

With his heart thudding, he ordered his syce to pull up at the entrance to the driveway. As he leapt from the car, the smell of burning filled his nostrils and the afternoon heat seemed even more oppressive with billows of smoke drifting from the garden to sting his eyes and rasp his throat. The screams of abuse from within the walls of his old home should have made him hesitate, but Alex began running frantically through the ornate gates standing ajar and along the driveway, until he was halted by shock.

Visible through the smoke were the long tongues of flame licking at the house. The verandahs running along the front of it, and the wooden shutters at every door and window opening on to them, were well alight and sending showers of sparks up into the still air. They fell into the gardens, where they set trees and shrubs aflame. Outside the house was a large gathering of hysterical people armed with knives, stones or knotted ropes, shouting for revenge and making threatening gestures at the house. A fire engine with its crew, held at bay by the furious mob, stood futilely in the driveway. The white walls of the house had been disfigured by paint, mud, rotting fruit, and all manner of filth flung in anger. The windows had been smashed by a hail of stones, coconuts, branches wrenched from the frangipani trees, and by fragments of what had once been the elegant sculpted fountain in the centre of the pool in which Alex had frolicked fully clothed with Thea during a monsoon storm.

As he stood trying to accept what he saw, a young English police officer Alex knew as Piers Johnson staggered through the undergrowth on to the path beside him. The man was filthy, hatless and bleeding profusely from a cut over one eye.

"Beresford, thank God you've arrived," he panted. "You have increased my available force to three."

"What?" cried Alex. "Where is everyone?"

"Elsewhere," came the brief response. "Since the newspaper report about those caged boys, Chinese anger has been running very high. We have protective cordons around the key men's homes and offices, but we never bargained for their frustration to drive them to your place. It was no more than abuse and a few random stones, at first, which was

327

why we thought my presence with two Sikh constables would disperse them easily enough. The revolutionary gang has moved in, however, and the whole thing is now completely out of my control." He dabbed uselessly at the cut with a handkerchief soaked with his own blood. "I had to send one of my men for reinforcements. Two detachments should be here at any moment. I've just made an attempt to gain the house. The bastards clobbered me with everything they have. With your help, I'll have another go at trying to get them out."

"Get who out?" yelled Alex in alarm above the din. "Do you mean the servants are still inside?"

Johnson gave Alex a straight look. "Servants, be damned. Your girlfriend and that madman Linwood are in there."

He had received so many shocks during the last few months, Alex took this news with astonishing outward calmness. "How do you know this?" he demanded through a dry throat.

"The girl tried to escape, but she was bombarded with stones and driven back inside," Johnson explained succinctly. "As I skirted the house just now in an attempt to bring her out through a side door, Linwood came racing through the garden from the tennis courts, said he'd seen and heard the disturbance from his bungalow down the road, then charged headlong into the building on hearing that she was trapped there. I tried to follow him, but the verandah went up in a sheet of flame and collapsed right in front of me. Then I ran to the front entrance, but was attacked the minute they spotted me. God knows if Linwood is still alive in that inferno. She is. I saw her at an upstairs window as I raced back here just now, hoping my men had arrived."

"I've got to get her," cried Alex wildly, moving forward.

He was held back by the other man, who yelled, "You'll never make it. Their only hope lies in our putting out the fire before it engulfs the entire house, but the engine can't approach near enough to do any good without my men to protect the crew. Where the hell are they?"

Alex was waiting for no one. With swift decisive words he told his companion so, and added, "If you can't put out the fire, turn the hoses on to the people. They'll fall back, leaving the way clear for me. I know the layout of the place," he shouted insistently at the other's protest. "It's my house, so I'm the one to go in. It's also my girl who's trapped in there."

"You're mad! In their present mood, they'll kill you on sight."

"Not if they're mown down by jets of water. Come on," he urged, starting to run down the driveway. "We're wasting time here."

"The crew has been threatened," panted Johnson beside him. "They may refuse to operate the pump."

"Then operate the bloody thing yourself," he directed. "I've got to get in there, and that's the only hope I have of succeeding."

They reached the fire engine unnoticed by the mob hurling rocks and abuse at the house. Alex had little time to reflect on the tragic destruction of his home as the police officer explained to the firemen, mostly Eurasian, what they should do. With Johnson himself and the Sikh constable helping the crew, it still took longer than Alex liked to connect the hoses and start pumping the handle up and down. When water suddenly gushed from the first hose held by the two policemen, quickly followed by a second guided by the fire crew, the element of surprise was all Alex hoped. Those directly in line fell back beneath the onslaught, crushing underfoot those on each side to create a panic.

At that moment, Alex broke from the trees at a run to take advantage of the gap forced by the confusion. Being the one man who was prepared for the force of water hitting him, he made full use of its power to hasten his progress as he kicked and shouldered his way through bewildered, sodden Chinese. Any resistance he countered with a vicious elbow or fist until he broke free of the crowd, panting and drenched, to face open ground leading to the main entrance. There, the door stood open as Thea had left it.

"Dear God, let her be safe," he prayed silently. "Let her be alive when I reach her."

He bent low as he ran, and zigzagged to avoid anything thrown at him, but the water jets were creating such chaos he was unhindered as he rushed up the steps and into the house. The real danger only then faced him, he realised. It was as dark as night in there. The smoke billowed out to meet him, filling his nostrils and throat. He began to cough; his eyes smarted unbearably as he looked desperately around the familiar hall almost obliterated by thick clouds of hot air.

Johnson said Thea had appeared at an upstairs window. That made sense; people always climbed away from fire. The main staircase was already flaming on the inner curve as he raced up it, wondering how long it would be before the whole structure collapsed cutting off hope of retreat that way. He made no attempt to call Thea's name. His throat was too raw, and she would never hear him above the roar of flames and crashing masonry as floors collapsed one by one. It was almost dispassionately that he noted the inferno raging in his own room at the far end of the branched corridor, into which he turned in the opposite direction. Praying that she was seeking refuge in her own room, that it had not yet begun to burn, and that she had not been asphyxiated by smoke, he raced on until halted by a sheet of fire, which was advancing toward him from a gaping hole in the floor. Thea's room lay beyond it, out of reach.

Chest heaving and bathed in perspiration, he tried to fight defeat. Then he remembered those nights when Fong had been so disapproving of his visits, and rushed into the nearest room to gain access to the verandah. *Oh God, poor Fong! Surely the mob had allowed him and the other servants to leave safely.* The french doors leading to the outside of the house were charred and smoking, but, thankfully, the flames had moved away from the verandah itself. Through the doors and on to it, he headed for the main entrance once more, intending to climb out over the large gable in order to reach Thea's room. However, once outside, he grew aware of a roar from below, and a veritable hail of stones and bricks began falling around him, flung by those who had caught sight of him and hoped to drive him back into the burning building. Dodging and ducking, he raced on until he turned a corner leading to the front of the house. A flash impression of the scene below greeted him. A crazed mob jostled and fought amongst the vivid blossoming trees, as jets of water swivelled futilely from hoses now in the hands of the aggressive Chinese. God help Johnson now!

Alex leapt at the sloping roof, clawing and grasping at the red-hot tiles as he attempted to mount and descend on the other side. He had cast aside his jacket and topee by the fire engine, and his thin shirt ripped as it caught a rough edge on the crest of the pointed gable. Over the top, he allowed himself to slide downward and almost came to grief as he misjudged the angle and hung in space for several moments above the excited Chinese watching him from below. Clinging to the rail with palms now raw and burning, he hauled himself over to safety with all the strength born of his many sporting activities. Upright again, he let out a sob. Thea's room no longer existed.

As Alex stared helplessly at the far end of the house which had collapsed in a cascade of fire, he heard a cry. It was faint and desperate, and came from the room by whose french door he stood. Swinging round, he charged inside, crying her name. She was hardly aware of him as she snatched up a light rug to beat at a man resembling a human torch, who had just entered from the inner corridor. Without hesitation, Alex seized another rug and beat at Martin's blazing trouser-legs alongside Thea. When she turned to acknowledge his presence, her eyes were wide with fear and incomprehension. Yet Alex saw something else in her glance which doubled his strength, and enabled him to knock Martin to the floor and roll him in the rugs to extinguish the smouldering remnants of material.

There was little time left to them, however. The doorway through which Martin had staggered was now well alight, with tiny rivulets of fire advancing over the floor of the room toward them. Signalling Thea to help him, Alex dragged Martin to his feet and helped his sagging figure toward the verandah by which he had just arrived, believing it to be still negotiable. They were too late! Fire had now travelled along outside the house to leave them trapped within that one room. Thea screamed his name above the roaring all around them, asking what they must do, and Martin was gazing steadily at him through the pain of his burns, clearly putting his trust in the only one who knew the layout of the house they were in. The responsibility of command hung like a great weight upon Alex in that split moment. He was not aware of clear reasoning, so it must have been instinct which drove him across to a door connecting with the adjacent room. Coughing and retching, all three staggered into an area not yet consumed by the conflagration, and across it to the integral bathroom.

Alex prayed. There was a narrow staircase used by the *kebun* when fetching water, which led down to the garden through the servants' quarters. That flight of wooden steps was their last hope of survival, if it still stood. Leading the other two, he found his prayer had been answered. Even so smoke was drifting up from the foot of the steps, suggesting that the ground floor was already alight. Hesitation would prove fatal. Another exchange of glances with Martin told him the other man still placed command fairly and squarely on him, so Alex pushed Thea between them both and began down the twisting way wide enough to allow passage for only one person at a time.

Although he knew it well, he had to feel his way through thick enveloping smoke, which had them all fighting to breathe between spasms of coughing. If the fire did not engulf them, the smoke would choke them to death before they reached the garden. The other pair followed him step for step, groping and stumbling in the obscurity, until he rounded a corner and was halted by shock. The kitchen was an inferno. It was impossible to cross to the safety of the garden beyond. They were trapped within a few yards of freedom. Even instinct proved no help to him now, and Alex turned in despair to stare at the two grim faces peering at him through the smoke.

At that vital moment, experience was of greater help than instinct, however. The man who had been through war, and to whom fire was a familiar foe, offered fresh hope. Above the swooshing roar of the flames creeping down toward them from the floor they had just left, Martin managed to croak the fact that fire moved swiftly to consume new wood. If they paused on that narrow stairway, there would be a moment when the flames would attack the lower steps, leaving the kitchen to smoulder and smoke. That would be their chance to break through the wall of flame narrowed by the confines of the stairs, and cross the area left as an ember.

It was immensely dangerous; it was a chance in a hundred. Yet it offered their only hope of survival. Martin's theory made sense, and Alex had to believe it by handing command to the man who had been forced to take it so often. In that instant of suspended time, Alex finally knew there was no sense of excitement or adventure in facing death; no justification whatever for envy of those who had been driven to face it time and time again. At this moment, he was deeply afraid and filled with such yearning for continued life, he knew he would use it to the full if it were granted him. Reaching for Thea, he pulled off his shirt and covered her head with it to protect her as she ran through the flames. Then, racked by deep coughs as his lungs burned with the acid smoke, he grasped her hand and made ready to dash at Martin's signal. It took all his courage to wait there as the fire crept gradually nearer and brightness almost blinded him, putting his life in the hands of the man he had dubbed a disgusting monster. Martin Linwood was no madman; he simply could not forget moments such as this. Alex knew he would never forget either.

When the flames were practically licking at his clothes and hair, the signal was given. Alex experienced no hesitation, no confusion, no fear. Holding Thea close he ran through the sheet of flame and into the blackened, smoking shell of what had once been the kitchen of his home. The burning sensation on his skin, the unbearable pain of fire on flesh, the dread smell of singeing assailed him as he raced onward, instinct once more coming to his aid to direct him along remembered routes. Then, the smoke began to clear, the stinging agony grew less. Grey ash changed to soft, green blades of grass beneath his raw feet. Still he raced on, dragging the girl he loved with him, until he crashed into a barrier which seemed invisible, yet was strong enough to knock him off his feet. He lay sobbing for breath, holding a trembling, retching girl against him as he solved the puzzle by identifying the wire surrounding the tennis courts well to the rear of the house. A few feet away, Martin hung against the wire, keeping upright by clutching it tightly with bright scarlet hands. He was shaking with such violence, the entire length of mesh was twanging metallically.

People came to them; great, tall, turbaned Sikhs in uniform. There were others in starched white coats, carrying stretchers. Alex refused to loose his hold on Thea, until they prised his fingers apart causing him such agony he must have momentarily fainted. When he opened his eyes again, he was being carried away by two strong Malays. At first, he thought they were taking him back into the fire. Then he realised that the fiery crimson glow was no more than the sun, setting behind the row of fan palms in yet another glorious twilight.

Chapter 19

The burning of the Beresford home hardened European attitudes toward their Chinese neighbours, and diluted much of their chagrin over the scandal of Randal Forster's dealings. The dramatic escape of three young people who had set the colony by its ears for almost a year, brought an almost total reversal of opinion. Alex Beresford became the hero of the day; a young man possessing all the qualities of the ideal colonial, who had been drastically repressed by a tyrannical father. Martin Linwood, sadly maladjusted though he was, had shown the typical British pluck which had earned him decorations for bravery during the recent war. He should be treated with compassion, not callousness, poor fellow.

Dorothea du Lessier was the only one of the three who remained unpopular. Two courageous young men had risked their lives to bring her from that inferno. What had she been doing in a house from which Margery had thrown her some weeks before? Why had young Alex apparently been jilted after the party at which they had claimed to be engaged? Had she set the two men against each other? Had Margery been right in her claim that the girl had been responsible for Austin's illness, which had led to his death? No one could offer a firm answer to any of these questions, but there was no doubt in anyone's mind that there was not one good thing to be said about Anna du Lessier's daughter.

George relayed all this news to Martin several days after the fire, as they sat together on the verandah of the bungalow from which Damien Lang had now moved all his possessions It was of Martin's former neighbour that George then spoke.

"I hear that particular lad is shortly to suffer a fate worse than death."

"Oh?" commented Martin, shifting his sore legs to a more comfortable position. "I trust the emphasis is on the word *suffer*."

"Didn't like him much, did you?" observed his friend.

"I've seldom disliked anyone more. Go on with the tale."

George grinned. "Lady Weyford's niece is all set to become Mrs Lang at a ceremony arranged with great haste and a strange lack of publicity."

"What?" cried Martin in astonishment. "Fay Christie is forcing him to a shotgun wedding? Good lord!"

With his grin turning into a chuckle, George continued. "You haven't yet heard the sting in this tale. Rumour has it that Lang is paying the penalty for another's pleasuring but, since he has no way of acquitting himself of the charge and the word of the lady in such cases must be believed, his only hope for survival out here is to take his punishment like a man."

"Well, well," was all Martin could think of to say, wondering why he should find himself feeling sorry for Fay, when she was thoroughly unlikeable and had asked for what she would surely get from Lang by way of revenge. "No doubt, Sir Hartle told the snivelling little wretch he must start 'pulling himself together'," he mused. "Well, well!"

"Lady Weyford is indisposed and not at home to callers," George informed him gleefully. "The residents are unanimously delighted at her downfall, naturally. She is such an insufferable woman. However, the most enjoyable part of the affair, for me, is that she was the undisputed leader of the anti-Thea campaign, yet it's her pi-faced little niece who has become the fallen woman instead. Isn't it grand?"

Martin nodded, then asked quietly, "How is Thea?"

"Fine—thanks to her gallant rescuers."

"You've seen her?"

"Before I came here today. They wanted to keep her in hospital for a few days, but she wouldn't hear of it."

"That sounds like Thea. I suppose Alex is with her."

"He wasn't when I called."

Martin was unhappy with that news. He guessed that his night with Thea had split the pair, but he felt that Alex deserved happiness from one direction when all else was falling around him.

"Have you discovered what she was doing in the Beresford house?"

"Yes. Collecting the last of her things, she told me." George leaned back in his chair with his hands linked behind his head. "It seems she had left her heavier travelling clothes there when she moved so suddenly to the hotel. Finding Alex away from the house, she took the opportunity to go in and collect them." He sighed. "What a tragedy there might have been if you two hadn't turned up when you did. It doesn't bear thinking about."

Martin studied the other man for a moment or two, then asked, "Are you in love with Thea?"

"Almost. Who isn't?"

"What's preventing your full commitment?"

With a faint rueful smile, George confessed. "Love for another."

"Good lord! You've never mentioned it before."

"You've never asked before. It has always been your own bloody love life we've had to sort out."

334

"Do I know her?" Martin probed.

With a shake of his head, George said, "We were together at a mission hospital some years ago. She refused to give up her work as a doctor with the Catholic nuns, and I refused to throw up the opportunity to enlarge my experience with tropical diseases. How wise we were! It was shortly after we parted that my condition worsened, and I very gratefully accepted my present post in Singapore. Francine is Franco-Siamese. She's the most stunning, fascinating woman I have ever met, but they would have made her life hell here with me. The French would have turned their backs, the native races would have despised her, our own countrymen would have treated her as if she were invisible. Nevertheless, no woman will ever take her place with me, and it's just as well. I'm no fit husband for anyone."

"Maybe not, but you're a damned fine friend," Martin said warmly.

"Well, I'm not so sure," George contradicted, straightening up to take the cup of coffee Wah had poured from the pot he had brought out to them. "I introduced you and the delectable Miss du Lessier to the Sing brothers. Who would have guessed those two wonderful old characters were engaging in such a diabolical trade?"

"Who would guess the dark secrets of most people's lives?" pointed out Martin, sipping his own coffee. "They lived up there in their self-confessed world of pretence, merely engaging in the financial transactions. You know, during the war it was extremely hard to bring oneself to stick a bayonet into someone a few feet away, yet it seemed more like fun and games to throw grenades and duck while they exploded. Men were killed in both instances, but when one didn't actually see them die it wasn't in the least like slaughter. Similarly, the Sing brothers didn't see those children caged like animals, so it was easy for them not to think of the gruesome side of a lucrative business. Forster did see them. In my book, that makes him a veritable fiend."

George added more sugar to his coffee, and stirred it slowly as he asked, "What put you on to Forster? No one else appeared to have the slightest suspicion of what he was doing, so what set you on his trail?"

"An anonymous letter," Martin lied deftly. "It was probably sent by one of his greedy, vicious associates who had fallen foul of him and wanted revenge." Wah had refilled his cup, and he took it from the Chinese servant with his bandaged hands before glancing across at George again. "If I had left well alone, Austin might still be alive, the Beresford house would still be standing, a number of men would never have lost their livelihood, and Sir Hartle would be free to twist arms *ad infinitum* in an unruffled society. I'm the real villain."

With a gentle shake of his head, George said, "It's not *what* you did, but the way you did it that they can't forgive. If you had only confided the facts to me, I'd have advised you."

"So you're on their side, are you?"

"In part." He frowned as he searched for the right words. "To attempt to govern a colony such as this is a thankless task. You've had no more than a year's experience with the complex problems caused by ethnic, religious and language differences. Due to your own struggle to readjust, you were hardly wholehearted in your commitment to Singapore's future. Your own was far too precarious. Most people out here genuinely believe they have something of worth to offer this island, otherwise they would never endure the climate and a lifetime's separation from their natural environment. However, a few are lured by the aura of the East into committing one or other of the unforgivable sins: exploitation, inter-marriage, or crime. When it happens, the elders of the colony convene to decide on how to deal with the offender."

Accepting a cigarette from the box proffered by Wah, George lit it, and leaned back with his cup on the broad arm of his chair.

"Unless the charge is one of murder, which has to be brought to trial, the accused is dealt with according to the severity of his crime. If he's merely adjudged a bounder—like Piers Massingham—he is put on a ship for home. Or he could be sent to the most uncongenial part of the Malay States, much as Austin sent his scapegrace brother Marmaduke. If he has really vicious habits or criminal tendencies, he's probably transferred to the most isolated and pestilential stations, such as the swamp area of the Gold Coast. Believe me, some poor devils suffer far more there than they would at the hands of the British legal system. The word is passed around the outposts of the Empire so that they are ostracised wherever they go. Their only hope is to turn native and eke a living amongst the rough, vicious underworld of the far or middle East. The majority of such men drink themselves insane within a few years, or take to smoking opium. Either way, they suffer a protracted and painful end."

"Justice is done without harming the fabric of rule; that's what you're trying to say, isn't it?" Martin claimed, in heavy tones. "I suppose I should have thought of that. After all, men accused of cowardice were taken off and shot in some place well behind the lines. If it had been done openly, morale would have been badly undermined." He sighed. "I suppose the decision to drum me out of the Department was justified. Do I now come under the heading 'bounder', or does 'half-witted Linwood' still suffice?"

George pursed his lips. "That comment deserves a piece of Thea's frank and caustic sermonising. What a pity she's not here to give it."

Facing Martin boldly, he asked, "When are you going to face up to the truth where that girl is concerned, and make an honest woman of her?"

Martin scowled across the distance between their two chairs. "That advice should rightly, and fairly swiftly, be offered to Alex Beresford, from what I understand of their relationship."

"Mmm, interesting," mused George, still studying Martin closely. "If she's committed herself as far as that, what do you suppose is preventing the marriage?"

Knowing the probable answer, Martin returned smartly. "If you feel it's any of your business, why don't you ask her?"

"There's hardly time now. She sails for England on Thursday."

"With young Beresford?"

"She didn't say." George paused for a moment before adding, "A lot has happened to that girl lately, robbing her of that precious, sparkling quality which made her so rare. There's a new pensiveness about her that I find slightly disturbing, for some inexplicable reason."

Martin looked away over the garden to the spot where another of the unusual green jade-flowers had unexpectedly bloomed. "If it's true, there's some hope for her. Instead of mistakenly trying to emulate her mother, she might one day produce a novel of some worth."

"Oh, she's finished the novel."

"Finished! Are you certain of that?" Martin asked in curiosity. "She hinted to me that the project had been abandoned."

"I was told no more than an hour ago that she was taking the completed manuscript to a publisher in London. I can't wait to read it, can you?"

With disappointment gathering fast, he said, "I have no intention of reading it . . . *if* it ever gets into print. In any case, where I'm going there are no bookshops."

Everything stood packed and ready. The liner was due to sail at dawn, and passengers were required to board by midnight. It was now four o'clock in the afternoon, and Thea could no longer pretend that it would be easy to leave without seeing him once more. Telling herself it was only because she had nothing else to do, she ran lightly down to the hotel lobby and told the doorman to summon a rickshaw.

The heat hit her the moment she walked from the building, and she wondered if the stifling brilliance of the tropics would be swiftly forgotten once back in the cool northern island of her birth. Gazing around at things she was seeing for almost the last time, the astonishing truth dawned on her. She was sad to be leaving this land of contrasts and complications; regretful that the scent of the hibiscus, the song of the oriole, and the heavy heat-hung glory of dying day would be lost to her. Even the sight of women in modest pale muslins, accompanied by escorts with coffee-coloured monstrosities on their heads, gave Thea a pang of wistfulness. Singapore had been an entire world within the world for a short period of her life. Emotions and experiences previously unknown had touched her here; standards and attitudes had been changed by the undeniable spell of the East. Would there ever be another time to compare with it?

On arrival at the bungalow, she paid the rickshaw-boy, then went along the side of the building to the steps used to reach Martin's verandah. She climbed them to walk unannounced into the bedroom where she had once found him lying bleeding and shocked after a flogging. That memory was heavy in her mind as she surprised him filling boxes and packing cases, which stood around with lids open. He turned on hearing her footsteps, and it took some moments for him to absorb the sight of her exotic lilac silk tabard, with matching shoes, before he said, "I thought you were sailing in the morning."

"Without saying goodbye?" she murmured, her dismayed glance registering the significance of what he was doing.

"You've already said goodbye at least three times."

She looked up into dark-brown eyes filled with resistance. "Where are you going, Martin?"

"Up-country. To Serantinggi, as it happens."

"*Serantinggi!* How can you be going there, of all places?"

"Knowing you, you'll appreciate the bizarre quality of this piece of news," he told her. "Now that Austin is dead and buried, Marmaduke is breaking loose. He's planning a grand tour of Europe where, no doubt, he'll twinkle over the floor of every ballroom available. A cabin has been booked for him in the name of the Duke of Beresford." With a strained smile, he asked, "Don't you think it's priceless?"

"What has that to do with your going to Serantinggi?" she asked woodenly.

"The old boy had heard I intend to become a planter and, in the manner of we eccentrics, promptly forgot that he hated me and offered the freedom of his home as a base while I look around the area."

"You're a bigger fool than I thought, if you intend to go ahead with the plan to shut yourself away in some jungle nightmare with only the bottle for company," she declared, with some heat.

"Is that what you came to tell me, Thea? You've already said that at least three times, too."

Had she hoped for a miracle; a last-minute flash of elucidation which would prove his salvation before she sailed in the morning?

"I came to thank you for helping to save my life. I haven't said that once, yet, have I?"

"Have you thanked Alex?" was all he replied.

"In a letter." She forced a smile. "I couldn't get near him for all his old friends and colonial colleagues. They've finally recognised his true worth, and are hailing him as a hero. Isn't that splendid?"

He nodded. "Yes, I'm glad."

Feeling more defeated with every minute, she moved nearer him, accidentally scattering a pile of books with her foot. "When are you going to allow people to recognise your true worth?"

His mouth twisted. "I think they've recognised that already. I've been kicked out of the Civil Service and every club in Singapore, for rocking the system they guard so jealously. Due to my behaviour, Sir Hartle has been cold-shouldered and issued with the chilly directive to get rid of me as swiftly and unobtrusively as possible. To that end, he has released enough of my money to cover the purchase of a plantation. There, I shall be free to run my own life with no embarrassment descending on the Weyfords, who have enough with Fay's hasty marriage to deal with. I intend to travel up to Serantinggi on Monday, where I shall find the peace and solitude I want. I sincerely hope never to see Singapore again."

"I can understand that, Martin. I've always maintained this island is the wrong place for a man like you, but Serantinggi is worse than wrong. Retreat isn't the answer. Can't you see that?" she demanded urgently. "Haven't you proved to yourself that, when faced with the most extreme danger, you're in total control of your actions and probably more courageous than most? The shell shock, that involuntary retreat into something you can't yet forget, is no worse than another's claustrophobia or fear of heights. Society doesn't shun them; why do you allow it to shun you?"

A shadow crossed the face which had lost its tan and returned to the original pallor. "Don't turn *me* into a hero. I only ran into the Beresford place because it was something I'd done before, and understood. It was instinctive."

"You really believe that?" she cried incredulously. "You truly believe that your actions in that inferno were as involuntary and uncontrolled as your behaviour at Alex's party?"

"In the main, yes. One attack of battle madness resulting in some good certainly doesn't cancel out a dozen others that do the reverse, Thea, and you're wrong if you think otherwise."

"So I failed," she exclaimed with deep sadness. "That night here achieved nothing; meant nothing to you."

His hands, pink from burns, rested lightly on her shoulders as he said, "That night is one I shall regret all my life. You possibly saved me from self-destruction, yet I wish it had been any woman but you who had been there when I reached out my hand."

"Your father apparently said much the same thing to my mother," she revealed quietly, knowing it now had to be said. "It's plain that you are unaware of the facts concerning Frere Linwood and Anna du Lessier. When we first crossed swords I believed your animosity was a reflection of that bitter relationship. Later, it was clear to me that you knew nothing of events which must have occurred when you were away at school. I hadn't intended to tell you, but I think you'll now understand what your father did."

His hands fell to his sides as he asked, "Tell me what, exactly?"

"May I sit down?" Her heart was hammering because she wondered whether instinct had led her astray, for once. How would he take the news? Sweeping a pile of shirts from a chair, he waited for her to sit although remained standing himself, with stony gaze fixed on her face. She wondered wildly how to begin.

"Our parents became lovers much the same way we did, from what I recall of the affair."

"My father would never have consorted with that woman," he declared harshly. "He hated her, and adored my mother so passionately there's no way he would have betrayed her with anyone."

"I was there when it happened, Martin," she told him gently. "Frere Linwood came to the apartment to confront Mother at a time when he had just lost the wife he loved so deeply. She baited him, played her usual heartless tricks on him, and they quarrelled with such passionate intensity, he broke down under the stress of his grief and loneliness. I can remember the sound of his sobbing, even now. It brought tears to my own eyes. He stayed all night with her." When Martin continued to gaze in silence, she continued with as much understanding as she could muster. "Their affair was voracious but brief, and Mother took full advantage of your father's vulnerability. By threatening to ruin his career by publicising their true relationship, she forced him to drop his attempt to stop publication of *Girl in a Plate of Strawberries*. He had no choice but to direct his counsel and friend accordingly, and the book enjoyed enormous sales when released to the public. Even so, Mother never forgave Frere for ceasing to worship at her shrine. I believe his hatred was rooted less in the content of the book he found so vile than in his sense of shame for having turned to a woman like her, in his grief for the lost Rosanne Linwood." Gazing up at Martin, she said, "It's slightly different with you. Your sense of shame for turning to me that

340

night is due to a sense of treachery to Alex, rather than to a beloved ghost."

He appeared silenced by what she had told him, yet she sensed that it had provided the final bar in the barricade he had always erected between them. Rising to face him again, she attempted a fourth farewell from a man who had been the first to possess her mind as well as her body. It was extremely difficult, she discovered. The pose of light-heartedness for once failed her.

"Let's not emulate them and part despising each other, Martin."

"I could never do that," he said, in tones so low she only just caught his words.

"Think of me sailing off into the dawn tomorrow . . . if you happen to be awake then."

"Yes, I will."

"I've finished the novel, you know."

"So George told me."

"I'll send you a copy when it's published."

"You won't know my address."

"That's no problem. By that time, everyone will know where half-witted Linwood can be reached." She gave him a last searching look, wanting it for her long empty future. "Please don't go to Serantinggi."

"Don't worry. There's unlikely to be another tiger yet awhile."

"It's not the tigers I'm worried about."

"Goodbye, Thea."

He had forced the issue. She had no choice but to leave. They made no attempt to kiss, or even shake hands. She simply turned away and left him standing in a room filled with the trappings of his own imminent departure.

Alex could hardly believe he was finally leaving. After a hectic cabin party with friends he had known all his life, the call had come for non-passengers to go ashore. They had moved boisterously to the jetty leaving him to face the moment deferred by almost seven years. He now stood quietly by the rail, gazing down on those throwing streamers across the widening gap between ship and shore. In the pale dawn, the dinner jackets and evening gowns seemed inappropriate. He watched the wild antics of youngsters with surprising detachment, feeling a great deal older than they. The last few months had brought changes and loss to hone the remnants of his maturity. Responsibility had been his in abundance after years of longing for it, and he had coped very adequately. The break with his family over which he had hesitated for so long, had been sudden, inevitable and sobering. That his father had died still hating him would cause him pain for some time to come, but he hoped for a reasonably close relationship with his mother and Lydia on reaching England.

The band was now playing "Auld Lang Syne", which always marked the moment when the great ocean-going vessels turned their bows toward the open sea and broke the last frail link with shores being left behind. Alex thought then of that day in 1914, when he had blinked back tears of yearning as others had gone to the war he had been denied. His life had been in a kind of limbo from then until the tennis party which had brought a return of that yearning. Martin Linwood had changed everything, sending him toward this present moment. They had not said goodbye. The strange relationship between them had never needed words. Each would never forget the other, so farewells would have been superfluous. It was of Martin rather than his old friends that Alex thought as his gaze wandered over the Singapore shoreline growing clearer with the advancing dawn. There was no similar escape for the man whose memories of war had extracted such a cruel penalty.

Alex sighed. Back there on the island *kebuns* would be hosing gardens and verandahs, birds would be active and joyous in the cooler hours before heat slowed everything to a somnolent pace. Europeans would be eating papaya, followed by bacon and eggs, before donning coffee-coloured monstrosities and joining the daily procession into the mercantile heart of the colony. Life would be continuing as it always had. The Forster affair, like every other tidal wave rising in that calm sea, would finally subside to leave only slight ripples to disturb the smooth surface. The residents would resume their beloved rituals at the Cricket Club, Raffles Hotel, military ballrooms and polo fields before returning to their airy homes set back amongst trees bearing the most fragrant and colourful blossoms.

A lump formed in his throat as the distant line of the island began to blur. Twenty-five years could not be dismissed easily. As he continued to lean on the rail gazing back at his youth and early manhood, he recalled the pleasures and companions of that sun-washed period. Parting from Fong had been mutually emotional. How could one define the relationship formed between an English boy and his Chinese servant? It was unique, very special, and difficult to sever. Saying goodbye to Ling and the other members of the household staff had been almost as painful. Being Chinese, they read mystic significance into the destruction of the house so soon after the death of its master, and the departure of its mistress with her daughter. That mysterious element known to them as *fung shui* had plainly changed from good to bad on that spot. Nothing would now induce them to go near that blackened shell. Alex had found employment for them all with pleasant European families. Fong had taken charge of a Belgian boy, whose bright red hair had been seen by the Chinese as symbolic with the fire which had destroyed the past. In the curious way they had of relating all things, Alex believed Fong saw young Alain as a phoenix-like reincarnation of himself eighteen years ago, and was happily preparing to live those years over again.

Turning his gaze from the far-off passenger jetties to the area where *Berondel* ships were tied up ready for loading, Alex hoped the line would prosper under the new consortium. When Lydia reached the age of twenty-one, the power of attorney she had granted him would end unless she wished to extend it. When she married, her husband would then control *Berondel*, he supposed. He could not imagine his gentle, sensitive sister ever following modern thinking and becoming the head of a prosperous shipping line. If Lydia were a girl like Thea, she would. If Lydia were a girl like Thea, how different the past year in Singapore would have been.

Turning away from the East, he leaned back against the rail to study decks empty now of those more interested in breakfast than a colony no longer clearly visible. Within moments, Thea was walking toward him, and the black and white of his visions leapt into colour once more. He recalled their first meeting; her vivid pointed face and laughing amber eyes as she had said: "Take off that damned silly hat and I'll greet you properly." There was no laughter in the eyes which now met his, as she reached his side.

"I promised in my letter that I'd leave you to say your private farewell to Singapore, didn't I?"

"Yes, you did," he agreed, "but until this moment I wasn't sure you'd actually be sailing with me. So it really was a case of 'Thanks, and goodbye', was it?"

"I'm afraid so."

She looked so much a shadow of the girl he had first encountered on the deck of a ship, he had to ask, "I suppose there's no chance of that wedding on the high seas?"

"No, darling . . . but I'll be your lover, companion, friend for as long as you need me."

"Is that what you offered him?"

"He didn't give me the chance."

Pulling her gently into his arms, he said quietly, "Your heart has been blinded by your absurd drive to find salvation for all who crossed

343

your path. You've never been in love with either of us, Thea. All you wanted was to make things come right for us both."

Sighing, she said, "I failed where he is concerned."

Alex smiled, and took her arm. "Fifty per cent success isn't bad, and you can carry on the good work for as long as I need you, just as you promised. Come on, let's find some breakfast. Neither one of us wants to watch those damned shores slowly vanish over the horizon."

The whole of Serantinggi Valley was blotted out by thick reddish mist, so that it was possible to see only as far as the nearest tappers' huts and the bungalow of the Eurasian overseer. Rain thundered on to the broad palm leaves, the shrubs and the creepers that constantly threatened to close over the entire plantation. It thundered on to the red earth tracks which provided the only means of movement around the area, turning them into muddy rivers. It thundered on to the tin roof of the bungalow in deafening fashion. It had been like that for four days and nights.

Inside the bungalow, two oil lamps augmented the feeble light filtering through shutters which could be opened no more than a crack. Any more and puddles formed on the floor, the furniture grew unpleasantly damp, and green mould began to sprout on the pale washed walls. Cicadas throbbed incessantly in dark corners where they had sought escape from the deluge. Lizards and cockroaches scuttled over the ceiling and walls unhindered. Inch-long ants formed two-way columns in all parts of the building as they industriously carried away scraps from the kitchen, crumbs from the floors, and the corpses of their less fortunate brethren to store until outdoor activity was again possible. Spiders as large as a man's hand had been driven from hiding by the rain which penetrated every nook and cranny. They crouched in sinister immobility, ready to run the moment they were disturbed by movement. Rats, timid in the brilliant sunlight, became lively in this half night and ran boldly along sills and ledges to seek food. They carried off fruit and nuts from the bowls on the table, paper from the wastebasket, and stuffing from a burst cushion. They gnawed the soap on the washstands and in the antiquated shower cubicles, leaving needle-sharp tooth-marks in the scented tablets. The only creatures not on the move were human ones. They remained under cover, shivering in the dank chilliness which had followed excessive heat.

Martin had been drinking since noon. It was now a short while before nightfall, although the present grey twilight had lasted ninety-six hours. He had been sitting in the same chair since opening the first bottle, so there was no way of telling whether or not he was now too drunk to stand. As he had no intention of trying to do so, the likelihood of his finding the answer was very remote. It had taken him no more than three weeks to realise that he had made the greatest mistake of his life. Serantinggi was not the same. The sun still shone, most of the time, and the valley looked as inviting at early morning and at twilight. There was still peace and beauty to be found, horses to ride, brown smiling rubber tappers, vivid birds and exotic blooms, yet it had become the loneliest place on earth because it was filled with memories.

Voices whispered in the silent rooms; the echoes of youthful laughter hung in the air. Wherever he looked there were reminders of that other time. The gramophone and pile of scratchy records to which they had danced by the light of the moon; the verandah rail where he and Alex had balanced with such bravado; the familiar rooms through which they had chased the girls before indulging in the horserace.

I used to twinkle across the floor . . . Very impressive place you have, Your Grace . . . Been in the family since Oliver Cromwell . . . The same gentleman who installed the showers, I presume . . . Oh, Martin, this has been the most marvellous night of my life . . . No, there'll be others twice as marvellous, but perhaps not quite like this one . . . Whoever knocks all six cubes into the garden will win a stupendous prize . . . What was the war really like?

Pouring another drink, he tried to drown those voices by downing it swiftly. Instead, his restless glance moved once more to the tiger's tail on the wall. It was an obscene symbol of killing; a cruel reminder of the act which had shattered the happiness he had discovered there. Voices invaded that dim room once more.

I'm glad you didn't shoot the tiger, Martin . . . He's nailed it on the wall . . . It's beastly . . . No, no! Lydia, for God's sake, no! . . . I'm desperately sorry, Martin. I couldn't let you do it . . . It's this damned place. The jungle is too elemental. No wonder planters go out of their minds.

Suddenly, Martin could bear it no longer. Struggling to his feet he lurched across the room to tear down the trophy, fling wide a shutter, and hurl the tiger's tail as far from the bungalow as he could. With his knees buckling, he clung to the windowsill staring out at the solid wall of rain, the reddish-brown rivers which had once been paths, and the oversized swollen plants crowding in on that clearing in the middle of nowhere. At that moment, he spotted another rat making its way along the adjacent ledge. Stealthily removing his belt, he wrapped the unbuckled end around his left hand for the best grip.

"Come on, you little bugger," he enticed drunkenly, fixing his gaze on the rodent's twitching nose. "Just a little further."

The rat spotted him, but he swung the belt again and again until the creature was no more than pulp. When he realised what he was doing,

345

he slid down to slump against the wall, head in hands, feeling as if he were the only person left in the world. There was no one to reach out a hand in the darkness, as she had once done. All he could do was try to concentrate on the memory of her fingers curling into his, in the midst of an earlier darkness. Another day died. He could no longer see the rats, the mud, and the fat, shiny encroaching undergrowth. Nothing blotted out the sound of the rain. That went on and on and on, beating into his brain the truth he had refused to see. Serantinggi had been wonderful only because they had been there with him. Alex, Lydia and Thea had put youth back into his heart and limbs; they had made him care again. It *was* possible for him to laugh, live and love like normal people. They had shown him it was possible.

Chapter 20

The heat was dry and invigorating. The sun blazed from a sky of gentle blue on to the bare heads of young men, and on the straw panamas of the more elderly; it enhanced the bright defiance of close-fitting hats sported by modern young girls determined on making their mark on the world, and it played over the romantic extravagant confections in pastel lace still preferred by matrons who deplored the loss of graciousness and decorum they had known before the Great War. London was enjoying an Indian summer in that autumn of 1922. The parks had seldom looked as beautiful as they did now, when the leaves were all gold, red and russet, the flowerbeds were filled with a mass of vivid dahlias and late-blooming roses, and the grass was dotted with nursemaids amusing their golden-brown robust charges amidst a scattering of shy young lovers. There was still the occasional war-casualty in hospital-blue to be seen, but most had now been discharged and sent off to make what they could of the remainder of their lives, or had been incarcerated in institutions from which they would never emerge until death claimed them.

Despite the return to peace and optimism, a new mood of awareness was developing. The initial aftermath of the war, which had created a drive to forget pain and misery, scrub it out as one would a blasphemy written on a churchyard wall, had swung round to give birth to a sense of social responsibility. Four years after the end of the débâcle, questions were suddenly being asked. The relief over the ending of something the world had never before experienced faded, beneath the inescapable legacy left in almost every home in Britain. The comforting lies sent by the fighting men to their anxious families at home, the soothing propaganda issued by the government to maintain morale, was now shown for what it had been as the shattered participants slowly emerged from numbness to tell the real story of their experiences. The horror of that four-year conflict and the unimaginable suffering of those caught up in it, was finally revealed. Beneath the struggle to rebuild, beneath the growing power of women who had been freed from the kitchen sink and refused to be chained to it again, and the longing for colour and gaiety after those khaki years, was a growing sense of shock and outrage at what the world had allowed to happen.

There was no doubt in Thea's mind that the success of her novel *The Jade-Flower* owed much to the present surge of public awareness of the victims of war. As she stood receiving the fulsome congratulations of the parasites of artistic achievement, and the more sincere compliments of complete strangers who could identify with the story she had told, the knowledge that her work, at a less perceptive time, might have been overlooked did nothing to lessen her sense of pride. Dorothea du Lessier had certainly eclipsed her mother, even if it was mostly due to a reversal of public attitudes, and should rightly feel vindicated for the cruelty perpetrated in *Domino*. Yet, somewhere along the way, the desire for revenge on a shallow, selfish woman had vanished to be replaced by the desire to force enlightenment on the socially blind. It was her success in this direction which flooded Thea with pride as she autographed copies of her novel, chatted with giants of literature and patrons of all forms of the arts, in the elegant salon hired by her publisher for the event of his year.

If the flatteringly large attendance at the light buffet luncheon was due to a secret hope of witnessing confrontation between the artificial Anna, and the talented daughter who had usurped her, the hope was frustrated. The author of the scandalous *Girl in a Plate of Strawberries* and *Domino* was said to be recovering from a malady in the south of France, from whence had come a message of brief congratulations on "a creditable first attempt at the literary art". Many were the sniggers behind signed copies of Thea's novel as guests read her mother's message, pinned on to the wall with great deliberation by the author herself. The nature of Anna du Lessier's malady was no secret to anyone present that day.

In a short swathed dress of imitation snakeskin with a brief purple matador cape hanging from the shoulders, and a close-fitting hat of curled purple feathers, Thea did all that was required of her while guests gushed, guffawed and guzzled the champagne liberally offered by a publisher who knew he could afford all this, and more, to launch his new discovery. Throughout the first hour and a half, however, she watched the flower-bedecked doorway knowing that the affair would mean nothing to her if they did not come. Her heart lifted when she finally spotted his curly head above those of a group surrounding her. Murmuring excuses, she pushed through the cluster of admirers to where Alex stood accepting two glasses of champagne from a waiter. The girl beside him was blonde and petite, but she was not Lydia. Then Alex caught sight of her. His face lit with pleasure and with the love he could not yet quite put aside.

"Thea! Sorry to be so late, but I was on duty last night and some damned fool borrowed my motor for a spree which used all the petrol. Had to beg a tow to the nearest garage before I could set out this

348

morning." He kissed her rather more intimately than he should with another girl beside him, and his green eyes were warm with feeling as he said, "I've eaten all my words, darling. It's a knockout of a novel."

"That's all I needed to make me believe it," she told him with a glowing smile, realising how badly she had missed him over the past six months. "Oh, it's so good to see you."

"I'd have gone absent without leave, if necessary, to be here," he declared, with the ardour she remembered so well. "After all, I suffered the birth pangs of your talent, didn't I?"

"Poor you! Was I *very* temperamental and difficult?"

"Frightfully." He made to drink his champagne, realised he had a glass in each hand, and turned to find that his female partner had gone. Giving the second glass to Thea instead, he shrugged. "She didn't really want to come. Knows very little about literature."

"Who is she, Alex?"

"Someone. I've had rather a lot of them since you left."

"I didn't leave, darling, you did," she reminded him. "When you joined the RAF your flying career provided all I had given for as long as you needed it. Besides, I could hardly have moved into your service quarters with you, and created a scandal that would have had you kicked out again very fast."

"You could have married me." At her silence, he went on, "I suppose it wouldn't have worked. You were never the dutiful matrimonial type. I still love you, Thea."

"I still love you," she told him. "Ours is a special kind of love that will endure, even when you eventually find the dutiful matrimonial partner you deserve."

He gave a rueful smile. "I'm not looking that far ahead. Flying is all-important to me now, and we're all so keen to develop new machines and techniques there's little time to think of anything else. The future for aviation is so exciting, and I'm very fortunate to be in on it at this stage."

"You're a born aviator, darling. Think how terrible it would have been if you were still cooped up in that office in Singapore, listing *Berondel* cargoes and walking out on paddle guards to find your excitement."

He grinned. "I still indulge in that kind of madness, occasionally."

"Mad Alex, they used to call you," she mused, studying him closely and thinking how well the blue uniform suited his strong physique. "You look happy. No, that's not the right word—*fulfilled* is more accurate." Slipping her hand through the crook of his arm, she led him toward a quiet corner, saying, "Come over here where it's more

349

peaceful and tell me all the news. Why didn't Lydia come with you?"

His gaze searched her face as he replied, "You must surely be able to guess the answer to that. She's read the book. It upset her a great deal."

"It has upset a large number of people. That was my whole purpose in writing it," she told him gravely. "All the same, I hoped it might make Lydia and me friends again."

He shook his head. "Just the reverse."

Thea sighed. "How is her marriage with Geoffrey working out?"

"His name is Gerald," Alex reminded her, then frowned. "I suppose everything is fine. Being so much older than Lydia, he shoulders all responsibility, leaving her and Mother to their afternoon teas and charity work. He's really very good to them both, you know. It's not every husband who'd provide rooms for his mother-in-law in his own home, although it's so large they don't have to meet up all that often." He drank the last of his champagne before saying, "He's decided to sell *Berondel*."

"Do you mind a lot?" she asked, in quick concern.

He shook his head. "I think Father would have approved, which is really more to the point. The outcome is slightly ironic, as it happens. The ailing *Rochford-Kendal* took on a bright youngster in a bid to save the line, and he has worked a miracle to the extent of offering to change the name to *Rochford-Berondel*. The new company will have the prestige and assets of two respected lines, plus the drive of modern thinking to ensure its future."

"Does that mean they'll also take over Serantinggi?"

"No, the plantation was bought three months ago by a fellow who had blotted his copybook in Singapore, and had been advised to leave by the first available means."

"I suppose it wasn't the abominable Damien Lang with his feline wife and twin sons, by any chance?" she asked hopefully.

Alex laughed. "I'm afraid not. The fellow's name was Carter."

"Poor devil! I wonder which colonial rule he broke," she reflected. "Where's Marmaduke, at present?"

"God knows. The last news I received was a tattered postcard from Monte Carlo. That was eight weeks ago, and it had chased me from our old apartment through several RAF addresses before it reached my present airfield. It's my guess the old reprobate has become a professional house guest on the Riviera."

She laughed up at him. "Well, he was only a slightly *grey* sheep, as he was fond of pointing out. They probably adore him out there in that relic of an era no one wants to surrender."

Alex gave her a long loving look full of hunger. "God, but it's wonderful to be with you again. You make me come alive just to look at you."

Touched by the same sentiment, she told him softly, "You know you're always welcome to visit me when your 'someones' pall."

"If I did, I wouldn't want to leave again."

"Yes, you would, Alex. Flying has become your first love."

"It always made me bloody airsick," put in a new voice beside them.

Thea turned to him, offering a prayer of thanks to the god of eternal hope as she studied him, while the two men shook hands and exchanged warm greetings. Apart from looking younger and slightly more sturdy, Martin was just as she remembered him from their last meeting over a year ago in his bungalow where the jade-flower grew. He turned from congratulating Alex on gaining his commission in the RAF, and the familiar dark-brown eyes met hers to reveal something so startling it robbed her of immediate words.

"Hallo, Thea," he said, attempting no physical greeting. "I feel honoured by your invitation to attend today."

"I never thought you'd come," she managed, at last.

"Well, I do have a prize mare about to foal down at Larkswood, and I'm supposed to be addressing my prospective constituents this evening. The acclaimed Thea du Lessier naturally took precedence over my time, as you see."

"Do you really mean to follow your father into Parliament?" she asked eagerly, pursuing his comment about prospective constituents.

"I know the plan won't meet with your approval but, like him, I am what you once called a knight at heart. I still believe in the old values, and mean to campaign for them if enough people support me." After a moment or two, he asked, "No outburst of condemnation? No frank, unexpurgated defence of socialism? Whatever has happened to the Miss du Lessier I once knew?"

"Singapore happened to her," she said quietly. "A foolish girl went out there intending to create a grand novel of the East, and wrote instead the story of a shell-shocked soldier trying to find a future after war." Pausing, she then asked, "Did you read the copy I sent you?"

"Yes, despite earlier prejudices. It's very, very good."

"You're not angry?"

He shook his head. "It's not about me: it's the story of them all. Your book says what needed to be said, but what most people tried to avoid. We all thank you."

Feeling dangerously emotional, she looked around for Alex. He was no longer there.

351

"I think he has just realised what George knew all along," said Martin, as she turned back to face him. "There's some inescapable bond between us, isn't there?"

"I've never been really sure," she confessed softly.

With his dark gaze fixed intently on her face, he asked, "Shall we go somewhere and find out?"

"If that's what you really want."

"What I really want," he told her, with his rare smile, "is to set tongues wagging when that shocking, meddlesome du Lessier creature is seen everywhere in company with half-witted Linwood. The news should reach Singapore by Christmas, if not before."